RUN

BEAUTIFUL

RUN

HOW FAR WOULD YOU GO
TO KEEP A PROMISE?

MEL A ROWE

Also by Mel A ROWE

Receive exclusive insights, and news on upcoming releases by joining: <u>https://melarowe.com/newsletter/</u>

COPYRIGHT

**Caveat: As a courtesy, since there may be some sparse language choices in this story that may represent an obstacle for the reader, I am offering this warning. Please note this language and cultural references are purely for fictional purposes only and not designed to offend any individual persons, culture, or religions implied.

The Following Is Written in Australian English

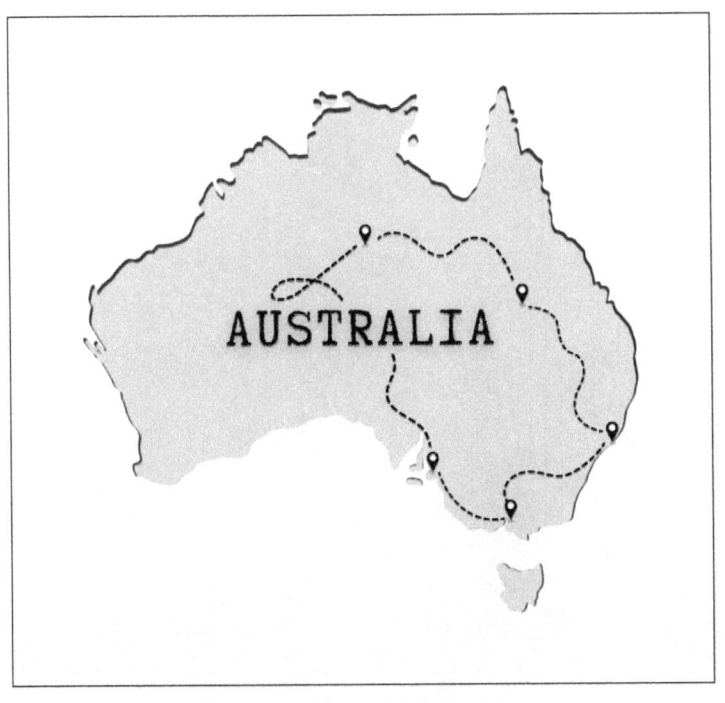

How far would you go to keep a promise?

"The most important person to keep your promises to, is yourself."

Anonymous

One

'How does the white rabbit get away with *I'm late! I'm late!* — because I'm freaking late again.' Maddison ran across the road as seagulls glided on the sea breeze that carried the deep-throated horn blast of a freighter docking at the wharves.

She pushed on the glass doors to Lou's Sports Bar and darted behind the bar. 'Sorry I'm late.'

'Been diving again, have we, Maddison?' Wearing his permanent scowl, Laurie tapped on his watch face. 'And today's excuse is …'

'The boat was late because the tourists kept wanting to extend their scuba diving adventure on the wreck. I don't know why they bothered; the water was that murky this morning.' She tossed her loose plait off her shoulder dampening her shirt's collar, then tightened the straps on her black work apron. 'When you take up my offer for those free diving lessons, I'll make sure it's clear with the tides.'

'If man was meant to swim underwater, we'd be waving around webbed fingers and toes.' He then sighed. 'Why do you do that?'

'Do what?'

'I'm supposed to be giving you a lecture on being late, again.'

'I'm sorry.' Maddison gave what she hoped was her best suck-up smile yet. 'You know I'm good for it.'

'Get to work. I'll be out the back.'

'Will do, boss.' She got busy behind the bar, where time flew, serving a steady stream of customers.

'There she is,' said Paul, a junior detective, strolling in through the front doors with his partner. 'I've been waiting all day to ask you to have dinner with me, Maddison.'

Maddison placed a freshly poured beer on the counter in front of Paul, and hesitated. She'd taken this bar job to help grow more of a backbone, to learn to be more assertive with people, but where was Laurie when she needed him?

'Say *no*, Maddy.' Senior Detective Mick Hetter leaned against the bar, scooping up his beer. 'You're better than that.'

Paul sneered at his partner. 'Are you for real?'

'Never date a cop. The hours suck… My two ex-wives will tell you that.'

The phone behind the bar rang.

Laurie stormed out of the office. 'Lou's Sports Bar.' He paused, listening to the phone cradled to his ear, as his frown deepened. 'Yeah, who's this?' He waved at Maddison. 'Hang on, I'll get her.'

'For me? Can't be, no one rings me.' *And that sounded sad.*

'Well, this modern piece of annoying technology is a phone that allows people to disturb your day and mine.'

'Is the phone for me, or am I getting another lecture?' Maddison grinned at the sizeable man, shaking his head at her. 'Hello?' She asked over the phone.

'Maddy—thank God—it's Bob. Listen, hon, I haven't got much time, I need a favour?' Uncle Bob's raspy breath wheezed with urgency. 'Can you meet me at the train station by the casino? Please, I'm begging you.'

'Are you in trouble?'

'Um … I'll meet you at the front entrance to explain everything. I'll see you soon.' Bob hung up.

'Is everything all right, Maddison?' Laurie asked, hovering nearby. Which was rare – she hadn't seen her boss all shift.

'Just Uncle Bob being Uncle Bob.' But he didn't sound right.

'Does Bob need you to bail him out again?'

'No, to meet him at the train station near the casino.'

'Don't tell me, Bob's lost all his money at the casino and needs time to hide out at your place, so the bookies don't find him?'

'Excuse me?'

'Yesterday, two men came in here looking for Bob. Don't worry, I told them nothing. But Maddison …' Laurie stepped in closer and with a lowered tone, he said, 'They were the tough henchmen variety.'

Henchmen? Who says that anymore? 'How do you know?'

'Trust me on that one, I've seen enough to know from working on the job for thirty years. Your uncle must be into something deep for those two men to walk into a known cop bar like this. I just hope Bob doesn't drag you down with him.'

'Uncle Bob wouldn't do that to me. Besides, I can take care of myself.'

'Make sure you do. Now get out of here.'

'Thanks, I will.' Maddison ripped off her apron and rushed out the door.

At the train station a steady stream of people flowed back and forth, accessorised with headsets and smartphones. The heady scents of coffee, train exhaust fumes, and assorted colognes were torture on the sinuses.

But Bob was a no-show.

Not the first time Bob had failed to appear, so she'd give him ten more minutes, then head home, or go back to work to make up for being late.

'Excuse me, miss?' A pimply-faced kid, carrying a skateboard approached. 'Are you Maddy?'

'Yes.'

'Your uncle told me to give you this.' The boy held out a cardboard beer coaster.

The scribble on the back read:

Maddy,
Go to platform ten and catch the first train out.
Get off at the first stop in Croydon.
I'll meet you there in the car park around the back.

'Where did Bob go?'

The kid shrugged his skinny shoulders. 'Some old guy told me to look for some lady with blonde hair, wearing a shirt that had *Lou's Sports Bar* on the pocket.' He pointed to the embroidered pocket of Maddison's collared shirt. 'He paid me ten bucks for it, too.' The kid grinned wider. 'He told me you'd give me ten bucks as a tip, once I'd done the job.'

'How do I know you got this from Bob? What did he look like?'

'Old guy, balding head, red face, big guts, wearing a crinkled-up suit like he'd slept in it. He looked like an old drunk to me. But he said you'd be suss and that I was to say *Bob bids it*—whatever that means.' The kid then held out his hand. 'Hey, ten bucks is ten bucks, lady. Are you gonna pay up?'

'*Bob bloody bids it*,' Maddison muttered under her breath. It was one of Uncle Bob's favourite sayings that he'd tell her when she was young. It was also Bob's handwriting on the beer coaster, and the kid's unflattering description of Uncle Bob were unfortunately true.

Maddison searched the large timetable boards. With five minutes to catch the train, she handed ten dollars to the boy. 'Thanks.'

'Miss, no offence, but is this some secret-squirrel kind of thing?'

'Why do you say that?'

'Because the old guy looked scared, sweating badly, looking over his shoulder all the time.'

Bob didn't sound too good on the phone either. Did the bookies find him?

As a flutter of fear shifted in her stomach, tightening her ribcage, she raced down the platform, hoping she wasn't too late.

Two

The train rattled away, leaving Maddison alone in the crisp early evening air. Her boot steps echoed along the station's platform. A flickering light buzzed overhead, causing her shadow to flicker over the stained concrete as she followed the ramp to the dark deserted car park.

Why here? Surely Bob wouldn't put her in any danger?

Peering into the shadows, her shoulders tightened as her heartbeat raced, reaching inside her handbag for her pepper spray.

Only to sigh with relief at the sight of Bob's decrepit car sitting at the far end of the deserted car park with Bob slumped over in the passenger seat.

'Bob?' She tapped on the car window.

'Hey, are you asleep?' She opened the sedan's door and Bob rolled onto the ground.

Great, drunk again.

Anger simmered in her chest at the man who weighed a tonne. 'Come on, Bob, help me out here.'

Bob groaned, as if annoyed at her for disturbing his sleep. But when she rolled him to his back the car park's dull lights exposed his face.

'Oh, no!' She dropped to her knees as a chill washed over her.

Bob's eyelids were swollen shut, with his lips swelling as if he'd been stung by a thousand bees. Blood from his flattened nose ran down his face and soaked his shirt.

'Maddy?' Bob slurred. He'd lost teeth.

'What happened? Who did this?' The blood was everywhere.

'Listen …' His groan was filled with pain between irregular gasps for air. 'There isn't much time.'

'I'm calling an ambulance.' She dug around in her bag for her phone.

Bob grabbed her weakly with a swollen, shaky hand, slick with blood. 'Maddy, please listen to me.'

Maddison stabbed the emergency numbers on her phone. 'You need help.'

'Do you remember my favourite place at the track?'

'Why are you talking about the track now?' Maddison frowned at the recorded message being played on her phone. 'No way! I'm on hold! Can you believe that? On hold for an emergency number!'

'*Maddy!*' Bob grabbed her shirt, dragging her down to face him. 'You know my secret place at the track?'

'Yes, of course.' Fear hammered in her heart so loudly it was a challenge to listen to her phone. She dropped it to the ground, the phone's speaker playing some eerie background music.

'Go to the track and find my leather journal. It's got a memory card in there. You need to finish what I started. Promise me you won't say anything to anyone?'

'It's okay, the ambulance will be here soon.' Why was Bob rambling about his journal? He only kept it for his article notes—but it'd been a long time since he'd published anything decent. 'Who did this to you? Laurie said some men came looking for you yesterday. Is this their way of debt-collecting?'

'That mob didn't shoot me. You can't get money out of a dead man.'

'*They shot you?!*' Maddison's voice echoed across the deserted car park. She frantically searched for wounds, but couldn't see anything through the blood, as she tried to remember her first aid while still on hold for an ambulance. Dragging her work apron out of her bag, she pressed it against Bob's wounds.

'Police. Fire. Ambulance,' said the nasally female monotone over the speakerphone.

'Quick, I need an ambulance to the car park at Croydon Train Station near a white sedan. My uncle's been shot and has lost a lot of blood.' Maddison was desperate to keep a grip before the panic truly set in. 'Hurry, please!'

'Ambulance and police have been notified and they'll be with you shortly.'

'They're coming, Bob.' Maddison pressed her apron harder against his chest to stop the bleeding as he laboured heavily for oxygen. 'Hang in there, help is on its way.'

'Trust no one, Maddison.' Bob groaned through gritted teeth. 'Promise me you won't tell anyone what I said?'

'You're not making sense.' His warm blood seeped through her apron and between her fingers. The rich metallic scent was distinct.

'Trust no one. Tell no one. Bob bids it, too.' He gripped her wrist as she pressed against his bleeding chest. 'Promise me, you'll finish what I've started. It needs to be finished. Promise me!'

'Okay, okay, I promise.' The tears welled up in her eyes.

'You were always a good kid.' Bob's pallor was a pasty grey as his chest rattled with each laboured breath. 'I just wish you'd find something better for yourself than working in a bar.'

'You can save your lectures on my lifestyle changes for when you're recovering.'

'No need for that, honey, just remember to keep your eyes and ears open. Watch your back. And trust no one— especially the police.'

'What?'

'Finish what I started. I know you'll do it, and you'll make me proud … I love you, Maddy.' Bob's words slurred into a whisper, ending in a sigh. It was so shallow and slow, it barely registered.

His head lay back. His shoulders relaxed and his entire body went limp, with his eyes staring vacantly across the car park.

The siren screams were too far away.

'*Bob?*' She couldn't find a pulse. No heartbeat. Nothing. 'No-no-no-no.' She desperately pushed down on his chest, trying to get his heart to work. Pinching his nose, she forced the air back into his lungs. 'Don't you leave me.'

A sweep of car lights blinded her as a deafening wail of

sirens filled the area. The emergency vehicle's red and blue flickering lights gave Bob's car a ghostlike psychedelic glow as they pulled up where Bob lay by the open passenger door.

Maddison continued with her compressions as tears streamed down her face, until the police officers pulled her off and the paramedics exposed Bob's chest.

'He's been shot in the heart,' said the paramedic to his offsider and shook his head.

Maddison hiccupped between tears, staring at Bob. The guy was harmless, he didn't deserve to die like that. Why would anyone want to kill Bob?

Three

With her hands hidden deep in her coat pockets, Maddison's shoulders sagged as she slowly strolled back from the funeral parlour.

Besides the priest keeping Maddison company at the crematorium today, no one else showed up for Bob Farley. It was as if the man had never existed.

But Uncle Bob had left a gaping hole in Maddison's world.

She kept expecting to find Bob on her couch, snoring like an out-of-tune cello. Or to see him stroll into the bar, tucking in his shirt, as he attempted to straighten the wrinkles on his suit. He'd never knock on her apartment door again, carrying beer and pizza with a story to share from his day out at the races.

He was gone.

And she was all alone, with no family left.

Uncle Bob's murder remained unsolved. Mick and Paul from the bar, worked for the Armed Crime Squad, and were the detectives investigating Uncle Bob's murder. No clues had been found as to why Bob had been murdered. But there were lots of rumours claiming it was a payback for Bob's gambling debt of thirty thousand dollars.

Who'd lend that much to Bob to drink and gamble away?

Was a life worth only thirty thousand dollars?

Rubbing the heel of her palm against her achy cold chest, her pain for missing Bob was only magnified by the crisp breeze nipping at her cheeks. In a daze, Maddison walked up the front steps of her apartment building and reached for the main glass door as her elderly neighbour pushed on it.

'Hello, Mrs Jenkins.' Maddison held the door open.

'Oh, hello, Maddison. You look nice, dear. I'm so used to seeing you in jeans and T-shirts.'

Maddison glanced down at her black woollen dress coat and black shoes. She'd aimed for vintage elegance. It was freaking sad.

'Are you just getting in, dear?'

Maddison's voice croaked as if she'd swallowed a handful of gravel. 'I've been at my uncle's funeral today.'

'Oh no! I'm sorry for your loss, dear.' Mrs Jenkins patted Maddison's hand, wearing sympathy in her eyes. 'But I thought you were home rearranging your furniture. I must be hearing things. Oh, this special delivery came for you too.' She passed an envelope to Maddison. 'Well, I must head to my bingo game. Wouldn't want to be late. You must come down for a cup of tea and a chat, soon.'

'Thanks, Mrs Jenkins.' Maddison stared at the envelope. It looked official, but with no return address, nothing. If it was from the lawyers, she wasn't in the mood to deal with that right now. She didn't want to think.

Shoving it into the inner breast pocket of her tailored coat, she trudged up to the first floor with a sudden craving for scotch. As Bob's favourite spirit it was perfect for drowning her sorrows.

She unlocked the door of her apartment. Its small balcony overlooked the neighbouring park's trees, giving her a grand country view in the city. Sadly, some days it was too cold to sit outside and enjoy it, but today it would be the perfect place to start her drinking party for one.

'Oh. My. God.' Maddison froze just inside her open doorway as broken glass crunched beneath her heels. Her eyes widened. Clutching her stomach, she found it hard to breathe.

Her furniture was tipped over with the stuffing slashed out of the couch. Curtains were stripped off the windows and strewn across the floor. Pictures that once hung on the walls were broken and ripped free from their frames. Dresser drawers lay on their sides and the cupboard shelves were barren, with her book covers torn and their pages flung everywhere.

The kitchen drawers were emptied. Her fridge and pantry doors were wide open, and torn food bags spilled nuts and assorted grains across the benches and all over the floor. Everything. Destroyed.

When her phone rang, she jumped, as she fumbled to tap the screen. 'H-h-hello?' Her tension-filled voice was unrecognisable.

'Hey, its Laurie. I thought I'd see how you're doing?'

'Laurie?' Her bottom lip quivered as she stared at a dishevelled war zone. 'I've been broken into. They've destroyed everything.' A loud smash of breaking glass carried down the hallway, she jumped, with a squeal escaping from the back of her throat.

'What was that?' Laurie asked.

'No idea? It came from my bedroom.' Her legs trembled and her hands were icy cold.

'Have you checked you're home alone?'

'I've just walked in.'

'Get out of there, *now*. Meet me on the street, you hear me.'

The loud toot of a car horn made Maddison scream.

'Move, young lady. *Now*.'

She slammed the door and ran down the stairs aiming for the light at the end of the hallway.

Too scared to look behind her, too scared to see if someone was chasing her, she didn't stop running.

She forced her way through the front doorway and out onto the street, to flinch at the deafening burst of traffic noise. She winced at the bright afternoon sunlight, as pedestrians brushed against her on the sidewalk. Taking in desperate, deep breaths, with the acidic taste of fear at the back of her throat, only then did Maddison turn to the building's front door and come face to face with her terrified wild-eyed reflection.

Four

Time stretched into aeons for Maddison, staring at the finite cracks and crevices that made up the steps to her apartment building's front landing, where she sat hugging her knees.

A sedan pulled up to the curb, with Laurie exiting from the rear seat. 'Maddy, are you okay?'

She barely nodded, sighing with relief to see her grumpy boss.

'How come Mick and Paul are here?' She pointed to the two detectives getting out of the car.

'They were at the bar when I called you, and they are the investigating officers into your uncle's murder.'

'Are you saying this is connected?' The fear she'd been trying to keep to a simmer jolted inside her chest.

'We're here to make sure you're okay,' said the senior detective, Mick Hetter, patting her upper arm. 'Take a deep breath, Maddy. Nothing will happen while we're here.'

She exhaled, pasting on a brave face.

'So, which is your place?'

'First floor.' She led the way.

'This is a swanky building,' said Paul, bringing up the rear as their footsteps echoed up the grand staircase. 'Can you afford to rent here on your barmaid's wage?'

'I can.' Maddison stabbed her door key at the lock, but her hands wouldn't stop shaking.

'Here, let me.' Taking the keys, Paul gave her hands a gentle squeeze.

His hands were so warm, and she was so cold, she had to bite down to stop her teeth from chattering. She hated being cold.

'Stand behind me, Maddy,' said Laurie. 'We'll stay outside while the boys check out the place.'

As Paul unlocked the front door, the detectives removed their handguns from under their jackets and headed inside.

Laurie listened from the corridor, poised and ready for attack, while Maddison was ready to run for the stairs.

'All clear,' called out Paul from inside.

'What the … They've ransacked the place.' Laurie squinted his eyes at the chaos.

It looked like a tornado had let loose in her apartment, tossing everything around. It broke her heart.

'Can you tell us what happened?' Mick asked, sliding his pistol back into its holster, while his partner poked around the tipped over furniture.

'I left to go to the funeral and came back to this.' Maddison shook her head at the mess. 'Why? Who?'

'Did anyone see you? Or go with you?'

'No one went with me.' Which dropped another smothering blanket of loneliness over her. 'This morning, when I left, I spoke to Mr Williams when he was collecting his mail. When I returned, I spoke with Mrs Jenkins.' She frowned at the spilled rice mixed with broken glass spread across her floor tiles. 'Mrs Jenkins said she'd heard noises while I was out. She thought I was home moving furniture around.'

'Do you see anything missing? Stolen?'

'It looks like all of your electrical equipment is still here.' Paul pointed to the wide-screen TV on the floor. 'You've got all the top brands for gear here. How can you afford this stuff on a barmaid's salary?'

'Um?' She glanced at Laurie beside her.

'You can tell them, it's routine questioning.'

'I have a trust …' She shoved her hands deep into her pockets, toeing at a broken coffee cup. 'From my mother— it's an inheritance thing.'

'Are you rich or something?' Paul asked, with Mick arching an eyebrow at her.

'It depends on what you'd call rich.'

'Do you own this apartment?' Mick tossed his thumb

back at the room.

'I own the building. Well, the trust does.' Maddison gave a meek shrug. She hated anyone knowing about her financial affairs; people treated her differently when they knew.

'How come you work as a barmaid?' Paul asked.

She repeated what she'd told many others. 'I like it. It's easy work and I get to hang out with some wonderful people.' She wasn't a part of the false world her mother belonged to. She'd escaped all that, hoping to reinvent her introverted self and find her spine when it came to speaking to people.

'Well,' said Laurie, scratching at his salt-n-pepper crew cut, 'they were searching for something. Do you have any idea what?'

'I don't know, not with this mess. Have you found Bob's murderer?' Maddison asked Mick.

Mick, in a suit that had seen better days, tugged at his loose tie. 'We haven't found anything new in our investigation. And the word on the street is Bob's death was a message from his bookie for others to pay their debts.'

'But Uncle Bob said it wasn't them. He said you can't get money out of a dead man.'

'Bob knew you had money, didn't he?'

Duh! The guy crashed on her couch because she didn't have a spare room.

'Did you ever pay his gambling debts?'

'Bob refused to take anything from me. I even offered him an apartment here in the building, rent free, but he refused. He was happy to just crash on my couch.' That now had its innards shredded across the floor. Pity, it was a good couch.

'I'll ask again,' said Mick, 'did Bob tell you what story he was working on?'

'No. Nothing.' Again, fear crawled over her chest like spiders, sending a rush of tingles to the top of her scalp.

'So where did your uncle keep his notes? Bob was a journalist; he must have written things down? What about a laptop?'

'I gave Bob a laptop for Christmas, but he hocked it for a bet on one of his sure things at the racetrack.' Maddison blinked hard at the floor, suddenly remembering Bob's words—*the track*!

She glanced at the detectives stepping over the wreckage. Her mouth opened just as the memory of Bob's words came to mind—*trust no one*.

She bit down on her tongue to stop the urge to spill all, and suddenly remembered the unopened envelope inside her coat. In her lower pockets, she squeezed her hands into fists trying to get the circulation back. She needed to focus. Time had slipped away from her, stumbling through the days ever since her uncle's death. She needed to wake up. And now.

'So, what happens now?' She asked the detectives picking over her place like it was a lawn sale.

'Do you have any insurance?' Paul asked.

Maddison nodded.

'We'll get the forensic boys to do a sweep on the place for prints,' Mick said to Paul who grabbed his mobile to carry out his instructions. 'Let's hope they can make a match with our database. There's no signs of forced entry, but I think they came in through your front door.'

'Who else has a key to your apartment?' Laurie asked, his shoes crunching on broken plates and cereal as he inspected her door's lock.

'Only Uncle Bob. Did you ever find his car keys?'

'No,' replied Mick, scrutinising the windows. 'I'd get a locksmith in if I were you.'

'I know one.' Laurie dragged out his phone and started scrolling. 'We'll beef up the security in here, Maddy, don't you worry none.'

'Why? Are they going to come back?' Maddison again swallowed that horrid acidic taste of fear. It was fast becoming a familiar friend you'd never forget. But she wanted to.

'I don't think so,' interjected Paul.

'How can you be so sure?'

'Calm down, Maddy, it's only a precautionary measure,' said Laurie. 'I'll make sure you're all nice and safe in here. Otherwise, you won't be able to sleep at night and you'll be no good for work. Have you still got that pepper spray I gave you?'

She nodded.

The buzzer for downstairs rang.

'Sounds like the forensic team's here.' Paul approached the panel by the front door, pressed the intercom button and spoke through the microphone, 'Hello?'

'Forensics,' replied the male voice over the speaker.

'Come on up. First level. Apartment four.' Paul then pressed the button to unlock the door to the main foyer entrance.

'Hey, how did you know which button to push for the intercom and the door?' It had taken her ages to work it out.

'Oh, that 6... my mum has the same type in her apartment.' Paul headed into the hallway.

'Well, Maddy, we can't do much more in here except let the forensic team do their job.' Mick jumped over her shattered coffee table and torn magazines. 'Listen, if you think of anything, and I mean anything, about your uncle or his notes, please call me or Paul, anytime. Trust me, every little bit helps us to catch these guys. Okay?'

She nodded, even though she was on the verge of spilling all. But she didn't know if Bob had been rambling. She needed to think, but she couldn't, not while the detective was watching her—the detective Bob had never liked.

Five

Stiff as a surfboard, Maddison lay in bed gripping the borrowed Taser to her chest. Under the low glow of the bathroom light, her wide eyes darted to the shadowy corners at every little sound.

She'd tried to find comfort in Laurie's words that she was safe. She had new locks and new security screens that ran like prison bars along her windows. They'd even installed cameras in the hallway outside her door. But Maddison still didn't feel safe.

'Why?' Maddison stewed over the same question she'd been asking since her uncle's murder.

Giving up on sleep, she turned on her bedside lamp, which only depressed her when she saw the dishevelled mess. She'd spent ages trying to restore some sort of order out of the chaos but hadn't even made a dent.

Tiptoeing into her walk-in closet, she slid on some socks and a baggy jumper like a security blanket.

At least she'd put her wardrobe back together, with her clothes hanging on the racks and her shoes back in pairs. Her mother's couture outfits, even her mother's authentic jewels, were all left behind.

Could they still be called thieves if they'd stolen nothing?

In the mirror's reflection, her long coat hung on the rack. She retrieved the envelope from the inner breast pocket. She'd forgotten all about it, too busy cleaning while getting lessons on personal security.

Inside the envelope was a first-class plane ticket and a small white card that read:

My darling Sweet Cheeks,
I have only just heard about your uncle. I am so sorry.
Call me because I've lost your numbers, again!
Then use the ticket to come stay with me.
From the wickedest of godmothers,
Nancy McCann.
Remember me—how dare you forget!

Maddison gave a weak smile, clutching the card to her chest.

The wicked godmother strikes again.

Maddison searched the time on her phone, who knows where her clock was? Was it too late or too early? Did she dare?

'To hell with it.' Putting it straight on speaker, she waited to leave a message.

'This had better be bloody good and by invitation only that someone should dare to wake *moi*,' grumbled the gravelly female voice of a heavy smoker.

'Nancy, it's me, Maddison.'

'Sweet Cheeks, is that you?'

Maddison rolled her eyes at the nickname. 'I'm sorry to call so late.'

'Darling, you've never needed an invitation to call me.'

Maddison heard the distinctive flick and hiss of a lighter, followed by a deep exhale as if smoking a cigarette. Sounds that were so familiar to Maddison.

'I could do with a midnight drinking session. You?'

'Um …' From her bedroom's doorway, Maddison faced a war zone.

'Darling, find something wet and alcoholic now. We'll call it a nightcap as we watch the sunrise together. Do it!'

'I'm doing it.' Well, she had been trying to have that drink all day.

She slipped into her hiking boots, then tiptoed through the torn furniture. On the kitchen bench, she left the phone on speaker and stared at her empty liquor cupboard.

Laurie had made her toss out any open bottles, while telling her scary stories about what thieves did with people's toothbrushes and toilets. It had made Maddison invest in a stash of thick gloves, garbage bags, and industrial-strength bleach as her weapons for a cleaning frenzy that began in her bedroom.

The rest would take a week to clean.

It might be easier to toss it all out the window and into a dump truck.

'*Are we there yet?*' Nancy cried out, as the distinct pop of a cork escaping from a champagne bottle carried over the phone. 'I'm pouring my coffee now.'

Champagne to Nancy was her water, coffee, and go-go super juice. It was always paired with a cigarette.

'Almost ...' Maddison opened her freezer, which held only her favourite vodka bottle. Did Laurie, the bar manager, sneak this in? Did she dare hope?

It was like drawing Excalibur from the bed of stone, pulling the bottle free as her eyes widened as if it was gold. And cold. She searched for the seal around the lid ... It was unbroken. *Yes!*

She scrounged around for an unbroken coffee mug off the floor and washed it twice. Cracked the bottle's seal, poured, and sipped. 'That tastes so good.'

'So, darling, I was starting to think my assistant, Farkwit, stuffed up that card I'd sent you with the air ticket.' Nancy spoke between sips of champagne and exhales of her cigarette.

'It arrived earlier,' replied Maddison, searching for a place to sit.

The stuffing from her favourite reading chair spilled from wounds like it had been slashed at with a sword. Five out of six dining room chairs had no legs. Only one survived, barely.

She flipped it over, then dragged it behind her as she cleared a path to her oak table, now bearing deep scratches. She positioned herself in the corner with her back to the wall, facing the door.

With vodka bottle, phone, coffee cup and Taser on the table in front of her, she tucked the pepper spray into her pocket. 'Okay, I'm ready.'

'Well, darling, you'd better have a bloody good excuse

as to why you're only ringing me now?'

'I buried Uncle Bob today.'

'Oh. Did many go?'

'Nope. Just the priest and me.' Maddison emptied her coffee mug and let the vodka burn inside her chest. She reached for the bottle, flicked off the lid, which disappeared into the crap crowding the floor. 'I wanted to have a drink for Bob, and so here it is … To Uncle Bob. May he rest in peace.' She raised her coffee mug to the room of rubbish.

'Oh my darling, drink up.' Nancy swallowed hard, again and again, no doubt emptying an entire champagne glass. Then came the glug-glug-glug of more being poured. 'I'd only just found out about Bob's death. Was he really murdered?'

'Yes, but no one knows why.' It sucked not having the answers. It was worse than being left with a cliff-hanging end to a TV series and having to wait to find out what happened in the next season, only for the studio to go broke.

'So, tell me everything and let's see if we can solve the problems of our world.'

'Most people say they solve the problems of *the* world,' corrected Maddison, feeling better from the icy vodka defrosting her limbs.

'Oh, my darling Sweet Cheeks,' crooned Nancy, 'there are only four things that matter to me in my world: me, myself and *moi*, and you. Not even my toy boys get that sort of attention. Now, tell your wicked godmother everything, it's been far too long between drinks.'

'Well, um, last week …' Maddison explained all, wiping at the tears, with her feet resting on the table beside the lidless bottle of vodka and bottles of water. 'And today, my place got broken into. They trashed it.'

'Was anything taken?' Nancy asked.

'Not that I can see. Laurie, my boss, said they were searching for something because the stuff that thieves normally take is still here, broken.'

'Is it something to do with Bob's murder?'

'I think so,' Maddison confessed in a whisper.

Dropping her feet to the floor, she faced the kitchen. Did she have any coffee in her cupboards because she needed to wake up.

'What does breaking into your apartment have to do with Bob's murder?' Nancy asked loud and clear over the phone's speaker.

'Bob was working on a story. He never told me what it was about, only making me swear to finish it.' But how?

'Oh come on, darling, Bob was always working on a big story.'

'I know,' said Maddison, skipping over the couch stuffing as she headed for the kitchen. 'But this time it was different because Bob didn't drink. He was busy on my laptop while he stayed here.'

'What was Bob researching?'

Yes! Another win. She'd found an unopened box of coffee bags she'd bought for Bob, who hated wrestling with the coffeemaker. But she couldn't see the kettle. Her microwave was smashed, so she dug around for a saucepan off the floor.

Again, as was her new routine, she washed it twice before filling up the dented pot, while hoping her stovetop worked. 'I have no idea what he was researching, and I can't check the history because my laptop got destroyed.' Like everything else in this place.

But the stove worked, so she could boil water. It was another small win.

'By whom? The criminals?' Nancy asked.

'No. Bob spilled his drink on it.'

'Scotch, no doubt?'

'No, it was coffee.' Bob's coffee bags were now her most treasured possession.

'I don't believe it. Darling, are we talking a straight coffee? Without the scotch?'

'Straight. Black. Coffee.' Just like the one she was looking forward to, since they'd spilled her sugar all over the floor.

Seriously, did some goons hire a bunch of kids armed with baseball bats and steel-cap boots for a trash party? The more she looked at the mess the more it hurt her eyes.

'Where is the laptop now?'

'The guys at the IT store said it was beyond repair. Bob said he needed to do more research, and that was the last time I saw Bob alive...' Her shoulders sagged as she leaned her back against the kitchen counter to watch the pot of water on the stove.

'Does Bob back up his notes?'

'Yes, he does.' Maddison stood taller.

'Do you know where Bob kept them?'

'I think so.'

'Well?'

Maddison braced herself for it … 'Bob told me to tell no one and to trust no one. He made me promise.' Those words of a promise whispered in her ear, curling around inside her as if committing it to her soul. 'I've made plenty of promises that didn't matter in the past, but this one,' she said, patting her hand over heart as if swearing an oath, 'this promise I have to keep.'

'FINE! Don't bloody tell me then. Just who the hell do you think I am? *Don't trust me.* Trust nooooo one!'

'I trust you, but it was Bob's last dying request. I didn't even tell the detectives.' Had she done the wrong thing by not confiding in those trying to catch Bob's killer?

'Fine, you can't break a promise made to Bob on his deathbed.'

'He died on the asphalt floor of a train station car park.'

'Oh, sorry, excuse the poor choice of words.' Nancy poured more champagne and lit another cigarette.

'What would you do if you were in my position?'

'Me? Drink.' Nancy's tone then softened as she said, 'But I know what your mother would do.'

Maddison frowned. 'What?'

'Janice would keep her promise and she'd start by finding those answers herself, like she always did. Just like you. You both were so—'

'Different.'

'My darling Sweet Cheeks, you have the same qualities as your mother. Even though you've run away to find yourself this past year, we both know you are your mother's daughter. And my darling Sweet Cheeks?' Nancy paused in her monologue for dramatic impact, as always.

'Yes?' Maddison poured the boiling water into her coffee cup.

'You come from a line of strong women. Your mother

was a queen who fought for everything she had, clearing the path for all those who followed, which was you and *moi*.'

No wonder Maddison struggled to get out from under Janice Farley's shadow.

'What I'm trying to say, my darling Sweet Cheeks …'

'Okay …' Maddison leaned away from the phone as Nancy wound herself up for a lecture.

'Don't you dare let your standards drop and forget who you are and where you come from. You never give up.'

'Uh huh.' Maddison sipped her coffee. It was black, bitter, and hot. *Best coffee ever.*

Inhaling the rich dark roast, while Nancy ranted over the phone, Maddison admired the sunrise creeping over the small park's treetops. The teeny tiny country view she used to adore was now ruined by thick ugly black bars.

'My darling, you've never been a girl who gave up and let others fix things for you. It's a quality you and your mother shared that I've always admired. You both have that inner strength to achieve anything you wanted.'

'Uh huh.' Maddison now pictured Nancy raising her champagne glass like a sword in the air and her cigarette like a microphone, talking to a crowd of … one.

It was a passionate speech.

'And darling, I truly believe with the utmost of confidence, that you'll run at full steam ahead like the day you worked out how to stand. So, what are you going to do? Hmm?'

'Well, I can't sleep here,' blurted out Maddison, surprised by her own words.

'Oh, I remember when my dingy flat got broken into; that's why I married my first husband. But darling, I do believe there's more to your home invasion, don't you agree? Hmm?'

'Yeah.'

'Good. So, how are you planning to fix it?'

'Um …' Maddison hesitated, staring at the aftermath of a bomb blast.

'HELLOOO! Have I got you so drunk you can't think?'

Maddison laughed, cradling her hot coffee cup. 'No. I'm stone-cold sober.' For the first time in a week, she was awake.

'Wonderful. Now, I gave you a first-class plane ticket, use it. Your room is always here and waiting for you, darling. Besides, it wouldn't hurt to come home and be pampered while you look at this situation from another angle.'

'You do have a point.' A pampering, even better.

'Of course, I'll take you shopping, and we'll go to all of my favourite restaurants. Oh, it'll be like a holiday for the both of us. So when can I expect you? Hmm?'

And just like that, Nancy had backed her into another corner.

Although, Maddison had no other offers, and she didn't want to be alone. 'Hopefully, today? But there's something I need to do first.'

'Well, don't bother touching that place, darling. I'll get my assistant, Farkwit, to send someone in to do the cleaning.'

'Yes, please.'

'So only pack a few things, it'll give us an excuse to go shopping,' said Nancy, all excited. 'Christ, who put the sun out?'

Maddison faced her window on a fresh new day with the sunlight creeping between the tall buildings. 'Sunrise is a daily miracle, you know.'

'Well then, my darling Sweet Cheeks, I'll see you before the sun sets?'

'Um?' Maddison needed to make a stop first and had no idea how long that would take.

'I'll book us a table for dinner.'

'I may have to call—'

'I'll get the stylist to deliver a new outfit for you, so don't bother packing much.'

'—if there's a change of plans.'

'I must tell Theresa to stock up on your vodka.'

'Is Theresa still there?'

'Oh my darling, as if Theresa would ever bloody leave. That old battle-axe will be so excited to have you home again. Well, until sunset, Sweet Cheeks?' Nancy said as if raising her glass in a toast.

'Until sunset,' replied Maddison, raising her coffee cup

for another sip.

'Be safe, my darling,' Nancy whispered as if in prayer.

'I will.' Maddison ended the call, smiling to herself while ignoring her chaotic surroundings. She knew exactly what she was going to do.

Six

An ornate curved iron archway framed the entrance of the heritage-listed Flemington Racetrack, home to Australia's most prestigious horse race, the Melbourne Cup.

Assorted rose gardens lined the wide curved walkways, where a tour guide led his wandering group of bucket-listers who were taking selfies. While the serious punters stood in the stands staring starry-eyed at the track, with racing programs in hand and their phones glued to their ears.

A loud bell rang. There was a pause in the air, as if gravity held its breath.

The crowd roared as the starting gates clanged open. A thunder of hooves barrelled down the track, holding everyone's attention. A dozen horses, with their colourful satin-dressed jockeys, shouldered each other for space, as they raced around the sweeping turn. The crowds' squeals, moans and yahoos increased as the string of horses made the final turn and powered down the straight for the finish line.

A cheer rang out as the horses slowed down, and shredded paper chits were tossed like confetti. Trackside, punters shrugged, picking up their programs they headed toward the stands to do it all over again.

'Aw hell, where did that wench go?' Eric stood on his toes, smoothing over his midnight-coloured lion's mane. 'Tom, can you see her?'

Tom stood a head above the crowd with his shaved scalp shining in the sunlight. 'Nah. Nah. Nah … Oh there, see?' He pointed with a massive paw to the stairs.

Eric craned his neck to spot the wide-brimmed fancy

lady's hat. 'Got her.'

'She sure looks different today, huh?' Tom said, loping alongside. 'She's got that confident stride like she owns the place. See?'

Eric tilted his head at Maddison Farley's hips swaying in her fancy frock that matched the hat, lugging around an oversized red handbag that didn't match the outfit.

'She sure scrubs up all right. See?'

'Will you stop perving and stay focused?'

'Don't you find her at all attractive?'

'Hell no.' They followed Maddison to the grandstand's first floor where the racetrack spread out in a grand vista as the warm breeze soon cooled in the shade of the food hall and betting areas.

'She looks out of my league the way she's all fancily dressed like that. See?'

'She's not my type,' said Eric. 'Her boobs aren't big enough, but I'll give her an eight on the legs and a good nine on that arse of hers.' It swayed lovely in that frock. 'But she's picked the wrong bag for that outfit, it's a crappy colour.'

'It's a blue dress. How can you call blue crappy?'

'So now you're a master of fashion, are you?' Eric arched an eyebrow at his idiot offsider in his outdated leather jacket, black slacks, and brown boots. All googly-eyed over their mark.

Tom gave one of his goofy grins. 'That Maddison looks like one of 'em glamorous models? Like she's loaded? See?'

Then the Neanderthal frowned.

Eric could hear its brain clunk into gear.

'How come she makes out she's just a barmaid?' Tom asked. 'She owns an apartment building, drives that fancy red Mercedes, and I swear on my two thumbs those diamonds she's wearing are real.'

'The lads-of-the-law reckon she's a trust kid.'

'A what?'

'It's an inheritance thing, where she gets so much spending money a month to live off. How the heck should I know? And I. Don't. Care.' Eric scowled up at Tom. 'We're here to follow the dumb blonde in case she finds anything.'

'At the racetrack? I'd doubt that. Why is she here?'

Eric rolled his eyes. Some days it was like babysitting a reject from *The Flintstones*. 'Maybe, she's here to pay tribute to her dearly departed uncle. Bob Farley was a known gambler who liked the ponies, and this racetrack was his preferred haunting ground.' He grinned, tapping Tom on the arm. 'Get it, haunting ground. Guys dead … Haunt—forget it.'

'Do you reckon she's here as a remembrance thing?' Tom asked as they went deeper into the building. The crowd thinned and the security tightened with guards and cameras everywhere.

'I don't give a toss why. All we do is watch her. That's it. We don't touch her. Don't talk to her. And she's not allowed to cotton-on that we're even following her.'

'Is that coz them coppers like her, huh?'

'Apparently, she's their favourite barmaid. Where is she going?' With the racetrack behind them, they followed Maddison up the stairs to an area that reminded him of a hotel foyer.

Maddison held out a white card to the receptionist waiting behind the counter. It was like an airline boarding desk, except with double doors and two security guards on either side.

'Aw hell.' Eric tightened his lips as he watched Maddison get escorted through the large automatic doors and disappear.

'Do we follow?'

'They won't let us in there, it's for VIPs. How rich is she?' Eric searched for options.

'Victoria Race Club. What's that?' Tom pointed his big paw to the sign on the wall.

'Members only, dickhead.'

'So, only the rich and richer go in there?'

Eric face-palmed himself.

'Didn't think she could afford that. I wonder if her uncle had a membership too.'

Eric eyed Tom in surprise. 'For a big bloke who annoys the absolute crap out of me, sometimes you ask the right bloody questions.'

'Um, thanks?' Tom scratched his head. 'Where are we

going?'

'To find out if Bob Farley is a member and what's in that member's area, because I bet Miss Fancy Pants in there isn't just having a flutter on the gee-gees.' Eric popped a mint, pasted on his billionaire's smile, and swaggered up to the female behind the counter. 'Hi there.'

'Can I help you?' The receptionist smiled politely, as if talking to a pile of overdressed horse dung.

But Eric kept on smiling. 'Do you have a member registered by the name of Bob Farley?'

'I'm sorry, I'm not allowed to give out membership details.'

'Are you sure, honey?' Eric leaned his elbow on the counter while holding out a folded fifty-dollar bill. 'I just need a yes or no. Easy as.'

The receptionist peeked around, then snatched the cash and started tapping away on the keyboard. 'Name?'

'Bob Farley.'

'Nope, sorry. Not here.'

'Are you sure?' Eric leaned over the desk to peek at her screen.

The receptionist turned her screens away. 'Yes, I'm sure.'

'Well, what about that woman who just walked in with the dress and matching hat,' Tom said over Eric's shoulder, 'who's she?'

'That was Miss Farley. Oh wait, she's a full member.' The receptionist's fingers hammered away at the keyboard like a drill on a factory line. It was impressive.

'What's the difference?' Eric asked.

'With a full membership you have access to our exclusive club rooms, which includes the dining rooms and private marquee areas. Their family receives the same benefits, especially for our main racing calendar days.'

'Like the cup?' Tom asked.

'*The* Melbourne Cup. There is the ever-popular Ladies' Day—'

'What about the uncle?' Eric didn't give a crap about fillies in overpriced frocks. He had his eye only on one prize, his job. 'Is there a Robert, Bob Farley on the list?'

The receptionist glanced at her screen. 'Oh, he was here

all the time.'

'Are there any lockers inside for the VIP members?'

The receptionist arched an over-plucked eyebrow at them. 'We're not a gym. It's a lounge area, boasting a fine dining menu for patrons to enjoy while overlooking an amazing view of the racetrack.'

The receptionist sounded like a salesman on commission selling a luxury car.

'Oh, and the loos are classy too.'

'Choice.' Tom grinned, nodding that big bald boofhead.

Eric wanted to gag. 'Thank you for your help.' He walked away with Tom shadowing him like a Great Dane. 'Stay.' *Well, what d'ya know the puppy stopped.* 'Stay here and keep an eye out for Miss Fancy Pants. Call me the second you see her. Just don't lose sight of her, okay?'

'Why? Where are you going?'

'To find a way to get inside.'

Seven

Maddison lounged back in the sumptuous leather chair with a grand view of Flemington Racetrack. It was so different from Lou's Sports Bar. Widescreen televisions were set above the luxurious brass bar. Warm floral scents filled the room from lavish rose bouquets, no doubt from the extensive gardens.

With phone and program before her, Maddison studied the race guide. She read the horses' bloodlines and past race performances, the jockeys and their riding styles, and the racing track's condition. All these details added up to the science of placing a bet, according to the teachings of Bob.

She used to annoy him by picking a horse because the colours were pretty, and she liked the name. But today, she was an eager pupil.

'Bob, you got me here, help me play the game.'

She signalled to the waiter, passing him her forms and credit card. He raced to the bookie's table and soon returned with her chits and coffee, she settled in to watch the show.

Between sips of coffee, Maddison peered through her binoculars as the horses lined up at the gates.

She checked out their form, like Uncle Bob had shown her many times. After all, this was how Bob did his babysitting; and she'd been accompanying him to the racetrack since she was six.

The bell rang. The gates flung open, and the mighty thoroughbreds leapt forward and were off and racing.

Grass flew behind their hammering hoofs as they rounded the turn in a tight pack. Down the first straight, the field of racers lengthened with a group of six fighting for the lead.

With binoculars glued to her eyes, her horse was nose to nose with another. 'Come on, do this for Bob.'

She held her breath as they barrelled down the straight, racing to the finish, where her horse gallantly dove through.

'Yes! A win.' *A bloody big win.* She pressed her knuckles against her lips to stop her cheer as the other punters in the room groaned at their loss.

Bob would have been so proud for her pick of the longshot. Would there be enough in the kitty now?

Again, she studied the form and the horses' history. Placed a few more bets and settled in to watch the next three races. She sipped rich coffee while having a long and luxurious brunch, ending up feeling overfull and sleepy. She was looking forward to napping on the plane.

Maddison approached the bookie's table, manned by a tall, wiry man with a peaked cap that Uncle Bob would call a classic newsboy cap.

She handed the bookie her chits, biting her bottom lip, hoping she'd made enough in the kitty to leave.

He swore under his breath with his arched eyebrows disappearing beneath his peak cap. 'Jeez, luv, you had the luck of the Irish today.' The bookie scratched the back of his head, then readjusted his cap. 'How do you want to do this? You're looking at well over twenty thousand in cash here.'

Holy crap! She pinched herself to stay calm and act like this happened every day. 'I believe there's a back room that's used for discreet cash transactions?'

'Yeah, there is.' The man squinted his eyes at her. 'Hey, aren't you Bob Farley's niece?'

'Um … yes.' Was this the bad bookie? Should she run? Wait, she wanted her winnings first.

'Bob would be proud of you today with winnings like this.' He then cleared his throat, while removing his cap. 'I'm sorry to hear what happened to Bob. I didn't mind the bloke myself.'

'Thank you.' She was surprised by his changed demeanour.

'Listen, luv, give us a sec and I'll get ya cash. I'll get the steward to take you to the back room, if that's okay?' He signalled to the steward on the far side of the room.

'Fine by me.' She was here for a reason.

'Listen, luv, are you sticking around for a bit, or are you heading off for the day?'

'I'll be leaving as soon as I get my winnings.'

'Well, seeing as how your Bob's niece and all, I'll get one of me lads to escort you to your car.'

'Why?' She swallowed hard, gripping the diamond on her necklace.

'We wouldn't want anything to happen to you out here, luv, coz this is Bob's backyard after all.'

She sighed, loosening the tension in her shoulders. 'Thank you, Bob would be pleased.'

'The name's Quid,' he said with a cheeky grin and a thick Aussie ocker accent. He gave quick instructions to the steward, then spoke to Maddison, 'Follow the steward and I'll see you soon, luv.'

'This way, miss.' The steward unlocked a side door. Her heels echoed down the slim corridor, where they were greeted by the aromas from the kitchens.

'Quid will only be a few minutes.' The steward unlocked the door to a simple square room where a small table and four chairs faced the large window. 'If you need anything, press that bell and we'll be right with you.'

'Thank you.' Maddison dropped her large red bag on the nearest chair and checked out the window view that stretched beyond the stables.

As soon as the door closed Maddison kicked off her heels, climbed onto the chair, and then the table. She reached for the white ceiling panel above the window, slid it aside and patted around the dusty edges.

She hoped it was still here.

And in a matter of moments, her fingertips brushed against the cold, thick plastic bag. She pulled it down, sneezing at the dust.

'Gotcha.' The pouch was heavier than expected.

Bob had explained, in significant detail, all the wonders this thick black waterproof, rodent-proof pouch had to offer, bragging about how much of a bargain it was. And she dumped it straight into her leather handbag, which was loud. Big. Red. And necessary.

Maddison returned the ceiling panel to its place. Climbed down. Dusted herself off as she slipped into her shoes. Pulled out her compact, touched up her lipstick and checked over her appearance. She then stood by the window, clasping her hands together, despite the itch to open Bob's pouch.

There was a knock on the door a few moments later.

'Hello there, luv.' Quid, carrying a leather satchel, was escorted by a dark-skinned man in a navy suit and maroon tie. 'This is Reggie, he's part of my security team. Reggie, this is Bob Farley's niece.'

'It's Maddy, isn't it?' Reggie asked, with the build of a compact rugby player.

'Yes, how did you know?'

'Bob used to talk about you all the time.' Reggie gave a tentative smile with a slight shrug.

'Didn't he just. Well, let's get to it.' Quid dumped his satchel on the table and opened its mouth wide.

It was a bag full of cash.

Maddison's eyes widened. 'That's not all for me? Is it?'

Quid nodded.

'How much is there?'

'Twenty-three thousand, four hundred and seventy dollars,' read out Quid, handing her the slip.

'Shiiiit.' She cupped her mouth, stunned.

Quid and Reggie chuckled.

'You'll need to sign for it.' Quid held out a pen and paper, all very business-like. 'Keep the receipt on you in case the coppers want to know what you're doing with all this cash.'

'Sure.' She signed on the dotted line. 'Did Bob owe you guys any money?' Bob would be whooping-it-up, dancing on the tables in the bar, shouting everyone drinks with this much cash.

'Nah, not me, luv. Heard it was the Talbots. I think Bob owed them about six grand?' Quin said, glancing at Reggie.

'Is that all?' Maddison had been told it was a thirty-thousand-dollar debt.

'Yeah, I heard the same.' Reggie, again, gave a slight

shrug.

'Is that enough to have someone shot over a gambling debt?'

'Jeez, luv.' Quid took a step back, rubbing his neck. 'We're bookies, not murderers. No one gets knocked off like that for spare change.'

'Is that what you got told?' Reggie asked Maddison.

She nodded. 'They said Bob's murder was a message sent to other gamblers to pay their debts.'

'Jeez, luv, if us bookies did that no one would wanna bet with us or ask us for tick. That's where we make our money—on the interest. It's just business. I've heard of a few getting a bit of a touch-up, but not murder.' Quid shook his head. 'And the Talbots, they had a soft spot for Bob, like most of us.'

'The Talbot's wouldn't knock someone off for six gees,' said Reggie, so sure of himself.

'Bob may be what he was, luv, but he always paid his debts,' said Quid. 'You know, you can't get money out of a dead man.'

'Uncle Bob said the same thing.' She stared at the cash in confusion.

'Who told you Bob's death was over a gambling gig?' Reggie asked Maddison.

'The detectives investigating his murder.'

'They're full of it,' blurted out Quid. 'I'd say them coppers are being lazy and not doing their job.'

Maddison blinked. Why would the police lie?

'Listen, luv, Bob was a good bloke underneath it all. I didn't mind the man. He was just down on his luck, is all. Most come good in the end.'

'Thank you.' She swallowed down the tears, grateful someone had a kind word to say about her uncle.

Quid nodded, again readjusting his cap. 'Do you wanna count your cash?'

'No, I believe you.' Strangely enough, she believed their side of the story more than what she'd been told by the detectives.

'Bob never counted his cash either. So, where do you want it then, luv?'

'In here.' She opened her red handbag and loaded it up with bundles of cash. 'For you two, gentlemen.' She gave them a hundred dollar note each. 'Thank you for your kindness and for being honest about my uncle, too.'

'Hey, I couldn't accept this, luv.' Quid held up his hands in surrender.

'Please, have a drink for Uncle Bob sometime. I insist.'

'Thanks, luv.' Quid grinned, plucking the cash. 'It's been a while since anyone gave me a tip.'

'Me too. Thank you.' Reggie slid the cash into his jacket's inner breast pocket, then opened the door. 'Now I'll escort you to your car. If you care to follow me.'

Maddison slung her heavier bag over her shoulder, yet it still looked half empty and was soon guided into the mainstream area of the racetrack.

Moving through the crowds, Reggie glanced back over his shoulder. 'Did someone come with you today?'

'No, just me.' Sad, but true.

'Did anyone know you were coming out here today?'

'No, it was all last minute. I thought I'd come and place a few bets in honour of my uncle. This was his favourite place. Why?' Her grip tightened on the straps of her handbag.

Again, Reggie looked back over his shoulder. 'What do you think is the real reason that got your uncle murdered like that?'

'What the—' She stopped and stared at Reggie. 'Bob was working on a story. That's all I know.' And that's all anyone knew, even if her handbag felt like a solid block of concrete that contained a ticking bomb.

Reggie stared long and hard at her, taking in all the details. 'Did anything else happen since his murder?'

'Um …' Trapped by his stare, she couldn't help but answer him. 'My place got broken into yesterday while I was at Bob's funeral.'

Reggie again frowned. 'Did they steal anything?'

'Not that I'm aware of, but they trashed everything.' She couldn't believe she'd spilled so much. She was lousy at this secret-squirrel stuff. 'Why do you ask?'

'Don't panic none, but you're being followed.'

Eight

'I'm being followed?' Maddison gasped, stepping back, but Reggie grabbed her by the elbow as people moved around them like they were stones in a stream. Everything was suddenly too loud, with the clashing chatter of a hundred voices drowned out by the next race being announced over the speakers.

She tried to breathe, but gagged on the overpowering aroma of sun-baked concrete, fragrant roses, and horse dung.

'Calm down, Maddy, just walk normally.' Reggie escorted her through the crowds. His grip was strong yet gentle on her arm.

She wanted to stop and see who was following.

'Don't turn around. Keep going.'

'But—' She glared at him. 'I want answers.'

'First, I want to make sure. We'll wander round for a bit and play the game, okay?'

If it meant her safety ... 'Sure.'

He guided her through the crowds, turning left then right, reaching for his mobile, while pulling Maddison along for the ride. But his face was dead serious.

She was itching to look. 'Can you see them?'

Facing straight ahead, he replied, 'Tall man, bald head, wearing a mid-length black leather coat. He's with a small bloke with Elvis hair.'

'Elvis hair?'

'Yeah, you know ...' Reggie let go of her arm to sweep his hand over his black curls. She had to grin with him. 'Hey, Croco? Reggie here. I'm on the south side near Tammy's TAB, can you get a visual on me?' He paused on the phone, stopping in the middle of the walkway. 'Maddy, pretend you're checking out the board for the odds on the next race,' he said, cupping the phone.

Maddison struggled to read the board and act calm while her brain rattled with so many questions.

'Yeah, you've got me … Do me a favour and check out if I'm being tailed by two blokes and ring me back with their descriptions … Cheers.'

'What are you doing?' Maddison asked Reggie.

'I want to be sure. So slow down your pace, keep your eyes ahead, and we'll aim for your car the long way round.' Again, he grabbed her elbow and resumed walking. 'Are you sure you don't know what your uncle was into?'

She shook her head, as they strolled past the gardens like the tourist groups she'd seen earlier.

'Who else have you spoken to about your uncle's murder?'

'My boss. The detectives. Now you. I can't believe I'm telling you.'

Reggie gave a crooked grin that soon disappeared. 'Was that the same detectives who fed you that BS about Bob getting murdered over a gambling debt?'

Oh, my God. 'Yes. Are you a detective?'

'No, but I know plenty. When did you see them detectives of yours last?'

'They were at my apartment after it got broken into, only yesterday.' Yesterday felt like a week ago.

'Homicide detectives interested in a break-in? That's rare, don't you think? Most coppers wouldn't bother to show up. They'd send in the uniforms with forensics to dust for prints and log in the job number for the insurance. Are you sleeping with one of them or something?'

'Hey!' She stopped and glared at him. 'They're regular customers at the bar I work at. They were there when I spoke to my boss, who rang to see if I was okay after my uncle's funeral. I thought an intruder was still inside my apartment, but the wind had knocked over a vase in my room.'

'Keep walking, Maddy.' Reggie expertly steered her around the other punters. 'Bit convenient, don't you think, to have the same detectives show up at your place like that?

The same ones who told you that BS about the Talbots knocking him off?'

'What makes you so sure the Talbots didn't do it?'

He stopped to stand squarely in front of her. 'I used to work for the Talbots. I used to be that guy who'd go around collecting their money. And the Talbots never ordered me to break a bloke's finger unless it was over the ten-grand marker. For someone to say your uncle got whacked for a lousy six-gee debt is pissing in your ear.'

Maddison gasped at Reggie as his words hit home.

Reggie's phone rang. 'Yeah … You sure? … That's them, same blokes I pegged. Hey, Croco, do me a favour? … Call the boys on the VIP car park gate and have them create a lockdown for me. I want the lady to make a clean getaway … Thanks, mate, we'll be there in a few.'

'Is it true? I'm being followed?' *What freaking nightmare is this?*

'There's a mirror over my right shoulder, you can check out your tails. You'll see a tall fella with a bald head?'

She narrowed her eyes at the mirror. 'I see him. He's so big. Black coat, with a shaved head that's shiny under the sun.'

Reggie nodded. 'Beside him, you'll see a smaller bloke with dark hair.'

'Oh, I get the Elvis hair now.'

It made him grin which calmed her down some.

'Have you ever seen those men before?'

'No, never.' She stared at the mirror, committing their faces to memory. The tall guy had big hands that made the racing program look like a sheet of toilet paper. He looked like everyone else who'd come to the track to place a bet.

The other guy, however, had this determined scowl on his face and beady eyes. Stylishly dressed as if he'd spent time in Milan, with some sharp shoes. 'I wonder if he has a pair of blue suede shoes?'

Reggie chuckled. 'Let's keep moving and get you back to your car. So, I'm not much of a gambler—'

'Says the man working for a bookie at a racetrack.'

'But I'm willing to bet they're the same guys who broke into your place, and they've tailed you from there, considering you'd told no one you were coming here.'

She'd take that bet, too. 'Am I safe?'

'Good question. But I wouldn't go home if I were you.'

'Why not?'

'They'd know all about you, your friends, your workplace, and your habits. They've probably tapped your phone, too.'

'Why?' She felt so exposed.

'Because whatever Bob was working on, my bet is that they're hoping you'll lead them straight to it.'

She gripped her handbag tighter. *What the hell, Bob!*

Reggie didn't miss it, squinting at her white-knuckle grip. 'Okay then ...' He sniffed and kept walking as he talked. 'How I see it, the way Bob was so brutally done over means he was into something deep.'

She grabbed Reggie's arm; he was the only who'd made sense and saw straight through her. 'What should I do?' Unbelievably, asking a complete stranger for advice.

'Leave town and lie low for a bit. Don't tell anyone where you're going. Don't ring anyone. Don't use any of your credit cards, or your phone, it's how I was able to easily track people. But you,' he said, tapping at her hand that clasped the big red bag, 'have enough cash in there to disappear for a while.'

'For how long?'

'I don't know, Maddy. Until you've worked out a plan.'

Early this morning, talking with Nancy, she'd had a plan—but this was not going to plan at all. 'Can I go to the police?'

Reggie arched an eyebrow at her as he guided her down the walkway. 'Look, you seem an okay person, and I liked your uncle, so I'm going to give you a bit of advice.'

'Uh huh.' Should she take notes?

'Don't talk to the cops, not in this state, because it smells like they're involved. Your uncle was brutally murdered, and if they've trashed your place who knows what they'll do to you or your friends ...'

She gasped as they walked through the gates, and the guards shut them without a word. 'Why do I feel like I've been evicted from the racetrack?'

Reggie grinned. 'Relax, your shadows will be stuck inside for a bit.'

'Relax, huh? Are you joking?'

'Where's your car?'

'Over there. It's the red Mercedes.' She dug around in her bag for the keys, among her purse, wads of cash and the black plastic pouch that she was scared to touch.

'Nice car. Easy to follow, coz it stands out like bloody dog's balls.'

'Sorry, I hadn't planned on playing secret spy and doing covert escapes from the city. If I had, I might have dressed more appropriately.' In her race day hat that matched her dress, Nancy would be so proud.

Reggie chuckled. 'I'm sorry.'

'Me too.' Sorry for … well, where did she begin? Sorry for making Bob that coffee he spilled over her laptop. Sorry for not having a spare laptop for Bob to use at home, so he didn't have to leave. Sorry for not making the time to teach Bob how to use her tablet. All sorts of sorry scenarios she could come up within the blink of an eye. The guy might still be alive, and she wouldn't be surviving on no sleep, standing in pinching heels, seeking help from a stranger.

But she'd cope.

She had to.

So she took a deep breath and faced Reggie. 'Tell me again, please. What would you do if you were in my shoes and had something they wanted, but you had no idea what it was? Does that make sense?' Bob had made her promise to finish what he'd started.

Reggie nodded. 'If my life depended on it …'

Again, she gasped, stepping away from him.

Reggie held her upper arms, trapping her with his stare. 'What do you think they'll do to you if they realise you've got what they're after? You're in the middle of some big boy's game now and they don't play by anyone's rules. Think of what they would do to your family and friends?'

'What do I do?' She croaked out with a dry throat. She couldn't risk Nancy, or anyone else, not until she knew what she had.

'Get in that flash car of yours and head to the airport. Let them think you've gone on a break to clear your head after the funeral.'

'Okay.' Not okay, but she was listening. This time she led Reggie to her car. 'Then what?'

'Stay away from your place and those cops who are telling you stories.'

'Okay.' Easy enough, she hadn't told Laurie when she'd go back to work yet.

'Once you get out of Melbourne, take a small charter flight or bus. Pay for it with cash. Stay away from big terminals that have lots of cameras, and that includes city streets. I'd go country if you can. Don't hire a car, as they'll want credit card details. Shame you haven't got any fake ID because that'd come in handy too.' Reggie opened her car door.

Maddison collapsed into the driver's seat, her mind working overtime. 'I do actually.' The Motor Registration Department had stuffed up her name on her driver's licence, and she'd never bothered to change it.

'Well, then ...' He paused, rubbing his eyebrow. 'Stay safe, keep looking over your shoulder and trust no one.'

'That's what Bob said to me too, just before he died.' A whimper escaped the back of her throat as the fear, as cold as ice-water, flushed through her bloodstream.

'If Bob told you that, he obviously knew what he was getting you into, so heed the warning from a dead man. Now get out of here. Go North. Head for the country if you can.' He pushed her driver's door shut and nodded at her. 'Good luck.'

She needed it.

Nine

After zigzagging through traffic and detouring down random side streets, Maddison craned her neck to stare at another tote board of numbers. Only this time the betting odds, race numbers, and horse's names were exchanged for incoming and outgoing flights.

Welcome to Melbourne domestic airport.

There were two outgoing flights departing soon. A flight to Canberra, but that place was too cold and too close for comfort. The other flight was to Adelaide.

The wheels on her small overnight bag rumbled behind her, its handle still warm from the boot of her car. She approached the flight attendant seated behind the airline's counter. 'Hi, is there any chance of getting a seat on the plane to Adelaide?'

'Well, they are about to board.' The flight attendant looked at the screens then at her watch.

'My uncle died and …' The tears welled up. 'I'm sorry.' Maddison grabbed a tissue to dab at her eyes. 'I need to be at his funeral. I'll pay whatever it costs.' An actress once told her that the secret to acting was drawing on her personal experiences. Would this brief show score her the golden ticket? Or should she fall in a wailing heap on the floor— which is what she wanted to do.

Keep it together, Maddy.

'Let me see what I can do.' The air hostess tapped away on the keyboard; her make-up glowed from the PC's screens. 'We have a spare seat, Miss?'

'Oh, thank you so much. It's Janice Fraley.' And thank you Motor Registration for transposing her first and middle names on her licence, along with the typo in her surname, which she'd never bothered to correct. Because that would have taken a tonne of paperwork and half a day sitting in a queue waiting for them to fix their department's mistake. *Huh, maybe things do happen for a reason?*

Maddison passed her fake-not-fake licence to the flight attendant.

'How would you like to pay?'

'Cash.' Maddison counted out the crisp bills, ensuring the rest of the bundled money was out of sight.

'Here's your ticket. It's departing through gate five. You'll need to hurry so you're not late.'

Late? Ha! Maddison snatched the ticket and rushed through the airport. Her skirt flicked up, and with her hair flying behind her, she charged through people as she ran in a very unladylike manner, dragging her overnight bag like a dog on a lead. Her mother would have been disgusted.

Maddison didn't care.

She didn't even have time to peek over her shoulder. Too scared if she did, those goons would be behind her, where she'd trip on her heels and crash into other passengers.

It suddenly felt far too dangerous to stay in Melbourne.

At the boarding gate, breathless from her cardio workout from running in heels on floor tiles, she shoved her ticket into the machine. She took deep breaths, just as she'd instructed her students to calm down before diving, until the machine gave her the green light.

Like an Olympic runner doing the hundred metre sprint, Maddison bolted down the carpet, through the open door then down a long corridor that felt like a rabbit warren, with one side made entirely of windows.

The corridor stretched on forever.

Around the corner and there, at the end of this marathon, were the doors to the plane with a lovely smiling air hostess waiting for her.

With five minutes to spare, a sweaty Maddison collapsed into her seat at the back of the plane with her overnight bag on the vacant seat beside her. She was next to the lavatory and the galley, leaving her with no privacy. The bonus was she had the entire back row to herself—it was a win.

With her luggage packed into the overhead locker, Maddison buckled into her seat, her heart still pounding. Not from running, but from pure fear.

She grabbed her water bottle with shaky hands, drinking it dry as the cabin crew performed their pre-flight checks.

If they didn't leave now, she'd rush for those doors again.

Maddison caught her reflection in the window, staring at that same wide-eyed, haunted look she'd seen only yesterday at her apartment.

Calm down.

Panicking was fruitless, a lesson she was learning these past twenty-four hours.

Finally, the plane doors closed, and the plane taxied down the runway.

This morning Maddison had planned to go to Sydney. Not Adelaide.

This morning she was meant to be visiting her godmother.

Nancy was going to kill her for not showing up.

None of that mattered as she clutched her red bag like a pillow, because Maddison hated flying. She'd rather sit in an aluminium wire cage surrounded by a dozen great white sharks than fly. It was something she'd never admitted to her boss, Laurie, who hated to swim.

But it was too late to back out now.

Ten

'Right, that skeezy dick said she'd be here.' Eric, in the passenger seat of the sedan, tucked away his mobile.

'Why here?' Tom steered the car as they scoured the airport's car park.

'She's supposed to be visiting someone in Sydney.'

'How do they know that?'

'I dunno, they're probably tapping her phone. Who cares? I hate this chasing game when there's no gain.'

'Huh?'

'We're chasing down a blonde because they *think* she might have something. Our job is to observe her movements, that's all.' It'd been a boring week, until today.

'Watching for what?'

'That, my friend, is the billion-dollar question. It's a waste of time. I mean, all that chick did was have lunch and place some bets at the racetrack.'

'The steward told me they had rooms in the back.'

'It's one big room from what I could tell.'

'Nah, out the back-back.'

Again, the moron wasn't making sense. 'English, Tom?'

'See, there's this room for members to conduct private transactions.'

'Like what?'

'I dunno, business deals. Counting cash. You name it.'

'So?' Eric didn't give a toss.

'But that steward said Bob Farley was a regular.'

'I know that, dickhead.'

'But you see, Bob visited that room the day he died.'

Eric sat tall, staring at his offsider.

'That's what the steward said. It cost me twenty for that info.'

'And you're only telling me this now?'

'There's her car.' Tom pulled up behind Maddison's bright red sports car.

Eric jumped out of the passenger's seat. 'Park the car and meet me inside.' This cat-and-mouse game was pathetic. Yet, the way the blonde had bolted from the track, she must have found Bob's notes.

It made sense. The chick was in a panic, and he was only too happy to make her panic some more. God, he loved the smell of fear in the morning.

Inside the airport terminal, Eric scanned over the line of passengers queuing to check in their luggage. He checked the large screens for departure times. The next flight to Sydney was in half an hour, boarding at gate six.

He pushed his way through the lines at the security check. Snatched a black plastic tray and dumped in his wallet, phone and keys, and put it on the conveyor belt to go through the X-ray machine.

A white-haired lady glared at him for pushing through.

'Sorry.' *Not sorry.*

'How rude.'

Eric didn't give a toss.

The only problem was, he now had the security guards and the other passengers taking notice of him. Not good.

'I got held up at work, then traffic, and I'm trying to catch my girlfriend before she flies out. I can't live without seeing her one more time before she leaves. She's in the army and going to be deployed for six months, I can't miss her.' Eric lied through his freaking teeth.

But the crowd lapped it up.

'Oh, how sweet,' gushed the elderly woman. 'Go right ahead, young man.'

Eric strolled through the main security scanner with no bells going off over his shoes.

'That's so romantic,' said the stern-looking female security guard manning the X-ray machine, personally handing Eric his belongings.

'Thank you.' He needed to use that romantic mush more

often.

'Good luck in catching her, young man,' called out the old woman.

'Whatever, schmucks,' Eric muttered under his breath, as he hurried down the main walkway.

At gate six, the passengers milled around rows of assorted plastic chairs near the walls of windows that faced the runways. Eric paced up and down trying to find Maddison, but didn't spot her anywhere. He rang Tom.

'G'day, mate,' Tom answered brightly on the other end of the line.

'Where are you?' It was irritating how nothing fazed the Neanderthal, while Eric was busting his hump, hunting a runaway barmaid.

'I'm in the security line, see. Are you upstairs already?'

'Yeah. And that female's not here. The flight for Sydney doesn't board for half an hour.'

'Maybe she's in the toilet or in the VIP section like she was at the racetrack.'

Again, Tom had supplied a golden nugget amid the rubble he had for brain matter. 'I'll check the VIP lounge. Call me when you get through.'

Searching for the VIP area, when he spotted a woman sprinting full pelt in heels. It was impressive. Her blonde hair was flapping away, with the skirt on her dress kicking up, dragging her overnight bag while gripping a large red handbag.

The red bag!

'What the …' Eric rushed to the wall of windows that faced the assorted planes waiting to load and leave.

As workmen in hi-vis vests and chunky headphones closed the luggage cargo hold on the belly of the large plane, above them he tracked Maddison through the windows in the air bridge as she ran all the way to the plane.

'Tell me that wench caught the wrong plane.' His hands pressed against the window, but Maddison didn't reappear.

'Dammit.' He thumped the glass.

'Hey man, I'm through,' called out Tom, coming up beside Eric. 'What are you looking at?'

'Maddison just boarded that plane.' Eric pointed to the

aircraft.

'Are you sure?' Tom stepped back and glanced around the terminal.

'I just saw her, with that big red bag of hers.' The bag did not suit the outfit, but it looked better now she had no hat.

'Why is she going to Adelaide?'

'How do you know it's heading for Adelaide?'

Tom pointed to the screens overhead and the large numbers displayed by the doors.

Eric reached for his mobile. 'Find out what time it lands.'

As Tom sauntered off, Eric made a call, watching Maddison's plane backing away from the terminal.

'What?' snapped out the overpaid Senior Detective Mick Hetter. There was no such thing as phone etiquette with this crooked cop.

'You were wrong. Your little friend didn't go to Sydney.' Eric smiled at his handsome reflection in the window, smoothing down the sides of his hair.

'Did you lose her again?' Mick demanded.

'I swear on my snake-skin shoes,' he said, leaning down to dust their silver tips, 'that Miss Maddison Farley got on a plane that is taking off, as we speak.' The large commercial plane raced down the tarmac chasing that white line. Its nose rose and the whole colossal beast of mechanical engineering lifted off the ground, heading high into the sky. 'It's amazing how something that big can fly.'

'To where?'

'Adelaide.' Eric grinned at the cop's frustration.

Eric hated dealing with coppers in his line of work. But ever since this job came up, he had to be in direct contact with this detective.

'Why Adelaide?'

'Beats me. You guys know the girl, not me.' Eric checked out his shave, then brushed down his shirt using the window as his private mirror.

He smiled widely at Tom, passing Eric a piece of paper with flight details. 'So, she's on flight QF691 and its scheduled to arrive in Adelaide at five this afternoon.'

'But Adelaide?' Continued the cop over the phone. 'Did she see you?'

'She had no clue we were following her.' Please, Eric was a professional.

'This isn't like Maddy.'

'Not my problem. I wasn't allowed to touch her, just watch her. So, my job is done.' Eric ended the call. 'Dickhead.'

'What do we do now?' Tom asked.

'It's up to the coppers to find her.' Eric laughed, imagining that smug detective pulling on that loose tie that never matched his outdated suit. 'In fact, I'll shout you a beer.' He patted his partner on the upper back and headed for the bar.

They were sitting on bar stools at the airport watching the constant flow of passengers when Eric's phone rang. 'Yep?' It was an unknown number, guessing it was the cop, as he took a sip of his beer.

'Where are you?'

'Boss!' Eric dumped his glass on the table and wiped his mouth. 'We're still at the airport.'

'Good. My assistant has you and Tom booked for the next flight to Adelaide. Someone will watch her until you get there. Find that girl and get what I want.'

Eleven

ADELAIDE, SOUTH AUSTRALIA

With the large commercial airliner safely parked at the airport, Maddison was the last to follow the passenger's mass exodus. She grinned at the small boy in front, being dragged along by his frazzled mother, who was overloaded with various bags that bashed the back of chairs down the skinny aisle.

Finally, she exited the stuffy plane and into the cool air of the terminal.

It had been a short, uninterrupted flight that had allowed Maddison to regain her focus from her previous blind panic.

But with no privacy onboard, she still hadn't been able to check through Bob's pouch.

The pouch itself was proving to be a mission to open, with its waterproof seal. So instead, she'd constructed a to-do list, hoping a new plan would keep her calm.

Inside the airport terminal, Maddison made her way through the passengers being happily greeted by family and friends.

No one was there to meet her.

No one even knew she was here.

The last time she'd visited this city was over fifteen years ago, when her mother had dragged her along to visit the grouchiest of grandmothers who'd refused to even acknowledge their existence. It was one of the few times

Maddison's mother had seemed sad or vulnerable.

'Right …' Maddison looked around the airport terminal. 'Toilet first, then phone Nancy and Laurie.' They were on the top of her list.

She spotted the sign for the public toilets.

Her heart dropped and her bladder squeezed at the queue of women waiting to use six toilets. Why, at nearly every public venue, were women expected to stand in line for a toilet?

She stood behind a dozen women of many shapes, ages, colours, cultures, and class, all waiting to use the loo.

'You'd think they'd put in more lavs for the ladies,' complained a middle-aged woman with short curly red hair to her friend beside her. They both waited in front of Maddison with everyone facing the six closed cubicle doors as if waiting to go to confession inside a cathedral.

'Betty, it's because it's designed and built by men,' said the friend with the deep brown bob.

'I'm hearing you.' Betty's cackle reverberated off the tiled walls of the public female toilets. 'So, Sal, when do you head off on your next holiday?'

'We're going north for our next trip.'

'To where?'

Their conversation echoed over flushing toilets and running water from the row of sinks that made those waiting in line cross their legs.

'To the Northern Territory. They've got these cattle stations that are like resorts that only allow a dozen people to visit at a time,' said Sal.

'Why would you want to go there?' Betty asked. 'It sounds hot and dusty to me.'

'To get my husband off his mobile and away from the laptop. They have no reception out there. And it's so remote you can only fly in and out in the wet season in one of those small charter planes. Or it's a five-day drive by dirt road from Alice Springs, just to get to the middle of nowhere.'

'What do you do out there?' Betty asked, as a few toilets flushed and the queue shunted forwards.

'Nothing but relax. Some have swimming pools, or you can go horse riding or bushwalking. They have various activities you can get involved in with running a cattle station. Mind you, I wouldn't go this time of the year, it's their wet season.'

'So?'

'It's got them ferocious storms. Mind you ...' Sal leaned toward Betty and stage-whispered loud enough for everyone to hear, 'Not being tourist season, it's half price. You can have the entire place to yourself because everyone avoids the humidity and rain. They say those monsoons flood everything.'

'Stop talking about water, will ya. Lordy, I wish they'd bloody hurry up.' Betty winced in agony, holding on to her bladder. 'Are you keen to fly in one of those little planes? Didn't see any of them around here at the airport.'

A little girl in bouncy pigtails skipped from the cubicle to the sink. She turned on the water and pushed on the soap dispenser, cupping the liquid soap in her hands. Added more water, then soap, with lots of gushing water that spewed from the taps.

'Lordy, girlie, there's a drought happening in this state. They have water restrictions here.' Betty scowled at the young girl. 'You could bathe a family of six for the next ten bloody Sundays with the amount of water you've just wasted.' Betty then started doing an awkward belly-holding, cross-legged, dancing jig.

The mother rushed from another toilet cubicle to stand behind the young girl, quickly washing her hands and turning off the tap. 'Sorry,' muttered the mother, pushing the child past the queue of waiting women. 'Sorry, I know how you feel. They never have enough toilets for women.'

Many of the women in line nodded.

'So, where were we?' Betty shuffled forward in the line. 'That's right, where do they keep them little planes?'

There was a chorus line of flushing toilets and those waiting in the queue paused, expecting all the doors to open.

But it was only two. Not six.

Everyone sighed from false hope.

'Are you sure you're not worried about getting into one of them tiny planes?' Betty asked Sal. 'I know I would be.'

'No, they're fine. And to answer your other question,

you go out to Parafield Airport, where they keep all of them smaller planes.' Sal too had succumbed to crossing her legs, gawking at the ceiling to not watch the sinks gushing with running water.

'Um, excuse me?' Maddison asked the two women who were now at the head of the line. 'I'm sorry to overhear, but where can I find out about these remote cattle stations you were describing?'

Reggie had suggested she head north and to the country, and those cattle station places sounded like they were remote enough. The bonus would be the price and having fewer people around to bother her made it even more tempting. She needed to go somewhere safe to trawl through Bob's notes.

'In the *Outback* magazine. It's a free magazine the travel agent gave us.' Betty rummaged around in her bag. 'Here, I've got a spare copy.' She handed the small brochure-styled magazine to Maddison.

'Thank you so much.' The cover advertised a scenic shot of Uluru, with thumbnail images of crocodiles. Not the normal magazine Maddison was used to reading, but it might be just what she needed. She slipped it into her red bag and waited in line.

Two cubicle doors opened; their occupants emerged wearing relieved expressions.

'Oh, thank God. My turn. I thought my bladder was going to burst first.' Betty snorted a laugh as she waddled into the cubicle holding her lower belly.

'No need to tell everyone.' Sal scoffed, performing her own awkward dash to the loo.

'Not like we'll meet any of them again, and besides,' called out Betty, closing the toilet door, 'all of them ladies are suffering too.'

'Hear, hear,' shouted out another woman a few places behind Maddison as mixed laughter filled the tiny, tiled room.

It was the same picture everywhere, there were never enough toilets for the women.

Twelve

Inside a hotel room in Adelaide's city centre, Maddison had showered and changed into her black suit with matching heels. Instead of being a woman on the run, she looked like a high-class businesswoman.

What she'd give to be in her jeans and boots, but she'd packed light to go shopping with Nancy.

Before she'd left the airport she'd rung Laurie and told him she was going to spend time with family in Sydney. Guilt gripped her rumbling stomach because she'd not only lied to Laurie, but she was also using him, hoping he'd speak with Mick and Paul—the detectives she didn't trust anymore.

Then she called Nancy with a lame excuse about a holiday to Queensland to find a coral reef to go scuba diving. Now her chest tightened from guilt for lying to Nancy. But she needed to protect her godmother.

It was like she was trapped in some B-grade suspense movie.

'What have you done to me, Bob?' Maddison said to her reflection in the bathroom mirror. Behind her, on the bed, was the big red handbag. Its enormous mouth lay open, spilling rolls of cash and Bob's pouch.

The pouch was proving to be a colossal struggle to open.

Vermin-proof, he'd said. Waterproof, he'd said. Was it Maddison proof too?

There had to be a trick to it, or she was going to hunt down a pair of scissors or a knife to tear open the damned thing.

Her stomach rumbled loudly.

From all the running she'd been doing, she was famished. Sadly, her hotel didn't have room service.

She grabbed her red bag and went in search of food. Maybe the hotel's reception would let her borrow a pair of scissors to open Bob's pouch. Her plan for the night was to go through Bob's notes in her room. Tomorrow, she'd look for a travel agent and shop for some suitable clothes for her outback expedition.

Too impatient to wait for the old clunky lifts, she took the stairs.

At nine-thirty on a Tuesday night, she hoped there was a place open nearby offering a decent feed. All she had in her bag were salted peanuts, some tiny UHT milk portions, and other airline delicacies.

As she approached the reception area, she overheard a man speaking with the female night clerk. 'Are you sure you don't have anyone staying by the name of Maddison Farley?'

It was the guy with the Elvis hair!

In the hall, Maddison froze with her back to the wall, staring at the guy's reflection from the glass that made up the picture frames.

'Sorry, sir, there's no one staying here by that name,' replied the receptionist behind the counter.

'Well, how many young women have checked in these last couple of hours?'

'I only started my shift half an hour ago.'

'How many exits does this place have?'

'Just this one. We have fire exits, but they're all armed with alarms.'

'I know she's here. Unless that idiot lost her somewhere.' He stroked over his Elvis hair and stomped through the automatic main doors and out onto the city street.

Maddison bolted for the stairwell. Thank God she hadn't used her credit card when she checked in.

Her first instinct was to run. But to where?

How did they know she was here?

Maddison had used a public telephone at the airport to call both Laurie and Nancy. She'd ditched her old mobile and bought a new one.

Reggie had warned her to get away from the security

cameras. If they had police on the payroll, it wouldn't take much for them to see her purchase her ticket and get on the plane to Adelaide. She didn't exactly sneak onto the plane with her *elegant* rush through the airport.

If they'd bugged her phone, they would have known she was going to Sydney to see Nancy. Maybe they already had someone at the airport waiting for her.

But why? What was so important to have Bob murdered with these goons chasing her across the country?

Whatever it was, it was too dangerous to stay here.

Thirteen

Eric opened the passenger door of their tan sedan and took his seat. The whiff of onions, plastic cheese, and Tom's cheap supermarket brand of deodorant was a slap in the face. He cracked open the window, scowling up at the hotel across the road. 'That woman is really ticking me off.'

'You didn't find her then?' Seated in the driver's seat, Tom bit his burger in half with one massive man-bite. Mustard, mayonnaise, and sauce oozed like slime around his mouth and fingers.

It made Eric sick. Opening the passenger window wider, he inhaled the cool city air. 'No. She's not in the hotel by that name. But I know she's there.'

'That Indian fella, the boss had watching her from the airport, he didn't lose her, did he?' Tom shoved the last of his burger into his gob, then wiped off the mustard and mayo with the back of his hand.

Use a napkin, dude. 'She's there. I know it.' Eric stared up at the hotel's ten stories. 'She must be under a false name.'

'So, what do we do now?' Tom slurped long deep pulls on the straw from his drink.

'We wait.' Like Eric had to wait to speak over Tom's noise. 'There's only one entrance and exit out of there.'

'All night in the car?'

'The Boss wants what that woman is carrying.' Eric leaned back, adjusting his chair rest.

Tom screwed up the burger's paper wrapping, salt sachets, cups, and straw, squeezing them all into the brown paper bag. It was so loud like he was scrunching that paper bag in front of a microphone in a stadium full of rock concert speakers.

The crusty aroma of the fast food's onions, pickles, and mustard created an overpowering gas bomb within the confines of the car.

Tom finally found a napkin. Wiped his hands and mouth. Added to the rubbish, crinkling the brown paper bag into a ball, before tossing it onto the back seat.

'There's no freaking way I'm putting up with that smell all night in this car!' Eric lowered his window all the way, then searched for a mint from his pocket. 'Get rid of it, will ya?'

'Sorry, man. I forgot how sensitive your nose was.'

'Oh look, there's a fancy bin right in front of us that's begging for you to go say hello.'

'All right, I can take a hint.' Tom chuckled.

Eric wanted to punch him for that, but he refrained.

Tom opened the back door and removed the offensive brown bag. He took a few long loping steps, dumped the rubbish, then headed back to the driver's seat.

It made a huge difference to the car's aroma.

'We might want to kill this interior light, eh?' Eric reached for the switch on the roof.

'Want me to take the first shift?' Tom asked, the car dipping with his weight as he clambered back into the driver's seat.

'Yeah, cheers, mate.' The Neanderthal had his good points.

Eric leaned back and shut his eyes. 'I'll take over at midnight.' Then he'd be recharged and ready to drag Miss Maddison down by the hair and onto her knees if she dared run from him again. And Eric was looking forward to it.

Fourteen

On the fourth floor of the darkened hotel room, with her body pressed to the wall, Maddison bit on her trembling lip. She peered out to the street through the tiniest of slits in the curtain.

Her shoulders tightened as she whimpered at the sight of the tall man with a bald head and mid-length leather jacket, walking to the bin on the street. She recognised him from the racetrack earlier today in Melbourne.

It was just like watching a thriller movie, she couldn't tear her eyes away from the guy strolling back to the driver's side of a sedan. In the passenger seat, illuminated by the interior light, was the guy with Elvis hair.

'Shoot—it's the goons!' Wherever that name came from, it fit.

'No-no-no-no …' Maddison stepped back from the window, ready to run for the door. But to where?

'Think!'

In the dark, she paced back and forth beside the queen-sized bed, chewing on her thumbnail.

When she peered through the fisheye lens of the door's peephole, it showed an empty corridor.

But how long was she safe in this room? Were those goons waiting for reinforcements to do a room-by-room search?

On the bench by the door lay the hotel's vinyl portfolio. Snatching it up, she closed herself inside the small bathroom, only then daring to turn on a light.

Her shaky hands fumbled to flick the portfolio's pages, as she searched for an answer. It spoke of tourist attractions and nearby restaurants, containing a small map of the city area, with the tram and bus timetables.

It was looking hopeless.

She turned to the folder's final page and in the sleeve of the cover was a hotel floor map as part of their fire emergency plan.

Had she found her escape?

Swallowing down that metallic taste of fear, she studied the hotel's laminated floor plan. There was a fire exit that led to an alley at the back of the building. She took out the complimentary tourist guide and found the small tourist map of the city centre. It displayed the network of major roads, as well as bus, tram, and train stops.

She tore the page from the magazine. Scooped at some water from the tap and nodded at her reflection. 'We can do this.' Her voice was so loud and foreign in the tiny room.

She grabbed her red handbag, her small overnight bag, and tiptoed out of her room.

Down the stairs to the ground floor, she followed the shadowy corridor to the *Fire Exit* light that was displayed above the door.

Her first instinct was to push it open, but there was a gigantic sign on the door warning that opening the door would trigger an alarm.

'Come on. *Think.*' Slinging her overnight bag's strap over her head and shoulder, she positioned it behind her back, spotting the nearby fire alarm panel on the wall. She strapped her large red shoulder bag over her other shoulder, making her feel like a pack horse, but her hands were free.

She tossed the hotel's fire plan to the floor and again studied the tiny street map. She took a deep breath, rubbing her fingertips together, she stared at the door.

In the blink of an eye, she pulled down the trigger on the fire alarm before propelling herself through the door and into the night air, to begin the race for her life.

Fifteen

An alarm bell pierced the night, it was deafening.

'Is that the fire alarm?' called out Tom, tapping Eric on the shoulder, dozing in the passenger seat.

Eric sat upright, blinking at the gloomy city street where neon lights displayed business names and sales. Traffic lights had paused on deserted intersections beside empty sidewalks. But the ringing bell and whooping alarm was enough to wake the dead. 'What's going on?'

'There's an alarm going off at Maddison's hotel.' Tom pointed at the hotel where the staff and guests were spilling through the main doors and onto the street.

'*Move.* I bet Maddison's done that. Quick, start the car and drive.'

For a big man, Tom sprang into action in a matter of moments. They sped across the road and turned left down a one-way street to the back of the hotel.

'There.' Eric pointed to the far end of the alley at a female's silhouette running toward the well-lit city street.

Tom followed in hot pursuit. 'How did she see us?'

'Don't care. Just don't lose her.'

Tom forced the car into the stream of traffic and onto Hindley Street's main drag. The place was crawling with cars filling both lanes, lit up like some Christmas parade. People crowded the bars and eateries as music pumped from various nightclubs and car stereos.

'There she is.' Eric pointed to the blonde running with her luggage, bumping into people.

'Man, she can run in them heels, see?' Tom was forced to slow down with their car trapped in the congested traffic.

'We'll lose her at this pace. I'll follow on foot. Catch up when you can.' Eric slammed the car door shut and gave chase. 'I'm not losing you now!'

Sixteen

Maddison ran blindly, her heart pounding against her chest as she bumped into people on the sidewalks. 'I'm sorry. Sorry.' But she couldn't stop. Only glancing back to discover that Elvis hair had jumped out of the car and was chasing her.

She turned to run, only to barrel straight into the chest of a tall man dressed in black. It was like hitting a brick wall.

'What's the rush there, sweetheart?' asked the bouncer, with red neon lights flashing above him. He stood next to an open door that led to a flight of stairs.

'Sorry.' All she saw was those stairs and ran for the red light at the top of the staircase.

'Twenty bucks, thanks,' said the bored hostess through the booth's box window.

Maddison grabbed the first note her fingers touched and threw it at the counter, then ran inside.

'Hey, don't you want your change?'

'Keep it.' It took a moment for her eyes to adjust to the smoky haze of the darkened room. On stage was a woman wearing only a G-string, swinging on a pole. Scantily dressed waitresses carried drink trays to men seated at scattered tables staring at the stage show.

At the back bar stood a group of bikers. Just behind them was the bar's small opening. It was her only shot. 'Sorry. Sorry ...' She tried so hard to dodge the bikers with her bags, to then dive under the wooden bar top.

On her hands and knees, she crawled behind the working side of the bar and found a gap between the sinks and kegs, to curl up into a ball.

'Hey, you can't be in here!'

'Help me, please. *Help me?*' Maddison pleaded with the topless barmaid who knelt in front of her.

'What's wrong, hon?'

'I'm being chased.' Maddison heaved for air, gripping her trembling knees to her chest.

'By who?'

'Two men. One short with Elvis hair, wearing a long black leather jacket. The other guy is tall, bald head, big hands, mid-length leather jacket. Please don't tell them I'm here, *please.*' Maddison was desperate to catch her breath with her heart about to explode.

'Hey, Karla? What's going on there?' A biker with a greyish beard and arms covered in ink, leaned over the counter with another younger biker beside him doing the same.

'Hello, sweetheart,' said the other biker with red hair. 'Didn't you just scamper in here like a little rabbit?'

'She reckons she's being chased, Reaper,' Karla said to the bearded biker.

Both bikers frowned. 'By who?' Reaper asked.

'Them.' Karla nodded to the front of the bar.

They're here. 'Oh God no-no-no-no!' Maddison gripped her bag tighter. Tears mixed with sweat streamed down her face. Crouching down on the dirty floor of a strip bar, she couldn't stop trembling.

'Hey, you'll be right, hon. I'll hide you. Don't move,' Karla said to Maddison.

'She looks scared out of her bloody wits,' said the younger man with flame-red hair beside Reaper.

'Excuse me, miss,' called out the voice of Maddison's nightmares, she recognised it from the hotel foyer. It belonged to the guy with Elvis hair. It was Goon One.

She cupped her mouth with both hands to stifle her scream.

'What do you want?' Karla stood in front of Maddison as she talked over the bar. Karla wore fishnets and some sparkly stripper shoes. As a barmaid, Maddison was impressed Karla could work in shoes like those all night.

Maddison peered through the cracks in the bar's wood

panelling and gaped at Goon One.

'I'm looking for a woman, blonde hair about yay big ...' Goon One raised his hand to his shoulder height.

Hey, she was taller than that!

'She's wearing a classy-looking black suit and heels, carrying a large red bag.'

'What's it to you?' Reaper said, as other heavily tattooed gang members lined up with their backs to the bar. Their patches displayed on their leather vests. In biker boots and jeans, it was a formidable scene from Maddison's peephole.

'So, you've seen her, huh?' Goon One grinned, swiping a palm over his Elvis hair.

'Now why would a woman dressed like that come into a place like this for?' Reaper said. 'Look around you, mate, all the women here are all half bloody naked.'

'I know she's here. Look, I don't want no trouble, and you don't want to get involved in this either, mate.'

Maddison's eyes widened as the second goon came up and stood behind his mate. He was big, with the lights causing a strange devilish-red effect on his shiny scalp. So, which one was the brains of the outfit and who was the sidekick?

'Piss off short-arse, this is our bar.'

'It's a public place, and I had to pay to get into this rathole.' Goon One seemed unfazed at facing a row of gang members. 'Just tell us where she is and we'll make it worth your while.' He reached into his pocket and Reaper reacted.

She couldn't see past the leather patches, jeans, and biker boots, but there was a scuffle of some sort, and then it was on. Fists hit faces, they smashed glasses, spilling beer and spirits. Women screamed and men grunted with each punch, in a barroom free-for-all brawl!

'Come on, little rabbit.' A gang member crouched down in front of her, holding out his hand. His short-cropped flame-red hair caught the neon lights of the bar like a halo. 'I can get you out of here.'

'Go with Match, he's a good bloke.' Karla, the topless barmaid had ducked down beside Maddison, holding up her drinks tray like a shield. 'Use the staff's back door, Match.' She pointed to the far corner of the bar.

With no other option, Maddison grabbed Match's hand. and followed him to the back door behind the bar. They scurried down a flight of dimly lit stairs before he pushed the door open onto the street. He didn't stop or let go of her hand until they stood before a row of Harley motorcycles, their polished chrome sparkling under the streetlights.

He passed Maddison an open-faced helmet as he slid on his own, then swung his leg over the seat of his bike. 'Get on.'

'I've never been on the back of a Harley before.' It would be her first bike ride ever.

Gunshots rang from the strip club above. Strippers and lingerie-clad waitresses screamed as they ran down the stairs of the nightclub with patrons spilling onto the street.

'Now's the time, honey.' Match kicked the bike over, and with a deafening roar it came to life. 'Get on.'

She hitched up her skirt and straddled the back of the bike.

'*Maddison*?' Goon One burst out onto the sidewalk, with the towering Goon Two close behind him.

'Go-go-go.' Maddison stared in horror at the goons, running towards her with guns!

'Hang on,' said Match, and she wrapped her arms tightly around the waist of a complete stranger, who gunned the bike and rode fearlessly straight into the stream of traffic.

Seventeen

The Harley roared down the road, the wind whipping around Maddison as she held on to a guy she'd just met as he hurtled through an unknown city. But not just some guy—a motorbike gang member.

He pulled up under the streetlight of a deserted car park.

The bike's noise was soon replaced by crashing oceanic waves.

Maddison unsteadily got off, still feeling the bike's vibrations. She removed the helmet to stare at the silent houses that lined the cliff face overlooking a darkened ocean. The salty air was invigorating.

Still seated on his bike, he removed his helmet and faced Maddison. 'They call me Match, but my name's Mitch. What's your name?'

'Maddison.' She shrugged while checking out the hero who'd helped her escape the gun-wielding goons.

He grinned at her, and *wow!* The guy was dynamite.

His nickname was obviously from his flame-red hair and freckles. She'd never seen a sexier redhead. This bad boy had presence. And baby, she wanted to get burned.

Which was so wrong!

'Thank you for your help. I hope your friends didn't get hurt?' A bout of nerves hit her. Was it the intense stare from the guy who was making her hot under the collar? Or was it the fact she was on the edge of a cliff, in the dark, alone with a biker?

'Doubt it.' Again, Mitch grinned, and she was flushed with a wash of heat. 'It's rare we get to save a damsel in distress.'

She frowned at his comment. *A damsel in distress! Are you kidding me?*

'And I've never seen a lady look as scared as you.' He sobered up, crossing muscular arms over his toned chest, his eyes slowly inched their way from the top of her helmet hair to the tips of her heels.

She'd never felt more exposed.

'Why were those men chasing you?'

'They followed me from Melbourne.'

'Melbourne? When did you get here?'

'About …' She glanced at her watch. 'About four hours ago. I was supposed to be in Sydney, but they followed me from Flemington Racetrack, so I caught the first plane out of Melbourne and ended up here.' *Wherever here was?* She searched for a street sign. In the distance a group of tall buildings stood near a long row of lights over the water, like a wharf.

'Where are you going?'

She faced the man who would normally have her drooling at the nicest piece of eye candy she'd seen in a while. But she wasn't helpless. She could stand on her own … kind of.

She was also in a life-or-death situation that didn't allow time for flirting with bad boys. And she sucked at flirting. 'I don't know.'

'Have you been on the run for long?'

'Since this morning. I had a plan, but that got lost back in my hotel room.'

'When was the last time you got some decent sleep?'

She sighed, staring up at dull stars hiding behind patchy clouds. 'Um, two days ago. Maybe?'

'You've been that busy, huh?'

She stared at the car park's asphalt, remembering another deserted car park at night. *Where did the time go?*

'Well, yesterday, my apartment got broken into while I was at my uncle's funeral who was murdered only last week. Since then, I've been told my phone's bugged, there's crooked cops involved, while copping the lecture on *life on the lam* by a bookies' bodyguard. So I fly out here, thinking I'm safe, only to spot the same two goons that followed me from the Melbourne racetrack asking about me in the foyer of my hotel. So I escape through the fire exit, tripping off the alarm, hoping they'd get distracted by the other people, but instead they chased me down in their car. I ran into my first strip bar, met my first topless barmaid and you. Got my first ride on a Harley escaping the scene of a barroom brawl and gunfire. And all of this happened in the last twenty-four hours!' She blurted it all out in one go, unbelieving she'd spilled all to a complete and total stranger.

Surprisingly, she felt better for getting it all off her chest.

'No way.' Mitch shook his head.

'I don't expect you to believe me. And you and your friends have already gotten too involved with what you did back there. I'm sorry for—'

'I believe you.'

'Why?' She could hardly believe it herself.

He shrugged, then gave a sly grin. It was divine.

'Are you going to ask me what they're after?'

'Nope.' His biker boots echoed across the car park until he stood right in front of her.

He was a wall of muscle. Tall and bad boy delicious. She wanted to lean against his toned chest and breathe him all in. He would be perfect for keeping her warm against the sea breeze that crashed over the waves.

'In my game, little rabbit, sometimes it's better not to know these things, especially with what you're apparently hooked up in.'

'Why did you do that? Help me?' Mitch was her hero, with the most amazing bone structure. Her wicked godmother, Nancy, would drool over him.

'You looked like a petrified lady in need.'

Again, his eyes slowly crawled all over her until she felt naked. Hot. And naked. She'd never felt so needy. Was it the adrenalin rush making this guy so desirable?

'We just weren't expecting those guys chasing you to have guns on them.'

That broke her trance. 'My uncle got shot to death.'

'Well, you're in somethin' deep, aren't you?'

'I know.' She sighed, turning away from the beautiful bad boy. 'And you've done so much already, I don't want you in anymore danger. So, if you could kindly point me toward a safe hotel?'

'I've got a better idea.' He swung his leg over the bike and tapped on the back of his seat. 'How about you hop on like a good little bunny?'

Tempting. So very, very tempting. 'To where?'

'I'll take you to a safe house,' he said, sliding on his helmet.

'Why? It's not, um, some bikers …' So what if he was a mouth-watering bad-boy biker, was he going to take her to some clubhouse to never see daylight again? Hello, he'd picked her up from a strip club.

Mitch held out her helmet. 'You need help and you need some sleep. You'll think better when you've had some sleep. Trust me on that one. It's okay, you'll be safe there. If I was going to hurt you, I would have already done it.' He let rip a killer grin as if he could read her mind.

Her knees knocked and she bit on her bottom lip.

'Besides, I know what it's like to be on the run.' He started the bike. 'Get on, beautiful, this ride isn't over yet.'

Eighteen

Eric sat on one of the twin single beds in their cheap hotel room, gingerly pressing an icepack to his eye as he inspected his reflection in the mirror above the tacky dresser.

'Aw hell.' He had bloodshot eyeballs and swollen eyelids, along with a pulsing lump in the middle of his forehead. 'Bloody bikers.' Eric was prepared for a punch, not a solid forehead smashing him in the face—they fought like animals.

'How are you feeling?' Tom strolled out from the bathroom wearing a towel around his waist.

'Just freaking peachy, mate. You?' Eric sculled back a mouthful of bourbon straight from the bottle. That was his medicine.

'I'm okay.'

'How?'

'Being a tall bloke, few people can swing that high. And now my nose has finally stopped bleeding …' He delicately dabbed a tissue at his nose. 'I had to re-straighten it again. That's the tenth time I've broken my nose. I reckon I can smell better each time it gets broken. See? I might get lucky and end up with a sensitive sense of smell just like you?' Tom chuckled. 'You look worse for wear.'

'Bloody arsehole bikers.' Eric reapplied the ice to his handsome face. Still, he had his teeth; he'd paid a fortune for his billionaire's smile.

'How come Maddison went in there?' Tom unzipped his canvas bag and started getting dressed. 'She's not the type of sheila to visit a titty bar or jump on the back of some patched member's bike.'

'Well, she did,' muttered Eric. The only problem now was she'd stared at him long enough to pick him out of a police line-up.

If he hadn't wasted so many rounds inside the strip club, he might have shot the bitch in the back. At least his firepower had stopped that gang from kicking his head in. If there was one thing Eric knew: you never take a knife to a gunfight.

He was also prepared for people to do crazy things when they were being chased. Usually, their panic made them rush into a corner. But not this little Miss Maddison— she was proving to be quite resourceful.

Tom lay back, staring at the ceiling, his enormous feet hanging over the end of the bed. 'What do we do now?'

'We wait until that copper, Mick, can give us an address from the biker's numberplate.'

'Did they find out what name she used for the plane ticket?'

'Nope. They're still checking on that, and the guest list at Maddison's hotel. How and when did that wench get a fake ID?'

'Where do you think she's gone?'

'No idea. But it won't be long before we find her.' Eric faced his reflection and made a solemn promise to himself. 'I'll get that little wench for getting my face punched in, and whatever else she's carrying, and we won't go home until we do.'

Nineteen

Face down on a king-sized bed, Maddison breathed deeply in a dreamless sleep.

A mobile phone started ringing, and she woke in a fright.

'Shh, it's okay. You're safe,' whispered Mitch, his hand gentle against her back. He reached over and grabbed his ringing phone. 'Yeah?'

Maddison wanted to sleep, listening to his voice while he rubbed her back. It was so soothing.

Hold the phone!

Her eyes widened, to dart around the room. *What the hell?*

'Yeah, we got away. Did anyone get hurt? ... Nah, I'm busy helping out a lady.' He smiled and tossed the phone to the floor. 'Morning, little rabbit.'

'Morning.' Flashbacks from last night crashed her slumber party. They'd ridden down small winding streets in the middle of the night, until Mitch finally parked his bike at the rear of a dark house. Then through a back door, down a corridor, and into this bedroom where he'd told her she could sleep, closed the door, and left her alone.

She'd heard Mitch talking to a female in the hallway, who Maddison had assumed was his girlfriend. But no sooner had her head hit that pillow, she'd succumbed to pure exhaustion.

So how did Mitch end up in her bed?

A baby started crying, then a door slammed down the hall.

A baby in a biker's house?

She ran a hand down her body, relieved to discover she

was fully dressed, with her red bag lying on the floor beside the bed. Right where she'd left it, beside an old dresser beneath a blanket that hung for a curtain, decorated with the southern cross flag.

Obviously, the guy didn't take advantage of her, even if he was only wearing a pair of Calvin's.

Under normal circumstances, she'd be admiring his body. The straight broad shoulders and muscular arms that matched the strong chest that narrowed into a washboard stomach.

It sent her pulse roaring, leaving her throat dry while her mouth watered. How was that possible?

'Where am I?' Maddison asked Mitch.

Footsteps passed outside the bedroom door accompanied by the soothing sounds of a female voice. The baby stopped crying.

'At my cousin's place.' Mitch rolled onto his side to stretch out like the god Adonis. Complete with ink, he was a red-headed, bad boy, Adonis. 'It's where I come to get some sleep. Not so much since the baby arrived.' He gave her a lazy grin that did wonders to her heartbeat. 'How did you sleep?'

'Great. Thanks.' She rolled to her back and stretched out her achy muscles. 'Although, I feel like I've been running a marathon.'

'If your body has been running on nothing but pure adrenalin, you'll be suffering something like a hangover from the impressive few days you've had.'

There was nothing impressive about being on the run, it was outright scary. 'You seem to know a lot about this?'

'I know what it's like to be on the run. Don't ask, coz I won't tell.' His grin grew, as he stroked her hair.

'Why are you helping me?' She asked in a whisper, grateful to her rescuer. Or was it the good girl attracted to the bad boy? And Mitch was a whole load of bad biker. *Oh mummy, save me from my sins!*

'Mm.' The low burr was commanding and all-male, sending a heat of arousal as her skin was set ablaze by his fingertip tracing down her face. 'Because I can.'

She was trapped by the warm amber of his eyes, which

held the dangerous heated animal-like intensity of a hunter staring at his prey.

It was hot.

His darkening eyes dropped to her mouth, where her teeth dug into her bottom lip.

He ever so slowly and gently leaned over and brushed his lips against hers. Upon touch, it was a scorching firestorm that pushed her back to the bed and sizzled all the way to her nerve endings.

He pulled back, his hooded, hungry eyes locked with hers.

'Jeezus, you look like an angel in my bed,' he whispered in a rough voice, swallowing hard.

Time stalled, her breath held, and yet electricity zipped through her bones. She couldn't take it anymore and pressed her lips to his.

He gently probed her mouth with his tongue, his chest pressed against hers as his body weight lay on top of her.

Her breath ran in short sharp pants as her fingers dug into his strong shoulders, shifting to moans when his slick tongue and lips stroked her throat. With his hot breath against her ear, her skin prickled alive everywhere.

BANG. BANG. BANG.

'Hey, Mitch,' hollered the female, hammering on the bedroom door. 'Did you drink all the bloody milk on me last night?'

'Damn,' muttered Mitch, exhaling heavily into Maddison's hair. His chest pounded as fast as her own heartbeat.

'I was saving that milk for the baby's brekkie, so I didn't have to go down to the shop 'til later.'

'All right, I'll get some.' He scowled at the closed door.

'Thank you,' called out the female, stomping down the hallway.

'I like milk in my coffee, too,' said Maddison.

His smile made her pulse jump. 'You stay right here, little rabbit. I'll be back.' He pushed off the bed and pulled on his jeans and boots. With shirt in hand, he gave her a wink and closed the door behind him.

'What was that?' Maddison lay back and covered her face in shock, taking deep breaths to calm the hot waves of lust still sizzling beneath the surface.

She sat up and faced her reflection in the tarnished mirror with its darkened edges on the off-white dressing table. It did nothing to hide her train-wrecked appearance.

Her hair was everywhere. Now she understood why women tied their hair up for bike riding.

Grabbing her overnight bag, she dug around for her hairbrush and set about correcting her appearance. It was all part of the morning routine that her mother and wicked godmother had ingrained in her for as long as she could remember. Hair brushed, she cleaned her face with travel wipes, noticing the dark rings beneath her eyes were gone. Applying a light make-up, the white terror in her eyes had disappeared too.

Mitch was right, sleep had done wonders for her.

Now she needed a plan.

She slid into her shoes, brushed down her suit, and stepped out of the bedroom in search of the toilet.

Down the hallway's threadbare carpet, Maddison found the lounge room where another old blanket hung as a curtain above a worn couch, beside a plastic milk crate of toys. The bookshelf was nothing more than a plank of wood on some bricks, holding a vintage television set.

From the end of the hallway came the sounds of cutlery falling on the floor, and water gushing into a sink.

Maddison walked to the doorway and took in the kitchen with its laminated table pushed against the wall, as sunlight streamed through the windows above the sink.

'Hello,' Maddison said to the young woman tossing her auburn plait over her shoulder while wiping down the hands of a baby in a highchair.

'Hey?' The girl stepped back, with a hand on her hip. 'Didn't realise Mitch had a woman with him. Are you his latest squeeze, huh?'

'I don't think so—'

'Well, I'll warn you now, he's a slut, that cousin of mine,' she said, wiping the baby's chin with the face cloth. 'Mind you, he's never brought a woman here before, especially one dressed like you.'

'My name is Maddison.'

'Ooh wee, fancy name for a fancy-dressed sheila, huh?' She rinsed the face cloth in the sink.

'And you're Mitch's cousin?'

'Yeah. I'm Tracey.' She faced Maddison with squinty eyes. 'I'm surprised Mitch told you his name, most only know him as Match.'

'And who is this little lady?' Maddison leaned down and smiled at the baby who gave a gummy grin. 'You're a cutie.' The baby gripped Maddison's finger, with eyes so big they reflected the window.

'That's Jamie.' Tracey put a protective arm around the back of the baby's highchair.

'I couldn't possibly bother you for the toilet, could I?'

Tracey raised her eyebrows. 'The loo's first right down the hallway. I'll put the kettle on?' She tilted her head with eyes darting all over Maddison as if trying to take in all the details at once. 'We've got no milk, but Mitch won't be long … I like your shoes.'

'Thanks, they were my mother's.' Maddison found the bathroom. It was old, but spotlessly clean, with an assortment of toys in the tub.

'Your mother's got great taste,' Tracey shouted from the kitchen. 'Don't she wanna wear them anymore?'

'No.' Maddison giggled at this shouting conversation from the toilet.

'How come you've got them?'

'She died.'

'Oh shoot. Sorry.'

What would her mother say about all of this?

'So where are you from?' Tracey asked Maddison as she returned to the kitchen.

Maddison took a seat at the table and Jamie's smile again lit up. She was adorable with those big blue eyes and light red hair. 'Melbourne. I lived in Sydney most of my life, but I was born here, in Adelaide.'

Tracey dumped two black coffees on the table. Her chair scraped across the worn tiles as she shuffled closer to the table. 'Whereabouts?'

'Elizabeth.'

'No freaking way. You came from that area?' Tracey passed a teething rusk to Jamie and dropped a few toys onto the highchair's table.

'My mother showed me the house I'd first called home from the hospital.' It was a dump, with tall weeds poking through rusty car wrecks littering the yard. The entire block was filled with graffiti-covered walls and smashed windows, condemned for bulldozing. 'Where are we?'

'In Parafield, pretty close to Elizabeth. So how did you get out?'

'Get out?' Out of Melbourne? This house? This nightmare she was living? She sipped on her black coffee as if searching for answers. It was strong, bitter, and magic.

'So, your mum, with those fancy shoes, lived out 'ere?' Tracey screwed up her nose.

'She grew up in this area.'

'True?'

'My mother had me at eighteen.'

'I'm eighteen.' Tracey sat taller and blinked with enormous eyes like the baby's. 'Your mum must've hooked up with a rich bloke to get those shoes.'

'No. I have no rich daddy.' Or any daddy.

'So how did your mum find the cash for those shoes?'

'She studied at uni and worked in some crappy casual jobs.' Just like Maddison had been doing this past year. 'Until her career took off.'

'What did she become?'

Queen of an empire. But with gravel in her throat she mumbled, 'The editor-in-chief of a magazine.' *Please don't ask for its name*.

'True?!' Tracey sat upright; it caused Jamie to pause mid-chew with drool running down her chubby cheeks. 'Lady, you're way out of Mitch's league.' Tracey's laughter echoed in the compact kitchen. It made the baby smile with her. Then she paused for a moment. 'You're in trouble, huh?'

Maddison took another sip of her coffee, unsure of what to say. She couldn't lie to the girl.

'Mitch doesn't tell me much. He only comes here when he's in trouble. I asked him if he was, but he swore he's been good, so he's here coz of you.' Tracey pointed at Maddison. 'Is that your natural hair colour?'

Which question should she avoid first? 'What do you do

with yourself?'

'Nothing.' Tracey dropped her head in shame. 'Jamie's father skipped out on me. But I'm thinking of going back to school.'

'And do what?'

'Don't laugh.'

'Why would I?'

'Interior decorating. But it's impossible to get into. There are only a few vacancies at the college I want to go to, but it's only for those with fancy apprenticeships. I aced my entry certificate but had to put it all aside when I had Jamie.' Tracey sighed, giving a weak smile to the cheerful baby gnawing on her rusk.

'How did she do it?' Tracey asked in a tone loaded with sadness. 'Your mum being like me.'

'My mother told me she was determined to provide a life for us.' A life she'd been running away from in so many ways.

'Well, ya mum must've done a good job to end up with shoes like those, huh?' Tracey grinned, raising her coffee mug in a toast.

Maddison stared at her Jimmy Choo's. As a kid she always wanted to fit into her mother's shoes—Gucci, Manolo's, Louboutin's, Louis Vuitton's—but she swam in them. As an adult she'd walked away from her mother's world, trying to get out from under that shadow. But she'd taken the shoes with her.

She'd never truly grasped how tough it must have been and how much her mother had done for her, until now.

'What are you going to do now?' Tracey asked Maddison.

Reality check—she was still on the run, in danger of what life she had! 'I need to get online.'

'I've got no computer or even a phone line here. I've got no credit until payday.'

'I only need a power point.' Maddison headed back to the bedroom.

'There's one here under the kitchen table you can use. I don't think the ones in the bedroom work. There's only the one in the lounge working, that's what the telly's plugged into. Mitch bought the place cheap to fix up later and reckons he'll get his mate in to fix it. But the whole house has to be rewired, and that's big bickies, you know,' hollered Tracey down the hallway.

Maddison carted her bags back to the kitchen. At the far end of the table, she plugged in her laptop.

'I like your bags. Wow, new laptop, huh? I've been saving up for one to do courses and stuff—Oh-oh.' Tracey sniffed the air and then the baby in the highchair. 'I'd better change this one's nappy and give her a bath. I don't know where Mitch has got to.'

'I didn't hear the bike,' Maddison said, waiting for her laptop to get online.

'No, Mitch took my car. All I needed was some bloody milk,' complained Tracey, carrying Jamie on her hip.

'Oh, hey, I forgot I had these …' Maddison rummaged around in her handbag. 'Will this do?' She pulled out the small UHT milk containers she'd kept from yesterday's flight.

'You're a bloody lifesaver, you are. I can give Jamie some cereal and maybe enough for our coffee too.'

Sometime later, the backdoor flung open and Mitch strolled inside with his tight T-shirt stained with grease, carrying an enormous bottle of milk.

'Did you milk a bloody cow for that bottle?' Tracey got up from her seat at the table where she'd been keeping Maddison company.

'Your car broke down, and I've been fixing it with Hammer. You've got a new battery, points, plugs, and all sorts of mechanical stuff you wouldn't understand.' Mitch handed the milk to his cousin.

'Is it still broken?'

'It's running better than ever. I'll take a shower and get this muck off me.' He ripped off his T-shirt and sauntered down the hallway.

Maddison's breath hitched at the impressive display of muscles on Mitch's torso and back, but the way those jeans cupped his beautiful behind—*yummy*.

Tracey flicked on the kettle as the bathroom door

slammed shut and the shower turned on. 'Mitch is a hottie and knows it. He's not shy with the ladies.'

'Uh huh.' Maddison cleared her throat and focused on her future, not the redhead getting all sudsy in the shower with the muscular body of a god.

'Do you want another coffee with milk?'

Could she have a cold shower? 'Yes, please.'

'Coffee's on the table when you're ready, Mitch,' hollered Tracey.

When Mitch rejoined them he smelled of soap, with hair damp and chin smooth. He sat beside Maddison and grabbed his coffee. 'Have you made a plan yet?'

'Yes. But I need to get into the airport. Undetected.'

'I hope not Adelaide airport, I'm sure they'll have a scout there.' Mitch sipped his coffee, watching her over the mug's rim.

'No, Parafield Airport.'

Mitch gave a tummy-swirling gorgeous grin as he sat back in his chair. 'Well, you're in luck then, aren't you?'

'In what way?' Seated at the table with a guy who looked like Mitch, that wasn't luck, it was torture.

'My mate works there. I'll call him to scout around.'

'I don't want to put you in any—'

'Hey, deep breath, little rabbit.' He grabbed her hand, his thumb brushed over the back of it sending a soothing warmth up her arm. 'I'm just dropping you off. It's the main reason I've been fixing Tracey's car.'

'Why?'

'Well, the blokes who chased you last night might've been smart enough to get the rego plates from my bike. And if you've got cops involved, they'll be looking for it. Not that I mind you on the back of my bike either.' He let go, grinning at her, as he took a sip of his coffee.

She felt cold without his touch and hid her hands in her lap under the table. *Stay focused.*

'Did you pay for your flight by credit card?' He asked her.

'No. Cash on arrival.'

'Give a false name?'

'Yes.'

His amber eyes narrowed at her. 'You sound like you've

done this before?'

'I'm learning fast. Do you have any tips?'

He gave her a long look; she felt naked under that stare.

'Get out of those fancy clothes. Change your hair length and colour, although…' He tenderly stroked her hair. 'I like the way you look now. Why mess with perfection?'

'Ugh, listen to yourself, will ya,' said Tracey, coming into the kitchen. 'Leave the woman alone, she's way out of your league.'

'Butt out, Tracey.' Mitch grinned at Maddison. 'I'll go make that phone call to the airport. Get your gear together.' With coffee in one hand, mobile in the other, he booted open the back door.

That man had so much presence he'd left a vacuum in the room.

'Mitch really must like you,' Tracey said, staring out the window to the backyard. 'He wouldn't go to this much trouble for just anyone.'

'Uh huh.' Mitch was too much for this little rabbit, he was a man who would have too much control over her. And that scared her.

Under normal circumstances, they would never have met. Yet, these people had done so much to help out a stranger.

'Here, Tracey.' Maddison closed her laptop and pushed it to the middle of the table. 'The laptop is yours. It's got a hundred hours of internet connection paid for; it should help you get back into your studies.'

Tracey screwed up her nose. 'Why?'

'You helped me out by letting me stay here, it's the least I can do.' It felt right.

'But—but—it's brand new.'

'Technically, I've had it a few days, so it's second-hand.' She could pick up another one easily enough. All she needed was a PC with an internet connection to work with the cloud.

Maddison scribbled on her trusty notepad and tore off the page. 'This is the name of an interior decorating company, here in Adelaide. Michael is the owner, gifted for his skills, but known for his acidic tongue. If he doesn't like something, he never holds back. It's what made him the best in the business. But sadly, he's forever hiring apprentices who quit when they've had enough of his layered sarcasm. If you can survive at least twelve months with Michael, then you'll survive anything and anyone in that line of work. Tell him I sent you; he may go a little easier on you.'

'But—but, you don't know me.' Tracey stared at the name on the paper, then gazed up at Maddison.

'But I remember what my mum went through as a single mother to give me a good life.' Maddison patted Tracey's slim shoulder. 'Sometimes, we all need a little help from a stranger. I should know.'

'I don't know what to say.'

'That'll be a first. But I hear *thank you* is a good start.' Mitch stood at the back doorway, tapping his wrist. 'Time to run, little rabbit.'

She rolled her eyes at the nickname; that only made him smile wider.

Tracey launched herself at Maddison's back and wrapped her arms around Maddison's neck. 'Thank you. Thank you. Thank you.'

'You're welcome.' Maddison laughed, trying to pry the young Tracey off her back to pick up her bags. 'Take care of you and Jamie, okay?'

'Will do.' Tracey grimaced with trembling lips and glassy eyes.

'Come on.' Mitch grabbed Maddison's hand and led her out the door. 'Tracey will start crying in a minute.'

'Nick off, Mitch, I'm allowed to.' In her holey socks and faded jeans with worn knees, Tracey waved from the back door. 'You stay safe, Maddison.'

'I'll try.'

'Don't worry, little rabbit, you're safe in my care.' Mitch flung his arm over Maddison's shoulders and kissed her cheek. He escorted her to an old Mazda hatchback that had different-coloured panels, like it was a metallic patchwork quilt.

Mitch opened the passenger door, it creaked in protest. Tossing her bag into the back next to the baby seat, he gave her a bow. 'Your chariot awaits, me lady.'

She giggled, climbing onto the torn passenger seat that was covered in a towel.

The door screeched shut and Mitch raced around to the driver's side. The whole car moved as he sat behind the steering wheel.

'My mate told me that, besides the staff, there's only a couple of passengers waiting at the terminal. We'll be taking the back entrance; coz the good lad has left the gate open.' Mitch drove through a maze of turns, giving Maddison a side street tour of suburbia, early on a Wednesday morning.

They followed alongside a tall wire fence on the outer edges of the airport where assorted small planes were parked in the distance. A tower stood in the centre near a criss-cross of runways that were spread out among the brown grass. It was so dry, with a hot wind curling off the tarmac carrying the aromas of dust and baking asphalt.

Taking a hard right, Mitch steered through an open wire gate. No security guards waited. No one was around. He zipped down the road to the gathering of buildings where a small plane was being loaded.

'How come you know so much about this airport?'

'Don't ask.' Mitch parked at the rear of the building.

Dumb question. Hello, biker. But where was his patch?

'Well, um, thanks for the lift.' She didn't want a long goodbye.

'I'm not letting you out of my sight until you get on that plane. It's a shame, I could have stayed in bed all morning,' Mitch said, getting out of the car. 'But then I doubt we would've got anything done for the next few days.'

The driver's door closed, and the car shook.

Her cheeks burned. Nothing could cool down her rampant thoughts—except for the screeching creak of the passenger door, with Mitch holding out his hand to her.

'This way, little rabbit.'

With ticket in hand, she sat beside Mitch in the sparse reception area.

Seated opposite, a married couple busily rummaged through their bags, talking in agitated whispers.

'Looks like you'll be travelling with them.' Mitch nodded at the couple feverishly going through their checklists while scowling at each other. 'Straight, conservative, middle-class kind of crowd. They're probably on their second honeymoon, trying to recapture their marriage spark before they get divorced.'

They seemed stressed, arguing in whispers while digging through their belongings. What did they have to be so stressed about?

'Thank you for everything,' she said to Mitch, admiring his smoothly shaven jaw. Cheekbones and freckles on a redhead had never looked so good.

'My pleasure.' Again, he casually put his arm around her shoulders as if he'd been doing it all his life. Stretching out his long legs, crossing them at the ankles, he was something to behold in his faded denim jeans, black motorbike boots and tight grey T-shirt.

She wanted to lean on his shoulder and chill.

But she couldn't afford to.

'Here, take this.' She held out a handful of cash. 'Take this, for all of your help.'

He closed her hand with his. 'Keep it. What you did for my cousin was enough.'

'*Boarding now for Elleron Downs,*' cried out the workman from behind the counter. He adjusted his baseball cap and large earmuffs. Eyeing off the married couple's luggage, he grimaced while wiping his hands on his bright orange work vest, before helping them with their bags.

Maddison stood and faced Mitch. 'Again, thank you for everything, I don't know how I can repay you for this.'

'I do.' Mitch pressed his lips against hers, holding her tight to his chest. It surprised her at first …

But then this kiss was her world.

Nothing and no one else mattered, just his lips against hers.

His warm hand cupped the back of her neck and that's when he took control. His tongue massaged hers as a hum murmured from the back of her throat as their kiss deepened. Her spine curved and their bodies aligned, their clothes a pressing barrier between them.

'*Oi, Romeo,* the plane's waiting,' called out the workman.

She pulled back giddily, blinking at the harsh light, only to drown in his amber eyes. *Wow, what a kiss.*

'Give us a second,' Mitch said, not looking away from her.

'It's not like you'll never see her again.' The workman chuckled.

'That's the problem,' whispered Mitch, his eyes roaming over her face as the back of his knuckles gently stroked her cheek. 'I don't think I will ever see her again.'

Again, he kissed her with a thirst that consumed her.

And then it was over. Far too soon.

'Take care of yourself, little rabbit. No more running blindly into strange bars, if you can help it.'

'Then I would have never had the chance to ride on a Harley.' His world was so different from hers. She clung onto him even as he squeezed her breathless from both his embrace and kiss. And then he let her go.

With fingertips grazing her swollen lips she strolled in a daze to the runway. At the steps to the plane, she looked back.

Mitch raised his arm in a wave. He gave a gorgeous smile with his red hair a halo in the sun. His shoulders were broad and strong, narrowing to the washboard stomach and strong thighs. Tall. Powerful. Beautiful.

She smiled, blowing him a kiss, then climbed into the plane, knowing that they'd probably never see each other again. But she would never forget him.

Twenty

ELLERON DOWNS, NORTHERN TERRITORY

ount Elleron was blanketed behind gutsy grey clouds that stretched behind the large homestead. Heavy rainfall had carved out long puddles that pooled over red dirt roads and empty cattle yards. Sheets of rain poured off the corrugated shed roofs that hid the silent machinery stored inside.

Within the shade of the farmhouse's deep front verandah, the family settled in for breakfast.

The front flyscreen door burst open as Glenda walked outside carrying a tray. She made short work of serving up plates of bacon, eggs, baked beans, and sausages to the three men.

'Thanks, Mum.' With cutlery in hand, Joe was ready to dig in. His little brother, Greg, doing the same. 'Did I hear the phone?'.

'Yes, dear, it was the travel agent. We've got three people coming out late this arvo.' Glenda poured out the tea, taking her seat.

'Three, eh?' Earl wiped down his greying beard, then scooped up his teacup. 'I thought we were only getting a married couple?'

'Please tell me they're not bringing out some little kid I have to keep entertained?' Greg whined, shrugging his skinny shoulders.

'Sucker,' Joe muttered low enough to avoid the glare from his mother but loud enough for Greg to frown.

Glenda tidied up her youngest boy's scruffy hair. 'You'll be right this time. It's a lady.'

'A what?' Joe frowned with his mouth full of toast.

'Don't speak with your mouth full.' Glenda slapped Joe's large hand. 'Can't have our guests thinking you boys have got no manners.'

'Boys? Luv, they're men,' said Earl over the rim of his teacup.

'Why do we let them come out here?' Greg really had the whines on this morning.

'Because they help pay the bills, son,' said Earl. 'Especially in the wet season.'

'I'm hoping by next muster we won't have to bother with them at all.' Joe wished.

'I enjoy having all these new people visiting,' said Glenda.

But both Joe and Greg groaned in between mouthfuls of breakfast.

'Even if some of them are demanding, most of them seem nice,' she said.

'But we have to say the same speech over and over again. *What we do? Why we do it?* Blah, blah, blah.' Greg whined, yet again.

'Who are our guests this round, luv?' Earl asked Glenda.

'There's the married couple, Analise and Zach Thurston. They're here for seven days. He's an accountant, and she's a homemaker like me, dear.'

'And the third one?' Earl asked as Greg gave a puppy-dog plea to not get stuck babysitting.

'No idea.' Glenda shrugged, sipping her tea. 'Only that she's booked herself in for two weeks and paid in cash.'

'Cash?' Joe looked up from his plate. No one paid cash. It was all electronic payments because they had no shops or banks out here.

'She booked in last minute and is paying at the airport when she checks-in.'

'No name?' Earl asked.

'Not until she boards the flight,' replied Glenda. 'All I

know, dear, is that she has requested the use of our PC and internet when she gets here. Oh, and sleep. Apparently, this poor lady is after an escape from all the stress she's been under lately.'

'Great, another pencil pusher, stressing over a broken fingernail she got from removing staples from paper reports,' mumbled Joe.

'Or she's a ninety-year-old hag covered in warts who scares little children off with a croaky voice and evil-looking eyes,' said Greg.

Earl and Joe chuckled.

The kid was a natural storyteller with a vivid imagination for horror stories; known to scare the absolute crap out of little kids who loved him for it.

Greg wound up, gripping his butter knife like a microphone. 'And this old woman will have a walking frame that creaks with each step like it's gonna snap. And she'll be demanding Mum waits on her hand and foot. Carrying around a deformed rat on steroids with fangs like a vampire in her handbag beside the knitting needles and poison.'

'Don't be like that, boys.' Glenda giggled. 'The lady's probably nothing like that.'

'Don't care.' Joe cleared his plate, then wiped his mouth with the napkin. He gulped down his tea, scooped up his wide brim hat off the chair beside him and stood from the table. 'I won't be here to see them.'

'Where are you going, dear?'

'I'll be busy checking out the floodplains. I'll be back in a few days.' He kissed his mother's cheek. 'Thanks for brekkie, Mum. Don't mind if I raid the pantry?'

'I'm coming with ya.' Greg got up from the table.

'Nope.' Earl landed a strong working hand on Greg's shoulder. 'You're staying put and helping me out, son.'

'Aw, come on, Dad.'

'Jeez, you've got the whines on today, bro. Suck it up.' Joe grinned at his baby brother flipping him the bird.

'You might need your raincoat, dear,' called out Glenda as the rain poured heavier on the roof.

'I've already got it, thanks, Mum.' In the kitchen, Joe slid on his Driza-Bone then stood at the open fridge with the esky at his feet, trying to work out his menu for the next few days.

'What are you driving and where are you sleeping?' His mother asked.

'I'm going in my ute, towing the dinghy. I put the canopy on the back yesterday; that'll keep me dry.' He sniffed at the cheese, then put it back. He grabbed eggs, bacon, sausages, steak, and milk for his cuppa. He opened the crisper where his mum kept the fruit and veggies, screwed his nose at it and slammed it shut. 'I've got the swag and the small gas cooker,' he said, adding potatoes, onions, baked beans, and the trusty dead-horse to his esky. His hand hovered over the mustard—did he or did he not?

'Clothes, dear?'

Why not go posh? He chucked in the mustard beside the salt. 'I've packed extra clothes in case I need them.' Not that he'd bother. It wasn't a fashion parade out there; cattle didn't care how he smelled.

Inside the pantry, Joe scoured the wall-to-ceiling shelves, searching for the junk food. His mum hid it from their dad, who loved the sweet and the salt.

'If you're in the pantry, dear, can you please take those tools that seem to show up out of nowhere?'

Joe looked at the shelf containing shifting spanners, screwdrivers, a drill, assorted rope, and cable ties. They cluttered a shelf all on their own.

'Leave 'em, son,' said Earl from the table. 'It's handy having them there if we need to make a quick house repair without bothering the guests.'

'The pantry isn't a part-time toolshed, dear. You have over a dozen sheds on the property to choose from.'

'Taking any guns, son?' Earl called out, ignoring his wife.

Victory! From the top shelf, Joe dragged out a jumbo bag of chips and the good ol' salted beer nuts. 'I cleaned my rifle yesterday and packed it with extra ammo and torches too.' His beer was already chilling in the fridge on the back of his ute. As always.

'Is that it?' His dad asked.

As if. 'The shotgun's in the boat with the spare spotlight and the flare gun is there to keep it warm. All I needed was this.' He walked outside, carrying his loaded blue esky.

'Have you got enough water, dear?'

'Mum, it's raining.' Greg pointed to the rainy grey skies.

Yeah, Joe was in for some crappy weather, but it beat sticking around to play polite with the tourists. 'I'll see ya in a coupla days.'

'Check in on the radio tonight, son,' said Earl.

'That's if the reception will allow it with all this weather, but I'll make sure I contact you in the morning,' said Joe, staring out at the rain.

Glenda got up from her chair and hugged her eldest around his large shoulders. 'You be careful out there; they're predicting some big electrical storms later on this arvo.'

'I'll be fine, Mum. Don't worry, Dad knows where I'm heading.'

'Man, I wish I was going with you,' said Greg, sulking in his seat.

'I don't.'

'Hey!'

'No offence, bro, but I want some time out to myself and don't need you nattering in my ear for the next two days. If I wanted that form of torture, I'd stick around to put up with the tourists.'

'Yeah, yeah. We all know you're jealous that I've been blessed with a gift the women love,' said Greg, wearing his big cheesy smile.

Joe laughed. 'I'll bring back some fresh fish and whatever else I drag out of the billabongs.'

In his four-wheel-drive ute, Joe tooted the horn as he drove out of the muddy compound towing the boat. There was nothing but open countryside and torrential rain surrounding him, and he was looking forward to two days of peace, free from tourists.

Elleron Downs wasn't a tourist resort—it was his home, and he hated all the tourists who invaded their privacy, even those flying in today, and he was going to do his best to avoid them all.

Twenty-one

I t was a plane ride into hell.

On the left, at the rear, Maddison was stuck in the smallest, pokiest, loudest plane of her life.

For six hours they'd been delivering freight here and there, bouncing around cattle stations and outback communities. The further north they went, the greener the landscape, the more they were tossed around by the fast-moving monsoonal storms. The turbulence had Maddison leaving indents in her chair's armrests from her white-knuckle grip.

She would never, ever, fly in anything this small again — ever!

If only she'd checked the weather reports before embarking on such a journey, she would have risked another day in Adelaide, even with the threat of the gun-wielding goons chasing her. It had to be better than this hair-raising plane trip to purgatory.

The married couple sat right behind the pilot, hurling continuously into paper bags. The stench was vile.

Maddison dry-retched, grabbing her perfume to spray the surrounding air again.

'Sorry about this, folks,' cried out the pilot, giving his assurances with his super-white toothy grin, which glowed against his spray-tanned orange complexion.

The pilot obviously loved it, cranking up the stereo to some whining-yodelling-dead-dog-dying country music that he sang out at the top of his lungs. 'Won't be long now, sweetheart.'

Maddison wanted to punch him in the mouth; he'd been

saying the same crap for the past four freaking hours.

And if that didn't make her day, his leering creepy stares only made her hug her red bag tighter. She missed her pepper spray.

For the first few hours of the flight, they had clear blue skies and straight flying. It had almost been a pleasurable experience, swooping low over the reddish-brown landscape.

Besides putting up with the creepy, orange-tanned pilot, the carry-on from the married couple added to the drama. Analise and Zach Thurston.

Mitch had pegged them perfectly as a long-time married couple trying to find their spark. Divorce would be kinder for this couple, who did nothing but bicker. They talked over each other, and everyone else, while asking the pilot a barrage of questions, they sounded like toddlers. *What's this? What's that? How come? What for? Why-why-why?!*

Analise's chalk-board scratchy voice droned on in her interrogation of the pilot.

The pilot, while leering like a lunatic from behind the controls, sprouted off absolute drivel, filling these tourists' heads full of hot air.

What's worse, the Thurstons lapped it up, behaving as if they'd never ventured beyond the bubble of their suburban street.

'Are you okay back there, beautiful?' The pilot flashed a gold tooth in his smile, like some sleazy real estate salesman. It matched his sickly brown dyed hair plugs.

Maddison nodded while squeezing the stuffing out of her seat's armrests.

Again, the plane plummeted a good five metres, leaving her stomach somewhere above her head.

'Gotta love that turbulence. *Yee-ha.*' The pilot yodelled as if in a rodeo, waving a straw cowboy hat he kept on the co-pilot's seat.

Again, Analise and Zach heaved loudly into their spew bags like it was a competition to see who could retch the loudest.

Maddison pressed her nose into the lapels of her jacket, inhaling her perfume.

A burst of brilliant white light illuminated the cabin's interior like a camera flash, and the plane jerked hard to the left. There was a deafening crack of booming thunder that vibrated throughout the entire plane, as if a god was shaking the plane like a child's toy.

The Thurstons screamed, flinging their spew bags into the air as they wrapped their arms around each other for dear life.

Maddison's scream caught in her throat. She should have stayed at Tracey's for one more night and given in to her lustful desires and spent the day in bed with a hot redhead. She'd rather be getting all hot and sweaty with a man than being cooped up in a stuffy, spew-smelling plane that was being tossed around like a yo-yo toy.

Another crackling flash of white light illuminated everything like a shot in an X-ray. This time the plane lurched to the right as a deafening boom detonated above them. It made her ears ring from shell shock.

'*Yee-ha*,' yodelled the pilot again, swinging his cheap straw cowboy hat in the air. 'Bring it on, Huey.'

'It's a storm, shouldn't we fly above it?' Zach cried out, with his wife clinging to him.

'Nothing to worry about, mate. It'll be all over soon,' said the pilot. 'You right there, sweetie pie? We'll be there soon.'

'Arsehole.' Maddison muttered through gritted teeth. Too scared to open her mouth in case she bit off her own tongue the way the small plane bounced around. Side to side. Up and down.

The Thurstons reached for more spew bags as Maddison stared out the window. Grey, angry clouds hid the world as the rain flew sideways creating a wall of water that was sliced at by the wide plane wing. How did the engine's propellers keep moving in this weather?

Another crackle started, creeping like a sky demon crawling on hands and knees across the clouds, it grew louder and louder, closer and closer. All the hairs on Maddison's arms stood on end as the cabin filled with static electricity.

The crisp crackle grew into a loud ear-splitting electrical

crack. It was soon followed by a *thwack* as a bolt of blue lightning slashed across the sky in a jagged flash. Its bolt-tip obliterated the aeroplane's engine and blew off half the wing.

Maddison froze in wide-eyed terror at the shower of sparks and flames exploding from where the wing once stood strong against the rain.

The plane plunged nose-first.

'Everyone, grab a life jacket under your seats and inflate them now!' The pilot gripped the controls as he called over the radio, *'Mayday. Mayday. Mayday …'*

The plane kept plummeting in an out-of-control spin.

Maddison screamed, helpless in this merciless runaway rollercoaster ride from hell.

With sheer determination, she pushed against the g-force and reached under her seat to grab the life jacket, struggling to put it over her head.

The plane's plunging pitch was ear-piercing, her eardrums threatened to burst from the pressure. It was worse than diving bends.

'Brace yourselves, we're going in for a crash landing.' The pilot fought with the controls, continuously calling *mayday* over the radio as they plummeted towards the earth.

Maddison clutched her large red handbag into her lap like a pillow for support. She inflated her life jacket, then with the spare she used it to wedge herself against the back of the chair in front of her and braced for impact. She blocked her ears to try and stabilise them and not panic.

The plane's engine, the roaring wind, and the Thurstons' screams made her blood run cold. She squeezed her eyes so tight there were stars behind her eyelids. She forced herself to breathe deeply as if about to go scuba diving, as the plane plummeted to the ground.

Was this it?

All that effort in running for her life—for this?

'Hold on everyone,' called out the pilot. *'May God save us all!'*

Twenty-two

Maddison woke to her face getting splashed by water rising around her lower legs. Still strapped into her plane seat, the entire front of the plane was underwater.

'Hello?'

Grey daylight streamed through the rear cabin windows, but heavy rain made it impossible to see outside.

Unclipping her seat belt, she threw off the cumbersome life jacket and removed her shoes. She shoved them into her handbag, putting it higher onto the seat out of the water.

The aisle was waist-deep with fresh water, the pilot must have landed in a river.

She dove under and swam toward the cockpit, where she found the Thurstons in a panic, struggling to get free from their seatbelts.

Maddison undid Zach's seat belt, pushing him to the rear of the rapidly filling plane.

Zach coughed and spluttered in the air pocket. 'My wife?'

'I'll get her, while you try to get that back door open.' Maddison took another mouthful of air and dove back under. In seconds she was beside Analise, where she wrestled with the frantic woman to undo her seatbelt, then dragged her to the back of the plane.

The air pocket was disappearing, and the cabin was getting darker the further they sank.

'Oh, my darling.' Zach reached for his wife where they jumped up and down, hugging each other like they'd won the lottery. But each jump made the plane lurch deeper into the river.

'*Stop hugging and open that door NOW*. We haven't got time, or we'll all drown!' Maddison's words bounced off the watery cabin. She'd never spoken to anyone like that!

'Right you are.' Zach grabbed a large tool and started banging on the door handle to force it open as the *tink* ... *tink* ... *tink* ... vibrated under the water.

It would help her find the way back from the darkening cabin, filling fast with water.

Maddison took another deep breath and dove toward the cockpit using the seats to propel her.

She found the pilot, strapped into his seatbelt, his glazed eyes staring at the darkness, his blood spilling like a pink ink cloud from the glass embedded in his throat and crushed chest.

She checked for a pulse and found nothing but cold glazed eyes, staring out through the broken window into the murky greyness.

It reminded her of Melbourne's oceanic dives, but here it was warmer and in fresh water.

Then something massive swam past the broken cockpit window.

A black shadow with four lizard-like legs, a snout, and a thick tail glided right past the broken window, mere metres away from her position.

'Crocodile!' The air bubbles escaped her lungs in a rush with her scream.

The beast turned around and aimed for the bubbles — straight for her and the bleeding pilot.

BOOM!

It was like a bomb exploding underwater, her ears were going to implode.

Desperate, she swam for the air pocket.

Spotting her red bag on her seat, she forced the strap over her head and right shoulder and then covered it with the spare life jacket, securing it over herself.

BOOM!

She covered her ears.

Was that the Thurstons opening the door, or the plane's fuel exploding?

She reached the air pocket, gasped a lungful of air, and tried to grab the roof. The top hatch opened and the luggage spilled out smashing hard against her head. A sharp, blinding pain exploded from her forehead; Maddison saw stars.

Twenty-three

Joe, in his dinghy, was puttering along the open floodplains. The rain cooled the humidity, turning red dust into slippery mud. But everything was green on the faraway jagged ranges, as the still waters reflected inky clouds alive with flashes of lightning.

KA-BOOM!

Joe flinched at the sound of a colossal explosion.

It wasn't thunder.

In the sky behind him, a large shower of sparks exploded like a firecracker, and the loud whining of a plummeting plane soon followed.

Joe stared in disbelief at the light aircraft doing a deadly nose-dive with angry flames and smoke pouring from its port side.

With his Akubra brim low and the collar high on his coat, Joe gunned the boat's engine and raced after it.

The plane crashed into the floodplain. A massive wave washed over the top of the aeroplane, sending out ripples that forced his boat to jump as if surfing rough seas.

The plane bobbed up and down, then the nose disappeared underwater, slowly sinking.

'Come on.' His small boat jumped the waves as the pelting rain stung his face. The wind was against him as the sky lit up with lightning and the deafening rumble of thunder.

He pulled up to the plane's rudder, wrapping a rope around the plane's tail to anchor the dinghy.

Tink ... Tink ... Tink.

'Hello?' Joe searched the murky waters, his hand on the

plane itself as if checking for a pulse.

Tink ... Tink ... Tink.

He felt it!

They're alive.

He threw off his hat, coat, and well-worn work boots, about to dive overboard when he saw the massive tail in the water.

Crocodile.

He gritted his teeth and reached for his shotgun, aiming at the water where he'd seen the large scaly tail.

BOOM. The shotgun blast echoed around him.

And he waited.

Tink ... Tink ... Tink.

He reloaded his shotgun, then aimed at the water. Through the shimmering surface, he could make out the back door of the plane a few metres below him. Inside, through the plane's windows, was some shadowy movement. The way the plane's tail was sitting high above the waterline, they must be in an air pocket. But how much air did they have left?

Yet Joe stood solid and waited with his finger on the trigger.

It glided like black lightning, the large scaly tail of one massive prehistoric beast.

He aimed and squeezed.

BOOM.

He'd hit it. Not enough to damage that tough hide, but it was enough to scare it off.

Tying another rope to the seat of his boat, he dove over the side with rope in hand.

He swam for the aircraft's door and peered through the plexiglass. Inside, a man and woman were trying to open the door.

Joe heaved on the handle with all his might, his muscles about to burst. With his feet on the body of the aircraft, he pulled with his arms and pushed with his legs until the door opened and the rush of water nearly sucked him inside. He gripped the rope and grabbed the man in front of him. He pointed to the rope and the surface where the bottom of his dinghy floated in the light.

With the rope in hand, all three of them swam upwards breaking through the watery surface, gasping for air.

'Is there anyone else down there?' Joe asked, pushing the woman into the dinghy.

'A girl,' called out the woman, helping the man clamber onboard. 'She got us out of our seats and went back for the pilot.'

'Right, stay there and watch for crocodiles.' Joe took a deep breath. Taking the rope, again he followed the side of the plane. He kicked his legs hard, keeping his eyes on the watery shadows for any lurking man-eaters.

Through the open door of the plane, the inside was barely visible. Luggage floated with other debris, when a hand floated in front of his face. Startled, all he saw was a mass of blonde hair. He cleared the silk-like wave to find her face, there was a cut on her forehead, but he found a pulse.

His muscles straining, holding her by the life jacket, he propelled himself off the side of the plane's shell, gripping on the rope to help drag her motionless body to the surface.

She was heavy, like something was dragging her down. But her body was limp with bare legs, skirt, and a life jacket.

Breaking through the surface, Joe gasped for air. 'Help me get her in.'

'She weighs a tonne for a skinny girl,' said the man.

Joe pushed until they dragged the woman onto the floor of the dinghy. He pulled himself up into the safety of the boat, his wet clothes clinging to him.

'*She's not breathing. What do we do*?' cried out the woman in a panic.

Joe made his way to the female unconscious on his boat's floor. He removed her life jacket and frowned at the waterlogged handbag. 'What the hell?'

'No wonder she was so heavy,' said the man.

'It's a nice red bag,' said the woman.

Joe grabbed the pocketknife sheathed on his belt and slashed through the bag's red leather straps. It landed with a heavy thud on the deck.

A large bump grew on the unconscious female's forehead, spilling blood into her hair, as Joe checked her airway. His hands were so big against her frail chest as he began compressions.

'Come on …' *Eighteen, nineteen, to hell with twenty.* He pinched her nostrils, pressing his lips to cover her mouth and forced air into her lungs.

Another breath.

Another round of compressions.

He was about to press his lips to hers again when she coughed out a gush of water.

He rolled her to her side and she spewed out water, gasping for breath while clutching his hand. And it was a tight grip he was glad to hold on to.

'You'll be okay now.' Joe rubbed her back, where he could feel her heart racing strongly. He wiped his mouth on his wet shirt, also taking deep breaths as his heart hammered at a thousand miles an hour.

'Where's the pilot?' Joe asked the other passengers huddled at the front of the boat.

'Dead.'

Her eyes were a stunning honey-brown, belonging to the blonde hair, blue lipped mermaid on his boat. Joe was at a loss for words.

'The pilot is dead.' And she laid her head down on the floor, shutting those eyes.

He wanted to hold her, to get her dry, with a fierce need to protect her.

The lightning flashed above him as the thunder rolled, but she still kept a grip on his hand. Her soft hand was cold, so he gave her a comforting squeeze.

He reached for his jacket to cover her and she huddled into a foetal position under his coat, which swam on her, hiding her from him and the world.

But she was alive.

Sadly, there was nothing he could do for the pilot, and they were losing light.

'I have a camp downriver. We should make it before dark.' Joe cranked over his outboard motor and headed downstream. 'Can you get me that spotty—'

'My name is Zach Thurston, and this is my wife Analise.'

'I'm Joe.' He was so sick of introducing himself to people who flew in and out, that he never bothered to even ask the names of tourists back home. He left the tour-guide-gig for his parents to deal with. 'Can you reach into the front for the large spotlight?'

The outboard motor whined as the rain poured and the boat fought against the wind. His heart was still pounding over what he had just done. So much for his quiet couple of days. No one was going to believe this back home.

'Is this what you're looking for?' Zach held up the spotty.

'That'll do. Thanks.' Joe shone the light while keeping his hand on the throttle of the outboard engine. 'So, who's the woman?' Normally, Joe never bothered to ask.

'Don't know,' replied Zach with Analise shrugging, both of them crouching down against the wind and rain.

The spotlight's reflection bounced off the water, as lightning competed with thick thunderheads crowding the sky. The rocky red ranges came into view, hiding the setting sun, which meant his camp was close.

'She never told us her name,' called out Analise over the sound of the outboard motor. 'She had her boyfriend drop her off at the airport, in such a romantic farewell. It was as if they didn't want to part.'

'He wasn't her boyfriend.'

'How would you know?' snapped back the wife to her husband.

'I heard the groundsman ask her if that guy she was playing tonsil hockey with was her boyfriend, and she said he wasn't.'

'So why did she kiss him like that?'

'I think *he* kissed her.'

Who the hell are these people? Joe rolled his eyes at the married couple bickering over a woman's boyfriend. 'Where were you headed?' Hoping the Thurstons would stop arguing over petty crap.

'Elor-All-Man,' Zach stammered.

'Elleron Downs,' said Analise with nose high in the air as if taunting her husband.

'Oh, great.' *The bloody tourists.* Joe glanced at the lump beneath his coat, the woman his brother had imagined to be a ninety-year-old scary witch.

Yet the way she'd gazed at him so trustingly while gripping his hand … His breath hitched and his heart pounded in his throat.

But that was only because he'd dived into a crocodile-infested river, rescuing people from a plane that had plummeted from the skies—not the woman.

It couldn't be her.

But he was dying to peek beneath his jacket to see if she was okay.

'Can you take us to that station?' Zach asked.

'You're already here, mate. But I'll take you to the homestead in the morning.' Joe searched the riverbank and there it was, his trusty ute. Home, sweet home.

'Why not tonight?'

'With all of this rain we're safer camping for the night.'

The Thurstons looked at him like he was lying to them.

Typical tourists!

But he imagined his mother giving him the eye, expecting him to explain. 'The runoff from this rain is enough to want to stick to high land and wait it out. We do not want to get bogged or caught in any flash flooding in the dark.'

'Where are we going to stay then?' Analise asked.

Joe aimed his flashlight at his ute with a large metal canopy on the back.

'That's not a camp.' Analise screwed up her nose.

'It might not be a luxury five-star resort, but it'll be a billion-star resort once them clouds disappear.' Joe nudged the boat's nose against the muddy bank and turned off the outboard. Thankfully, the wind and rain had died down.

'But where are we all going to sleep?'

'Who cares, we're back on land.' Zach jumped off the boat to splash his shoes in the red mud. 'I don't care if it's wet, *we're on land*.'

Joe cocked an eyebrow at the middle-aged man doing some weird rain dance of joy. 'Oi, dancing man, grab the rope from the front and I'll get your wife out, shall I?'

'So sorry, Analise, I got carried away.' Zach grabbed the rope and held his hand out to Analise, who stumbled off the boat. Then both husband and wife jumped up and down in the mud, hugging each other in rain-soaked muddy clothes.

Joe tossed the anchor high onto the bank. He then crouched by the huddled body on the boat's floor and gently lifted his coat. 'We're here.'

With her wet honey-blonde hair spilling around her, her light brown, golden-flecked eyes reflected the setting sun.

This time a hammer hit him hard between the shoulder blades with an erratic rise in his heartbeat that sizzled through his bones like a drum. *No way!*

Who was she?

Twenty-four

Maddison gaped at the man standing above her. With blue eyes and rich dark brown hair, the lightning flashed above him like he was the god of thunder. The man who'd saved her.

Wrapped up in his warm coat, she'd never forget his scent of earthy male spice, or his soothing touch against her back.

But what killed the moment was the voices of the married couple.

'Can I hide here, until the Thurstons leave?'

'Now that's tempting.' He laughed, with a warm smile that crinkled his deep tan.

It warmed her. Or his warm coat was doing the warming. *Ugh*, how much river did she swallow?

'I'm Joe. And you are …?'

'Maddison.' She shook his strong working hand. Men she'd met in her past never had hands like his. 'Hi, Joe.' She smiled up at her saviour, who had the nicest blue eyes that caught the flashes of lightning.

'Come on.' Effortlessly, he pulled her to sit up. 'How are you feeling?'

'Light-headed and bloated from having swallowed half the river.' *This was a daydream, right?* 'Ow …' She touched the lump forming above her right eyebrow, setting off a pounding headache behind her eyes. The smear of red blood was so bright against her waterlogged skin. She was a prune. A mess. And this guy was all male and gorgeous.

'You have a nasty bump there. I've got a first-aid kit in the ute.'

She tried to stand but the boat shifted, forcing her to latch on to his right arm. *Nice move, Maddy.* Except for the pounding headache and looking like a water rat, she couldn't have planned that any better.

'Do you remember what happened?'

She didn't want to.

She leaned into Joe's body heat as his arm came around her and he held her to his chest. The guy was built, but not pumping-iron, gym-body built. He had a workingman's frame—tall, solid, athletic and sturdy—yet with an unexpected tenderness. Just holding his hand made her feel safe.

No one did that.

Ever.

'Um …' Too soon the warmth was swapped for an icy wave of body tremors. 'The plane got struck by lightning, it crashed, and I must have blacked out. When I woke up, we were in the water. I got out of my seat and grabbed superman Zach there—' She pointed to Zach doing some awkward chicken dance.

Joe chuckled. 'And she's Lois Lane?'

'Lois Lane was a reporter. I doubt Analise would read anything else besides a shopping list.' She slapped her own mouth in horror. 'Sorry, that was bitchy.' And so unlike her. Although it was something Nancy would say.

How hard did she hit her head?

She tenderly touched her war wound. 'The luggage hit me from the overhead hatch … then I woke up to you.' The guy was her hero. 'Thank you for getting me out of there.'

'Glad to be there. Come on, let's get you out of this rain.' Still holding his hand, Joe led her to the front.

'There's our little hero,' called out Zach on the muddy bank. 'Thank you, young lady, for getting us out of our seat belts.' Zach hoisted her out of the boat. 'You're so much lighter now than when Joe first dragged you out of the water.'

'What happened to you?' Analise asked, 'And why did you have that bag over your shoulder like that?'

'My bag?' Maddison turned back to the boat.

'This?' Joe held up her waterlogged red leather bag in his

hand. 'It nearly dragged you underwater.'

'Thank you.' Maddison snatched it from Joe and gingerly climbed the gravelly wet bank. She removed her black heels, to tip out the water from her bag. The cash was all still there, and the rodent-proof, waterproof pouch had survived.

'Hope it was worth it,' Joe said.

Me too — if she ever opened the cursed thing.

'Didn't you know, women carry their entire lives in their handbags,' said Zach. 'Bet you could fit a kitchen sink in that bag.'

'Shame it's ruined now,' muttered Analise. 'It's a nice bag.'

'It's just a bag. It doesn't matter.' Maddison kept her back to them, not caring about the handbag itself. She could dry out the money, but the mobile phone was beyond repair. However, she was grateful Uncle Bob's documents remained sealed in the black pouch that had put her through hell.

'You don't have any dry clothes do you, Joe? A towel perhaps?' Analise asked as the rain slowed to a drizzle. 'All of our clothes are still in the plane.'

'Well, I'm not going back to get them,' stated Zach.

'I should have done what she did.' Analise pointed to Maddison. 'What is your name, anyway?'

'Maddison,' answered Joe. The husband and wife stared at Joe, who was anchoring the boat's rope to the bull bar of his ute. In his wide-brimmed cowboy hat, denim jeans and boots, the guy was a real-deal cowboy, tying his boat up like a horse in front of a saloon.

'How do you know her name?' Zach asked.

'I asked.' Joe grinned at Maddison.

She gave him a goofy grin, probably going to drool any second. Now she understood why rodeos were a thing — she had to be dreaming.

This morning it was the beautiful bad-boy biker and now this outdoors rugged cowboy.

'Well, I haven't got much, I wasn't expecting company.' Joe opened up the side of the ute's back canopy to create an extended roofed area.

Standing out of the rain, she watched Joe rummage

around in the back tray.

'Here's that first-aid kit.' Joe opened the tin box. 'Come on.' He beckoned her with a crooked finger.

'I'm okay.'

'It's disinfectant,' he said with his blue eyes sparkling beneath the brim of his Akubra. 'This is cattle country and with the humidity this time of year, any cuts and grazes can easily turn into septic tropical ulcers.'

'Oh? If I must, I must.' She'd had enough of the bad medicine that she'd take some good, especially when packaged like Joe.

* * *

'Welcome to the Northern Territory,' Joe murmured, cleaning up Maddison's forehead. The nasty bump was still bleeding. His hands trembled, trying to dab gently at her soft skin. He'd never seen skin so soft. He wanted to touch it, taste it.

Was he still so pumped with adrenalin that it was bringing the animal out in him?

Whatever it was, a surge of protectiveness demanded he take care of this stranger. He'd never reacted like this with anyone. Even with her wet hair and smudgy make-up, it only highlighted the honey in her eyes, and those plump pouty lips made him want to drag them between his teeth to settle in for a dominating kiss.

What the hell? He wanted to knock some sense into himself. *Think about it, mate. She's a tourist, with a boyfriend.*

'Only a slight cut, no stitches. It'll bruise a bit.' It was a shame to mark her beauty. 'I've got some ice to put on it.'

'That's okay. Thanks for everything. What you did was incredible.' Her voice was like honey, warm and sensuous, and the appreciation he could read in her eyes. They sure were pretty eyes with their golden flecks reflecting the dying light.

'So, Joe ...' called out Zach.

Great, the tourists speak. And that broke their spell, with

Maddison stepping away from him.

'I've got boxers on that'll dry out soon enough,' said Zach. 'Shall we start a campfire to dry out our clothes?'

'I'd like to see you try.' Joe rummaged through his duffel.

'There's no dry wood for a campfire, Zach.' Maddison pointed to the rain-soaked countryside. 'It's warm enough to not need a fire. Finally,' she said with a smile.

'Don't you like the cold?' Joe asked her.

'No.' She removed her jacket.

Hello. White. Wet. Shirt. He froze.

'Did you say you have some spare clothes?' Analise had a voice that could crack glass.

It shattered his daydream, with Maddison walking away in a figure-hugging wet skirt, wringing out her jacket.

They all needed dry clothes.

'I've got some shorts and a shirt for you, Analise. A spare shirt for you, Zach.' Joe passed out clothing to the Thurstons. 'And that leaves only a shirt for you, Maddison.' He held out his light blue collared work shirt. She was small enough for it to be a dress on her.

'You've got clothes for yourself, yes?'

Again, he cleared his throat. 'I've got my jeans, and it's only for the night.'

'Thank you, again.' As she accepted his shirt their fingers brushed and her breath hitched as she bit her bottom lip.

Was she feeling this too?

'Oh, God.' Maddison turned away with a shudder.

'What?' Did he smell?

'Behind you.'

Joe turned around and copped an eyeful of Zach stripping down, with his lily-white legs and butt cheeks exposed for all to see.

Then Analise started stripping. Joe turned fast to keep his back to the couple.

'Is he dressed yet?' Maddison whispered beside him.

'Don't ask me to look.'

'Why not?' She grinned up at him.

'I don't want to perve on some middle-aged guy and his wife.'

'Well, I'm too scared to look again. I've already copped an eyeful, thank you very much. I'm scarred for life.'

He matched her sweet grin. 'At least you have your sense of humour, considering the ordeal you've been through.' Her giggle only made him smile more. What would her laugh sound like?

'You have no idea.' She sobered up. 'Any discreet places to change?'

Right in front of him would be perfect. 'Um, the other side of the ute. I'll put up the canopy on that side so you're out of the rain. Didn't you have some shoes in that bag?'

She followed gingerly in her little bare feet, with bright red nail polish on her tiny toenails.

'My shoes are unsuitable for this terrain.' She showed him a pair of high-heeled shoes.

'Whoa, they're some sexy shoes.' He couldn't believe he'd blurted that out.

To save face, from the ute's back tray, he dragged out a pair of black thongs. 'You'll swim in them, but it's better than being barefoot around here, especially when it gets dark.' He opened the other side, creating a verandah from the back canopy's doors. 'You can get changed here, and I'll watch—I mean, I'll be at the back setting up camp, so Zach doesn't walk around by mistake.'

'Thanks. Any suggestions on where or how to air dry these clothes?'

'Um, inside the cab, I'll rig something up for everyone.' With his back to her, he removed his wet clothing and slipped into a pair of dry jeans and socks before putting his boots back on.

Although tempted to peek at Maddison getting changed, he kept a wary eye out for the Thurstons to not catch him naked either.

'So where are we all going to sleep tonight?' Analise asked again, while wringing out her wet clothes near the boat.

'I don't care if it's on the ground,' replied Zach. 'It's on land.'

'Don't crocodiles walk on land?' Maddison asked from the other side of the ute. 'I saw a big one under the water when I was in the cockpit.'

'How big?' Analise asked, stepping away from the water's edge.

'Twice the size of me. It swam right in front of me.' Maddison finished buttoning up his shirt like a dress. His thongs on her looked like snowshoes in the mud.

'Bull,' blurted out Zach.

'No, it's true,' said Joe, admiring his shirt on the lady. 'I saw the same crocodile circling above. I shot at it a couple of times with my shotgun.'

'That's what that noise was,' said Maddison. 'It sounded like a bomb exploding underwater.'

'I've never heard a gun underwater to know what it sounds like.' Joe began unrolling the canvas from the back of the ute's canopy and with two large poles he erected a tent.

Without waiting for directions, Maddison grabbed the fold-up chairs while he fetched the table and they set up camp together like they'd done it all their lives.

Until the married couple plonked down onto the chairs like they owned the joint.

'I've got an esky for you to sit on, Maddison.' He went back to his ute, grinning at her tiny steps following in his big shoes, as she rolled up the sleeves of his shirt.

'So where are we all going to sleep?' Analise asked for the umpteenth time. 'I could do with a shower from this mud. I wonder if it's any good for the complexion?'

'I'll take first watch from the crocodiles, if you like? This is quite a rig you've got set up,' Zach said. 'Got any drinks in that big box?'

With Maddison's help, Joe carted the esky and tucker box to the table.

'What's for dinner?' Zach sat back like some lord lump of the camp. 'I'm starving.'

'Me too,' said Analise. 'I'm thirsty too, now you mention it. I hope we have something decent.'

Was she searching for some restaurant menu?

'Seriously, how rude are you two?' Maddison stood with hands on her hips in front of the Thurstons. 'This poor guy is doing his best and you two are acting like Joe should cater to your every need. How about showing a bit of gratitude for what he's done? Because I've never heard you two, not once, thank Joe for what he did for us. He's really gone out of his way for us, so show a bit of respect to the man who has literally given us the shirt off his back.' She winced, touching her forehead's angry red lump. 'Normally I say nothing, but …' She then glared at the married couple. 'Stop arguing amongst yourselves like children. You could have drowned, so be grateful you've survived and have each other.' She then took a deep breath and turned to Joe and said in that honeyed voice of hers, 'Is there anything I can help with, Joe?'

Damn, she was good. The married couple were annoying him too, and he never had the patience for people, which is why he kept away from the tourists. 'Here's some thin rope if you want to hang it inside the cab for a clothesline.'

'Great, I'm onto it.'

Joe grinned, watching her flip-flop away in his thongs and shirt with head held high. He liked her spirit, and the way her arse and hips moved in his shirt.

'That's the most Maddison's said all day,' said Analise.

'But she's right. Real little spitfire that young lady is. I thought she was quite shy myself.' Zach approached Joe, holding his hand out. 'I'd like to apologise for my selfish behaviour, and to thank you wholeheartedly for what you did for us today. You're a proper hero in my books.'

'Yeah, right.' Joe shook Zach's soft hand.

'Me too, you're my hero.' Analise kissed Joe's cheek. 'Thank you for rescuing us.'

'No worries. I'm sure you'd do the same,' mumbled Joe, stepping away from the hugging, kissing tourists.

'So, what would you like us to do?' Zach eagerly rubbed his hands together.

'You can give Maddison your wet clothes to sort out. Zach, on the back of the ute, there's a mosquito net that needs to be pulled down before they hit. We'll all be sleeping on the back tray. Analise, how are you at cooking?'

'Good. I'm a mother of three grown children.'

'Well, inside that tuckerbox there's a small gas cooker and there's food in the blue esky. I'll get you some lights.'

Joe opened the driver's door to find Maddison's suit

already hanging up on the string line. 'Thanks for speaking out, Maddison. They were annoying me, too.'

'Like I said, we have a lot to thank you for.' She smiled at him, then hung up her white shirt.

Did she have any underwear on underneath his shirt?

Clearing his throat, Joe grabbed the radio and searched for a signal, flicking a few switches. 'Come in Elleron Downs … You there Elleron Downs?' He waited, listening to static.

Nothing.

'Are we out of range?' Maddison asked.

'This weather doesn't help. I'll radio in once we're on the move in the morning.' He turned the radio off and flicked on the lights, which gave a yellow glow to their camp. 'By the way …'

'Yes?'

'My shirt looks good on you, even if it is the last one off my back.'

'Thank you …' Delicately patting his old shirt she wore, her eyes filled with such a clear and deep appreciation it spoke to his soul. 'Because without you, I wouldn't be alive.'

He'd never felt more like a hero than in that one moment, just from the way she looked at him. He was only a cattleman. A simple bloke. Yet she'd made him feel like a king and he was damned glad she was alive too.

Pity she was only a short-term tourist.

Twenty-five

Maddison woke with a scream trapped in her throat. Sitting upright, she gasped for air.

'Hey, are you okay?' Joe whispered, lying beside her.

'Yeah ...' *Just a nightmare, it's not real.* She blinked at the dark void of no walls that stretched on forever, with a ceiling of stars shimmering with a marvellous brilliance.

Two people snorted and snored as the memory of where she was hit with a thud. She lay back down in Joe's ute with her head towards the cab and her toes pointed at their small camp, waiting for daylight to arrive.

She turned to face Joe where he lay to her right, Analise behind her, and Zach over on the far left, with crocodile infested waters surrounding them in the middle of the outback.

Close by there was a sound like a child screaming. She flinched, grabbing whatever was closest—Joe's arm. 'What's that?'

'A curlew.'

'A what?' *Oh no, not again*! Two days in a row she'd woken up in a strange place beside unknown men, and both men weren't wearing shirts.

Was Joe still in his jeans that fit the man perfectly, highlighting the muscular abs of a tanned handsome man with amazing blue eyes.

Was her intense attraction to the guy because he'd saved her, and she'd survived a plane crash?

'It's a bird.' Joe rolled over to face Maddison in the dim light. 'They're harmless.'

A loud screech whizzed overhead as it flew in the shadows of the night. 'What's that?' Again, she reached for Joe, his body warm against her cool trembles of fright.

'Bats.'

'Vampire bats?'

He chuckled. 'Fruit bats'

'Oh.' She pulled her hand away as the heat pricked at her cheeks.

'Have you ever been out bush before?'

'No. I've always wanted to. I've never been camping until now, and I've never been on a plane as small as the one that crashed.' She involuntarily shivered with the terror still fresh from her nightmare.

'Here …' Joe put a sheet over her and rubbed her arms. 'You're safe, nothing can get you here.'

His touch and soothing words had her sighing with relief.

The Thurstons continued to snore behind Maddison as if continuing their competition from the plane over who could retch the loudest.

When a hand landed on her backside.

'Is that your hand?' She asked Joe.

'Where?'

'On my bottom.' She wriggled to get away from the hand that clung to her butt. 'Get it off.'

Joe chuckled, putting his hand on her arm. 'This is my hand.'

'Well, whose hand is that?'

Joe leaned over and peeled the trespasser's palm from her posterior.

Rude much!

'That was Zach. I don't think he meant anything by it. He's still asleep.'

'I can hear.' The Thurstons snorted and snored among other grumbling gargling nonsense.

'Want to swap sides?'

'Yes, please.' She'd had enough of being kicked and knocked by Analise and with Zach's creepy arse grab—the further the better.

'You shift over.' Joe got up and Maddison scuttled

beneath him to the other side where she lay with her back to him.

'Thanks.'

'No worries. Here, you can have this too.' He dropped a pillow between them.

'I thought the Thurstons had the pillow?' They'd given the married couple everything to shut them up.

'I stole it. They won't notice.'

Not with that snoring they wouldn't.

'I'll share.' She adjusted the pillow and lay on her side, staring at the many galaxies of stars. It was endless. 'It's stopped raining.'

'About an hour ago.'

She shivered a little from the cool air. The sheet didn't do much.

'Cold?'

'A little.'

'Here …' Joe wrapped his arm around her, his bare chest against her back. 'Don't worry, I won't do anything.'

'Matter of survival, huh?' But she was grateful for the body heat and the sense of security he provided.

'Something like that.' His breath was warm against her skin; she wanted to hold his hand.

'I've never seen so many stars. They're beautiful.' It would have been peaceful without the Thurstons snoring along with the birds and bats screeching.

A loud splash came from the river.

'Was that a crocodile?' She wriggled closer to Joe.

'Probably a barra jumping out of the water.'

'A what?'

'Barramundi, that's a big fish. Don't worry, crocodiles can't climb up here, you're safe.'

'I'm sorry for being such a wimp.'

'That's okay. You're not used to it,' Joe murmured, giving her a gentle squeeze. 'You're still recovering from your big day.'

'Yeah, I survived.' *Plane crashes and goons.*

'That you did. What's your boyfriend going to say about you sleeping like this?'

'I don't have a boyfriend. Where did that come from?'

'The Thurstons said you did.'

'That's right.' She huffed, remembering the Thurstons bickering on the boat over Mitch being her boyfriend or not. 'No, that was Mitch, he helped me out yesterday because I was in a jam.'

'Is this *damsel in distress* thing a habit for you, eh?'

'No.' She frowned at the night sky. But, ever since her uncle's murder, there had been a sharp increase in her need of rescuing. It was pathetic. 'And for your information, he kissed me.'

'What's the difference?'

'I don't know how you do it out here in the middle of whoop-whoop, but there is an enormous difference.' She rolled over to face his smirk and shiny eyes.

'No, there isn't. A kiss is a kiss.'

'There's a big difference.' *Cowboy.* '*He* kissed *me*—in fact, he took me by surprise.'

Joe shrugged like she was some clueless idiot.

'I'll prove it.' And kissed his forehead. 'See that's me kissing you.'

'Meh. That's your version of tonsil hockey, is it?'

'Tonsil hockey?' She screwed her face up.

'That's how the Thurstons described it. Can't city girls kiss properly?'

'Excuse me? I'm no kissing-booth expert on how everyone else does it. And I certainly don't have any experience on how cowboys do it, I'm just trying to demonstrate there is a difference.'

'Yeah, right.' He shared a deep sigh, laying on his back, patting his bare chest. 'A demonstration on how to kiss your mother.'

She scowled at him. 'He kissed me.' How dare Joe dismiss her like that?

'Uh, huh.' Joe slid his hand behind his head and closed his eyes.

She sat up, ticked at this smug guy who knew nothing. 'I'll show you.' She grabbed the sides of his face and pressed her lips against his and eagerly kissed him for everything her self-pride was worth.

When she pulled back, swallowing hard, while staring at

Joe, dumbfounded at what she'd done. It had been unbelievably good. And he tasted unexpectedly delicious.

She lay back with ragged breath, staring at the stars. Her heart pounded and her stomach swirled as the heat from that kiss had her toes crinkling for more.

'What was that?'

'A clear and obvious demonstration on the difference of me kissing you. And who calls it tonsil hockey, anyway? What kind of stupid, degrading—'

Joe rolled over and kissed her with as much gusto as she'd done. Only, he took the kiss so much deeper, rubbing his tongue against hers. It was warm and welcoming; that only made her hungry. His hand cradled her face as his firm lips took control of their battle and she relished the attack.

Her itchy palms, with their need for skin, slid around the warm smooth contours of his broad muscular shoulders. Her body hummed with a burning desire for more as their mouths crushed against each other.

Analise snorted and spluttered so loudly she sat up, scratching her head. 'What's going on?'

Joe and Maddison froze with arms wrapped around each other, their hearts beating loudly against each other's chests.

Zach kept snoring.

Analise lay down and soon resumed snoring in sync with her husband.

Joe rolled off Maddison, where they lay on their backs and sighed as if they'd been holding their breaths.

Maddison rolled to her side, keeping her back to Joe.

What had she become? Yelling at the Thurstons earlier. Kissing two different, but very handsome men, two nights in a row. Her wicked godmother would be so proud, but Maddison grimaced with confusion.

'What was that?' Maddison touched her swollen lips, tasting him, her body awakened. The man could kiss.

She grabbed the sheet and wrapped it around herself. Who was she to suddenly start making out with a cowboy in the back of some ute? *Seriously!*

'That was me kissing you.'

She could hear Joe's smile. Obviously proud of his efforts, having proven his manhood for the pride of cowboys everywhere.

Okay, credit was due, but she would never tell him that, even if she felt safe beside Joe. How was she ever going to get some sleep now?

Twenty-six

Maddison woke slowly to a hazy pink ribbon of clouds that streaked in the distant horizon above a calm inland lake. On the other side, jagged red rocks and curvy hill crests stretched in the distance, where waves of olive-leafed treetops rolled into a green sea that met the sky.

Her tiny country scene from her balcony window never looked as magnificent as this.

Pity the bed was just a board on the back of Joe's ute.

Sadly, the snoring snuffling carry-on of Mr and Mrs Thurston continued. But having Joe's arm wrapped around her kept her warm.

Then she frowned as a flush of heat crept up her neck. She'd kissed Joe and they could have easily gotten carried away.

Safe wasn't meant to be sexy. And she felt safe with Joe, who was sexy—even asleep.

But that made it two different men in two days, in two different beds, in two different states. Attracted to the pair of them, even though the bad-boy biker and the cowboy were not the type of men she'd normally meet in her day-to-day life.

But both men had called her *a damsel in distress*.

Maddison frowned. She had never depended on anyone. She'd always relished doing things for herself. Never asking for help.

The men in her past either despised her independence or felt the need to save her from working behind a bar or her other casual dead-end jobs.

Stuff 'em!

That was Nancy's mantra, repeated every time the wicked godmother had separated from one of her many husbands.

Nancy would get bored with her latest male tryst and move on. Maddison's mother never needed a male to rescue her either. And Maddison was done being the distressed damsel, never more ready to kick that cliché to the curb.

She slowly removed Joe's arm and slipped out from under the sheet, wearing nothing but the guy's shirt.

Seriously? She needed to get her self-control back.

Maddison put the camping kettle on the gas burner, then tiptoed past the slumbering bodies, unsure why she bothered with the Thurstons' loud snoring.

Hiding behind the ute's bonnet, Maddison changed into her own clothes. They weren't fully dry, but they were hers and she needed to stand on her own two feet. She'd had enough of playing the victim.

She went through her wet red bag to see what she could salvage. She brushed her hair, applied deodorant, then moisturiser and other items that were part of a daily routine for as long as she could remember. And that routine helped her to regain her strength—even though she was in the middle of nowhere.

Maddison didn't care if she was over-dressed, she did this for herself.

The kettle boiled, and she made herself a coffee.

Sipping on the bitter black brew, she surveyed the vast landscape in the early dawn light. Black storks waded along the watery edge, with strange spoon-billed ducks and other birds parading by.

She inhaled the crisp morning air. Free from fumes, the invigorating scents of fresh water and damp soils blended with lush wild grasses and flowering native trees. A slight cool breeze skimmed off the glassy water, keeping the humidity down as the sun peeked over the horizon.

There was nothing and no one else around.

No cars. No houses.

Just Joe's ute.

If ever there was a perfect time and place to read her

uncle's notes, this was it.

With her red bag in one hand and coffee in the other, she followed the red dirt track up the tiny hill. She found a large flat rock and there, as the sun rose, she sat with a coffee beside her and pulled out the plastic pouch.

She stared at it.

The thick black plastic pouch reminded her of the slim waterproof bag she used for her mobile phone whenever she'd go out on the diving boat. *Duh!* It had the have the same principles. She hoped. Or she was going to pinch Joe's pocketknife and slash the thing open.

Taking a sip of her coffee she focused on the task. She pulled back the stiff clips and unrolled the thick plastic, then opened its mouth wide.

It was finally open.

She paused, expecting some magical genie or curse to float out on a wisp of smoke.

But nothing.

She emptied the pouch, placing each item on the rock beside her. There was a well-worn leather-bound journal with the gold initials *BF* in the corner. It was a birthday gift she'd given Bob years ago.

In addition to the journal was Bob's mobile phone and her digital camera, with both of their USB cords for charging. They were unusual items for a man who avoided technology, referring to himself as the old-school note-taker with ink-stained fingers, who refused to use the cloud.

Maddison stared at the simple items she'd been chased around the countryside for.

The camera and phone batteries were likely dead, so she'd have to wait and charge them wherever Joe was taking them.

Picking up the leather-bound journal, she recognised Bob's handwriting.

Tears blurred her vision, as she remembered articles that her uncle had read to her as a child. Many he'd had published, some fiction more than fact. He should have been a novelist, not a journalist.

Sadly, his gifts were wasted on drinking and gambling.

She hugged the journal, to watch the sun rising over the

floodplains that blended into the horizon. The river was calm and clear as water reeds waved with the breeze. Tiny red finches flitted from swaying grasses as flashes of blue kingfishers darted for bugs in aeronautical feats. As the pinks from the sunrise faded, giving way to an azure blue that filled a massive sky where flocks of geese flew by in V formations.

Uncle Bob would have appreciated the scenery.

Now, after surviving these past few days of hell, she was more determined than ever to keep her deathbed promise to Bob, she was going to finish what he'd started. With a deep breath, she opened the leather journal and began her search for answers.

Twenty-seven

Joe winced at the daylight, lying on what little swag bedding he had left. The wood-sawing snore of the Thurstons grated against his back. He frowned at the couple he'd rescued from the crocodile-infested river.

Then he smiled, closing his eyes, picturing Maddison. Her humour last night and the smile that shone in his eyes, and how she'd looked in his blue work shirt with her smooth creamy legs. Most of all, that kiss. And how Maddison tasted and how pliant her body fit against his.

It was a beautiful dream, that wasn't actually a dream. Maddison was *real*.

Joe spotted the blue shirt Maddison had been wearing, hanging over the side of the ute's tray.

A loud gurgling noise of a backfiring bugle heralded the most god-awful smell he'd ever encountered. It was worse than rotten eggs and eye-watering onions.

'Oh God!' Joe gagged, pinching his nostrils as his eyes watered at the nightmare.

He held his breath, too scared to breathe. Covering his nose and mouth, he scrambled as if his life depended upon it and dashed away from that poisonous gas, gasping for fresh air.

Yet the Thurstons still snored beneath the mosquito net, wallowing like pigs in the mud as that stench strangulated the open air.

'Bloody hell, Analise, what crawled up your arse and died?' Zach covered his mouth and nose and clambered out of bed.

'What?' His wife sat up with hair everywhere. 'Ew, what

is that horrible pong?' Analise too scrambled out to join them by the table and chairs. 'Is there a sewerage problem out here?'

'No.' Joe frowned at the newcomers disturbing his peace. 'I'll put the kettle on.' The kettle was still hot, so Maddison hadn't been awake too long and he scrounged for cups in the nearby tuckerbox.

'Where's the toilet?' Analise asked.

'Anywhere you like.' Joe dumped the dunny roll on the table. 'Just don't go near the water.'

'Why?' Zach asked.

'Crocodiles.' *Aw come on!* Playing tour guide was like being a babysitter for grownups. Joe didn't have the patience for it.

Wait, where was Maddison? Surely, she wasn't silly enough to be croc bait? But she'd never been camping or experienced the bush before.

Joe stepped out from under the tent's shade and scouted the scenery for her.

Seated on a rock on the nearby hill, dressed in her suit, Maddison looked like she was reading a book.

She was stunning to watch.

'Where's Maddison?' Analise asked.

'Over there.' Joe nodded in her direction.

'What is she doing out there?'

'How should I know?' Joe slid on his hat, grabbed his blue shirt and headed towards Maddison. Buttoning up his shirt, he inhaled the soft floral perfume that lingered in the material. He remembered it well, having held on to sleeping beauty all night.

'Morning.' Joe stood in front of Maddison, reading from a handwritten book in her lap.

Maddison gasped, slamming the book shut.

'Sorry, didn't mean to scare you.'

'It's okay. It's beautiful out here, isn't it?

She was more beautiful than a thousand sunrises. 'Yeah.'

She looked up at him and he realised he was staring at her like an idiot. 'You got up early. Catching up on some reading, huh?'

'Um, yeah.' Maddison clutched the brown leather book.

'I'm surprised that's dry.'

'Waterproof bag.' She slid the journal inside a thick rubber pouch she clipped shut, then dumped it into that big red bag of hers.

She'd never gotten angry at him for cutting the strap on that thing, but she'd improvised by tying the ends together.

'*Ah!*' Maddison screamed, clutching Joe's arm to hide behind his back. 'There's something in my bag. It's alive and scaly.'

He grabbed a large stick to peek inside her bag. 'Are you sure you saw something? You didn't mistake it for your lipstick?' He'd never seen so much junk inside a woman's handbag before.

'Yes, I'm sure. What is it?'

'Well, we do have snakes out here …'

Maddison stepped closer, clinging to the back of his shirt.

He licked his lips to hide his smile. 'Scorpions. Spiders.'

With each word she held him tighter.

He enjoyed playing hero.

'Get it out,' Maddison demanded.

But he didn't like the sound of fear in her voice.

Using the thick stick, he snagged the end of the bag and tipped out all of its contents. A frill-necked lizard scurried away. 'It's a frillie. They don't bite. He's probably been sunning himself right next to you on this rock before checking out your handbag.'

'Is it gone?'

'Yes.' He opened the mouth of the huge handbag. 'There's nothing left inside. You really could fit a kitchen sink in here.'

'A lizard, huh?' She squinted at him, pressing those plump lips into a thin line. 'You were trying to scare me about snakes, weren't you?'

Busted. 'There really are snakes, scorpions, and spiders out here. Pick your species, I'm sure it's made a home out here, right alongside the crocodiles.' He nodded at the vast wilderness.

'Great …' She gave her bag a good shake before filling it back up.

'Is that money?' Joe picked up two wet rolls of hundred-dollar bills. There were dozens of bundled wads of cash laying on the ground everywhere. There had to be thousands of dollars' worth.

'Hey, that's mine.' She snatched the rolls from him and filled up her bag.

'What are you doing with all that cash?' He'd never seen that much cash lying around like that. No wonder she clung on to that handbag as if it had her entire life in there. 'Did you rob a bank or something?'

'Excuse me?' She glared at him with so much fire in her eyes he stepped away from the blonde beauty. 'How could you say such a thing? I won this money.'

'How? Gambling?'

'Yes. I made a few bets, that's all,' she said, jutting out that dainty chin of hers.

'The pokies at the casino?'

'No. With the track's bookie, running places on the long shots.'

'Gamble often, do you?' Because she spoke like she knew all about that con's game.

'No.' She scowled at him. It wasn't her best look.

His mum had told them they were to expect a last-minute tourist, a woman who'd paid for her trip in cash. No one paid in cash for anything anymore. 'How much is there?'

'That's none of your business.' She shoved the last of her items into her bag, then gingerly stepped in the red dirt in her stiletto heels and black tailored business suit. Maddison was not dressed like the typical tourist that came to Elleron Downs. Scared out of her wits at anything that moved, clutching onto a bag of cash.

She didn't look like a criminal who'd rob a bank. They wouldn't hide out here—would they?

* * *

'Morning, Maddison,' called out the Thurstons in unison.

It was jarring, and so were the questions from Joe, who

watched her suspiciously as she approached their small campsite. 'Morning.'

'Is everything all right?' Zach asked. 'We heard you screaming?'

'There was a small lizard in my bag.' Maddison put her bag on the nearby box then washed her coffee cup.

'It's such a nice bag,' said Analise, staring at the red bag. 'It's such a shame Joe had to cut the strap like that to get you to breathe.'

'Uh huh.' Of all people to end up in the middle of nowhere with, was she being punished for something?

'Anything you want us to do, Joe?' Zach asked, rubbing his hands together.

'Let's pack up camp.' Joe dropped the ute's back tray and rolled up the mosquito net. 'I need to get into radio range and let everyone know you're okay.'

'Our children would be fretting,' Analise said to her husband. 'And all our friends and family too.'

Zach nodded. 'We should call them as soon as we hit that homestead. What about you, Maddison? I'm sure someone's worried about you?'

Maddison hesitated. After all, she was meant to be hiding. 'I'll help do the back tray.' Her shoes weren't going to handle walking around in the dirt for much longer.

'I'm sure your family and friends are concerned. I know all of my work mates would be,' Zach said, wrestling with a fold-up chair.

'And our church group. And all those people I deal with at the school,' proclaimed Analise, coming to his rescue on the chair.

Joe put the large plastic boxes and other items into the back as Maddison rolled up his swag, trying to keep busy.

The Thurstons kept rattling out names of people who'd miss them, moving on to their sports clubs and local supermarket.

Maddison paused. If she had died in that plane crash, who would have shown up for her funeral? Would they have buried her under her false name? Or would they have eventually worked out who she was from her remains? If so, would anyone bother to come to her funeral?

'You can call your family when you get home,' said Joe, packing the chairs on the tray beside her.

She frowned at the emptiness of her life. 'I have none, okay? My mother died years ago and my last living relative, my uncle … I buried him three days ago. I quit my job and really no one even knows I'm out here, so there is no one.' She then said through gritted teeth, 'So leave it alone.'

Alone.

It landed with a thud across her tired shoulders where a cocoon of loneliness smothered all hope inside her. Maddison had no one—except the goons chasing her with guns.

She hid her face in her hands as her miserable reality hit, she couldn't stop the tears and the achy sobs escaping her tight throat.

Joe jumped onto the ute and wrapped his arms around her. 'Hey, everything will be okay.'

She tried to find comfort in his words, sobbing against his chest, her tears dampening his shirt. She wished she could believe him, because, after what she'd read in the journal, she knew that she'd never be safe again. And, just like her uncle, she could never tell a soul.

Twenty-eight

'This is Elleron Downs. Come in, Joe.' Earl's voice crackled over the radio speakers of Joe's ute. Even though it was loaded with worry, damn, it was good to hear his dad's voice.

'Hey, Dad, Joe here, and before you ask, I'm okay.' He held the radio handset with one hand while steering the ute with the other. They were driving past swollen river beds, climbing the rocky ranges in a slow slippery slog on the muddy red tracks.

Zach acted like a king in the front passenger seat, with Analise seated behind him in the back seat.

Maddison sat behind Joe. She hadn't said a word to anyone since she'd stopped crying.

But the second Joe had turned on the ute's engine, he'd copped a thick and fast interrogation from the Thurstons.

He hated tourists.

As a rule, he kept well away from them at all times. But the confined space and constant ear bashing was going to kill him.

'Listen, son, the plane didn't come in last night,' said Earl over the radio speakers. 'There was a mayday call from the pilot, and no one knows what happened.'

'I saw it, Dad. I've got the three passengers with me, all safe and unharmed.'

The Thurstons grinned from ear to ear. Through the rear-view mirror, Maddison remained expressionless, hiding behind her sunglasses, staring out the window. Joe couldn't tell if she was awake or asleep, but he worried for her.

'And the pilot?'

'He didn't make it.'

'Where did the plane go down?'

'In the river by the twenty-mile billabong. I've left a marker tied to the plane's tail rudder.'

'That's good, son. The authorities gave a list of the passengers, I need to confirm their names. Do you have a Zachariah Thurston with you?'

'Yep,' said Joe, with Zach nodding his head up and down like a pogo stick.

'An Analise Thurston?'

'Yep.'

Analise nodded as energetically as her husband.

'And a Janice Fraley,' called out Earl over the speakers.

'Who?' Joe frowned at the rear-view mirror.

'Isn't your name Maddison?' Analise asked.

'I have the name Janice Maddison Fraley here on the list, son.'

'That's me,' said Maddison, rummaging through that big red bag of hers that she never let out of her sight.

'Oh, you're known by your middle name,' said Analise. 'How come?'

'Janice is my mother's name. See ...' Maddison showed her driver's licence to Joe.

'Yeah, she's here, Dad,' said Joe over the radio's microphone. 'Cute picture.' He grinned at Maddison, handing back her ID.

'Sounds like a bit of confusion there, son?' Earl asked.

'Janice goes by the middle name of Maddison.'

'Your mother had uncles who did the same. It was a common thing in the olden days. So, when will you be home?'

'In a few hours. You'd better warn Mum, these people have nothing but the clothes on their backs.' He also wanted to warn his family to prepare for the continuous barrage of questions from the dotty Thurstons.

Casually dressed, the Thurstons had nothing else on them. While Maddison wore a classy black suit and sexy heels, like she was going to work or — a *funeral*.

She'd only just buried her uncle, the poor woman.

'No worries, son, drive safe. We'll let the authorities

know the situation. Over and out.'

'Authorities?' Maddison's honeyed voice sounded strained.

Glancing at Maddison through the rear-view mirror, Joe returned the radio's handpiece to its clip on the dash. 'We'll all be interviewed by the police.'

'Oh, hell no,' whimpered Maddison, clutching her handbag tighter.

A bag carrying a tonne of cash.

'They'll need divers to retrieve the pilot's body and the plane itself,' said the all-knowing Zach.

'Will reporters be there too?' Analise asked.

Zach tapped his chin in thought.

'There would have to be reporters. This is big news, honey. We survived a plane crash.' Analise sat forward, with wide shiny eyes. 'We'll be on *A Current Affair*. Or we could sell our story to the *Women's Weekly*. We'll be famous and on national television. Just imagine it. Us, famous.'

'Great.' *Not.* Joe shifted in his seat, looking back at Maddison in the mirror for help of some kind.

'It'd be terrible publicity for this station, don't you think, Analise?' Maddison sat higher, lifting her sunglasses to expose her red, tear-stained eyes.

'I thought all publicity was good publicity,' said Zach.

'Oh, we'll all make money out of this,' said Analise, dreamily. 'We'll be famous.'

'Elleron Downs is a family-owned tourist destination,' said Maddison in that no-nonsense tone. 'Joe and his family don't need this kind of publicity. It could ruin their livelihood. Considering how Joe, being one of those family members, rescued us …'

'As if you'd know. I know news reporters only report facts.' Zach spoke to Maddison as if she was nothing but a simple child.

Joe arched an eyebrow at the know-it-all in the passenger seat.

But before he had a chance to respond, Maddison spoke again.

'Reporters will twist and turn whatever you say and make you into something you're not. What you see today is sensationalised journalism, milking the truth to then embellish it for ratings.'

'Bull.' Zach, the smart-arse, sat with his nose in the air.

'It sounds like Maddison knows what she's saying there.' Joe was tempted to knock the pompous twit down a peg or two. But his mum would kill him if he hurt the tourists.

'I agree with my husband, it's not all fibs,' blurted out Analise. 'Not everything we see and read is made up?'

'Most of it is the truth that gets twisted to leave it up to others to make their own interpretations and assumptions. It's all about the spin they put on it to make it sell. Fear, sex and scandal sells papers.' Maddison pushed up the sleeves on her jacket, as if going in for round two against the Thurstons. 'They do it to hook you in to sell their papers or magazines. And the more they sell the more than can charge for advertising.'

'How would you know, you're just a fancy-dressed receptionist?'

Joe frowned at the married woman over his shoulder. He did not like that tone.

'I am a journalist, who used to work for the largest media publication company in this country. I saw firsthand how decent, hard-working people had their reputations destroyed for thirty seconds of fame.' Maddison glared at the Thurstons as if daring them to say something back.

For once it shut them up.

No wonder Maddison had defended Lois Lane earlier.

'Do you still do it, now?' Joe asked. 'Reporting?'

'No.' Maddison sighed, slumping into her seat. Clutching that bag, she stared out the window. 'I quit. Well, I took a year off to try out other things.'

What things?

The sturdy drone of his ute's diesel engine was the only sound as they drove down the red dirt track. It was bliss.

'So, what you're saying there, Maddison,' said Zach, breaking the peace, 'is that we shouldn't talk to the reporters about this?'

'For the sake of Joe's family station, including the family of the deceased pilot—no.' Maddison's softer tone, was loaded with sympathy. 'It's not just one business or family involved here either. You've got all those people we saw working at the airport when we caught that plane. There's the mechanics, the pilots, the ground crew, the caterers, the cleaners, the office staff, and all of the other connected businesses. This accident could damage that small airline's reputation, maybe forcing all those people out of work.'

'What should we do?' Analise asked, in wide-eyed wonder.

'Say nothing.' Maddison again lifted her sunglasses to face the married couple. 'Leave it to the authorities to deal with the press. They're trained for it. They would have released a press statement already, saying only the minimum, while the Transport Safety Bureau conducts their investigations.'

Could Maddison convince the Thurstons to stay quiet? A couple that never shut up!

'Very well …' Zach gave a decisive nod. 'Analise and I won't say anything to the reporters. We'll leave it up to the authorities.'

'I wouldn't want all those people jobless.' Analise reached out and touched Joe's shoulder. 'Don't worry, Joe, we won't say anything.'

'Thanks.' Talking to the press was something Joe hadn't thought about. In the rear-view mirror he caught Maddison's eye and mimed, 'Thank you, again.' *What a lady.*

Her lips curled into a slight smile before she turned to stare out the car window. It wasn't a full smile, and he still wanted to hear her laugh. But why was Maddison so keen to *not* have anyone talk to the press? Did it have anything to do with that bag of cash?

Twenty-nine

The working dogs barked in the early afternoon at Elleron Downs homestead. Through the teeming rain the headlights on Joe's muddy ute highlighted the rails in the cattle yard, before sweeping across the house windows. The windscreen wiper blades furiously swiped backwards and forwards across the ute's front window, as Joe slowed down.

His parents rushed through the front door of the house, with his brother, Greg, pointing at them, with large umbrellas ready to meet their latest load of tourists.

'Wow, it's a huge house.' Zach peered through the front passenger window.

'It's lovely,' Analise said.

Joe's lips shifted into a slight smile as the tension released from his shoulders at the sight of the stone house with its deep verandahs. Large bay windows stood open catching the breeze, while assorted cane couches and plush armchairs waited along the verandah, perfect for a cold beer on a warm night.

It was home.

'Who's that?' Analise asked, as Joe parked his ute by the front steps.

'That's my parents, Glenda and Earl Charter, and my younger brother, Greg.'

Joe's family members rushed forward with umbrellas raised.

'Welcome,' called out Glenda, approaching Analise and Zach.

'We're glad to be here.' Zach ducked to stand under the

umbrella.

'We could do with a phone to let our family know we're okay,' said Analise, sharing Glenda's umbrella.

'Of course, dear. We've put out some clothes on your bed. You can shower and change into them, just this way …'

'Oi, bro?' Greg rushed up. 'Heard you've had some adventure, huh? So much for escaping the tourists.'

'Here, give us that brolly.' Joe opened the ute's back door.

'Whoa!' Greg stopped still with widening eyes as Maddison got out of the ute. It was those sexy shoes first, leading her lean legs and figure-hugging suit.

Yep, he could relate to his brother. Maddison looked like someone who had stepped out of a classy business magazine. She was not the typical tourist to Elleron Downs, that's for sure.

'Thanks,' replied Maddison, ducking under the umbrella.

Joe admired her perfume as she raised her sunglasses. Gone were the red tear-stained eyes; there was a shine in them now.

'Hi,' she said to Greg who was gawking like a dork in the rain.

'Oi.' Joe slapped Greg's arm.

'Er … hi …' Greg's face turned a cooked mud-crab red. Greg was never shy. And never blushed.

'Maddison, this is my kid brother, Greg.'

'Hi, Greg.' She held out her hand.

The seventeen-year-old shook her hand, while getting soaked from the rain.

Joe seriously considered slapping his brother over the head to wake him up.

'Let's get you inside.' Joe escorted Maddison up the cemented pathway to the house with Greg following like a lovesick puppy. Greg then rushed ahead and gallantly opened the door. Was the kid going to bow too?

'Thank you,' Maddison responded with a giggle.

Joe frowned at his brother. How come the kid got her to giggle and not him?

'You're more than welcome,' gushed out Greg.

It was sickening.

'Behave … She's way out of your league, bro.'

'Yours too,' Greg whispered, following Maddison inside.

'Whoa.' Earl raised his grey eyebrows, faltering in his step from the kitchen. 'You must be Maddison, eh?'

'Yes, and you're Earl.' Maddison shook Earl's hand like a businesswoman at the start of a meeting.

'Oh, my …' Glenda patted at her hair as she came down the hallway. 'I'm Glenda.'

'Hi Glenda, I'm Maddison.'

'Can I get you a cup of tea or something, dear?'

'I'd kill for a beer.' Maddison gave a timid shrug.

'A girl after me own heart,' said Earl. 'Greg, get the lady a beer, and I'll have one too.'

'Make that three.' Joe bloody well deserved one.

'Do you want to take a seat?' Glenda asked Maddison.

'I'd rather stand, I've been sitting all day. You have a lovely home, Glenda.' Maddison inspected the photos on the wall.

It made Joe cringe.

He'd begged his mum to take down their family photos. It was bad enough that they were allowing strangers, tourists to come here, so why keep it looking like the family home it always was? But his mum had insisted.

Yet, all those tourists had never even bothered to look at the photos, not the way Maddison viewed them now with keen interest.

He tugged at his collar. Should he fetch his own beer and go unload the ute?

'Elleron Downs has been in our family for generations,' said Glenda with pride shining in her eyes. 'No doubt Joe told you little about the place. Our boy's not much for tourist talk.'

No, Joe saw all tourists as invaders.

'Joe was quite the informative tour guide.' Maddison grinned at Joe.

'That doesn't sound like Joe.' Glenda raised her eyebrows at Joe.

'Joe didn't have much of a choice because of the Thurstons' interrogation.'

'Here you go…' Greg returned with three beer cans, passing one to Maddison.

'You could have opened it for the lady or got her a glass, son,' said Earl.

'No need. Fewer dishes to wash.' Maddison expertly opened her can, then swallowed again and again. 'I needed that.'

'Righto?' Earl mumbled with a cocked eyebrow.

Joe grinned. Almost reading his dad's mind over a fancy-dressed sheila drinking beer like a bloke. The woman was a surprise.

'I'll show you to your room, shall I?' Glenda led the way.

'That'd be great.' Clutching her red bag in one hand, with a beer in the other, Maddison asked, 'Hey, Greg, where's the bar?'

'Down the other end of the lounge.' Greg pointed to their homemade bar, which sat in the far corner, complete with bar stools. It stood near their large dining table, already set for dinner.

The roast cooking in the kitchen had Joe's stomach rumbling. He wanted to kick off his boots, drink beer, and eat a tonne of food. But couldn't, not with the tourists around.

'Do I leave my money on the fridge?'

'Yeah.' Joe knew she had cash, a tonne of it. But she wouldn't even look at him as her heels click-clacked down the hallway.

'It amazes me how a woman can walk in shoes that tall.' Earl cracked open his beer can.

'I'm in love.' Greg sighed, sliding his hands into his jeans.

'What's happening with the authorities, Dad?' Joe asked.

'They're arranging helicopters to come out tomorrow, to assess the damage and to retrieve the pilot's body. With all of this rain, it'll be a logistical nightmare.' Earl then rubbed the back of his neck. 'I'm worried about the publicity and the damage it may cause for the next tourist season. Are these tourists the type to say nasty stuff?'

'No. Maddison's already convinced the Thurstons to keep their mouths shut and to leave it to the authorities.'

Why did Maddison do that? It wasn't her problem.

'What do you know about our guests there, son?'

'Zach's an accountant and Analise stayed at home with her three kids, but their youngest left for uni so now they're home alone. They've never left the state before and have always wanted to see a cattle station. No joke, I could tell you their entire life story because they both never shut up, asking hundreds of dumb questions.'

'Sounds like they'll annoy the crap out of me,' said Greg.

'They did with me.' Joe cracked open his beer and took a long, deep pull. He deserved a dozen more for his sanity's sake.

'I hope you showed a bit of patience, son?'

'Maddison put them back in their place a few times, so I didn't have to.' The woman was a champion. How he'd survived that road trip without kicking the married couple out was a miracle. 'I'm going to unpack the ute, there's a load of washing to do. I've got no clean clothes left.' Joe headed for the bar to grab another beer.

'Why? You had heaps,' Greg said.

'The tourists wore them last night.' *Typical tourists, taking everything.* 'I'll be in the shed.' That was his tourist-free zone, since his home now belonged to paying customers.

He had to remember Maddison was just another tourist to steer clear of—even though he couldn't stop thinking about her.

Thirty

On the back verandah, just outside the kitchen of Elleron Downs homestead, Maddison sipped her coffee as the soft shell-pink sunrise stretched over the expansive landscape. A blanket of trees stood before a vast flat land of red soils that led to a large hill, or maybe a mountain.

There were no cars. No people. Instead, birds twittered and whistled, mixing with the bellowing of cattle. A soft breeze rustled the leaves in the trees, to then whisper over tall grasses spread across the plains. The crisp smog-free air was alive with an invigorating aroma of rich damp soils and lush green growth, accompanied by a beautiful warm rain that fell like soft snow sparkling under the porch lights.

Relaxed on the outside, basking in the glorious morning view, Maddison was still worn out from having gone to hell and back to get here.

Last night she'd survived dinner with the incessant chatter of the Thurstons at the large dining room table. Maddison had to admire the patience of both Earl and Glenda in taking it all in their stride. Greg looked bored. Joe's mixture of boredom and annoyed frustration amused her more.

But then the table conversation had turned to the police arriving this morning. It had Maddison pacing the floors of her bedroom last night. Dog tired, she could sleep for a week, but her mind kept ticking over.

She didn't dare touch the evidence, which she'd hidden in one of the sheds, until the police left, because she didn't know if the Northern Territory Police were involved with the

Victoria Police.

Telling lies to strangers was one thing, but to the police was downright incriminating. And she sucked at telling lies.

Technically, she hadn't lied to anyone, especially to Joe and his family. She'd only told part of the truth and let them make up the rest.

But dealing with the police in an interview was entirely different.

Her boss was an ex-cop, and as a barmaid she'd spoken with fresh-faced rookie constables, she'd served detectives, superintendents, including the chief commissioner of police, and his underlings.

Now, as she sipped her third cup of coffee, she tried to remember every titbit of advice they'd ever shared about routine interview techniques. She'd heard many versions, from the good-cop, bad-cop routine, to start the story from the beginning and let the criminal trip themselves up. *Gulp.*

But Maddison wasn't a criminal. She'd broken no laws. Yet, worry pressed upon her shoulders for carrying the colossus mother of all problems she couldn't deal with—not until the police left.

So today's main issue, without running blindly into buildings, bars, or planes, was how to deal with the police.

'Morning, Maddison,' called out Glenda, through the window above the kitchen sink. 'Another coffee, dear?'

'Morning. And yes, please.' Maddison headed into the kitchen.

'You're up bright and early. Sleep well?'

Maddison shrugged. Her stomach clenched; it made her ill lying to these people. She just couldn't do it.

'Joe said you've been having a bit of a hard time, dear.' Glenda blended the beans, releasing a rich coffee aroma into the big country kitchen.

Maddison leaned against the kitchen bench to watch the coffee drip into the waiting pot. Rich. Hot. And black. Just the way she liked it.

'Joe told us your uncle had recently passed, I'm so sorry for your loss, dear.' Glenda patted Maddison's upper arm. 'I can understand your need to get away and grieve, dear. We've had a few guests who've done the same. They try to get as far away from their problems as they can, to look at it with a whole new perspective.'

'I've never been this far north, and I came here for its remoteness, to get out of phone range.' And at racetrack Reggie's recommendation.

'While I have you here, dear, can I ask you something?' Glenda poured the rich coffee in a steady stream into Maddison's cup.

'Go for it. Don't be shy with me.' In Maddison's old world, she was the one who was shy. Anywhere near the shadow of her mother's brilliance, no one else noticed her.

'We've offered the Thurstons some extra days because of the accident.'

Maddison narrowed her eyes. 'How long are they staying for?'

'Eight days.' Glenda's nose twitched into a grimace, but for only a second.

Maddison screwed up her face. 'You poor buggers.'

Glenda giggled, pouring her own cup of coffee. 'We're hoping they may change their mind and go back as scheduled. We can't refund their money. We want to offer you the same.'

'Me? No. I don't want any refund or any extra free days either. I'm quite capable of paying my way, thank you.' This family was opening up their home to strangers. She'd expected a tourist resort filled with reprinted images found on hotel walls or local art they'd try and sell. Instead, the walls were lined with images proudly showing off a long family history in weddings, babies, school photos, cattle wearing blue ribbons, and old vintage photos of the buildings that made up Elleron Downs.

It was a beautiful home, rich with a family history she'd never been privy to before. It made her want to tie her hair back, walk around barefoot, and forget wearing make-up or jewellery. She'd never felt so at ease in a place.

'Please don't offend me by asking. I won't accept. If I stay longer, I'll gladly pay you.' With a big tip, too.

'Joe said you'd say no,' said Glenda, sliding on an apron.

An apron. A proper, well-worn apron in a homely country kitchen. Did Martha Stewart die and get reborn as an

Aussie version in Glenda?

'Joe said you seemed the type to not accept a free ride.' Glenda opened the fridge to grab eggs, bacon and proper butter.

'Oh, really?' As if Joe knew her so well after twenty-four hours.

'Joe told us you'd quit your job as a journalist, calling it a world full of lies. That shows you've got morals, dear.'

Ouch! Not that she advertised it, or anything, but she did live by her own standards, and they were pretty damned high. Yet lying went against her morals—but in her current situation she had to, just to keep everyone safe.

Maybe she shouldn't have come here and put these people at risk?

'Can I help?' Maddison needed to stop her mind running all over the place.

Glenda shook her head. 'You should relax, dear. You're paying for the privilege.'

'I'll do plenty of relaxing later.' Not giving in, Maddison rolled up the sleeves on her borrowed shirt. 'I haven't wound down from everything, and it'll take me a few days to do that. So, please, give me something to do.'

'If you insist, dear.' Glenda held out a fresh folded apron to Maddison.

Maddison smiled widely and slipped on the faded yellow apron with daisies all over it. Should she put flour on her nose to look the part too? 'So, what do you cook for breakfast?'

'Bread. Bacon, snags, and eggs. Have you made bread before?'

All carbs were forever banned from her mother's house. 'Never, but I'm keen to learn.'

'Hands first, dear.' Glenda nodded to the sink.

The smile never left her face as she washed her hands, while staring at the glorious morning view that stretched on forever. Her small apartment's teeny-tiny country view was pathetic compared to this; this was almost bliss.

Thirty-one

After dumping a load of hay for the calves waiting in the pens behind the shed, Joe closed the gate. A honk overhead came from a pair of lean grey brolgas flying across the flamingo-pink sunrise. Heavy grey clouds gathered on the horizon, in the direction the police were coming from.

He wasn't looking forward to the interruption. The tourists were bad enough—the police were worse. The last time he'd dealt with them hadn't been pretty.

Heading for the house, the aromas of baking bread, coffee and chocolate filled the fresh morning air as Joe's boot-steps echoed along the back verandah.

His mother's cheerfulness filtered through the kitchen window, joined by the sound of Maddison's light laughter.

Joe paused to take his boots off, peering through the flyscreen into the kitchen, and there was Maddison. Her smile was so wide her eyes shone; it was gorgeous. And her laugh … It was a tinkling sound that only made him smile.

What's going on? He'd never bothered to stop to listen and smile at a woman laughing.

No female had ever affected him like this—over one simple laugh.

'Morning.' Joe hung his Akubra on the rack inside the kitchen. 'Something smells good.'

There were cooling racks filled with bread and other baked goods all over the kitchen table, where his dad sat at the head digging into a plateful of tucker.

Joe washed his hands in the sink, then poured himself a coffee and grabbed a warm muffin from the trays. 'Are you cooking, Maddison?' She looked cute in his mum's old apron.

'Maddison's been helping me out, dear. We've been having such a lovely time together.'

His mum looked rapt with her cooking companion.

With her dainty chin raised, Maddison looked pleased with herself too.

Damn, he could sit and watch that smile of hers all day. It made him forget about the cops coming—for a moment.

'Maddison cooked?' He eyed off the beautiful blonde standing beneath the morning sunlight streaming through the windows.

'Maddison made those muffins, dear.'

Joe sniffed suspiciously at his muffin. 'What did you put in it?'

Maddison faced him with hands on hips. 'Don't you think I can cook?'

'I didn't say that.' But he liked the fact he got a bite out of her. Last time she'd done that, he'd tricked her into kissing him. He wouldn't mind another one of those kisses. 'But then again …' He put the muffin back onto the cooling rack.

Maddison narrowed her eyes at him as her plump kissable lips thinned into a line.

'I like what little I have in taste buds. Besides, I have this feeling that if I eat that muffin, I'll have to say it tastes good even if it doesn't. It'd be like telling a woman she doesn't look fat in a dress when in reality she does.'

'You jerk.'

Joe sipped on his coffee to hide his smile.

'Morning,' called out Greg, coming into the kitchen. 'Something smells great.' He snatched up a muffin and took a bite.

'Is it any good?' Joe asked his brother.

'Oh, man.' Greg's eyes widened as he stared at his half-eaten muffin. 'Mum, these are awesome. They're the best you've made yet.' Greg devoured the thing in a couple of bites, then snatched a few more as he took his seat next to Earl.

'See, they're edible.' Was Maddison going to poke her tongue out at Joe like a three-year-old kid?

'Apparently Maddison baked those muffins,' Joe said to Greg. 'Just so you know, I've doubled the value of your life insurance policy this morning. So, eat away, bro.'

'Hey!' She scowled at him.

Although he preferred her laughing with him, this game was good. And he hadn't even finished his first coffee yet.

He sipped and stared at the most stunning woman he'd ever seen, standing in his mother's kitchen. Even if she was getting angrier at him by the second, she was worth the watch, the way the sun highlighted the different strands of blonde in her hair. He wanted to stroke her silky hair, to trace the outline of her face. And her lips …

He swallowed down the lump of desire clawing up his chest like an animal.

Should he stop teasing their paying guest?

'*Good morning, everyone,*' sang out Zach and Analise as if they were singing in some out-of-tune choir.

Joe groaned into his coffee. Mood destroyed.

'And that's my cue to leave,' Maddison whispered.

Best idea yet. His eyes followed her as she removed the apron and grabbed a coffee mug.

'Is it okay for me to check out your library?' Maddison asked Glenda.

'Yes of course, dear. Thanks for your help this morning, it was fun.'

'I should thank you, Glenda.' Maddison then wiped away her smile, stopping in front of Joe.

He inhaled her soft, floral perfume, admiring the amber flecks in her eyes.

She grabbed a muffin off the cooling rack. 'Go on, try one—if you dare.' She took a bite. 'Mmm …'

It was hot. And he swallowed hard, not at the food, but at the woman he couldn't stop watching.

Joe chuckled, watching her cute arse sashay down the corridor. His brother's jeans looked damned fine on the lady, but he liked her dressed only in his shirt best.

Tourist, mate. She's a paying customer. And the guests always leave.

Still, there was no harm in playing … was there?

Thirty-two

With its folded doors open, the library stood near the front door. It had a cosy colonial feel to it, with wall-to-ceiling shelves filled with assorted books. A sumptuous leather couch stood at the foot of a rich tapestry rug stretching over the polished floorboards. Table lamps were positioned near comfy overstuffed armchairs, creating perfect reading nooks. On one side, a large desk dominated the room, set before the wall of windows that gave a grand view of the property.

Maddison plucked a book off the shelf from among the collection on cattle, farming, and assorted fiction. She nestled into one of the comfy armchairs with her coffee beside her. Cracking open the cover of the book about crocodiles, she was keen to learn about the prehistoric creatures, considering she'd been up close with one twice the size of her, hoping to take her mind off her pending police interview.

'You know,' said Joe, walking into the library with that sexy swagger amplified by his figure-hugging jeans. The leather squelched as he dropped into the chair beside Maddison. He slurped on his coffee before taking a bite from one of her muffins. 'Everyone who comes here reads that book.'

Maddison tried to ignore him, but it was impossible. Not with his aroma, a divine, earthy mix of denim, hay, musky spice, soap, and male. A rugged outdoorsy male.

She drank down the last of her coffee to stop her mouth watering. 'Are you here to annoy me?'

'And to get away from the Thurstons.' He shoved the last the muffin into his mouth, wearing a smirk as he chewed.

'Don't you have some farming thing to do?'

'Yeah, there's always something to do.' He again slurped on his coffee, leaning back in his chair. 'The thing is, I can't leave the house until the police arrive.'

Maddison's hands trembled at the mention of the police. 'Really?' Even though she hadn't read the page, she flicked it over.

Joe narrowed his eyes at her. 'Are you worried about seeing the police or something?'

She sighed, holding the book open in her lap, unable to read the words. 'I'm not looking forward to reliving the entire ordeal of the plane crash.'

'Have you ever been interviewed by the police?' Joe asked in a low, tender tone. It was soothing.

'Only over my uncle's death. I don't remember most of it.' Back then she'd been stuck in a cloud of grief and guilt. 'I've never even had a traffic ticket.'

'It's nothing to worry about, they're only trying to find out what happened. It was an accident, it's not like they'll interrogate you, beat you to a pulp, and then press charges on you for assault or robbery.' He scowled at his hands cradling his coffee cup.

'That's twice you've said that to me.' She frowned at him.

'What?'

'Robbery. I can prove to you I won that money fair and square. The bookies gave me a receipt for it. Anyway, why do I have to justify myself to you? Are you trying to annoy me on purpose?'

'I didn't mean it like that. It's just that I've never seen that much cash out here. Most people would deposit it into the bank?'

'I never had the chance.'

'Why not?'

'Why should I? And pay bank fees and charges. Hey, what I do with my life is none of your concern.'

'I needed to know. That's all.'

'Why?'

'Because you intrigue me,' he said with a blue-eyed stare

that had her trapped in her chair.

No one had told her that before. 'I thought I amused you?'

'That too.' He chuckled.

'You ...' Her anger smouldered like a heated fire, angry at Joe and at herself for being in this situation.

'Oh, look at this room and all of these books,' gushed Analise, walking into the library with Zach beside her. '*Farmer's Guide. How to Grow Vegetables. Animal Husbandry* ...'

'*Moby Dick. Sherlock Holmes*,' said Zach on the other side of the room. The husband-and-wife team read aloud every book title.

'Forget them and finish what you were saying,' urged Joe in a rumbling tone to Maddison.

It was sexy and annoying all at the same time.

She leaned closer to him with gritted teeth. 'You annoy the crap out of me sometimes.'

Whoa! Where did that come from?

She was always the polite Maddison. The perfectly poised private school–educated Maddison. The shy girl in the shadows, not this outspoken person who'd put the Thurstons in their place twice, and now this—with Joe.

She slammed the book shut and headed for her room.

'Hey, hang on a minute ...' Joe followed her down the corridor.

She put her key into the lock of her room.

'Hey, I'm talking to you.' He grabbed her arm.

'Sure. It's been such a great conversation. We'll do it again, maybe *never*.'

'I'm sorry.' His brow wrinkled as if in pain. 'I don't mean to annoy you. I've only been having some fun with you, that's all.'

'It's irritating. Why do it?'

'It's my dry sense of humour.' He sighed, staring at the hallway floor. 'I like the way you react. You've got a good sense of humour, with your comebacks and stuff.' He studied her as if trying to read her. 'Just not today?'

Did her humour disappear with her manners too?

'You don't know me.' She was beginning to wonder if she knew herself.

'No, I don't. You're a hard person to work out, Maddison.'

'Why bother? I'm only a tourist who'll leave in a few weeks. You would've seen people come and go on a weekly basis.'

'Because ... Because ...' He took a deep breath. 'Ever since I've met you all I ever seem to want to do—no, I *need* to know everything about you and be near you.'

His confession glued her to the spot.

'I'm no creep, and I always do my best to steer clear from all of the tourists, except you, who I haven't been able to get out of my head, not since we kissed.' He scrubbed his nails through his short hair. 'I know, I'm damning myself for saying this, but it's true ...' He looked at her, really looked at her, as if she was his entire world.

'Why?' Her heart raced, pressing her palms against the wall to stop herself falling.

'Because ...' Joe shrugged. 'I don't have the words for it, but, there's this—' He pulled her towards him and kissed her. Hard. As he pressed his lips against hers, Maddison struggled.

But he only held her closer, and the kiss deepened to a whole new level.

Stunned, her anger was soon swapped for a heated passion. But it was more than that, there was a power to his kiss, his soft warm lips, his body heat, and his gentle touch. Again, an incredible spark of an internal firecracker exploded inside her and that animal magnetism burst forth, hungry and alive. Just like their first kiss.

The Thurstons' voices carried down the hallway, their footsteps coming closer.

Joe opened the door to Maddison's room and hustled her inside. Their lips didn't break apart for a moment.

She'd never experienced a kiss like it. Or a guy like Joe. He made her feel safe, from the second she woke to him from the bottom of his boat.

But Joe was also safe *and* sexy. But safe shouldn't be sexy? Right?

He pushed her against the wall, slamming her door shut, and then it was as if all hell broke loose, with her self-control tossed out the door. Her lips crushed, bruising against his, as her fingers raked through his thick hair, with his muscular arms enveloping her. She moaned as he found the bottom of her shirt to caress her skin with work-hardened palms that had such a gentleness it sent pleasure-trembles up her spine.

'Seriously, lady, you're driving me crazy,' he murmured, swallowing hard, pressing his body against hers. His hand fisted in her hair, controlling their kiss with a vivid thirst.

'Hey, Joe?' Greg yelled in the distant corridor.

Joe and Maddison kept kissing.

'Oi, JOE.' Greg's ear-piercing whistle echoed down the corridor jolting the couple apart.

'What?' Joe scowled at the closed door. His hard body pressed against hers with their hearts hammering in erratic beats.

'The police are landing. They want you to show them where the plane went down. Where are you, man?'

'I'll be there in a minute … Damn.' Wiping over his mouth, his strong chest rose and fell with each breath, while staring soul deep at Maddison. 'The reason I've been trying to work you out is because you're unlike any other woman I've ever known.' He leaned down and softly grazed his lips against hers, then opened the door. 'I'm sorry if I forced myself on you.' And was gone.

Maddison leaned against the wall, staring across the room where a double set of glass doors stood. The stream of morning sunshine highlighted her king-sized bed. Taking shaky breaths, her legs trembled, but her body was on fire.

She slid down the wall to the floor and hugged her knees. With her fingertips, she brushed her blood-filled lips, still tasting him. Still thirsty for him. 'What was that?'

'*Focus!*' She had more important matters to contend with than indulging in some holiday fling, not with the burden of the deathbed promise to her uncle hanging heavily over her. Once she'd dealt with the police, she could then tackle the bigger issue without endangering everyone around her, including herself.

Thirty-three

ADELAIDE, SOUTH AUSTRALIA

In the city centre, at the end of Rundle Mall, Eric and Tom sat at a small outdoor café, finishing their breakfast. Assorted pedestrians, shoppers, workers, and school kids shifted in waves from buses, cars, and trams early that Friday morning.

Eric sat back, sipping his coffee, now sporting two black eyes hidden behind his sunglasses. His broken nose was covered with a large white bandage. But he could still eye-off the delectable ladies giving him a personal parade as if contestants in a beauty pageant.

'I'll give her a six for the legs.' His head tilted at a woman in a short business skirt, teetering on stylish red stilettos. 'Shame about the face.'

He sipped his coffee and scouted around for the next contestant.

'Eight for the arse.' He arched his good eyebrow at a woman wearing tight black pants then winced at her bright pink jacket made from shaggy bath towels. 'Shame about her dress sense.'

A group of teenage girls in private school uniforms paraded past.

'Too young and dumb,' he muttered.

Tom said nothing, reading the newspaper, drinking his coffee.

'I'm tired of all this waiting around.' Eric hadn't seen a

ten in his ratings game for a few days now. That's when he'd launch himself from his seat, slip on his billionaire smile and chat-up the chickie babe. But not with a face full of bruises. *Bikers are arseholes.*

'You heard the boss, we sit tight until they locate her,' said Tom, flicking over the newspaper page. 'Who knew Maddison Farley would get hooked up with a bike gang, huh? Did you see that Match's bike? It was nice.'

'I would've loved to have smashed that fancy Yankee Harley crap up just to teach that arsehole a lesson, then shoot his dick off,' muttered Eric, bitterly. 'And then I'd shoot that other overpaid dick too.'

Senior Detective Mick Hetter had located Match's registered address. Of course, it was false. Leaving only the clubhouse address where they waited for that lowlife, Match, to arrive.

It had been a couple of nights since Maddison's disappearance on the back of Match's bike ...

For hours Eric sat with Tom inside their sedan, watching the coming and goings of the gang's clubhouse. It was an old shopfront with a red metal door and blacked-out windows, standing amongst a block of deserted shops on a quiet street on the outskirts of the city.

Guarding the red door was a long row of shiny assorted Harley Davidson's. Every time someone rode up, parked their bike, and knocked on the red door, a metal viewing slot slid open to the gatekeeper.

That gatekeeper had told Eric to nick-off.

But it was the only way in.

'I'm getting sick of staring at blokes on loud motorcycles, wearing leather vests with some silly logo on the back. Just who do they think they are?' If he had a grenade launcher handy, he'd blow that red door up, just for kicks and giggles. But this wasn't his turf to start any gangland wars — even if he was itching to play.

'It's the patch they wear,' said Tom, in the driver's seat, reading some cowboy dime-book.

'It looks like some bad boy scout's patch they get for

pinching some old duck's purse as she crossed the road. I wonder if they get promoted for pilfering boxes of girl guide cookies too?' Eric was sick of sitting in this car, staring at a bunch of wankers. He wanted to sit in the pub and have a beer and watch a fight.

How hard would it be to make those silent over-sized bikes that stood in a row topple like dominoes? He was in the mood to see some overpriced, polished chrome kiss the curb.

'The patch is their coat of arms they wear with pride. Those higher in the chain of command you wouldn't even know they were bikers, they look like businessmen.' Tom put down his cheap book to stare at the passing cars.

'How do you know?'

'I've had a few mates who were patched members, see.'

'What happened to them?'

'A couple got killed in their war over drug territories.'

'What happens in them clubhouses?' Eric narrowed his eyes at that red door.

'Not much. They drink, do a bit of drugs, get a few strippers and play pool. See, it's like any other bar or football club. Except they're heavily protected.'

'Don't they plan what they do?'

'Do?' Tom chuckled, returning his attention to his easy-read novella. 'Most of them gangs own legitimate businesses like nightclubs, tattoo parlours, nudie bars, or run strippers around. I reckon that bar, where we got our heads punched in last night, was their turf.'

'I remember that bloke said something about it being their bar.' Eric sat back staring at his cuticles. He'd already finished his crossword, and the paper.

A low mechanical rumble had him peering over his sunglasses at a pair of incoming Harleys.

'There's our boy.' Eric pointed to the large Harley with the numberplate *Match* on the back. It parked alongside the other bikes in front of the clubhouse. 'Enough of this waiting crap, it's time to play.' Eric jumped out of the car.

'What are you doing?'

'I'm going to find out what he's done with our little Miss Maddison.'

'You can't confront him on the street like that, not in front of his clubhouse.'

Eric straightened his jacket. Ignoring Tom, he crossed the road. '*Oi.*'

Match muttered to his mate, who bolted for the red door, while he removed his helmet.

'Are you Match?' Eric had his eye on the prize. The redhead. Now he understood the nickname Match.

'Are you lost? The kiddie's playground is two streets over.' Match swung his leg over his shiny metallic beast. He stood tall, glaring down at Eric, sliding his right hand into his jeans back pocket. 'Or you're here to get another punch in the mouth, little man?' Match said coolly, with a hint of a grin.

Eric wasn't little. He was a big bastard. A dangerous mother. Not some toy for bullies to kick around in the schoolyard. Nah-ah, Eric was the big bad bully now!

'What did you do with Maddison?' Eric reached for his gun.

Before he got a grip on the holster, Match leaped forward and punched Eric hard in the face with a set of brass knuckledusters.

Boom. Boom. BAM.

Three lightning quick punches and Eric was flat on his back staring up at an angry redheaded biker.

Eric saw stars. The biker was beautiful.

Over a dozen burly tattooed men spilled out of the red door, rushing to Match's side, brandishing assorted weapons ready for a fight.

'What the hell do you want with Maddison?' Match grabbed Eric by the shirtfront and punched him again.

Eric's bones crunched in a splintering crack all the way to his cheekbones. Blood exploded across his face, he could taste it trickling down the back of his throat. This was going to cost him a packet—as long as they didn't touch his teeth.

'Leave her alone or I'll kill you.' Match swung back, his brass knuckles dripping with blood.

'Don't, man,' said an older biker with the *President* tag emblazoned on his vest below the patch bearing the name *Reaper*. He held back Match's fist. 'Step away, Match.'

'Why? It's because of these wankers, Maddison's running.' Match growled with pure hatred at Eric.

It was enough for Eric to swallow fear. Genuine fear. With his one good eye open, gasping for air, as a killer, he recognised the look in Match's eyes—this guy was going to kill him.

'Leave that trash to lie in his own blood. I told you they were waiting for you. I told you not to come until that lady was gone,' said the President.

'Maddison left hours ago.' Match then yelled into Eric's smashed face, 'Okay, dickhead? She's gone. As much as I would've wanted her to stay—she's gone because of YOU.'

'Check out his mate, there.' The President tapped Match's upper arm.

Match looked up.

Through his fast-swelling eyes, Eric followed his gaze to focus on Tom.

There the big boof-headed Neanderthal stood like an angel in the sun, holding a large semi-automatic weapon aimed at Match.

Atta boy.

Match dropped Eric who landed hard on the road, groaning in pain. Why couldn't he breathe? Rolling over he tried to crawl to his saviour.

'These aren't simple thugs there, Match,' said the President. 'That lady is involved in something heavy for them blokes to carry that much firepower. Leave it be. She got away.'

Under a bright sun, every miniscule millimetre over the gravelly asphalt seemed like miles as Eric tried to crawl out from under the biker's shadow.

'Look, fellas,' called out Tom.

Eric frowned, spitting out a glob of blood. Tom spoke in that same casual tone as if having a beer with ol' mate at the pub. Whatever, as long as it distracted the thugs while Eric crawled towards Tom's cheap boots.

Tom approached, keeping a steady aim at the gang members. They crowded the front entrance with handguns, sawn-off shotties, machetes and metallic baseball bats. But the serious weapon Tom had in his hands would wipe them all out in a spray of gunfire and they all knew it.

'I don't want any trouble, see,' Tom said. 'You'll have to excuse me mate there, his temper gets away from him.'

Eric wanted to scowl but his smashed face was tight from the swelling. *Arsehole*.

'Get up, Eric.' Tom's boot tapped Eric on the shoulder.

Eric tried. But the world kept spinning in red blood as he wheezed for air. Stones stung into his palms as he pushed himself onto all fours like a dog in the middle of the road.

'I won't ask where the girl is, coz I know you won't say nothing. See, I know how it is with your codes.'

'Take your mate and nick off, then,' said the President.

These bad boy scouts didn't fight fair. If Eric could only reach Tom's gun, he'd paint the road red.

'Consider us gone, mate. We won't bother you again.' Tom raised the gun's barrel as he yanked Eric to his knees. 'Get in the car now, Eric.'

Tom's big hand went right around Eric's arm like it was a scrawny twig, and he dragged Eric to the car like a doll. He tossed Eric the way a bodybuilder chucked his gym bag into the car. Sprawled across the back seat, Eric's blood splashed everywhere as the door slammed shut behind him. Seconds later, Tom drove them away.

'I hate motorbike gangs,' muttered Eric bitterly, gingerly touching his broken nose. He reached for the painkillers in his pocket. Popped the lid, swallowed a bunch of pills, washing them down with water. 'Arsehole wannabe bloody bullies they are.'

Tom chuckled. 'You were rude. Especially the way you demanded it like you did. And in front of their clubhouse.'

'I wasn't expecting the guy to react the way he did. You'd think she was his girlfriend or something.' Eric scowled at the passing parade of people from their position in the cafe. 'It did look like that Match was expecting us?'

'I reckon he rode over to that clubhouse just to punch you out.' Again, Tom gave a low chuckle. 'Come on, that mob does more underhanded dealings than what we do.'

'So how did this female suck them in?'

'I dunno? Pretty girl scared out of her wits, hell, any man worth their salt would jump to her defence, see? If I wasn't chasing her for the boss and getting paid to do it, I would.'

'Would what?'

'Rescue a lady. Any lady if they were in trouble. Wouldn't you?'

'No. Dammit.' Eric held his hands over his throbbing nose. He couldn't wince without a sharp pain blinding him. 'I wouldn't get involved in anyone else's crap but my own— unless they paid me.' Eric pointed at Tom. 'That's what makes us so different. I don't give a toss about anyone else but myself. And you shouldn't either. Remember who you are, what you do for a living, and who pays your bloody wages, mate.'

Tom had the facial reaction of a pet rock, only to shrug his bulky shoulders before returning his attention to the newspaper.

Eric glared at the caveman's cousin. You could hit Tom with a lump of wood and he still wouldn't react.

But he owed Tom his life.

Taking a deep breath to calm himself down, Eric glanced at the passing stream of pedestrians. 'Anything interesting in the news?'

'Nah, usual crime, corrupt politics, and gossip. Australia lost against England in the cricket.' Tom gripped his coffee cup by the sides.

'Why do you do that?' Eric held his cup by the handle like a high-class gentleman. His mother had tried to instil manners in him.

'Do what?'

'Hold the cup that way. They have handles for a purpose, you know.' Eric could be sipping mud for all he knew, because everything was tasteless from his broken nose.

Tom again shrugged those shoulders, plonking the cup back onto the saucer. 'I can't get me big thumbs inside the holes. See ...' He held up his large hand. 'It's how I got me name Tom, from Tom Thumb. Nan gave it to me because I was all thumbs as a kid.'

'But your name's Tom?'

'Nah, it's Melvin. Melvin Thomas.' Tom turned the newspaper page over. 'Says here there was a light plane crash up north yesterday. Three survivors and the pilot missing.'

'Another bloody plane crash, so what?'

'You have more chances of getting into a car crash than being in a plane crash. But to survive a plane crash is rare.'

'Where did it happen?'

'Up north, heading to some cattle station opened to tourists.' Tom scanned the small article. 'It doesn't say much except they've been experiencing some large tropical electrical storms with fifty millimetres of rain in twelve hours. That's a lot of rain in one night, even if it is the wet season.'

'Wet season? What's that?' Eric half listened as he continued his search for that perfect ten.

'Hot as hell, thick with humidity. It's like walking around in a wet blanket. But when it rains, it's like nothing you've ever seen. None of that icy rain either. See, they get roaring walls of water.' Tom shook his boof head like a boulder between his shoulder blades.

'Why were you up there?' Eric asked.

'I took me Nan up to Darwin for a holiday before she died. We took the train and stuff, hired a car and checked out Kakadu National Park. But I've always wanted to visit a cattle station, see, like this place in the paper where that plane crashed.'

'Why?' Eric winced, tears blurring his vision for daring to screw up his beautiful nose. 'Do you have some unresolved childhood fantasy of playing cowboy?'

Tom grinned a full set of caveman teeth. 'I've always wanted to have a look. I like the country. See, I could handle retiring in some shack in the hills near some river or lake and go fishing.'

Funny, Eric could picture Tom squatting in some cave in the hills.

'I couldn't think of anything worse. Stuck in the middle of nowhere, with no phone, no shops, and no women to perve on.' Eric looked at the pair of female office workers. 'I'd give that pair a seven just for a threesome.'

'Well, there'd be no traffic and no nosy neighbours. You'd disappear out there and no one would bother you,' said Tom, sighing to himself. 'That's my ideal paradise, it'd be the perfect getaway location.'

'Hey, hold up.' Eric sat upright. 'How many people did you say survived that plane crash?'

Tom searched the newspaper article spread across the table. 'Three passengers, a husband and wife and one woman. No names.'

'I bet that's where our girl went.' Eric grabbed his mobile and scrolled through the numbers. 'Sometimes, mate, you're a bloody genius.'

'Huh?' Tom scratched his shaved head.

'Think about it, if you were on the run, wouldn't you hide out in a place in the middle of nowhere like this …' He angled his head to read the name in the paper. 'Elleron Downs Station. It'd be perfect.' He pressed dial and waited for the copper to answer. 'Hey Mick, Eric here. Did you hear about that plane crash up north? … Yeah, that's the one. Can you find out the name of that female survivor? Coz I bet that's our girl … Sure, no worries.' Eric disconnected the phone, amused at his own politeness to the scummy cop. 'Mick said thanks. That detective has never said thanks before. He almost sounded like a nice bloke—for a crooked cop.'

'What did he say?' Tom folded his paper to display the plane crash article.

'To sit tight while he checks it out. He reckons the police will swarm all over the station for a bit. But once they process the interviews through the system, he'll be able to tell us then.' Eric took a deep breath, the boredom lifting as he took a sip of his coffee.

'What happens once it's confirmed?'

'We might go and see a cattle station, just like you've always wanted, Tom.' Eric was looking forward to it.

Thirty-four

ELLERON DOWNS, NORTHERN TERRITORY

Maddison lay on her bed mid-afternoon waiting for her police interview. She was well and truly ready to get on with it.

Finally, someone knocked on her door.

'Maddison, dear? They're ready to see you now,' said Glenda in the hallway.

'Okay, coming.' Maddison popped a mint and checked herself in the mirror with a critical eye. She inhaled deeply, with none of the terror she'd recently seen staring back at her. 'Let's do this.'

'Here's Maddison now, gentlemen,' said Glenda, opening the library's concertina doors.

'Hi,' she said to the three men.

Their suit jackets hung over the back of their chairs, with their ties loose around the collar. Seated at the oak library table covered in paperwork, they glanced up, did a double take and sat taller. One of them straightened his tie.

'Maddison?' I'm Detective Sergeant Karl Hunter.' He rose from his seat and approached Maddison. 'Seated on my right is my partner, Detective Michael Hanslop, and on the left is Brian Chatswood from the National Air Investigation Unit. Please take a seat.'

'Care for a drink or anything?' The younger detective, Michael asked, as Karl returned to his seat.

'No, thank you.' She sat gingerly on the dining chair placed in the middle of the room, facing the table. It was like a job interview in front of a scary panel of judges.

But she wasn't a criminal and had to remember that.

Like a well-trained lady, Maddison crossed her legs at the ankles and tucked them to the side, kept her knees together and her hands clasped in her lap. With straight back and shoulders, and with chin up, her mother would have approved. She was ready.

'Can you confirm your name is Janice Maddison Fraley,' Karl asked, reading from his paperwork.

She maintained steady eye contact, the way her mother and her scary godfather had taught her when talking to the media. But she was about to lie to the police!

'I-I-I have my licence with me.' She dug it out of her pocket, only for it to practically fly from her fingers to slide across their table.

Michael caught it with a smile. 'The Thurstons said you'd managed to get your bag off the plane.' He showed it to Karl and the aviation investigator at the end of the table, and they took notes. He then gallantly walked around the table, handing it to Maddison with a smile.

He really was cute.

'So, let's proceed. Hopefully,' Karl said, glancing at the men on either side of him, 'this shouldn't take too long.'

Maddison gave a nervous giggle. 'The Thurstons, huh? I can imagine.'

'Yeah …' Karl loosened his tie more while chuckling with the other men.

It lightened the tension in the room.

See, I'm not a criminal. I'm not.

'Okay, Maddison, can you tell us what you remember of the plane crash in your own words, please. Start from when you boarded.'

'I got on the plane in Adelaide …' With tight throat, fighting her tears, she gripped her thighs and retold one of the most harrowing experiences of her life. She rubbed her forehead where the lump was barely there, but the bruising was ugly. 'The luggage from the overhead compartment knocked me out and the next thing I know, I'm lying on the floor of a boat, throwing up water with some man standing over me who had just resuscitated me.'

She owed Joe her life. What man would dare to dive into a crocodile-infested river to rescue strangers from a plane?

She wanted to thank him, again. As the tears trickled down her face, she wanted Joe to hold her, to speak in that deep masculine soothing tone that reverberated through his chest, while telling her everything was going to be okay.

But would she ever truly be okay?

She sniffed and faced the officers. She'd done her job and reported the facts, and only the facts, just the way she'd been trained. Now she waited for any follow-up questions.

The aviation investigator cleared his throat, staring at his notes. 'How would you describe the pilot's demeanour and his skill level during your flight?'

'The pilot was extremely patient with the Thurstons and their continuous questions. The poor man was stuck giving them a six-hour tour.'

All three men groaned, having spent the past few hours with the Thurstons.

Maddison didn't want to sit here that long, keeping her answers as brief as possible.

'Anything else?' Karl asked Michael and Brian. They both shook their heads. 'Right, we'll type up your statement for you to sign. Shouldn't be long. Can you wait around for it?'

'Sure, I'll be in the kitchen if you need me.'

'Good. Hey, are you okay?' He patted her shoulder, concern worn across his face. Laurie, her boss, used to look at her like that.

So no, not all cops were crooked.

'I'll be fine, thank you.' Hell, yeah. She'd been torturing herself over a ten-minute interview.

In a daze, she headed for the kitchen.

'That was quick,' Greg said, seated at the large kitchen table with his mother and the Thurstons. A teapot and assorted cups and cakes were set out for afternoon tea.

It was just what she needed. Sugar.

Maybe Glenda had a stash of ice cream somewhere.

'Are you okay, dear?' Glenda asked Maddison.

She wanted a hug. A big hug, nuzzling into a broad chest, with a set of muscular arms wrapped around her. A hug from Joe.

But she shouldn't be relying on others. She needed no one and couldn't afford to get involved with anyone, not while she had the mother of all problems hanging over her.

'I'm okay.' The lonely burden made her drop into the nearest empty seat, staring at the grains in the wooden table. She'd survived a plane crash and lived to tell the tale. How much was this going to cost in therapy?

'I found it to be quite a harrowing experience …' Analise's voice clawed at Maddison's brain like someone scratching a chalkboard. '… To re-tell that accident was horrible.'

'Terrible …' Zach stared vacantly into the teacup he held with two hands. 'We told them about how rude that pilot was to you.'

'The pilot wasn't rude,' Maddison said in defence of the dead.

'He was. Even I felt uncomfortable with the way that pilot kept sleazing onto you.' Analise took a deep breath, opening her mouth to rabbit on some more.

Maddison snapped. 'Don't you two ever shut up?!' She glared at the Thurstons seated at the other end of the table. 'That pilot died, okay? He's dead! Have a little respect for the guy. He could have flown us into a cliff or landed on something hard, but he found water where we survived, and he didn't. Christ, I wish you two would think about what you say before you speak.'

The room fell silent.

Everyone stared at her with wide eyes and mouths open, as if she'd gone and bitch-slapped the lot of them.

Where did that come from?

'I'm sorry for that outburst, I don't normally speak out like that.' Who was she? 'I didn't mean to yell like that.' But she'd seen two dead men in under two weeks and had run from men with guns and survived a plane crash.

The tears stung as they flowed freely down her cheeks. She cradled her face in her hands, lowering herself to the table, and wept. There was no stopping the sobs that escaped her tight throat. She mourned not only her uncle, but also the pilot who had died while she had lived.

So how many more were going to die before she fulfilled this damned deathbed promise?

Thirty-five

On the banks of the river, near the Twenty-mile Billabong, stood a makeshift camp. Open styled tents, two boats, and three large helicopters made up the rescue investigation team for the plane crash.

Joe and Earl loaded up their vehicles with cargo pulled from the plane wreckage, including the waterlogged luggage belonging to their guests. They'd been on site helping the teams all day.

In Akubras and Driza-Bone jackets, the father-and-son team dashed out of the rain to the large tent and waited for their cue to leave.

Inside, everyone had gathered around a table covered in paperwork.

'Thank you both, Earl and Joe,' said Anthony McGuire, the head of the task force. 'I appreciate all your help today and the use of your boats, too. It made it easier for my team.'

'No worries,' replied Earl. 'We're sorry it happened.'

'At least we have survivors, thanks to you, Joe. God knows what would've happened if you weren't in the area.' Anthony peered at the remote wilderness. 'It's a pretty place, out here. I wouldn't mind coming back one day for a holiday.'

'There's plenty of room up at the homestead.'

'Thanks for the offer, Earl.'

'So, what happens now?' Joe was over answering their never-ending questions, being made to relive the day of the plane crash. It pained him to remember how Maddison had looked when he'd pulled her out of the water and resuscitated her.

She'd been on his mind all day.

Even while he'd been dealing with the task force officers and police divers on his boat, while he'd kept watch for crocodiles, Maddison had been on his mind.

But nothing had prepared him for coming face to face with what the officers called *the swamp monster*.

It was the pilot. Bloated and eaten by fish, he was wrapped in plastic so his skin didn't slide off. The odour was horrific.

He wanted to shower and scrub his mind free from that memory. Joe wanted to see Maddison, to help him forget.

Would she be at the homestead playfully bantering with his younger brother at the bar? Or would she be in the kitchen helping his mother cook dinner, like she'd done with breakfast? Would she be curled up in an armchair in the library reading a book?

The corner of his lips curled at the memory of their passionate moment this morning. He wanted to finish what they'd started.

'I'm waiting on my offsider's report. He's up at the homestead interviewing the survivors. Mind you …' Anthony glanced at his watch and then at the silent radio on the table. 'He's never taken this long to interview three people.'

The Thurstons. Joe's grin mirrored his dad's.

'At least we can take the pilot's body back to his family.'

Joe wiped the layer of grit from around his tired eyes, he did not want to think of the pilot again.

The radio crackled, coming to life on the table.

'You there, Anthony? Brian here,' called out the male's voice over the radio.

Raising the microphone, he replied, 'Anthony here. Go ahead, Brian. You took long enough.'

'We interviewed that married couple first and got the whole in-flight conversation. I swear I know their entire life story,' whined Brian.

Earl and Joe chuckled.

'I see,' said Anthony over the microphone, glancing at the two cattlemen. 'What did they say?'

'Both husband and wife couldn't tell us how the accident happened.'

'Where were they seated?'

'Directly behind the pilot. All they knew was the plane was falling and that they couldn't get out of their seatbelts after it crashed.'

'How did they get out?'

'Maddison. She's the other passenger. She dove to save them one by one—and it took two hours each to get that much information out of the Thurstons!'

'And the female passenger, this Maddison?'

Brian's voice softened over the radio. 'Her version of the facts took less than ten minutes. I swear we should've interviewed her first. She saw it all happen.'

'Which was?' Anthony asked and everyone stopped to listen as the rain fell on the tarpaulin tent on the hill near the swollen river.

'It wasn't pilot error. Maddison saw a lightning bolt blow the wing off. She even described the static electricity build up too, that plane was a flying magnet for a direct hit. There was nothing the pilot could've done to avoid it.'

'Did she describe the impact?'

'No,' replied Brian. 'Maddison blacked out from the air pressure. She woke up soon after they'd crashed, with enough wits to save the other two passengers.'

'Did she try to rescue the pilot?'

'Yes. But, by the time Maddison got there, he was dead.'

'So why didn't she pull the pilot from his seat like the other passengers?'

'She got too close to the biggest crocodile she'd ever seen through the windows of the cockpit. It scared the hell out of her.'

'I'd believe it. You should've seen the size of the crocodiles we've spotted here today. I'm never going swimming again unless it's in a swimming pool,' said Anthony.

The other men in the tent nodded.

'What happened then?' Anthony asked Brian over the radio.

'The Thurstons said a bloke named Joe dove under the

water and helped them into his boat.'

'Did Maddison say how she got out of the plane?' Anthony asked while staring at Joe, who had already given his statement.

'Maddison tried to swim back to the airlock, but something knocked her on the head. She's got a nasty bruise where she got hit. The next thing she remembers is waking up on the floor of a boat with some guy standing over her, having just resuscitated her.'

'Crikey,' mumbled Earl, looking at his taller son.

Joe wiped a rough hand over his mouth. She'd been so close to not making it.

'Poor thing,' continued Brian over the radio, 'you could see what a terrible impact it had on her.'

Joe frowned, looking back at the muddy track to home.

'What did you find from the wreckage?' Brian asked Anthony over the two-way.

'We've retrieved the body …'

'Swamp monster?'

'Yeah. I'm not eating seafood for the rest of the year.'

'And the plane?'

'The divers' pictures showed the missing left wing and burn marks along the port side.'

'Those divers must have hustled to get photos so fast.'

'Crocodiles are a helluva motivator. We had to let off hand grenades around the wreckage to scare off the crocodiles, then stand guard with guns.'

'What do you plan to do now?' Brian asked.

'We've got what we can from the wreckage. With these weather conditions and this area's remoteness, we can't do anything else, so we're packing up and heading home.' Anthony waved his finger high in the air in a circular motion as the signal to the team. A flurry of movement began as they started loading up their helicopters.

That left Anthony, Joe, and Earl near the radio.

'Are you bugging out tonight?' Anthony asked Brian through the radio.

'Nah, the plane's coming to pick us up in the morning, at first light. I reckon that young detective is going to make a play for the young girl.' Brian laughed.

Joe glared at the radio's speakers as an angry flash of jealousy surged through him. Shoving his fists into his coat pockets, he lowered the brim of his Akubra to stare at the muddy ground.

'Are you okay, son?' Earl asked.

Joe gave the slightest of nods.

Brian continued over the radio speaker ... 'But I'd doubt the bloke's got a chance in Haiti's of getting near that girl.'

Joe sighed with relief, flexing his fingers free from fists. He hadn't realised how tense he'd gotten in the shoulders. He shouldn't be reacting over some guy being attracted to Maddison. Joe didn't own her.

Damn. It's because it was a cop.

If it had been a ringer, or some road train driver, he wouldn't care. But a cop—now that made his blood boil.

But it'd been years. He should've gotten over it by now.

How could he? Not when he was still paying off the freaking debt caused by a cop!

'I feel sorry for this young Maddison. We all do,' said Brian over the radio.

Earl leaned over and whispered to Joe, 'These blokes gossip worse than women.'

Joe tried to grin, but all he could muster was a sluggish shrug.

Anthony shoved paperwork into his briefcase, making fast work of clearing the table.

All while Brian yakked on the radio. 'The poor kid just buried her uncle a few days ago. Hops on a plane to get away and deal with her grief, only to see another dead guy right in her face while having her own near-death experience. That's two dead men in less than two weeks. No wonder the girl's such a mess.'

Maddison. Joe's heart dropped like a heavy bag of galvanised fencing nails. 'I'm going back.' He was done waiting.

Dashing through the rain, he jumped into his ute and took off down the slippery track. Throughout the steady slog from the billabong back to the homestead, Joe thought of nothing else but getting to Maddison's side.

Back at the homestead, he parked beside the verandah.

He jumped the front steps, kicked off his muddy boots. The main door creaked, as the smell of roast beef greeted him. It was good to be home.

'You're back quick.' Greg rushed up to greet him. 'Are you trying to break some land-speed record, huh?'

'Remember, I've been up and down that track half a dozen times these past few days.' Joe hung up his hat and wet jacket, glancing at the few guests seated at the bar. They'd introduced themselves this morning before he drove out to the crash site.

The younger detective, apparently vying for Maddison's attention, nodded at him.

Joe nodded, keeping his frown in check. He headed straight for the kitchen with Greg hot on his heels.

'You're home early, dear. All done?' Glenda asked.

'Yeah, they're all leaving or gone by now.' Joe scrubbed his hands at the kitchen sink. 'We've got the guests' luggage and our freight. Some is salvageable. Been draining on the back of the ute since we pulled it free from the plane.' Joe fell hard into his seat at the table.

Maddison was a guest. He shouldn't be getting worked up over a guest like this. He blamed his past for making him want to punch the cop in the lounge room for no reason.

He blamed his ex.

Inhaling deeply, resting his elbows on the table, Joe tried to forget his past and not get into any more trouble—especially over a woman he'd just met.

Glenda placed a plate of roast meat and vegetables in front of Joe. 'You should get the luggage out for our guests, Greg.'

'I'll get it in a minute,' said Greg, sliding into the seat beside his brother.

Glenda sat opposite Joe. 'Is everything all right?'

'Yep.' Joe began shovelling food into his gob. He was famished a few minutes ago, but now he couldn't taste anything with his guts solidified into stone. But if he didn't eat, his mum would worry.

'What happened out there today?' Greg asked eagerly.

Joe explained, grateful for the distraction while he ate his meal. 'So, I heard that the interviews with the Thurstons went for hours?'

'Not wrong,' said Greg. 'But dude, you should've seen Maddison, in and out in ten minutes.'

'Poor thing ...' Glenda's shoulders stooped as she folded her hands in her lap.

'What's going on there?' Joe asked.

'Maddison comes out looking all shell-shocked,' said Greg. 'Not like the Thurstons who wouldn't stop yakking, until Maddison shouted at them to shut up.'

'Really?'

'Oh yeah.' Greg shared a lopsided grin. 'Maddison gave them a lecture too. Didn't she, Mum?'

'In all honesty, they were blabbering a bit, dear.'

'It worked. We haven't heard boo out of that pair since.' Greg's grin grew.

'How's Maddison doing?' Calm on the outside, Joe's chest squeezed with worry.

It wiped the smile off his little brother's face. 'Maddison's a mess.'

Joe frowned. 'Mum?' He didn't want an embellished story, he wanted facts. Fast.

'As soon as Maddison signed her statement, she went back to her room. The poor dear has been in there all day.'

'Has Maddison eaten?' Joe dropped his cutlery onto his empty plate.

'Not since breakfast. That nice young detective suggested trauma counselling. He gave Maddison a card, and I guess it's only time now. Still, she is all alone, grieving for her uncle.'

'I'll get Maddison's bag from the car and check on her.'

'You'll be taking a shower before you bother any of our guests, young man.'

'Yeah, you're right.' He needed to wash off this crappy day. His chair scraped across the floor as he got up from the table. His mum was already taking his plate away, with Greg following him to help unload the gear from his ute.

Freshly showered, he carried the small black overnight bag through the house. Even though the contents were wet, it still wasn't as heavy as lugging Maddison's big red leather bag into his boat.

Joe knocked on Maddison's door.

There was no reply.

Again, he knocked on the door where he'd kissed Maddison only this morning.

The Thurstons' delighted voices carried down the corridor where Greg and his mum were delivering their soaked luggage, and they had a lot of luggage.

Maddison only had a tiny case, that red handbag had to be bigger. It wasn't the typical luggage he was used to seeing from the tourists.

'Maddison? Are you in there?' Joe opened her door. 'I've brought your bag off the plane.' His eyes adjusted to the darkened room, where she lay on the bed, huddled on her side. 'Maddison, are you okay?'

He'd never seen anything so fragile. She was like a flightless baby bird fallen from its nest, laying on the ground. Alone. And defenceless to the outside elements.

Would he ever see her smile or hear her laugh again?

'Do you want anything to eat?' He closed the door, putting her bag on the floor beside her bed. He now understood his reasons for getting here so quickly. He just wished there was a way he could help her.

'No,' she whispered as if in some catatonic state.

'Come here.' Joe lay down beside her and pulled Maddison into his arms and held her close to his chest. He had no idea why he did it, he just did.

Her breathing was quiet but steady. Her hair was soft, and her floral aroma was as delicate as the lady herself. With no idea how to remove her pain or sorrow, all he could do was be there, to let her know she wasn't alone. And after such an intense day, they soon fell asleep, just like the first night they'd met.

Thirty-six

How did Joe end up in her bed?

Fully clothed.

'You're awake.' His deep baritone made Maddison want to curl up into his chest and hear his heartbeat.

Instead, she rolled over and stretched out her spine, blinking at the slow-moving ceiling fan with the air-conditioner humming. For more than a week, nightmares had plagued her sleep, but last night she'd slept safe and sound.

'Are you okay?' Joe rolled over to his side to watch her.

'What's the time?'

He checked his watch. 'After nine.'

'What time did you get into ...' *My bed?* Yet she wasn't alone. And it had been her first decent sleep since Uncle Bob had died. *Oh, snap!*

Reality check.

She'd survived yesterday's ordeal and now had an even bigger problem to tackle.

But all she could do was lie there as if tied down with heavy chains on the bottom of a swimming pool of jelly. Where was her strength to carry on?

'At about eight o'clock last night. Mind you, I don't normally sleep this long either.'

'Up at dawn?'

'Yeah.'

'Big day for you too?' She'd been told Joe helped the police with the plane, and he'd apparently rescued her luggage. The guy was faultless.

'Let's hope I don't look like I'm carrying the world like you do. And we can't lie in bed all day,' he said with a shine to his blue eyes.

'I can.' Great, now the man could read her mind and body language too. Maddison rolled over with her back to Joe, wrapping the blanket tightly around herself. She wanted to hide from the world.

'I brought your case in, so you'll be able to wear your own clothes. They'll need a wash first.' The bed shifted, then the floorboards creaked, followed by the swoosh of opening curtains.

She winced at the bright sunshine swamping her bedroom.

Joe opened the double glass doors that led to the verandah and inhaled the outdoors air.

Maddison covered her head with the blanket. 'What are you doing?'

'Waking you up.' It was that same teasing tone she recognised from yesterday. 'Come on, daylight's wasting.' He tugged on her blanket.

'Go away.' The blanket muffled her complaints.

'No.' Again, the bed shifted as he sat beside her. The air-conditioner beeped and shut down. 'I reckon I'm going to annoy you all day.'

'No need. Go away.'

But he pulled the blanket down from her face. She glared at him, not caring that her hair was everywhere or that she had morning breath. His cheeky grin, which was sexy at the same time, only irritated her more.

'No. I won't go away. At least I'm getting a reaction out of you, not like last night's catatonic state.'

'All the more reason to stay in bed.' She reached for the blanket, but he ripped it free from the bed like a magician whipping off a tablecloth, leaving the dining setting all in place—except she was a train wreck.

'You are going to get up. Have a shower and get dressed. We'll have breakfast and then I'm taking you out for the day.'

'To where?'

'Sweetheart, the sun is shining. So I'm going to get you

out into that fresh air and sunlight and show you around the property.'

He called her *sweetheart*. Only condescending adults said that to her. Yet the way Joe said the word, it was caring.

'What if I don't want to?' She sounded like a kid trying to skip school.

'I'm not giving you a choice, Maddison. Now, come on.' Effortlessly, he scooped her up off the bed and placed her down by the bathroom door. 'Listen, you've been through hell these past few days, so let me show you around.' He put a hand over his heart and said, 'I promise to be a gentleman as your tour guide.'

'Careful what you promise, it can get you into all sorts of situations?' She should know.

'Go on, try me then. '

She narrowed her eyes at him. 'You're willing to answer all of my dumb touristy questions?'

'I swear I won't fill your head with bulldust, like I'm tempted to do with the Thurstons.'

'Ugh, the Thurstons.' She hid her face in her palms. 'They must hate me after what I said to them yesterday.' She'd been so harsh to them, which was so out of character for her. As was how she was speaking to Joe, who was only trying to help.

'Not that the Thurstons' didn't deserve it, but this way we can both avoid them. Now get in there.' He turned Maddison around to face the bathroom.

She stood still like a robot. A day out would be good. Not that she could think straight. Was she hungover?

Joe picked up the overnight case he'd retrieved from the plane, hooking his arm through hers he walked her into the bathroom. 'Here, go through your luggage and sort out everything for Mum to wash and get on the line, because a day of sunshine is rare this time of year.'

Joe turned on the shower, leaving her bag by the sink, he closed the door.

'I didn't say yes.'

'You can thank me later.' Joe laughed on the other side of the door as the shower's steam filled the white-tiled room. 'I'll tell Mum to put the kettle on for you.'

She grimaced at her reflection in the mirror, with her hair a wild bird's nest, her face blotchy, and her eyes all red and puffy.

Today had to be better, she couldn't take much more of this pressure.

It couldn't get any worse than what she'd been through.

Could it?

Thirty-seven

Cruising past the expansive floodplains, which reflected the cloudless, blue sky, Joe steered the large quad motorcycle along the rich red dirt track.

Maddison held on to Joe's waist, taking in the sprawling countryside.

Wallabies lounged in the shade of scraggly silver gums beside red lumpy ant mounds that stood like cathedral spires. Wild water buffaloes wallowed in billabongs, while cattle meandered in herds grazing in grassy fields. The air was so fresh and invigorating, filled with assorted swooping birds performing complex aeronautical displays chasing bugs, from the flash of the tiny Gouldian finches through to the majestic wingspan of the sea eagle.

It was a private safari with Joe as her personal tour guide in this unexpected adventure, filled with unfamiliar sights and sounds, that made her feel so alive.

Joe had dragged her to the kitchen to eat breakfast while he packed an esky for lunch. To then give her a tour around the homestead. They had various sheds filled with assorted machinery where Joe kept his ute and quad bikes. In the smaller fenced pens, she got to see her first cow. Up close and personal.

Under Joe's gentle encouragement, she'd patted the white neck of the large brahman with its huge hump and big doe eyes. He'd even let her bottle feed a calf. She hadn't been able to wipe the smile off her face.

But getting on the quad, she'd hesitated. The last time she'd gone for a motorbike ride was with Mitch, when escaping her gun-wielding goons.

Swallowing down her fear, she refused to think about the goons and climbed on board. Soon, the warm wind whipped around her, as the humidity defrosted the fear free from her bones.

The vast scenery was of flat lands holding silver-leafed trees with black trunks to stark red soil. Around the bend they entered a gully and into a forest where the canopy of trees was so thick they blocked the sun. On its borders were grasses that towered above them like a green wall. Lorikeets flashed by in fluorescent colours. Black cockatoos with red underwings were just as spectacular, as the screech of nesting fruit bats captured her attention.

Joe headed for the rocky ridge. As they climbed higher she caught glimpses of deep gullies and hills that rolled like gentle waves in a never-ending sea of green. Pregnant grey clouds dragged their shadows behind them to water the sparkling floodplains that seemed to stretch out like an inland sea.

With a sharp left, Joe steered them downhill on a winding gravel track filled with deep ruts and rocks. 'Hold on, it gets a bit steep here.'

She peeked over his shoulder as she gripped his waist. 'Oh, my God ...' Her eyes widened, as they made their descent.

Before her was a towering waterfall, so tall it hid the sun. Water tumbled from the clifftop with a roar, pouring into a large crystal-clear pool nestled among red rocks. A scattering of salmon-coloured ghost gums and soft mossy grasses ran along the edges. A fine watery mist filled the air, the spring water tasting sweet on her tongue.

It was an oasis. No, this was paradise.

Joe parked under the shade of a tree.

Maddison scrambled off and approached the escarpment that opened to a massive vista. Water tumbled into the floodplains, with what seemed like the entire world laid out like a blanket before them. The river spilled like a floating ribbon, sparkling in the sun. Various shades of green made up gradual curvaceous hills dipping into deeper valleys. It stretched on forever.

There were no houses. No cars. No city buildings.

Just a big wide-open land.

It was the Northern Territory outback in all her glorious splendour.

'What do you think?' Joe asked while untying the esky from the back of his quad.

'It's amazing.' She approached the water's edge and stared up at the waterfall—only to jump back. 'Are there any crocodiles here?'

'Not unless they're part mountain goat and vegetarian. Come for a swim. I am.' He kicked off his boots, tearing off his tight T-shirt.

Maddison's head tilted as he removed his jeans, watching the way his back muscles shifted and the tan line above his shorts. The heat in her body scorched like a rocket breaching the earth's atmosphere. She licked her lips, tasting the waterfall's fresh water, as she watched the thick cords of muscles in his thighs and strong washboard stomach. He was pure working man's muscle.

He then dove in like a merman with the splash aimed at her.

'Jerk.'

Sweat trickled down the sides of her face as the humidity thickened the air.

'Come on, get in,' said Joe, floating on his back like a sexy starfish.

Why was she being such a prude in this hot sticky weather?

'Fine ...' She slipped off her borrowed clothes. In her white lace underwear, Maddison dove in and was soon cocooned in the crystal blue water. Her fingertips grazed the white river sand that made up the soft floor. White water churned beneath the falls as the only muffled noise in this underwater wonderland.

She broke through the surface and floated, staring at the plump clouds shifting in a sapphire sky. She'd never seen the sky so big.

She smiled, and for the first time in a long time, she was filled with peace.

Maddison swam to the rocky edge near Joe and faced the expansive vista before her. 'Thank you for bringing me here, Joe. This place, this whole station, it's so beautiful. Where are we?'

'Mount Elleron herself.' Pride filled his chest from simply speaking those words. From their rooftop view of the rocky ranges that towered over the lands below, everything before them was his home.

'How much land is part of this station?'

'The boundaries blend in the wet season.' Unable to resist the opportunity, he swam close to point his arm over her shoulder. His breath on her supple neck with his chest barely grazing her bare back, it was the best view of her cleavage. 'Elleron Downs runs from that river there and across to the other side, and of course, what we've driven through as well.'

'I didn't realise this place was so big.'

'Not compared to other stations, but it's manageable,' he said, admiring her lashes, which shaded her eyes reflecting the world below.

'How come you've opened your family home to tourists?'

Bugger! Joe frowned, swimming back to the esky waiting by the grassy bank. 'Do you want a beer?'

'Sure. You don't like playing tour guide, do you?'

'Only for you.' He closed the esky lid and swam back with beers in hand, handing one to her.

'I saw how you and Greg were with the Thurstons. Your dad seems to put up with it. Your mother, who is the perfect hostess, told me you've only been doing it for a few years.'

'Yeah, it's a new venture we're trialling. Diversifying.' He cracked open his beer, took a deep drink of the crisp ale, then rested his arms on the rocky ledge, letting his legs float behind him. What could be better than having a cold beer on a hot day, swimming with a beautiful woman by a waterfall? 'Hopefully, after this muster, it'll be the last year we have to do it.'

'Why?'

Joe stared ahead, as the leaden weight of worry settled across his shoulders. 'I'm hoping we'll have our loan paid off by then and we'll no longer need to put up with strangers in our home.' He hated it, but it was all for a purpose.

'I see.'

'Although Mum doesn't mind it, and Dad's okay with having different people to talk to at night. But we'll start scaling it back to eventually not have them here at all.'

'So, opening your home to tourists was only a temporary measure?'

'Yeah.' Joe sighed, rolling his tight shoulders. 'We went through a bad patch a few years back.'

'Drought?'

'We'd had a few poor wet seasons, nothing like the droughts down south.' He took a deep pull of his beer and wiped his mouth with the back of his hand. 'Then the market fell with the live export freeze. Dad had some dodgy ringers who ripped him off, stealing a couple hundred head of cattle—'

'Oh no.'

He could just hug her for the empathy she displayed.

'Then Dad got sick. And then there were the legal fees, school fees, medical fees that all came in at once. It was five years of hell. I should have never left.'

'Why? Where were you?'

'Mum and Dad kicked me out—not in a bad way. Don't get me wrong, this is home for me. I knew I'd end up working here and I've always wanted to. But they pushed me to go and try other things.'

'How long were you gone for?'

'Five years. I worked on other stations, different farms, mine sites, building sites and road crews. All around Australia and overseas.'

'Wow, I'm impressed.' She gave him a playful nudge.

'You thought I was living a sheltered life here out in the sticks.' He nudged her back, and there it was, a wide smile that shone in her eyes with that tinkling laughter that made him smile with her. He'd thought the best part of his day was watching her sleep. Then watching her smile grow in the rear-view mirror of his bike was special. But this was better. Damn, it was pretty.

'What brought you back?'

He wiped a rough hand over his face. 'I got into some trouble.'

'There goes my mental picture of you being the perfect little country boy who helped little old ladies cross the street.' She grinned.

But Joe didn't have the heart to smile back.

'What happened?' She asked in that sweet tender honey-tone.

Joe avoided the tourists and all conversations like this. Yet the way she looked at him, prompted him to continue. If he wanted to know all about Maddison, it was only fair he shared.

He cleared his throat. 'Working down in the mines in Western Australia, I'd been dating this girl, Kate, for a few months. We were at this party near the city and I lost sight of her. When I found her, she was screwing another bloke on the bonnet of my car.' He scowled at the scenery, tempted to crush his beer can and throw it over the edge.

'What did you do?'

'I punched the crap out of him.'

'Really?'

'It gets worse.' Joe took a deep breath, looking away from her as the burn of shame clawed its way into his guts. 'I told Kate to rack off too. And then I did a stupid thing.'

'What?'

'I got into my car and drove off.' He shook his head with disgrace. 'I was a drunken idiot, angry at what Kate had done, all fired up from punching that guy.'

'Where were you going?'

'My place. But I never got close.'

'What happened?'

'The cops chased me. They came out of nowhere. I over-steered when one of their cruisers cut me off and ran into the side of a building, totalling my car.'

She gasped with hands covering her mouth.

Again, he wanted to hug her for the sympathy and fear

she wore for him.

'Were you hurt?'

'Only my pride. I walked away from that accident without a scratch on me.'

'You were lucky—even if it was a stupid thing to do.'

'I know. But it didn't end there… It turns out that the guy shagging my girlfriend was a cop, so I got arrested for drink-driving, dangerous driving, running from the police, and whatever else they could think of, including assault. The officers that had arrested me were friends with the cop I'd punched out, and they gave me such a hiding they had to drag me to the hospital.'

Her face screwed up horrified. 'Did the medical staff say anything?'

'The cops told the doctors my injuries were from an earlier fight and that I'd caused an accident while DUI.'

'You said nothing?'

'Who was going to believe me over four police officers? I was in hospital for a week. The broken bones and injuries took months to heal.'

'Do you hate all the police?'

'At first, yes. Now it's only Western Australian cops.' He rested his back against the rocks and craned his neck to watch where the waterfall met the sky. 'Anyway, as part of my bail conditions, I couldn't come home until I settled my interstate court appearances. And that's when Dad got diagnosed with prostate cancer.'

'Oh, no. Is Earl okay?'

'It was hell for a year, but Dad's good now.'

'That's a relief,' she said. 'What happened with all those charges?'

'I pleaded guilty. Because I was guilty and felt guilty for what I'd done too. And because I pleaded guilty, the prosecutor dismissed the smaller charges, but the big ones remained.'

'And …'

He winced as the weight of shame clamped around his ribs like a machine's vice that just kept squeezing. 'I was convicted. As it was my first offence, and I was young and dumb, they gave me a two-year good behaviour bond. I lost all of my licences for over a year and ended up with a thirty-thousand-dollar debt for property damage, lawyers' fees, and fines.'

'That's steep.'

'That doesn't include the travel and accommodation costs to appear in Perth court. Back then, I'd been driving those large dump trucks for the mines, and with no licence I lost my job.' He shook his head, annoyed at himself. 'Everything I'd saved for, all those years working, I'd lost the lot in one night for not thinking clearly over a two-timing girlfriend—who'd been screwing around on me the entire time we were together. I was such a moron.' Was he an even bigger fool to dare chase a girl like Maddison?

Hell, this should really scare her off ... 'And then with me being in and out of court, and Dad in and out of hospital,' he said, scowling at the countryside as his beer can crinkled in his tightening grip, 'our station hands were stealing from us. We'd trusted these people.'

'I'm so sorry.'

'Me too. I only discovered it when I'd landed home straight after my final court appearance. Soon after that, Greg quit boarding school and come home early too. We didn't want him to leave school, but he got himself kicked out, knowing we were struggling to keep him there.'

Maddison rested her fingertips on his arm. It was such a tiny gesture, but it spoke volumes.

He wanted to shrug it off. He wanted to swim away.

Instead, he grabbed her hand. It was so tiny and soft compared to his. 'With all of Dad's medical bills, my legal bills, and the losses on the station, we signed a loan to cover everything. We couldn't afford to pay for workers, and we didn't trust them either, but it was enough for us to scrape through the musters. But when the market dropped and the drought hit, it got tough.' Dropping his head to his chest, he admitted, 'It was hell.'

She gave his hand a gentle squeeze; there was no judgement in her silence either. He was glad she was there.

But Maddison was only here because his mother had an idea.

'It was Mum who talked us into renting out the rooms

for tourists.'

'Against your wishes?'

'At first, Mum, Dad, even Greg, were keen on the idea. I wasn't.' He hated the idea of invaders traipsing through his home.

'I can tell you're not keen on playing with tourists.'

'That obvious, huh?' He hid his grimace behind his beer can.

'So, what did they make you do? Play tour guide?' She said with a sweet grin on those kissable lips of hers.

'Hell, no.' He even raised a grin. 'I remained in the background, managing the station. I never spoke to the tourists that took over our home.'

'So why do it?'

'For the extra money. Most who stay want to help. They liked the idea of playing pretend station hands. It was free labour, even though they were paying for the privilege, and some were more of a hindrance than a help. The other advantage was it saved on freight, because it all comes in on the tourist planes.'

'So, with all of that sacrifice, please tell me it's worked?'

He nodded to the tourist, who was also paying for the privilege. But she was the only one he'd ever bothered with. 'We put in everything we had together as a family. Dad got better, I got all my driver's licences back, and Greg's doing school by correspondence at home. From the past few musters, we've paid off a chunk. Enough to breathe again. We're back on track, so by end of this muster, or next year we'll have that debt paid off. Then we won't have to put up with people like the Thurstons, unless Mum wants to. We'll be able to hire some staff to help with the cattle too.' Did he dare believe the end of the battle was near? 'So there, that's the skeleton in my closet.'

'Everyone has a tale to tell.'

'So, what's yours?'

'Nope.' She coyly pushed away from the rocks to swim to the centre of the rock pool. 'I don't want to ruin a perfectly good day.'

Thirty-eight

Later that same afternoon, heading homeward from the waterfall, Maddison sat behind Joe on the quad motorcycle. He steered them along the dirt track that sliced through the wide, flat land.

She pointed to a narrow valley that looked like a graveyard. 'What's that?'

Joe stopped on the side of the track and turned off the engine.

'What is that?' She'd seen nothing like it. It was as if there were rows and rows of tall thin rectangular shaped tombstone structures. She got off the bike and walked towards them.

The surrounding lands were green from the rain, yet this area was dry, cracked, and desolate as if in a desert.

'They're termite mounds. White ants,' Joe replied, climbing off the bike.

'I've seen termite mounds, they're those huge pyramid shaped ones that are red, but these are grey and flat.' Taller and wider than her, there were dozens of them, set in rows like a giant's graveyard.

'They're all termites, just a different species.'

'The mounds look like tall tombstones.'

'Don't get too close.'

'Why? Are they going to attack me or something?' She'd been through worse, surprised at her burst of bravery.

Joe laughed. 'No. Not unless you attack them first, and they bite hard considering they chew through wood.'

'Well, I won't upset them. I want to see.' Maddison took a step closer; her fingertip touched the flat, smooth grey clay structure. It stood three metres high and over one and half metres wide, yet it was only as thick as her outstretched hand.

She took another step closer when the ground crumbled under her boots as if dry. It didn't fit the lush green wetlands that surrounded this wasteland. It was as if they'd sucked away all life.

'Careful.' Joe warned her.

'*Augh*.' The ground collapsed under her like she had broken the delicate crust on a pavlova, leaving nothing but air. She was falling.

'Gotcha.' With his hands around her waist, Joe pulled Maddison back from the deep hole in the ground, alive with a whirl of tiny white termites running from the light. 'This is where they consider you attacking them.' Joe dragged her back to safety where they watched the whirl of irate insects gather.

'What is this place? You said you'd explain my touristy questions.'

He chuckled, even playfully rolling his eyes. 'If I must ... In this valley, these termites all burrow underground. I'm not sure on the technicalities and terms, but they have this network of tunnels that run from one mound to the other. The mounds keep them cool from the heat of the outback sun, while they eat away all the trees in this area.' Joe pointed to the gaping hole now swarming in a mass of moving ants. 'Because of their underground tunnels, they've made this ground unstable. We've lost cattle in here.'

'How deep do these holes get?'

'I've never seen them get any deeper than a metre, but it's enough to bog a cow or break a leg, stranding them there to get eaten alive.'

'That's terrible.'

'That's nature. The only thing we can do is put the cattle out of their misery.' With the Akubra shading his eyes, he stood tall and pointed to the wide desolate valley. 'We call this place *Dead Man's Gully*.'

'Why? Because it looks like a graveyard with these mounds?'

'Do you see that billabong at the back of the mounds?'

Joe pointed through the scattering of tombstone mounds to a glistening blue billabong behind it. Tall ghost gums stood beside pandanus palms, shading slender grasses that waved in the breeze.

'Billabong?' She stood on her toes, holding on to Joe's arm so as not to fall into anymore termite holes.

'During the height of our dry season, animals are attracted to the water and will walk right through here. If they get past the termites' territory in one piece—'

'How would you get past the termites?'

'You run as fast as you can and hope for the best.' Joe gave her a lazy side-grin, his eyes sparkling with mischief. 'We used to do it as dares when we were kids.'

'Why?'

'It seemed like fun to dash through there to get to the billabong.'

'Uh huh?' Didn't they have an X-box or Netflix? 'Is that part of the river?'

'In the wet season it is. That billabong has water all year round from a natural spring. It's good for Barra fishing.'

'It looks pretty.' Wild lotus flowers and wide lily pad leaves spread over the watery surface like a holey carpet, while overhanging olive-leafed gum trees hugged the banks of the calm waters.

'Don't let that fool you,' he said with a laugh.

'I'm guessing it's got crocodiles?'

Joe gave a nod, his Akubra shading the depth of his blue eyes. 'It's got the biggest mother we've ever seen, and that's her nesting ground.' He pointed to a large muddy bank on the right side of the forsaken valley. 'If you ever want to die, you go to the right where you'll find her nest on that floating croc-grass. It's a territory she guards fiercely.'

'Aren't you scared of them?' She asked the man who'd dived into crocodile-infested waters to pull her free from a sinking plane.

'We're always wary of them. So here's a tip, if you ever get chased by one on land—never run straight, because they're fast and love to lunge.'

'How do you escape them?'

'You run in a zigzag like how a rabbit runs.'

'For how long?'

'Until you find a tree that isn't hanging over the water, because they can jump a full body height out of the river.'

'You're telling me to do a rabbit sprint until I can climb a tree?' She licked her dry lips, staring at the distant billabong's calm surface that glistened like diamonds in the late afternoon sun. 'How do you get away from the crocodiles in the water?' Why were they still standing here?

'Don't go swimming with them in the first place, that helps.' Joe chuckled, making her grin, loosening the tension in her shoulders. 'If you find yourself in the water, try to wedge yourself under some tree roots. Grab something to poke at them and aim for their eyes, nose, and mouth. Their skin is like armour, you'll never get through.'

'So you just let this enormous crocodile breed here and eat your cattle?'

'She's been in that spot for over sixty years. Usually, it's the males who rule the territory, keeping a harem of females, but she's the queen here. It's the best spot for her to nest. As soon as her eggs hatch, those baby crocodiles have a billabong full of fish to eat. But then they have to fight for their territory. If they're not quick enough, the other crocs will eat the younger ones, if they haven't floated off downstream in the wet like most of them do to survive. But it's good fishing here in the dry too.'

'You fish there?' She screwed her face in horror. 'What's left to eat from the crocodiles?'

'There's a group of rocks and a lot of tree roots the crocs can't get into along the far edges.'

'So, you let her have at it?'

'My dad and grandfather tried to destroy her breeding grounds, to even hunt her for destroying our cattle, but she's tough and cunning, unlike any other creature we've ever come across. Now we leave her alone and fence it off from the cattle, so they don't go near it.'

'It's such a dangerous place, living out here.' It was so beautiful, but also terrifying beneath its surface, as she stared at the mass of termites swirling near her feet.

'No more dangerous than living in the city with all the crime, pollution, people, and traffic jams. I wouldn't want to live there. At least I know what I'm dealing with out here. We all co-exist and do our own thing.' He then tugged on her shirt sleeve. 'Come on, I'll teach you something you can't do in the city.'

He led Maddison back to the bike. 'Get on.'

She climbed onto the back.

He laughed at her. 'You can't steer the quad sitting that far back.'

'You're going to teach me how to drive this thing?'

'Yep.' He helped her slide to the front, where she gripped the wide handlebars of the four-wheeled bike. 'Just don't roll or run into a tree. Lesson one, before you even turn this sucker on, here's the brake.' He then muttered under his breath, 'women drivers.'

'Oi, I heard that.' She tried not to smile.

'Good, that means you're listening. Lesson two, if you ever think you're losing control, don't look at what you fear the most. Always look to the open spaces.'

'Why?'

'People in a panicked situation turn without realising it. They'll aim for what they're scared of hitting, like a tree.'

'That makes no sense.'

'If you're running scared, look for safety first and nothing else. Always keep your eye on the target.'

She knew her lesson well on that one. 'Point taken.'

Joe showed Maddison how to start the bike and with him seated behind her, they headed back to the homestead. Her confidence grew under his tutelage, even if he teased her, she was soon in command of the gigantic machine. The stress she'd been carrying had left her shoulders, nothing like this morning's depressed state.

She steered them onto the main track of the homestead as the sun set, with Joe pointing her toward the shed. His presence was enormous, even comforting as he kept his hands resting on her hips, with his chest pressed against her back. The times his breath brushed against her bare skin as he spoke close to her ear, made it almost impossible to steer.

She stopped with an awkward jerk near his ute, where a few more quads were parked.

'We finally made it back before the next century. Now I

remember why I don't let women drive me anywhere.'

'Jerk.' Maddison laughed as she scrambled off the bike. She'd done it. Rode a bike. A big bike.

'I'm glad to see you smiling again.'

Her jaw was aching from smiling. 'Thank you.' She gazed up at the man in the tight T-shirt that only accentuated the shift of his muscles across his chest. 'I mean that, I had a fantastic time.'

'Good. I was hoping it would help. But being a bloke, and seeing as how I'd promised to be a gentleman while we were out, to which I behaved and controlled all my inner …' He paused while his eyes scanned all over her. She felt naked under his intense inspection. 'I'm demanding a thank-you kiss.'

Before she could even respond, he'd stepped in close, his palm cradling the side of her face, and he leaned down to gently press his lips against hers. He ever so tenderly kissed her, stroking her upper lip as her lips parted for more. A tiny moan rolled free from her throat in a plea as he pulled away, looking at her intently as if taking in the details.

He was a lethal combination—a man who was skilled at kissing, with a chiselled body to match

But he was heartbreak with a capital H, no matter how she looked at it, especially as she'd forgotten everything just from the way he gazed at her. She should duck away from his touch and find her willpower to focus on …

'What?' she said with a ragged breath. Did she do something wrong? Besides keeping a promise that led her to this place, to this man whose kiss made her skin sizzle into a sweet delirium that was leaving her a trembling mess.

This magnetic attraction between them would never last.

It couldn't.

Could it?

* * *

She trembled like a small kitten, but only for a second, until her eyes locked on his. Then she licked those plump lips of hers like a woman in charge.

'Four kisses, same girl and yet all different.' All of them were sensational. 'Damn, I've got to do that again,' he muttered with his throat so tight he couldn't swallow. He gripped her hip to bring her into his chest to kiss her again, pressing his mouth hungrily over hers. And he wanted to really kiss her. To kiss her so powerfully it would take away all her pain.

He'd been craving for her touch since the first time they kissed in the back of his ute. Hell, if he was honest with himself, it was from the second the blue-lipped mermaid lying on the bottom of his boat had opened her eyes and stared up at him with trust. It was a feeling so foreign, but it felt so right.

He tightened his grip, pulling her body closer it moulded perfectly against his. With her fingers entangled in his hair, her soft gasp purred as he settled into the kiss.

It had started out gentle and controlled, but it soon became punishing and hard with the hunger of a hurricane — and he was ready to batten down and ride out this storm.

'You *lucky* bastard,' called out Greg, standing by the shed's open doorway.

'Oi.' Joe frowned at the interruption, his arms wrapped around Maddison as she burrowed her face into his chest. 'Can't you see I'm busy here?'

'That's obvious.' Greg chuckled, wearing a cheesy grin.

Maddison giggled against his chest. He smiled down at her.

'Good to see Joe's got you laughing again, Maddison.'

'What do you want, bro?' Joe could never stay angry at Greg.

'Mum said to wash up. Dinner will be ready soon. She sent me out here to see what was taking you two so long.' Greg's smile ripped wide as he rocked heel to toe in his boots. 'Now I know why.'

'You hungry?' Joe asked Maddison, ignoring his brother. Food was not an issue with his current train of thought.

'I'm starving.'

'All right then, let's go feed the lady.' Joe held her hand like he never wanted to let go, heading to the large house together.

It had been one of the best days he'd had on the station and he wanted to show Maddison all of it. Yet, he had to remember she was a tourist, only visiting for a short time. Too short a time.

Thirty-nine

Dressed for dinner in her own clothes—a strappy summer dress and slip-on jewelled sandals—Maddison walked into the station kitchen to find Joe's mother busy with the meals. 'Do you need a hand, Glenda?'

'Well, don't you look pretty. It's so nice to see you smiling, too. Have a good day, dear?'

'It was great.' Spectacular even. 'Can I do anything?'

'You can carry that dish in for me, dear.' Glenda grabbed a plate of assorted sliced meats. Carrying the vegetable platter, Maddison followed Glenda into the dining room where everyone had gathered by the bar.

'Beer, Maddison?' called out Earl.

'Yes, please.' She placed the food platter on the table and spotted the Thurstons. It was the first time Maddison had seen them since her outburst. She rubbed her fingertips as she took a deep breath. 'Zach, Analise? I want to apologise for the way I spoke to you both yesterday. I don't know what—'

'Oh no, you don't.' Analise cut her off.

'It's us who should thank you, Maddison,' said Zach, sliding his arm around his wife's shoulders.

'What for?'

'For putting us back in our place. Thank you.' Analise reached over and hugged Maddison, swamping her with a face full of hair lacquered in products so thick, each strand was as stiff as a bras underwire.

'Thank you from me, too,' said Zach, also hugging her.

'Um ...' Maddison blinked at Zach's vintage cologne.

Handshakes and air kisses near the cheek were considered the fashionable custom from her world. It was done in such a way that it never smudged make-up or wrinkled clothes. Hugs from acquaintances never happened.

Where's the nearest exit?

Joe chuckled from behind the bar. He knew she didn't want to see the Thurstons. Again, just his mere presence stopped her urge to flee the room.

'So, we're good?' Maddison asked Analise and Zach.

'Absolutely.' Zach gave a firm nod.

'Dinner's served,' called out Glenda.

Maddison was seated between Glenda and Analise, with Zach talking to Earl about tax and accounting issues for most of the meal. Afterwards she was glad to escape, helping Glenda carry the dishes to the kitchen, only to be shooed away and told to go and play the part of a paying houseguest.

In her bedroom she opened the back doors to sit on the wicker couch on the verandah, facing the night sky. Rain fell softly, hiding the stars, but bringing fresh scents to the night air. It was accompanied by the clashing chirp of crickets and screeching cicadas, which created a chaotic insect choir that beckoned the bass of green tree frogs. But it worked.

'I was wondering when I was going to get you alone...' Approaching from the far end of the darkened verandah, Joe held out a delicate frangipani flower; its warm heady fragrance was breathtaking. 'Beautiful flower for a beautiful lady,' he whispered with a half bow.

'Thank you.' The romantic gesture made her heart melt.

'So ...' He slid onto the couch and put his arm around her shoulders. 'I must've done something right, if you're smiling like that.'

'You did good, all day. Thank you, Joe.' He had been a big help in her survival, right up to this very point. But they were on borrowed time.

Not wanting to waste a second of the precious time they had left, she surrendered to her own need to end this frustrating game. She cradled his face with both hands. 'I believe you need more than just a thank-you kiss for what you've done for me.'

The guy was her personal hero, and heroes needed a reward, so she kissed him with as much sensual passion as she had, hoping he got the message.

She pulled away to stand at the open doorway of her room, then peeked at him over her shoulder. 'Are you coming?'

She bit her bottom lip, waiting for the right answer, because she wanted this. No, she needed this. With all of the near-death disasters that had brought her here, she deserved something deliciously physical from a man who was not only sexy but made her feel safe. It was an impossible combination to ignore, and one worth dreaming about. If only he said yes.

* * *

Joe swallowed hard, gazing at the angel in the doorway. With her thick eyelashes shadowing her stunning eyes, in a dress that kissed her curves, she was extraordinary.

'Hell, yeah.' He stood to gaze up at the heavens, praying for no more interruptions.

The woman had been driving him insane with her breathtaking kisses, which grew in intensity every time their lips locked. He had to follow her, closing the glass doors behind him.

At the bedside table Maddison turned on the lamp; its dim light illuminated the room in a soft glow. Nervously, she chewed on her bottom lip, shying away from him as she unclipped her hair. He couldn't resist reaching out to caress the strands.

Her sweet floral aroma enveloped him as his lips brushed over her bare shoulder. Her skin was so soft and warm as he traced his way to the base of her neck. There he watched a shiver of goosebumps scatter across her supple skin as his palms slid down her bare arms.

Lifting her small hand to his lips, he tasted her skin, the smoothness of her knuckles, the tenderness of her palms. With an unhurried touch, his kisses followed from her fingers to her slender wrist, climbing up to her inner elbow to linger there as he caressed her skin. He wanted to remember every pore of her skin.

He slowly turned her around to face him, her breath a bare whisper but her heart hammering like music, as his thumb traced over the pulse in her wrist.

Joe looked into her eyes, their gold flecks highlighted by the soft lamp glow. His knuckles brushed against her cheek, admiring her delicate facial features, her flawless complexion, her high cheekbones and plump lips. Even without any make-up she was incredibly beautiful.

As he inhaled deeply, she held her breath as he brushed his lips with hers. First grazing on her delectable top lip, then nibbling and suckling on her plump bottom lip as if it were the sweetest of summer fruits, ripe for the taking.

With both hands, he cradled her face and stared into the deep pools that reflected his world in her eyes, and whispered as if with his soul, 'You're so beautiful, Maddison.'

He saw the slight smile in her eyes, he tasted it on her lips as he pressed his mouth against hers. Her entire body quivered with a warmth radiating from her skin. And he wanted skin. Now.

He made quick work of her dress zip, his fingertips trailing down the curve of her spine, pulling the thin spaghetti straps down past her smooth shoulders. He licked his lips as her dress slipped from her body and fell to the floor, looking at her in awe with his throat tightening and his body hardening.

The small lamp illuminated her body, emitting a halo appearance of a goddess with the body of an angel.

He couldn't speak, touching her flat waist, tracing the soft delicate details of her lace bra. Resisting the urge to rip it from her skin, he tore off his shirt as she helped him shuck off his jeans.

His lips traced down her throat while his fingertips circled her nipples hardening under his touch. Her breath came in a pant and her chest heaved, as her body bowed to beg for his palm to knead her firm breasts that swelled under his touch.

With her head tilted back, her eyes closed, she moaned in a way that made his skin shiver while her fingers dragged a firestorm from their feather-light touch across his shoulders. He wanted her to grip him, as hard as he wanted to grip her.

Feeling his manners diminishing as the hunger to have her surged harder, he unclipped and removed her bra, then he lay his prize down on the bed. There his mouth suckled each of her breasts, following her body's tremor down her sides to her hips, to her lace underwear.

In a fight against his own desires, his fingers fumbled to savour every second. He pushed down the fine lace to allow his fingers to glide and explore every inch of her. Fascinated, he watched her succumb to his touch. And when he looked at her as he inched his way inside, her sigh was like a goddamned symphony of sensuality. It married perfectly with the heat, the intense moisture, and the tight velvetiness of their joining.

His mouth closed over hers, igniting a blast of passion in the long kiss that followed. The licks of their tongues twirling and tasting, as if breathing each other in.

With a small gasp, her grip tightened in his hair, and her hips rocked against him as he filled her.

She stared at him, and all he saw was her. A connection deeper than the physical in a space with no shields to hide her pure and beautiful vulnerability. Naked before him, as if giving him permission to bend her to his will—and just for this moment she'd allow it.

Giving a gentle tug on her hair made her lips part so he could kiss her deeper, worshipping her mouth as his long powerful movement rocked inside her, again and again. She was drugging him with her flavour, along with a perfect synchronised rhythm as she met his forward motion to sheathe his full length. Every time they surged deeper, as if they were long-time lovers, until he lost all common sense under her spell.

Captivated by the surging fury in their lovemaking, her thighs trembled as whimpers escaped her lips. Her back arched and an intense tremor shot throughout her body. She clung onto him; her legs wrapped around his waist. Again, he ground into her, giving her everything until his inner body twisted and erupted into euphoria. She had blinded him, and he'd lost his ability to breathe. Her body squeezed his and he groaned as if his entire life force spilled inside her.

Stunned and powerless to move, they lay there with their fevered bodies entwined, staring at each other, while their hearts hammered against their chests.

Never had he ever truly made love to a woman.

Never had he ever truly understood the meaning of what it was to make love to a woman—until now.

Forty

ADELAIDE, SOUTH AUSTRALIA

Basking on an outdoor sun lounge, poolside, Eric dabbed suntan lotion sparingly over his yellow and purple bruised face. Having regained his sense of smell and taste, he sipped on a cool beer, soaking up the sun's rays.

Tom did slow, lazy laps in the swimming pool.

When a mechanical roar shook their glasses on the table, as the shadow of an incoming plane passed overhead.

Then a phone rang.

Eric cracked an eyelid to peer at his mobile phone, lying on their table beneath the sun-faded umbrella.

Tom stopped swimming and searched for the noise from the pool.

It was a foreign sound, the phone's ring was jarring as it vibrated against the pen and opened newspaper displaying an unfinished crossword.

Eric tapped the phone's speaker, frowning at the interruption as he side-glanced at Tom, now standing chest height in the middle of the large swimming pool. 'Yeah?'

'We found her,' said the gravelly male voice over the speaker.

Found who? 'Boss?' Eric sat up, mentally kickstarting his brain, while Tom waded to the pool's edge. 'Where is she?' Eric listened with phone to ear as he scribbled on the crossword puzzle, filling in the blank squares with instructions. 'Yeah … Okay … How? … The idiot …' Eric laughed. 'Nah, you can count on me … No worries, Boss. I'll get the job done. We'll call as soon as we return.'

Conversation over, he stared at his phone with a devilish grin.

Tom hoisted himself out of the pool and snatched up a towel. 'What's going on?'

'They found her.'

'Who?'

'Maddison Farley. We've got her.' Eric snatched up his beer, suddenly in the mood for bourbon.

'Where?'

'At Elleron Downs.' He could just hug himself. 'Just like I'd suspected.'

'How did they figure out it was Maddison?'

'That silly wench had a false name on her licence. Didn't think she'd be that clever.' Had he finally found a worthy opponent in a female?

'How?'

Eric tapped on the crossword puzzle. 'She's got a dodgy licence that has her correct licence number, but it's in the name of Janice Maddison Fraley.'

'But she's Maddison Janice *Farley*?' Tom scratched the top of his boof head. It'd be enough to confuse the caveman for a few days, just hearing that brain clunk its gears while peering at the crossword puzzle. 'It's her real name, but it isn't. How—'

'It doesn't matter.' Eric gave a limp wristed wave. 'All that matters is that we've found her. Typical dumb female, thinking she could hide in the outback like some tourist on holidays.'

'It feels like I'm on a holiday.' Tom sat back in his chair where the sun glistened across his damp skin.

While Eric stayed in his room recovering from his war wounds, Tom was playing tourist. Every afternoon the Neanderthal would return showing off his happy snaps of museums, beach scenes, wineries, or some other tourist crap. It bored Eric to tears.

But neither of them could go home until the job was done.

'So, we'll be going to a proper cattle station?' Tom's eyes lit up like a kid hoping for a pretty pony for Christmas.

It's a good thing Eric didn't mind playing Santa Claus today.

'Yes, Tom. In five days, we'll be flying out from this small airport where they don't have any X-rays or airport security to bother us.' Eric tapped on his handwritten instructions that filled the crossword as if it were part of the puzzle itself. He was such a genius.

'Why can't we fly out today?' Tom's shoulders sank like a saggy birthday balloon.

Aw, the poor little boy's gotta wait.

'Relax. Maddison can't leave this place because its flooded, and we don't wanna spook her. We're gonna let her think she's all safe and sound at this Elleron Downs.' Eric resumed his spot on the sun lounge and closed his eyes still wearing that devilish grin. 'And in five more days I'll meet Miss Fraley. Face to face.'

Forty-one

ELLERON DOWNS, NORTHERN TERRITORY

Inside the homestead's kitchen, Maddison made coffee, leaning her hip against the cupboard to gaze out at the view over the sinks. Every day the view was different. Today, subtle pinks and blue greys mixed with warm sunlight. They peeked through inky clouds that spilled rain over the ranges, fuelling the muggy air. It mixed with the appetising scents of freshly baked bread, cakes and scones spread across the large wooden table. Breakfast was a feast in this household.

The flyscreen door creaked, and a familiar footstep soon followed.

'Hey, beautiful.' Joe slid his Akubra onto the hook where many other wide-brimmed hats waited.

Her smile started a giddy roll in her tummy that spread warmth throughout her chest at the mere sight of the man, who'd only just left her bed to start his pre-breakfast chores.

'You know,' he said, sliding his large hands around her hips with his fiery breath against the side of her throat.

'Mm…' She arched her neck as goosebumps squirrelled to the top of her head, inhaling his outdoorsy aroma.

'I'd rather stay in bed with you all day than service the tractor with my dad.'

'Can't you leave that poor girl alone.' Glenda share a cheeky grin as she carted in a loaded laundry basket dumping it onto the large chest freezer.

'Morning, Mum.' Joe took his seat at the table.

Maddison carried their coffee, to sit beside him. These people ate proper homemade sit-down meals, no microwave, home deliveries, or eating on the run in this place.

Greg and Earl soon joined them, all in a jovial mood this morning.

'What's happening with you today, Mum?' Joe asked, tucking into his plate of bacon and eggs.

'Your father and I are taking the Thurstons to meet the plane. We'll be picking up two more guests, dear.'

All the men groaned.

'The Thurstons have been great,' said Glenda. 'What are you mob complaining about? They're holding two-way conversations, now.'

'Where's our break from the tourists this time of year?' Greg's cutlery scraped over his plate as he slurped up some beans mixed with runny eggs and dark sauce.

'Young man, remember our guests.' Glenda, motioned towards Maddison.

'I didn't mean you, Maddison. I forget you're only here on a holiday.'

'That's okay.' Maddison ignored Joe's fleeting frown over his coffee cup.

She had to keep reminding herself why she was here, too. She could easily slip into the station's lifestyle and pretend she belonged here. She was going to miss this place, the family, and especially Joe when it came time to leave.

'Dunno if you'd call it a holiday,' said Greg, using his bread to sop up the sauces on his plate. 'The way you're always on the library's PC all day, when most people come out here to get away from that stuff. What are you doing anyway?'

'Research.' Technically, she'd never lied to these people; it would kill her if she did.

'For what?' Greg shoved the last of his toast into his mouth.

'I've been working on a piece that my uncle started before he was …' She cleared her throat.

Under the table, Joe squeezed her knee. It was

reassuring. But she couldn't afford to get comfortable.

Yet, she drew his hand into her lap to trace the lines, the ridges, and calluses that made up his large working palm. His hands held a strength in them, unlike any other man she'd met.

'I thought you hated journalists and stopped doing all that sort of stuff?' Joe closed his hand over hers. It swallowed it.

'Not all journalists.' She pulled her hand free to pick at the muffin on her plate. 'Like any business, there's always a few rotten apples that ruin it for everyone.' It was a constant struggle to shut down her feelings for Joe, his family, and this station.

'So really, you're like on a working holiday, huh?' Greg had the same lopsided grin he shared with his father and big brother.

'You could say that.' Even if it was all completely unplanned. Strangely, she hadn't thought about her life in Melbourne or her godmother in Sydney. She'd been so consumed by her research, and with Joe, who'd demand her attention at the end of each working day.

'So how often do you do that?' Earl dabbed at his greying beard with the napkin.

What? Run for her life? 'Do what?'

'Do this writing thing you do?'

'I'm a freelance journalist,' replied Maddison with a shrug.

'What's that?' Glenda sipped from her delicate floral teacup that matched the saucer, while the rest had chunky coffee mugs.

'If I come across something of interest that inspires me, I'll write it up and send it in to get published. I aim for a magazine piece once a month.' *Please don't ask the name.*

'Which one, dear?'

Seriously! Maddison took a big bite out of her muffin, hoping to avoid the answer.

But the table remained quiet, waiting for her response, except for the scrape of cutlery across their plates and the other sounds of an eating family.

'I, um, send them in to this publishing company that

manages an assortment of magazines and newspapers all under the one roof.'

'Such as?' Glenda brushed down the crumbs on her yellow apron with white daisies. They were two of Glenda's favourite things, the colour yellow and daisies, she also had a fondness for talk-back radio, and none of them had any form of social media.

'Fishing ones, cars, fashion magazines, that kind of thing.' Maddison needed to change this conversation. 'May I ask who these guests are, arriving today?'

'We have two young men joining us this week.'

Maddison flinched, a sip of coffee going down the wrong way. She fumbled and spilled the coffee on the table and all over her dress, coughing loudly while gasping for air.

Joe was quick to react and patted her back. 'Hey, are you okay?'

She nodded, as that all-too-familiar flutter of fear flared in her chest, while Glenda grabbed a cloth and started cleaning the table. 'I'm so sorry, Glenda.' She reached out to help, but her hands wouldn't stop shaking. *Calm down. Maybe it's not related at all.*

'Are you sure you're okay?' Joe grabbed her hands.

'I'm fine. Sorry, it went down the wrong way, that's all. Excuse me, I'll go clean up.' She practically fled the kitchen, remembering not to slam her bedroom door and dashed to the bathroom.

At the basin, she forced herself to take deep breaths, staring at her reflection in the mirror. It was that same panic filled terror in her eyes, like the first time she'd fled her apartment.

Turning on the tap, she started to clean the coffee spilled across her dress.

There was a quick tap on her open bathroom door.

'Are you all right, Maddison?' Joe asked, leaning his broad shoulder against the doorframe.

'Yeah, fine. Clumsy, that's all.' She couldn't look at him, concentrating on calming herself down, while dabbing away at her dress.

'You're not clumsy. You look scared.'

She faced the mirror where Joe's reflection stared back.

How could he read her so easily after only a week? 'I don't think so.'

'It's the same look you wore when you had that lizard in your bag, or when you nearly fell into that termite hole.' He took a step closer, the sheer size of him filled the room, with his blue-eyed stare pinning her to the spot. 'What's going on?'

She hesitated. Unable to lie to Joe, she'd been careful with the little she shared about herself—which was normal in her old world.

'You're shaking.' Gently, he grabbed her hands. 'Why are you reacting like this over Mum mentioning the new guests arriving?'

Again, that spike of fear made her tremble. She bit her lip, scared she'd draw blood.

'Are you in some kind of trouble? You've been okay this past week.'

'This week has been amazing.' She pulled her hands free to cover her face, taking a deep breath, desperate to calm down.

'I'm not moving until you tell me.' He pulled her hands free from her face, forcing her to look at him. 'I want to help.'

'Find out who those two men are. That'd help.'

'Not until you tell me why.' Standing tall, he narrowed his eyes at her. 'You're on the run, aren't you?'

She gasped, trying to step away from him, but he only held her in place.

'Come on, Maddison, let me in. I only want to help you.'

'Okay ...' She took a deep breath, preparing to go against her better judgement. 'I'll tell you everything, but I doubt you'll believe me.'

'Finally.' Joe led her by the hand to the end of her bed and made her sit beside him. 'You have this habit of only sharing snippets about yourself, so I'm keen to know your story.'

'Fine. You asked for it.'

He gave her an encouraging nod. 'I'm listening.'

She was helpless to deny him, and so she began ...

'About three weeks ago, my Uncle Bob was murdered in Melbourne. Shot three times in the chest. He died in front of me. But before he did, he made me promise to find his journal and finish the piece he'd been working on.'

'You made a deathbed promise?'

She nodded. 'My uncle made me swear to trust no one and say nothing.' Was she breaking her promise now?

'Go on,' urged Joe.

'The detectives investigating the murder told me that my uncle died for a thirty-thousand-dollar gambling debt.'

'Was your uncle a gambler?'

She nodded. 'And an alcoholic. But he was a really nice guy, the last of my family.'

'Hey, it's okay. I'm not judging,' he said, slipping his arm around her shoulders.

'Anyway, a week later, on the day of my uncle's funeral, I go back to my apartment to discover someone had broken in. They'd destroyed everything, as if they were looking for something.' Did her godmother, Nancy, get her assistant to clean up the place?

'What were they searching for?'

'My uncle's notes. But they didn't find them.'

'Where were they?'

'At his favourite place, Flemington Racetrack. It's where I won that money.' From under her bed, she dragged out her big red bag. The leather was worn, and the strap was tied with a big knot. It was ruined.

Maddison pulled out a receipt along with the black plastic waterproof pouch. She'd kept them close ever since the police had left. 'This is what I won that day—what you accused me of robbing from a bank.'

'I only meant that as a joke.' Joe read the receipt. 'Damn. You're carrying twenty grand in cash! How?'

'I got lucky on a couple of long shots.' She gave a meek shrug.

'The only time I bet on a horserace is if it's Melbourne Cup day and we're near a pub. But you?'

'Since I was six years old my Uncle Bob taught me all about the world of racing, from the signs of a good horse, racing conditions and more, while babysitting me at various race tracks.' She tenderly patted the bulky pouch containing Bob's journal. 'Uncle Bob wasn't a bad man, and he certainly didn't deserve to die the way he did.'

'From gambling debts?'

'So the cops told me. Until I met Quid and Reggie, at the track. They told me my uncle only owed six thousand, which isn't enough debt to even get your thumbs broken.'

'So, he wasn't killed over a gambling debt?'

'My uncle may have been a gambler and an alcoholic, but he was also a good investigative journalist. In the week before his death, Bob didn't drink. And the only reason he'd visited the racetrack, on the day before he died, was to hide this.' She held up the cursed black plastic pouch.

Joe wiped a palm over his face to hide the disappointment and confusion in his eyes. 'Do you mean, this entire time the research you've been doing isn't about your uncle's memoirs?'

'No.' And now she felt like a big fat liar. 'When I arrived, I hadn't had a chance to read this cursed thing.' She dropped the black pouch onto the floor and glared at it for all the trouble it'd caused. And it still wasn't over. 'The day I collected this pouch at the racetrack, I had originally planned to catch a plane to Sydney to stay with my godmother. But it all changed quickly when Reggie spotted the goons following me.'

'The who?'

'The goons. Here ...' She unclipped the waterproof pouch and pulled out a bunch of printed images. 'That short one with the Elvis hair, that's Goon One.'

'Elvis hair, huh?' Joe's eyes narrowed at the images. 'It fits.'

'His offsider, the tall guy with the bald head, that's Goon Two.'

'Who are they?' Joe studied the images.

'I have no idea what their names are. I can't even tell you how long they'd been following me before they were spotted at the racetrack.'

'Did you tell the police all this?'

'That's the thing, my uncle made me swear to *not* tell the police. Then Reggie warned me that the cops were lying about the reason for Bob's murder.'

Joe's eyebrows shot up. 'And you believe him?'

'It's a lot to swallow, but here …' She passed Joe another photo of four men. 'This photo was with my uncle's journal. The two men with the goons are Senior Detective Mick Hetter and his junior partner, Paul. They're the detectives in charge of my uncle's murder case. In that photo they're exchanging keys and cash.' She tapped on the image. 'That's my uncle's missing car keys.'

'How can you tell?'

'I recognised the good luck charm hanging off it. I gave that to my uncle when I gave him the spare key to my apartment.' She glowered at the photo. 'Those detectives knew all about the break in. I can't believe I trusted them.'

'Hey, I believe you and you know you can trust me.'

Oh, she wanted to.

'Remember, I've had my own run-in with questionable cops,' said Joe. 'How did you end up here?'

She gazed up at the ruggedly handsome cattleman beside her and filled him in on her chase from Flemington, through the streets of Adelaide, to her crash landing.

'Why did you pick this place to stay?' Joe asked, having listened intently.

'I'd overheard these women talking about stations in the airport toilets. One of them gave me their tourist magazine to do a search. Elleron Downs had a flight leaving the same day, and you advertised internet and PC access available to guests. I figured no one would ever find me here.'

'What did you find from your uncle's notes?'

'The reason they murdered him.'

'No way?' He hissed through his teeth, as if to keep his composure, but his grip tightened around her shoulders as if to comfort them both.

Maddison pulled out another photo, but hesitated. She was risking his life if she went any further.

'Babe …' With his hand covering hers, he made her show him the photo. 'Who's that?'

'Antonio Cottillard.' She frowned at the man with dark olive skin and cold black eyes.

'Never heard of him.'

'He's a businessman who turns old warehouses into high-rise accommodation. He also owns an import shipping company that includes a stash of warehouses that sit along Melbourne's docks.'

'He's a property developer?'

'And a people smuggler. He uses them for slave labour,' she said coldly, showing the photos her uncle had taken. All in fabulous grainy colour. 'Those illegal immigrants become his building labourers, to work off their debt to him for coming to this country. While this guy sells those sea-view apartments—making millions.'

'No way,' muttered Joe.

'They arrive by boat, landing on the far north coastline, where they get transferred into sea containers that are then shipped down the east coast to Melbourne. There they're kept in large warehouses before they're shipped off to whorehouses, sweatshops and work camps to pay off their debt for freedom. He's making a fortune out of these people's misfortune. Do you realise we've had over one hundred illegal boats caught in Darwin harbour alone in the past three months, with more coming every week only for those people to become slaves?'

'No offence, but if you've found out about all of this from out here, how come the government has done nothing to stop this?'

'The immigrants won't say anything, they're illegally smuggled into this country with Cottillard promising them a set of immigration papers to stay.'

'How much is that costing them?'

'Two years' manual labour, working fourteen hours a day, wage-free. They get two meals a day, and sleep on a factory floor. That's just the men.'

She passed another photo to Joe. 'Cottillard owns everyone.' She tapped on the photo showing four men standing on a golf course. 'That's the same two detectives handing the same envelopes they been given by the goons to these two men. The one on the left is a Police Superintendent and the guy on the right is about to be promoted to Deputy Commissioner.'

'You're kidding, right?'

'Oh, it gets better...' She pulled out another photo. This one had Antonio Cottillard talking with another man. Her uncle must have been hanging off some fire escape to take that photo, but it was the money shot with both men staring straight into the lens. Busted. 'The man talking to Cottillard is our country's Federal Minister for Immigration.'

'He's obviously getting a payoff if his office is doing nothing.'

'Correct. The Minister is being paid to clog up the federal investigations with red tape, while also supplying unlimited working visas to Cottillard's company, that I'm assuming he's using as bait to keep these people working for him.'

Joe glanced over the images. 'Don't take this the wrong way, but to me, these photos show a few blokes getting money as if they were having a wager over a golf game.'

She sighed. 'I agree. Thank you for your honesty.' Seriously, were there any faults to this man?

'But you've found more, haven't you?'

'Yeah. A tonne of trouble, all on video.' She dragged out her uncle's old phone.

'I'm guessing this is the reason they murdered your uncle?'

'You should back out now. You can't unsee—'

'Hey, I'm with you all the way, babe.'

'Babe?'

'Meh.' He shrugged with shoulders that were as heavy as hers. 'Go on.'

'Okay then.' Not that he was giving her a choice.

Activating the phone, she scrolled to the video image. 'This is a recorded conversation between Antonio Cottillard, the Police Superintendent, and the Federal Minister. They're talking about a combined Federal Police and Customs investigation that is about to raid the sheds where the illegal immigrants are kept.'

'Did they bust them?'

'No. Because on this recording they're tipping off Cottillard about the raid. Cottillard gets angry over the costs to his smuggling business and does this huge dummy spit over diverting ships, missing collections, and finding places to hide these people.'

'All on this?' Joe tapped on the phone screen frozen on Cottillard's portrait.

'Yeah. It's not the best image, but the voices are crystal clear,' she said. 'The man heading up the Federal Police side of the operation has been causing serious problems for Cottillard. On this tape, Cottillard demands information on this Federal Police Officer, saying he's going to kill him personally. The guy even describes how he's going to do it!'

'Where did your uncle discover this?'

'He taped it down at the wharves one night. It all happened right in front of my uncle. The three men, having this little conversation, must have thought my uncle's heap of crap was a deserted vehicle. I recognised it from the dashboard you can see at the bottom of the screen.'

'That's what got your uncle killed?'

'I believe so, and his money shot where Cottillard's staring straight at the lens. Because five days after this taped meeting, the Federal Police Officer was found shot dead, exactly how Antonio had described it. And that's the day my uncle sobered up, knocked on my door asking to crash on my couch and to soak up my wi-fi.' Maddison turned on the phone and played the video for Joe.

'Damn …' Joe wiped his hands over his face when the video finished. 'Have you made copies?'

'Yes, I used a few of your brother's memory sticks and there's also a copy in the cloud.' She stared at the paperwork in front of her. 'You're the only one I've spoken to about this, and it may sound stupid, but I'm glad I could talk this through with someone.' If only she could dump the burden pressing heavily against her chest. 'Do you believe me?'

'Yes …' He gave a slow nod, staring at the paperwork spread across the floor.

'Have you got questions?'

He gave another heavy nod. 'Have you been carrying this load all on your own?'

She shrugged, unsure how to answer that one. 'I can't put anyone else in danger.'

'What are you planning to do now?'

'No idea. My only reason for coming here was to hide out while I worked on these notes.'

Joe frowned hard at the photos on the floor. 'Is there anything else?'

'Um, ask me my name?' She winced as guilt screwed a hole into her stomach. She wanted to be sick.

* * *

Joe raised his eyebrow at her. Had she been lying to him this entire time? Including the story she'd just told?

'M-M-Maddison is my actual name.' She dragged out some ID from her purse. 'The motor registry made a mistake with my licence when I renewed it. I never bothered to get it corrected, and I'd forgotten about it. This is my name, I'm Maddison Janice Farley.' She showed him her scuba diving licence and credit cards.

It was the same smile, the eyes, the dainty chin and full lips. Maddison Farley.

She held his hands in hers, pleading with him. 'I hated doing this, but I had to. I didn't mean for us to get involved and was doing it to protect all of you. I never lied, I—'

'You only told us a part of the truth and let everyone assume the rest of the story.'

She sat straighter. 'Yes. How did you know that?'

'When you talked the Thurstons out of selling their story to the press, you warned us of how the truth gets twisted by leaving it up to others to make their own interpretations and assumptions. That's why you've never said much about yourself, no matter how many times I asked you.' It was like pulling teeth getting answers out of her at times.

'I couldn't tell you.'

'You told the truth, didn't you?'

She nodded with glassy eyes. 'I just couldn't tell you the whole story. I couldn't risk it … or you.'

Bloody hell, the woman was protecting him. 'I understand.'

'You do?' Hope filled her enormous eyes, melting his heart.

His thumb wiped at the tears threatening to spill down her cheeks. 'Well, you answer to your name like you've had it all your life.'

He had hoped for a smile, but she grimaced instead.

With the burden she'd been carrying on her own, Maddison was far stronger than he'd ever imagined.

'Was it that obvious that I was on the run?' Maddison asked.

'No. Well, at first I was suspicious, after I saw all that money in your handbag, that you clung on to like it was your life.' He toed the red bag with his boot. 'I thought you were running from some ex-boyfriend or employer.'

'The money helped me hide.'

'You paid cash for everything.'

'That's what made you suspicious?'

'Yeah, and you had this ridiculously small overnight bag and wore a suit. Most women who've come out here have five times the amount of luggage for their new cowgirl's wardrobe. You didn't have a pair of jeans or boots, not even a hat in your suitcase. But that's okay, you don't need to wear anything for me.' He nuzzled her slender neck, hoping to put her at ease.

'You have been a distraction while I've been trying to do my research.'

'Annoying you is one of my favourites pastimes,' he said, kissing her cheek. 'Right now, I'll find out who these two blokes are.'

'I'm coming too.' Maddison shoved everything into that big red bag and booted it under the bed.

'Mum?' Joe called out, with Maddison beside him in the vacant kitchen.

'Out here, dear?'

The screen door gave its familiar creak, where he found Glenda by the laundry area on the verandah. 'Mum, who are those new tourists coming out today?'

'They're cousins. Jonathon and Christian Nelson.'

'How long ago did they book their stay?' Maddison asked.

'About six months ago, but Jonathon broke his leg and they had to postpone their vacation. They paid extra to hold their booking because we can't give refunds, dear. It was what Joe stipulated as part of the terms for when people booked.'

'Really?' Maddison peeked at Joe over her shoulder.

'Didn't want anyone ripping us off,' said Joe, 'especially when we're shipping in food for some of them.'

'Smart move.'

Well, didn't that make his ego soar?

'Jonathon's wife rang a few days ago, asking if we had the room, her husband had fully recovered now. Why do you ask, dear?'

'Did they say why they're coming out now, especially after a plane crash?' Maddison blurted out.

Joe frowned at the memory, drawing Maddison closer to his side.

'Christian's work insisted he use up his holiday leave, or he was going to lose it, and she said they wanted to show their support to our business. That's rather sweet, don't you think?'

'Isn't it unusual for two men to visit without their wives?' Maddison asked.

'No.' Joe's scowl was a permanent fixture whenever he talked about the tourists who invaded his home. 'Most people try and live some childhood fantasy of playing cowboys. They're nothing but a bunch of soft —'

'Earl takes them fishing,' interrupted his mother. 'Don't worry, dear, your father will be keeping them entertained.'

'Good. Keep 'em away from me,' he said, crossing his arms over his chest. 'All right?' He asked Maddison, who gave an unconvincing nod.

'Hey, Joe?' called out Greg, barging through the house.

'In the laundry.'

Greg pushed open the screen door. 'Can you give Dad a hand with the tractor? I'm a bit worried he might blow his own personal gasket or something?'

Joe didn't want to leave Maddison's side, but he also didn't want his dad hurting himself.

'Go on, I'll be fine.' She pushed on his arm and stepped away.

He didn't like her stepping away from him, especially when he had so many questions. But Maddison also wasn't the type to allow him to hover over her shoulder either.

'I'll be in the shed if you need me.' Joe kissed her cheek.

'I won't be far.'

His reward was a slight smile.

Damn, she had the power to make him feel like a king and he was going to do his best to protect her—if only she'd let him.

* * *

Maddison watched the brothers in Akubra's, matching jeans and boots, take steady strides along the verandah. They even walked the same, with Greg yet to fill out like Joe.

'Is everything all right, dear?' Glenda asked, as the washing machine whirled into life behind her.

'Yeah, fine thanks.' On the outside she seemed fine, on the inside she was fighting with her fear.

'Come on, let's make you a fresh cup of coffee.' Glenda hooked her arm through Maddison's and guided her back into the kitchen. 'How long are you thinking of staying, dear?' Glenda sat opposite, putting a coffee cup down in front of Maddison. 'I have you down for another week and the airline contacted me to confirm your return dates.'

Maddison took a deep sip of her coffee as if searching for an answer. 'Is there another way of getting out of here? By road?'

'I doubt you'd get through with all the rain we've had. The crossings are flooded. Are you scared to fly?'

'Yes.' Maddison had always suffered from a fear of flying, but it was worse now. 'Where's the nearest major city or largest regional town from here?'

'That'd be Alice Springs. Are you thinking of extending your stay?'

'I'm not sure ...' *about leaving or staying*.

'Joe would love for you to stay longer, and you'd be no bother.'

It felt more than a holiday fling, and unlike any relationship she'd ever had where they'd only spent one night apart since the day they'd met. Joe had taught her so much, like how to fish and ride a motorbike, while sharing his incredible patience with her as he answered all her questions about this place. There were also plenty of times they didn't need to speak, where they sat back and watched the sunset stretch across a never-ending outback horizon. It had truly been a wonderful experience being with Joe.

'You know, Joe really adores you, dear,' said Glenda over her teacup.

Maddison sank into her seat with a deep sigh. It was obvious how Joe felt about her. The guy was caring, attentive, funny, charming, and so near perfect. 'But ...' With all her other dramas, she didn't dare put Joe at risk, or even allow herself to fall for anyone while her own life was in danger.

'Are you wondering what it would be like when you go back to living in Melbourne and with Joe here on the station. Is that what's got you worried, dear?'

'It'd be impossible.' Even if there wasn't a promise to keep, would they be compatible as a couple? 'It's a long way. I'm a city girl who's never been to the country, and Joe loves it here. This is home to him.' She didn't have a home, now she thought about it. Nothing like this place where there was a family who sat around the table sharing meals, who were friends too.

'You seem to be enjoying yourself here.'

'I am.' She kept forgetting she was here to hide as the place was so comforting, and she loved the immense country views. She enjoyed her baking lessons with Glenda and had found kneading bread surprisingly therapeutic. There was the teasing banter with Greg as they tried to hustle each other over the pool table. Earl would patiently explain the station's history. And Joe ...

'I bet Joe is thinking about the same things, dear,' said Glenda.

'Really?' Or would the poor man be glad to see the back of her after what he'd just learned. She wouldn't blame him.

'Joe has lived in the city and travelled a fair bit, too. He knows what goes on out there and has lived in both worlds. What you should be asking yourself is how would you feel if you met Joe in Melbourne? Would you look at Joe any different to the way you look at him now, if Joe walked into your world, like you have walked into his?'

Maddison stared at Glenda, stunned at her question. Would she react the same way if she'd met Joe in her world? A world she'd run away from long before she'd made her uncle a promise.

Forty-two

The shed's corrugated roof creaked under the day's heat as the breeze floated through its wide-open doorway, where Joe was busily working under the tractor's cab. The aroma of diesel fuels hung heavily in the humid air, as Joe wiped the perspiration from around his eyes on his shirt's sleeve.

Greg's music played in the background, as he'd demanded he be in control of the playlists while getting a lesson on engines. Earl stood on the other side, supervising, as they gave the large engine an overhaul so it would be ready for some heavy lifting as soon as the rains stopped.

As Joe worked, he kept thinking over what Maddison had been through alone. Her story was astounding. He could tell she was going to complete that deathbed promise to her uncle, who deserved some form of justice for what had happened to him.

Joe also wanted to punch the bloke for daring to put Maddison in danger like this. Yet, if this poor Bob hadn't discovered this story, making Maddison promise to go through with it, then she wouldn't be here now.

'Oh no,' moaned Greg, behind Joe's shoulder.

'What?' Joe peered up from the engine, spotting Analise and Zach Thurston coming towards them. 'Just great.' The shed was meant to be a tourist-free zone.

'Behave, boys,' warned Earl as he greeted the couple in the doorway. 'We'll be leaving in the troopie over there.'

'We came to say goodbye to the boys,' called out Zach, rubbing his hands together.

Boys? Joe arched an eyebrow at Greg, frowning.

'Come on, boys.' Earl beckoned them to come forward.

'Dad, we're in the middle—' Greg stopped at Earl's dead-eye stare, which had been known to make cattle pull up in their tracks. 'Coming.' He scuffed his boots beside Joe to face the Thurstons.

'We've come to say thank you for everything,' said Analise with a wide smile. 'I had the greatest time.'

'No worries, mate,' said Earl. 'Come again anytime.'

Both Joe and Greg cleared their throats to stop the smartarse comebacks and grabbed a rag each to wipe away the grease on their hands.

'Thank you for saving us, Joe. We'll never forget you.' Analise lunged at Joe to hug him.

Joe cringed into a face full of hair that reminded him of sticky fencing wire. 'Anyone would've done it,' he mumbled, peeling himself away from the married middle-aged woman. He never displayed his affections in public with anyone, except with Maddison. And only Maddison.

'You're still my hero. I'm going to tell everyone about you.' Analise gave Joe's bicep a squeeze.

'Yeah, right.' Joe stepped back from the woman feeling him up.

'Joe, if you're ever in the area, our house is open to you and your family. Anytime.' Zach grabbed Joe's grease covered hand and shook it. 'Um ...' His face screwed up in horror at the grime covering his soft accountant's hands.

'Here ...' Joe tossed a rag to Zach. 'Take care and have a safe trip home.' Joe watched the couple walk arm-in-arm back to the house with Earl, where their luggage waited for them on the front verandah. It was quite a change from the bickering couple he'd first met.

'Reckon you'll ever take them up on their offer to stay, Joe?' Greg asked.

'Hell, no.' Joe focused on the tractor's engine to finish it up. 'They're tourists.' It astounded him how people paid to come and see how they lived. He was always grateful when they left.

Joe glanced back at the grand house, its windows reflecting the fast-moving rain clouds.

People came and went every week, that's what guests

did, they came in and out of their lives so quickly, never to be heard from again.

'Greg, you can finish up.' He washed his hands in the large industrial sink. 'It only needs a de-grease.'

'Why? Where are you going?'

'To check on something.' Joe dried his hands on his shirt and headed into the sunshine peeking through the heavy clouds.

'Or someone,' called out Greg by the tractor.

Joe leaped up the front steps of the verandah, letting the screen door bang shut behind him. 'Maddison?'

'Here.' She sat in her familiar spot at the library desk facing the computer screen.

Joe dropped into the chair beside the mahogany desk. It used to be a spot where he'd work with his dad doing the bills, now kept clear for the tourists while he worked on the accounts in the shed.

But Maddison wasn't a tourist.

'What are you doing?'

'Trying to figure out what to do.'

He'd only had a few hours to digest her story and was trying to catch up. 'Can't you email it to the police or something?'

'But will they be honest or corrupt police? Would it get lost in transit? They might not even act properly with this information either, and I'll still have these goons chasing me. I can't send copies; I have to give them the originals.'

'You've really thought about this, haven't you?'

'I'm at the point of obsessing over it.' With elbows bent on the table, she rubbed her face in her palms. 'I can't take this information to Victoria because of the police involvement. With the Federal Minister involved that rules out the ACT and I don't know anyone there. It needs to go to someone I can trust to do the right thing.'

'What was your uncle planning to do with all of this information?'

'Publish it, I guess.' She sat back in the chair, frowning at the screen. 'Uncle Bob told me this would help him get back into the game.'

'What game?'

'Journalism. Frontline reporting. Bob used to love the adrenaline rush he'd get from the job.'

'Aren't you a journalist too?'

'Well, yes, and no. News reporters go for crime, scandals, and politics.' She dropped her head to fidget with her fingers as she said in a softer tone, 'I got into other topics for a women's magazine.'

'The latest in botox and eyeliners, huh?'

'No,' she said, lifting that dainty chin of hers. 'A lot more than you'd think.'

'Well, tell me.' He wanted to know her story; even if it came with a tonne of baggage, he had to hear it. He was just grateful she was finally opening up to him.

'I'd report on current affairs and women's issues. I'd report on my travels or amusing incidents and did a lot of work like my mother used to.'

'Your mother was a journalist too?'

She nodded, with her plump lips clamped tight into a thin line.

'So it runs in the family, huh? Like us, with this station.'

'It's a publishing business that aims to make a profit for its shareholders.' She pointed to the family photos on the wall. 'It's nothing like what you guys have; this is a home.'

'True.' His home and he didn't mind sharing it with only the few, not the mass of unfamiliar faces that trudged through the front doors every week.

'You're lucky you have this, and such a wonderful family.'

And he'd do everything in his power to protect this station and his family too.

He then realised the woman was an orphan, her uncle who'd died had been her last relative.

He reached for her small hand and they sat there in silence, watching Earl and Greg through the window. They were loading up the troop carrier with luggage for the Thurstons' flight out. No dust stirred as his parents drove toward the airstrip to collect the next lot of strangers.

'Who would your uncle see about publishing this story?'

She sat forward. 'Sydney!'

'You're leaving?' And his heart fell as if sprinkling into

shattered glass across the floor.

* * *

Maddison didn't want to answer Joe's question. But they both knew the truth. 'I have to finish this. I made a promise I would.'

'Is it because of these two guys coming out today? Is that what's pushing you?'

She rubbed an eyebrow, trying to put this as delicately as possible without hurting them both. 'Look, okay, I panicked earlier. And I've made copies of all my work and stashed my uncle's pouch in a place nowhere near my room, but I can't live like this.'

'Like what? Here?' He thumbed to the window that gave a glorious view of the outback.

'No, the running. Constantly watching over my shoulder in fear because two men, who'd booked to visit six months ago, sent me into a panic. I struggle to trust anyone, looking at everyone warily, wondering if I'm going to make it. And I can't put you and your family at risk anymore by being here …' She hiccupped, drowning under the sorrow threatening to spill from her chest. Her throat was tight, as the tears blurred her vision of the man she would have to eventually leave behind. She couldn't risk anyone, especially Joe.

'Hey …' Joe pulled her close, holding her against his chest. 'It's a lot to deal with on your own.'

'You're telling me.' With the heel of her palm, she desperately tried to brush away the tears.

'What do you say we disappear for a few hours?'

'And go where?'

'It's warming up out there, let's take the ute and drive to the falls?'

'The ones at Mount Elleron?'

'Yeah, they seemed to do you the world of good last time.'

'That place is spectacular.'

'So is the company,' he said with a cheeky wink. 'Come on, step away from that computer and clear your head for a bit, then we'll tackle this thing together.'

Together? 'Listen Joe, we, you and me, with what's going on over my uncle—'

'Hey.' He pressed a finger to her lips. 'You've missed your chance to fly out of here today, so you're still a guest for another week. And I'm not interested in hanging around for the next mob of tourists to arrive. I think we both deserve a cold beer on a hot day while swimming in a private remote location.' With his hand on her hip, he pulled her close to his chest to nuzzle her ear. 'And I can show you what I wanted to do to you the first time I took you out there.'

'What about your work? And it's going to rain.'

He chuckled. 'We're going swimming—we'll be getting wet, anyway. And I'm not taking no for an answer.'

Maddison squealed with laughter as Joe scooped her up and carried her out the door.

Forty-three

The small light airplane circled above the Elleron Downs red dirt runway. Eric sat at the right rear of the plane, gripping a fresh spew bag, having lost his lunch an hour into the flight from the bumpy turbulence and shifting monsoonal storms. 'I hate these little planes.'

'I don't mind them.' Tom sat opposite, staring out the window while chewing on another lolly like a cow. 'Hey, did you know this was the same type of plane that crashed the other week? I wonder where it went down?'

'Will you shut up!'

'Man, that must've been a plane ride from hell, huh? Can you imagine it? That little plane being tossed around in all of them storms. The turbulence sending it up and down,' Tom swung his body as he spoke, 'and side to side.'

Eric hurled into the bag.

Tom laughed.

Arsehole.

'We're coming in to land now,' said the pilot, busily flicking dials in the cockpit.

'No worries, mate.' Tom gave a thumbs up.

'Is your friend okay?'

Not my friend. Eric couldn't speak but only glared at the Neanderthal.

'I reckon he'll be one of those people who'll play Pope and kiss the ground when he gets off the plane.' Tom gave a cheesy grin.

If Eric weren't so sick, he'd wipe Tom's smug smile off with the back of his hand.

'Want a lolly? They're mint green ones.' Tom held out a green jelly to Eric. 'Mind you, they're a bit warm and they've gone all soft and gooey. Do they remind you of anything?'

The horrid green squashed monstrosity in Tom's large hand, made Eric press the spew bag over his mouth to dry retch. He had nothing left, only his stomach lining.

Tom chucked the lolly into his big fat gob. 'I didn't realise this place was so big. I reckon it's ten times the size of Adelaide. Did you know South Australia is Australia's driest state suffering with drought? You'd think they'd work out a way to ship all that surplus ground water down south.'

Eric didn't care if they landed on Mars, as long as it was land and soon.

The small plane made its descent, then bumped along the small dirt airstrip. It taxied toward a group of people waiting under a small tin lean-to, and when the engines switched off there was blissful silence.

Made it. Eric sat back in his chair and sighed.

'I'm really looking forward to this.' Tom unclipped his seat belt and scooped up his brand new ten-gallon cowboy hat. He tucked his flannelette cowboy shirt into his new Wranglers, then bent over to dust off his new American cowboy boots, momentarily blocking the shine from his fake rodeo belt buckle. 'How do I look?'

Were they trapped in a nightmarish episode of the Flintstones gone cowboy?

'I can't believe you went and bought all that bloody cowboy crap,' said Eric.

'Mate, I'm livin' the dream. See?' The caveman had gone cowboy with his boof head at a crooked angle, as he was too tall for the plane.

While the pilot got busy outside, Eric clambered out of his seat. 'Do you remember what my name is?'

'Christian,' replied Tom. 'Are you part of the catholic denomination or one of them hand-clapping Mormons?'

'Go to hell, ya moron.'

'Nah, I didn't peg you for a choir boy.' Tom chuckled, hoisting his backpack over his shoulder.

Eric was surprised Tom didn't carry a set of saddlebags.

'What's the plan, Christian?'

'We've got four days until the plane returns.'

'Can we call anyone?'

'No. We don't want them to trace the calls or know who we are.' Eric slid his overnight bag over his shoulder, and faced his partner. 'That's the plan. Find the girl and get the gear. Simple.'

'Righto.'

Eric winced at the bright sunlight as a whopping wave of heavy heat washed over him as if he'd stepped into a sauna. He didn't care; he was back on land, aiming for the shady trees.

'Welcome to Elleron Downs. I'm Earl Charter and this is my wife Glenda, and we'll be your hosts for the week with our boys.' Earl spoke in a well-rehearsed speech.

Boys? 'I'm Christian and that's Jonathon.' Eric shook the couple's hands. These Aussie rednecks looked simple enough with their deep tans, dust-stained jeans and worn boots. They were old, with a couple of boys, and no threat to Eric and his plans.

Tom stumbled down the plane's steps like a newborn calf only to walk bandy legged like some spaghetti western movie hero, going for a quick draw showdown at high noon. 'G'day.'

'My word, you're a big man.' Glenda craned her neck back at Tom, so much taller with that bucket on his head he called a hat. 'New hat, eh, Jonathon?'

'I bought it for the occasion, see.' Tom tipped his hat at her. 'Please, call me Tom.'

Idiot. Eric glared at the freak playing dress-up.

'Tom's me nickname, see, I only get called Jonathon when I'm in trouble.'

'Tom, eh?' Earl squinted his wary eyes.

'I've had it since I was a kid. My nan called me that after the movie *Tom Thumb* on account of me big thumbs. See?' Tom showed them his large thumbs that made both Glenda and Earl nod.

'Your nan sounds like a nice lady,' said Glenda.

'She was. I brought her out here, well up in Darwin, a few years ago, see, and that was her last trip before she died.'

'Well, I'm sure she's watching over you, dear.'

'You think so? Nan was a good ol' stick. I reckon she'd love being out here. I've always wanted to see a cattle station.' Tom's boof head whirled around to take in the view of nothing but a dirt airstrip, a crappy plane, and a mud-covered four-wheel drive.

'Let's get you blokes into the troopie and we'll head back to the homestead, eh.' Earl hurled the luggage into the back of his vehicle. The other couple were climbing into the plane with the pilot preparing for departure.

'Will you shut up?' Eric said to Tom through clenched teeth.

'Why?'

'You sound like a bloody yapping tourist. And the way you're dressed, come on.' Eric waved his hand at the oversized man-boy playing cowboy. It was embarrassing.

'You said we're to act like tourists on holidays and that's what I'm doing, see. You know, that Glenda reminds me of me nan.'

'I don't give a flying toss!'

'Good to see you've recovered from your flight there, Christian.' Tom laughed as his boots clomped behind Eric.

'Hey, Earl, Glenda,' said Tom, taking his seat in the troop carrier, right behind the couple. 'No doubt you get the usual three hundred and thirty questions from people. How about you tell me about the place?'

Eric glowered behind his sunglasses, his shirt sticking to his clammy skin, as he slunk down into the back seat of their vehicle. The scenery was nothing but foreign spindly trees and red dirt.

He blocked out Earl's regurgitated speech. Eric didn't care about the owners or anyone else, just one little woman.

With the taste of triumph rising in his chest, he was safe on land, and had four fun-filled days to find his answers. It was payback time.

Forty-four

Through the pouring rain, Joe steered his ute over the muddy terrain to park beside the house. 'I'll drop you off here and park the ute in the shed,' he said to Maddison, seated in the passenger seat.

'Thank you again for another amazing afternoon.' She reached over and kissed his cheek.

'My pleasure.' He was pleased to see the fear gone from her eyes. 'Could do with a hot shower. You?'

'I'm way ahead of you.' With a laugh, she dashed through the rain.

'I might come and scrub your back,' Joe called out through the driver's window. Her tinkling laughter matched her wide smile. It only made him smile with her.

He drove into the shed where Greg was refuelling their quads. 'Are you getting ready for the tourists, huh?'

He hated the way strangers would use and abuse their equipment. Nothing was their own anymore.

Still, he shouldn't complain. The tourists paid the bills, and Maddison was one of them—although her reasons for visiting were completely different.

Joe's lips curled into the hint of a smile. He enjoyed teaching her the everyday things he took for granted, watching her confidence grow as she rode his quad bike. Today, he'd shown her how to shoot using the rifle he kept in the ute. Most of all he enjoyed watching her, the soft look when she'd first wake, or when they'd made love. Her openness and how she looked at everything in awe made him feel proud of who he was and where he lived.

'You can fill my ute too, Greg. I'm running a bit low.' He

was keen to go share a shower.

'Sure, not! Your ute, your fuel.' Greg put the fuel cap on the bikes and returned the fuel drum to the rack. 'So how was your afternoon?'

'Good.' *Damned good!* The passion from one little lady was amazing.

He grabbed the esky from his ute that had been a part of their picnic. Yes, he was now doing picnics. If anyone had told him he'd be picking flowers, going for sunset walks or picnics, he'd tell them to nick-off. But it made the little lady smile.

'Did you meet the new guests?' Joe asked Greg.

'Oh yeah.'

'What are they like?'

'The usual. New hat, jeans, and boots, playing wannabe cowboy. The tall bloke likes being called Tom from these massive thumbs he has. He seems okay, happy hanging with Mum.'

'Mum's feeding them, huh?'

'Yep. But he's real tall and got this shiny bald head. I reckon he shaves it.'

'What did you say?' Joe dropped the esky and grabbed his brother's shirt. 'Tall man, shaved head?'

'Yeah.'

'The other guy, is he short with hair swept back like Elvis?'

'Who?'

'A lion's mane.'

'How did you know?'

'Dammit.' Fear kicked a surge of adrenalin through his spine as his guts churned hot concrete. 'Where are they now?' Joe grabbed his rifle from behind the seat of his ute.

'Why? What's wrong?'

Joe loaded up his rifle and shoved handfuls of bullets into the pockets of his jeans. 'Where are they?'

'With Mum and Dad in the kitchen.' Greg gripped his brother's arm. 'What's going on, Joe?'

'Those two men have been chasing Maddison around the country, and they're armed and dangerous. We need to make sure Mum and Dad are okay. I want you to go into the kitchen and check it out. I'll come in from the other side.'

And he prayed Maddison was safe in her room.

'But—'

'Just do it. Mum and Dad are in danger.'

Forty-five

The rain spilled off the roof like a shimmering satin curtain, cooling the day's heat and pooling over the lawn. Hope and happiness brought a spring to Maddison's step all because of Joe. He pleased her on so many levels, from tenderly treating her like a lady, making love to her, to then teaching her how to shoot a rifle. She was clumsy and missed their targets and the noise was a shock. But he gently supported her, giving her the right form of encouragement, unlike anyone.

She strolled down the wide verandah to the double glass doors of her room. Inside, she grabbed the towel from her freshly made bed.

She paused at the bathroom with its door open, lights on, but her red leather handbag sat on the floor tiles with its mouth open wide. Empty.

The rolls of money filled the sink, and her make-up was everywhere. Tubes of creams were emptied. The facial wipes torn from their packages. Her tube of lipstick smashed, and her hairbrush broken in half. Someone had ransacked her toiletries just like her apartment.

'Oh, no.' Maddison walked backwards to the glass doors, her eyes widening as the door handle from the hallway shifted.

She froze on the other side of the room. It was Goon One.

'Hello, Maddison. My name is Eric. After chasing you through three states, it's so nice to make your acquaintance.' Eric grinned at her like an evil Cheshire cat.

The air crackled between them as the rain poured on the

roof. The sounds of laughter floated down the hallway, along with the smells of a roast cooking. Sounds and scents that once brought her comfort in a scene that now terrorised her.

In the blink of an eye, she bolted out the double doors. Throwing them shut behind her, she ran blindly into the rain as fast as her legs could carry her.

'*Come back here, Maddison.*' Eric flung open the doors hard against the wall, their glass panelling shattering in an almighty crash.

BANG was the gunshot.

Maddison screamed as she flinched and ducked but kept running like a jackrabbit being hunted by a fox, through the torrential rain and across the wet muddy grass. Her nightmare was real.

Forty-six

'**M**um, Dad, are you okay?' In muddy boots, Greg skidded across the floor from the kitchen doorway, he was forced to grab the kitchen bench to stop himself from falling.

'Watch yourself, son,' said Earl, seated at the kitchen table with that big man.

'Greg, you know better. Why didn't you take your muddy boots off before coming inside?' scolded Glenda. 'How many times have I told you—'

'*Come back here, Maddison.*'

There was a horrific sound of smashing glass.

BANG.

Everyone in the kitchen flinched.

'That was a gunshot,' said Earl.

'*Eric*?' Tom jumped to his feet, knocking his chair backwards to the floor. He ran for the hallway, pushing past Greg, but Tom's fancy cowboy boots slipped on the wet floor tiles and he lost his balance. He fell on his side. Slammed into the kitchen wall, landing on his chest with arms and legs splayed out like a newborn calf that had yet to learn how to walk.

'I thought his name was Christian?' Glenda asked, still seated at the table beside Earl.

Joe burst through the back screen door. 'Don't move, arsehole.' Hatred dripped from each word, while he aimed his fully loaded rifle at Tom.

'Hey, I'm not here to hurt you lot, I swear it.' Spread-eagled on his stomach, Tom held out his hands in front with fingers and big thumbs spread wide in surrender.

'Greg, get the slip ties from the pantry.' Joe pressed the rifle's muzzle into the back of Tom's shaved head. He wasn't playing games.

Greg ran past the kitchen table to the large pantry that was a part-time toolshed.

'What the hell's going on?' Earl demanded, with Glenda beside him.

Joe shook his head at his dad, then glared at Tom on the floor. 'Hands behind your back, arsehole.'

'Okay, mate, I'm doing it. See …'

Greg soon returned.

'Tie him up like you're going to brand a feral cleanskin,' ordered Joe.

Greg tied Tom's hands behind his back and then at the ankles. 'How's that?'

'Here …' Joe handed the rifle to Greg. 'If he moves shoot him, and I don't care where.'

'Look, fellas, I'm cooperating. See?'

Joe checked the ties were secure, then rolled Tom over to his side. He roughly patted down Tom's shirt and found the handgun and wallet. 'Melvin Thomas,' Joe read from the Victorian driver's licence found inside the leather wallet. He chucked it onto the table. He then checked the handgun for ammunition, tucked it in his belt and grabbed the rifle back from Greg to poke the tip against Tom's cheek. 'Where's your mate?'

'*What the* HELL *is going on*?' Earl demanded with flushed cheeks. 'Why is our guest tied up on our kitchen floor like a backwards steer at a rodeo?'

'These men are here to hurt Maddison,' said Joe, scowling at Tom.

'Hey, only cops and criminals carry handguns,' blurted out Greg, pointing to the wallet, 'And he lied about his name.'

'Get the other shotgun, Greg.' His brother ran off. His parents stared on in shock while his baby brother tried to be brave. 'You okay, Mum, Dad?'

'Ah, yeah, we're fine' replied Earl, scratching his grey hair. 'You?'

'I will be once I find Maddison. Come on, Greg.' He

would not leave his parents unarmed with this cretin on their kitchen floor. The seconds felt like hours as the rain hammered from the sky and the sweat trickled down his face.

Where the hell was Maddison?

Forty-seven

Maddison ran through the rain, past the calving shed and around the rear of the homestead. She had to get Eric away from Glenda and Earl in the house.

She made a sharp left at the fence line and aimed for the main shed with Eric in hot pursuit.

Mud splashed her legs, her dress stuck to her skin, and the rain was blinding. She tasted perspiration mixing with fresh rain and that all too familiar metallic taste of fear.

Dodging her way through the fencing barricades, she fled past the cattle pens, loading ramps, and assorted machinery to shove open the rear door and dash inside the main shed.

'JOE.' Her words were muffled by the pouring rain that pounded on the tin roof. She wiped the hair, sweat, and rainwater from her eyes, searching for someone, anyone.

But no one was there.

What was she thinking? This burden was hers to carry alone. She couldn't afford to rely on anyone and certainly didn't want to put anyone else in danger.

Her pulse raced as her blood boiled, her breath so shallow it burned her throat, with her energy depleting and fast. Where could she go?

She spotted the quads facing the front doors and jumped on the nearest one. She turned the key, gunned the accelerator, and kicked it into gear.

'*Maddison, stop.*' Eric burst into the shed aiming his revolver at her.

BANG.

Maddison screamed, releasing the clutch. The bike lurched through the open doorway and into the stinging rain, scared she was going to flip it. In a blind panic, she sped through puddles, sending muddy water in all directions. But she couldn't stop because the further she ran the safer it would be for everyone.

Forty-eight

'*Maddison?*' Joe rushed through the front doors as Maddison sped past on the quad with the second goon in close pursuit.

Joe aimed his rifle at the goon's back, but with the angle he had he might accidentally shoot Maddison. 'Dammit.' He let out a warning shot, hoping Maddison heard it to spin around.

Both riders flinched, but the two bikes kept racing down the eastern track.

Was Maddison deliberately ignoring him to draw the danger away from his family?

He had to have faith in Maddison. She was much stronger than she realised, hoping she'd use that inner strength to keep going until he could help her.

'Dad, keep him tied up with your shotgun aimed on him at all times,' said Joe over his shoulder. 'Shoot him in the leg if he tries anything.' That man, Tom, was not only taller he was stronger and more streetwise than his baby brother and father combined. 'Greg, get your own gun and back Dad up.'

'Where are you going?' Greg asked, coming from the kitchen.

'I'm going for Maddison.' Joe ran through the rain with rifle in hand toward his ute. Before the driver's door had shut properly, he sped out of the shed.

He flicked on the spotlights that lined the roof of the cab and the bull bar, hoping Maddison would notice them. But visibility was poor through the rain.

His large vehicle slipped sideways in the track's sludge and he punched the cab's roof in anger. 'Bugger.' He'd just remembered Greg had filled both quads, so they were running on full tanks, with twice the amount of fuel Joe had in his ute, with the rain washing away all of their tyre tracks.

Forty-nine

The rain whipped against Maddison's face blurring her vision. Her teeth chattered as the wind chilled her to the bone. She struggled to not only breathe, but to keep a grip on the handles.

Peering over her shoulder, she saw Goon One was gaining on her.

'Not fair.' She desperately searched ahead for a solution. All she saw was the floodplains and nowhere to hide.

She flew over a rise in the dirt road, skidding in the slippery mud. The wheels bounced over the track and she held on for dear life, scared of rolling the beastly bike she'd only learned to ride a few days ago. Yet, the way Eric was gaining on her, he seemed the more experienced rider.

Maddison screamed out her frustrations and lack of skills, gunning the bike harder. She would not surrender.

Then she spied ahead on her left the giant's graveyard. *Dead Man's Gully.*

It was her only hope.

Maddison skidded the bike to a halt, then on her toes, she sprinted, praying the ground would support her.

Light as a feather. I'm light as a feather … Over and over in her mind. Head down, hands in fists, she ran the race of her life straight down the middle of the silent towering headstones. She didn't dare stop, heading for the billabong at the end of the valley, less than two hundred metres away. *Run.*

Fifty

Eric skidded to a stop beside the deserted quad. *Did Maddison run out of fuel?*

He grinned, spotting Maddison running through the rain. Steering the quad off-road, he drove past tall rectangular towers of mud. He'd seen nothing like it. Irregular shaped tombstones scattered around like a giant's cemetery.

He didn't care, returning his focus to the female only fifty metres in front.

He pulled out his handgun, slowed down the bike, and aimed at Maddison's back. 'Too easy.'

Suddenly the ground beneath the front wheels of his bike crumpled. The tyres sank deep into a collapsed crater smashing into the dirt wall, sending Eric hurtling over the handlebars.

'*Augh* …' Tumbling through the air, he slammed hard against a muddy mound. Its solid shell cracked against his chest, and he fell to land on his back with a hard thud.

'YOU BITCH,' he screamed to the grey skies that pelted down relentlessly. He rolled over onto his knees, wiping the dirt off his tender nose.

Maddison kept running for the river ahead. Her blue dress and blonde hair a stark contrast to the grey muddy graveyard. It was like he'd landed on the moon.

Covered in grey mud, Eric searched for his gun. It lay a few metres ahead. Dragging himself up, flicking off the mud from his good shoes, Eric had never wanted to catch anyone as bad as that bitch in the blue dress.

Grinding his teeth, the hatred raged almost uncontrollably inside, he reached over to pick up his gun when the ground beneath him collapsed. He sank down half a metre into the ground.

'What the hell?' He'd fallen into another hole where a cloud of dry dust greeted the rain as he landed on his backside, getting completely caked.

Again, climbing to his knees, he scanned an alien scenery, devoid of life. The crusty soil with its soft edges cracked like ice and fell to expose a widening crater.

Now he understood why Maddison had drawn him here.

'*I'm going to kill you slowly, Maddison.*' Eric yelled out bitterly from his dusty hole.

You'd think, after travelling through three states, being beaten up by bikies, and then being crammed into a crappy plane with a Neanderthal, that he'd give up. Hell. No. Eric was just getting started.

With his trusty pistol in hand, he scrambled out of the hole. Wiping away the rain and grit from his face, he scowled at his shoes, now covered in cakey mud. They were ruined.

With clenched teeth he sprinted down the valley of tombstones when something itched at the skin on his leg. It was if something had become trapped with the mud among his leg hairs.

A blasting flash of pain tore into his lower leg. 'OW.' It burned. But he kept running, grimacing at the pain as he ran for the water twenty metres in front of him.

It was almost serene, with its vibrant green circular leaves offsetting the white lotus flowers. The calm waters reflected the cluster of storm clouds as the pelting rain relented into a hazy drizzle.

The muddy structures gave way to a wide glassy billabong. Or was it a river? And what the hell were those muddy tombstones he'd just run past?

He didn't care. All he wanted was the wench, and it didn't take long to spot her muddy footprints. 'You're mine.'

As he raced after her, something bit into his lower leg. Then another. Then another. 'Ow.' It was as if his legs were under a vicious attack. The pain was sharp, pure white-hot fire.

'What the hell?' He slapped at his legs, back, and shoulders, crying out in agony as if something was eating his flesh.

Lifting his muddied slacks, his shins were covered in white ants with large pincers that crawled all over his bloodied skin. He was being attacked.

Wiping away at them, they bit into his hand, crawled up his wet sleeves. His entire body was on fire.

Beckoning before him was the glistening riverbank.

Eric ran and dove deep beneath the murky, cool surface.

Coming up for air a good five metres from the bank, he stood on the muddy floor, chest deep in water. Facing the riverbank, he splashed at the termites, hoping to drown them.

'*I'm going to kill you for this, Maddison*.' His words echoing over the water. 'Ow, little bastards.' Submerging himself fully, he did a strangulating rain dance to ensure he'd rid himself of all the termites. The cool water was easing the heat of their bites.

But where was Maddison?

There was a flash of blue high on the bank, the colour of Maddison's dress.

Gotcha.

Fifty-one

Maddison had run to the edge of the billabong where her first instinct was to dive in and swim for the other side. But then she remembered the crocodiles. And this was their breeding ground. Joe had warned her the right side of the billabong was home to the mother of all crocodiles, so Maddison turned left and went upstream along the soft grassy bank.

When she skidded to a halt, gasping, with her heart in her throat.

There, in the mud, lay the largest crocodile Maddison had ever seen. It had to be three times her size and four times her width.

It was a massive land-dwelling prehistoric monster. From the gnarly tip of its tail, over the scaly leather ridges along its back, through to the deadly teeth that protruded from its snout. Then its eyes opened, to roll and peer straight at her.

Maddison swallowed the biggest lump in her throat and stepped back slowly.

Her eyes widened at not just the enormous crocodile, but the five other smaller crocodiles that basked beside her, camouflaged by the mud with their snouts facing the water.

They were all bigger than Maddison. And they all stared at her.

It was as if time slowed as the rain stopped, and nothing moved in the thick muggy air.

'I see you, Maddison.' Eric's laughter came from behind her.

Maddison didn't move, staring at her more immediate danger—the six man-eating crocodiles.

Joe had warned her they could tear a massive bull to

pieces in seconds. What would they do with her?

Run for the trees. It was as if Joe was whispering in her ear.

Olive-leafed gum trees waved on the crest to her left, and she ran as one of the smaller crocodiles lunged for her, snapping at her heels.

She jumped, running in a zigzag pattern in pure blind terror. She ran around the smaller trees, leaped over fallen logs that scratched her knees, and headed for the biggest tree she could find.

Heavy thuds, snaps, and snarls followed close behind her as the crocodiles bashed through the brush.

She didn't dare look back.

There before her, shining in the sun's rays, stood a towering solid ghost gum. She leaped high into the air, reaching for a sturdy branch. She then scrambled up its smooth bark that scraped against her skin.

A sound like a crashing truck smashed its way behind her as the ground shook beneath the tree as another large snapping noise came within a hair's breadth of her feet.

Something slammed into the tree's trunk, and the whole tree shook.

She screamed, swinging her legs up, scrambling higher up the slippery trunk. Bark and twigs fell, embedding into her skin, but she still climbed higher.

Below her, a menacing guttural growl echoed. The sinister sound made the hair on her arms rise.

Her grip slipped as she reached for a higher branch. But she didn't dare look down. Joe had told her to keep her focus in her driving lessons, that when in a panic aim for what you want. *Keep your eye on the prize.*

Powered by the memory of his words, she reached for a stronger branch and kept on climbing, higher and higher. Until she straddled a thick branch and hugged the trunk in a secure grip, and only then did she dare look down.

She was at least ten metres high, while three crocodiles stood directly beneath her. *Three!* They'd surrounded the tree trunk, staring up at her with wide-open mouths full of razor-sharp teeth.

She couldn't take it. Her body trembling in terror,

trapped in a tree, she screamed at the horror of the monsters beneath her.

'What are you screaming at, you stupid girl?' It was Eric, only fifty metres away, standing waist deep in the billabong.

'*Help. P-please help*,' Maddison whimpered, tasting the tears that mingled with the sweat streaming down her clammy face. Her heart hammered in her ears, as she tightened her grip on the tree trunk that swayed on the edge of a billabong with three man-eating crocodiles lying in wait beneath her.

'I've got you now.' Eric aimed his pistol at her.

'Oh, no.' Who would kill her first? The crocodiles or the man with the gun?

Either way, she was a dead woman.

Fifty-two

With an evil smile, Eric aimed at the woman with her legs and arms wrapped around the top of a swaying tree trunk and pulled the trigger.

The trigger's click echoed off the water.

But nothing happened.

Only the breeze.

'*Bugger*. Gun's jammed.' Eric shook his gun in frustration.

But he had her, that girl was going nowhere.

'You're a bloody sitting duck, you know that.' Eric laughed as he released the clip from his jammed pistol. His shoes sank into the mud, standing waist deep in the fresh water, it created a cooling effect against the stinging insect bites covering his lower legs and back.

But he was in no rush, not with Maddison stuck up a tree. *Silly girl.*

Now for the finale and his favourite part in this game of revenge.

'It's only fair that you tell me where your uncle's notes are. I want all the photos and stuff.' He had no clue what it was, no one did, only that they'd spotted her bumbling Uncle Bob taking photos, asking questions he shouldn't be asking.

Now Eric was here to collect, then he could go home.

Christ, he'd been dealing with a moronic man-child playing dress-up wannabe cowboy, a woman who baked biscuits like it was the fifties, stuck in this hellhole of heat. But he finally had her.

'Even though you've been a royal pain in the arse,' he

said to Maddison, 'I'm willing to put you out of your misery quickly. And I swear to not hurt that family up there either. But you see …' He checked the ammunition clip, shaking the handgun free of water. 'I still owe you for what your biker boyfriend did to me in Adelaide. Yeah, Match, that was his name. What sort of dumb nickname is that?'

He slipped the clip of bullets into his top pocket and pulled back the gun's barrel slide a few times to empty the automatic chamber. Empty, he squeezed the trigger. It clicked. Loud and clear.

Pulling the loaded ammunition clip from his shirt pocket, he shook it vigorously to remove any excess water.

'So, because of what that biker boyfriend of yours did to my face, I'm returning the favour, unless you tell me where you hid the stuff.' His wicked laugh bounced off the water as he slammed the clip back into the base of the gun.

'Still, it doesn't matter to me if you tell me where you stashed that gear, because I have four days to tear that place apart to find it. I know from personal experience that dead men don't talk.' He frowned at his watery reflection, raking fingers through his hair. The water rippled, distorting the image of Maddison clinging to a tree. 'Mind you, that's what I thought with your uncle being a dead man. But he told, and dead men normally don't tell tales.'

Eric took a step forward to discover he was stuck in the mud with his handmade, Italian leather shoes.

'What did you do to my uncle?' Maddison bellowed out, high in the tree. 'Did you kill my uncle?'

'Yeah, okay, I'll admit it …' Eric flung his arms in the air as if surrendering in waist deep water and laughed. 'Who are you going to tell? Not like anyone is going to hear my confession here in the outback. So, yes, I did it.' Eric tried to wriggle his shoes free from the sludge as he spoke. 'It was an easy kill too. The fat drunk was just sitting in that crappy car of his for ages. I reckoned he was waiting for someone. But I got bored waiting to find out who. To disguise my noise, I used the train pulling into the station as the perfect cover, too. So while Bob was gawking at that train, I opened the door, and bang—Bob's your uncle. Hey, he was your Uncle Bob, too.' Eric laughed. He was such a genius.

'I watched you,' he said, waving the gun at Maddison, 'trying to revive him.'

'To kill me?'

'To see if he'd tell you his dirty little secrets.'

'Why kill him, you monster?'

Good. It's what he was after. She'd shifted past the fear and into rage. And people made mistakes when angry, giving away their secrets through their blind fury. From there they'd become frustrated before sliding into self-defeat, begging him for mercy before their imminent death.

It was all part of the game.

'Because that's what I get paid to do, sweetheart. To fetch and kill for the highest bidder.'

'Who paid you? Cottillard?'

'Listen, my little tree fairy, after all the trouble you've put me through, this job became personal. But I'll be taking all that cash I found in your bag as a personal bonus. You've ruined that bag, you know that. It never matched that frock you wore at the racetrack, which looked better without that hat. Hey, is that where you got all that cash?' Eric struggled to get his shoes free from the mud.

'Go to hell.'

Eric chuckled. He finally had his shoes free and tried to swim forward with his pistol in the air. 'This mud is pathetic. You owe me a new pair of shoes.'

'Hey, arsehole?'

'Now, there's no need to be like that.' Eric was enjoying her fire.

'Didn't you call me a sitting duck before?' She pointed to the water behind him. 'Look at who's the sitting duck now.'

'What?' Eric turned around, his shoes again sinking into the mud.

Silently, over half a dozen floating logs with beady eyes came towards him from all directions.

'What is that?' He'd never seen anything like it.

'Man-eating crocodiles.'

Eric's eyes widened at the immediate danger. He aimed his gun at the encroaching creatures and squeezed the trigger.

Again, his gun jammed.

Fifty-three

'AAAGGGGGHHHH' Eric's screams echoed as monster teeth crushed into bones and flesh.

Maddison winced at the sight of the enormous crocodile lunging at Eric. They'd come from everywhere. All differing sizes in all directions, the scaly slithering water monsters had snuck up on Eric, who was helpless against them.

Even if he'd fired his gun, there weren't enough bullets for the swarm that surrounded him.

She hid her face against the tree's trunk, gripping it tightly. With eyes clenched shut, she wanted to block her ears from Eric's terrifying pain-filled screams amid the splashing water.

It seemed to go on forever.

Then Eric's screams stopped.

But the loud tumbling water thrashing continued.

She peeked through her fingers and gasped.

The water had turned red and Eric's lifeless body was trapped in the jaws of the mother of all crocodiles. His arm torn free and hung from the mouth of another crocodile, his leg and other body parts were savagely torn apart by monsters that came from everywhere.

The water bubbled as their scaly bodies rolled in a feeding frenzy as more prehistoric beasts lunged for pieces. Until Eric's body was dragged underwater, and the waters became still.

Then all those other crocodiles that had missed out, turned and made their way to the tree Maddison clung to, where only one crocodile had remained, steadfastly waiting for her below.

Trapped. She blubbered helplessly.

Stuck in a tree surrounded by blood-thirsty crocodiles with not another living soul around to save her.

Fifty-four

With rifle in hand, Joe traced the muddy footprints to the billabong the colour of blood. His heart went ice cold. 'MADDISON?'

Was he too late?

'JOE, STOP.' Her screams echoed around the billabong. 'I'm over here.'

He could breathe again as relief swamped him at the sight of Maddison frantically waving at him high in a tree.

'I'm trapped and there's more crocodiles coming right behind you.' She pointed to the water's edge.

Joe spun around to face a line of crocodiles coming up fast. 'Damn.'

He raised the rifle and started shooting at them, sending them back to the water.

Downstream, more crocodiles were clambering up the muddy banks towards Maddison, where one stumpy beast had her trapped.

Joe kept shooting.

Yet the beasts were out of control. The larger animals had turned on their own kind and were attacking the smaller crocodiles, ripping at them in a ferocious frenzy in the billabong. Joe didn't have enough bullets to pierce the cannibals' tough hides, who were now ignoring the noise of his gun.

'Hang tight, I'll get the ute.' He sprinted back down the track to his ute, parked nearby.

Using its large front bull bar, he cleared a track through the scrub on the far side of the valley of termites. He pushed his way through the trees, stopping only to hook a wire cable around a group of strong sturdy tree trunks. Then the diesel engine roared as he flew over the ridge where crocodiles thrashed their mighty tails to scramble out of his way.

Mud flew as his beefy ute tyres sank into the sludge. He pulled up directly beneath the tree and slammed his hand on the horn. BEEEEEP in a long deafening stream, his air horn bellowed through the air.

It sent every man-eating predator scurrying to the water.

Joe hung out the driver's window and took a few pot-shots with his rifle while keeping his other hand on the horn.

Above him, Maddison covered her ears in the tree.

Scrambling onto the back tray, then onto the roof of his high-clearance four-wheel drive, he kept his rifle aimed at the billabong that still ran red. The banks were clear of crocodiles, only leaving the slide marks in the mud as a clear sign of their escape.

'You can come down now.' He craned his neck to watch Maddison. Leaves and twigs fell as she climbed down trembling limbs. It seemed to take forever.

Joe reached for her ankle, putting his body beneath it to help her climb down. Her legs were covered in scratches as he grabbed her hips.

'I've got you.' He pulled her free from the tree to the roof of his ute, then wrapped his arms around her frail figure and breathed her all in, holding her tight. 'You're safe now. I've got you.'

'Thank you,' she muttered again and again.

A slight breeze returned. A flock of magpie geese honked as they flew overhead, as cicadas and crickets began their chorus warning of more rain.

Finally, the couple were able to breathe normally, and her all-over body trembles had subsided.

'Are you okay?' He winced at her scraped inner arms and torn dress.

'Thanks to you, I'm okay.'

Swamped with relief, he kissed her forehead, wrapping his arms securely around her.

'I'm assuming your goon ended up in the billabong?' Joe

glanced back at the still waters now reflecting the stormy clouds.

'Yeah. The termites attacked him and he went into the water to wash them off. He admitted to murdering my uncle before the crocodiles got him.'

'Speaking of crocs, we'd better move before they get game again.' He spotted the ripples running against the current, a sure sign of the beasts beneath.

He helped Maddison climb into the cab and followed closely behind, then put the ute into gear and backed out. But the tyres slipped on the soggy ground and spun in the mud.

'We're stuck?' Maddison cried out with fear flaring in her eyes.

'I expected to get bogged. Remember, this is my backyard.' Joe grinned, flicking the switch on the dash and a loud whining whirling noise began from the back of the ute.

'What's that?'

'My winch.'

'Don't you have one on the front?'

'And back.' Joe liked his gadgets. The tourists only saw them as toys, but to him they were tools of the trade.

There was a hard tug from the back of the ute and slowly they were dragged backwards from the mud to the safety of solid ground.

Joe unhooked the winch cable from the trees, and from behind the seat he scratched around for an old towel and wrapped it around Maddison's shoulders. 'You're safe now.' He wiped the wet hair free from her face.

'Thank you.' A deep gratitude flooded her eyes.

'I'd do anything for you, Maddison,' he said, holding her against his chest. 'I thought I'd lost you when I saw the blood in the billabong. I thought you were dead.'

'I remembered what you told me, how to run from them, find a tree, everything. It's because of you I'm still alive.'

'That's twice I've had to rescue you, and I'll keep rescuing you to keep you safe, because I love you, Maddison.' He lifted her chin so their eyes met. 'I'm not expecting you to say anything, but I almost lost you, so I have to say it ...' He took a deep breath, and the words spilled so easily, filled with an overwhelming emotion that came from his soul. 'I love you, Maddison. I'm in love with you.' Admitting it for the first time in his life to anyone. He pressed his lips to hers, relieved she was safe and in his arms again. But for how long?

Fifty-five

Among the teacups and assorted plates of biscuits and sandwiches lay a loaded shotgun. Earl, Glenda, and Greg sat at one end of the wooden kitchen table. At the other end, bound tightly at the wrists and ankles, sat Tom.

The kitchen clock ticked, the fridge motor whirled, as Greg's boot soles tapped on the floor.

There was a splash of tyres churning through puddles, with the rumble of an engine pulling up. It was Joe's ute.

Both Greg and Glenda rose from their seats.

'Wait,' commanded Earl, putting his hand on the shotgun's sturdy stock handle. 'Wait and see who it is.'

The front screen door opened and a set of familiar sturdy boot steps tromped inside.

Glenda smiled and nodded at her husband. Greg's chair legs scraped across the floor as he headed for the door with his own rifle.

'Dad? Mum? You right?' With the rifle in one hand, Joe led Maddison into the kitchen.

'We're good. You?' Earl replied, keeping his eye on Tom.

Joe patted his baby brother's tight shoulders where worry hung heavy in the lad's eyes. 'You good, bro?'

'Yeah, I'm cool. What happened to you?' Greg pointed at Joe's mud-covered jeans.

Glenda swamped Joe with a hug around the waist. 'You're safe. Oh, Maddison, you look a fright, let me get you a towel, dear.' She rushed to the nearby laundry basket and handed out thick towels.

Joe helped wrap the towel around Maddison. Her lips

were trembling, her skin cold and scratched, her hair wet and dress torn. 'We should get you into a hot shower.'

'In a minute,' she said, wrapping herself tighter in the towel. Then she stopped and stared at the far end of the table.

'Where's Eric?' asked the stranger intruding in their space at the table.

Joe gritted his teeth and stormed over to Tom with white-hot hatred pumping through his veins. With clenched right fist, he swung putting everything into the almighty punch, connecting with Tom's face.

It sent Tom hurtling backwards on the chair to land with a heavy thud.

'*Are you going to try to kill Maddison, too? JUST like your mate tried to kill her?!*' Joe was livid.

His family gasped, standing around the table staring down at Tom on the floor.

'NO,' cried Tom, still tied to the chair. 'I don't do that.'

'Bull!' Joe pulled out Tom's handgun waved it in Tom's face. 'Carry this for fun, do we?'

'It's blanks. Check the clip yourself, you'll find it's nothing but blanks,' pleaded Tom. 'I swear, I would never hurt you and your family. I don't do that.'

Joe didn't move with his finger on the trigger.

'Take a look, son,' said Earl, coming up beside Joe with the shotgun.

Joe unloaded the handgun, spilling the bullets onto the table.

Earl picked one up and checked the end. 'He's right, it's got a crimped hollow point to allow the gas to escape coz there's no ammunition cartridge. It's similar to what we use to scare the birds when we're planting seed.'

'Why are you here?' Joe asked Tom.

'For Maddison.'

'*Wrong answer!*' Joe dragged Tom up by the shirtfront, chair and all, and slammed his fist into Tom's face again.

'Joe, no,' cried out Glenda. 'Earl, do something.'

'Why are you after Maddison?' Joe snarled, mere millimetres from Tom's face.

'Because she's got something that the boss wants.'

'What's that?'

Tom shook his head. 'They never told me. The boss only spoke to Eric, and that's all Eric told me.'

'Who is Eric?' Earl asked, standing beside Joe.

'The bloke I came out here with. Where is he?'

'Dead!' Joe dropped the bulky seated Tom flat to the floor again.

'How?' Greg asked.

'*Can we all please calm down?*' Glenda's raised voice made everyone stop and stare at her. 'Thank you. Now, I'm sure we all have the same questions. So as to not repeat ourselves, can we all please take a seat and behave like civilised human beings? And please, boys, let's get Tom off the floor?'

Joe, Earl and Greg pulled Tom into an upright position.

'Thanks,' mumbled Tom, using his shoulder to wipe at the blood trickling from the side of his mouth. 'You pack quite a punch, mate.'

Joe grunted, pulling his clenched fist back.

Tom winced, bracing himself for it.

'Stop, Joe.' Maddison cupped her small hands around Joe's fist. 'Tom can't go anywhere, and he knows it.'

Joe stepped back, bringing Maddison with him to take a seat. He didn't want her anywhere near the cretin at the other end of the table.

She stopped and turned to face Tom. 'Your mate, Eric, got eaten by crocodiles. They tore his limbs apart.'

'And we can do it to you, too, and no one will ever know.' Joe was so tempted to drag this guy into the back of his ute to take a one-way tour of the Territory he'd never forget. This man, at the end of the family table, had threatened everyone in his home and Joe would do anything to protect his family, which included Maddison.

Tom's Adam's apple bobbed up and down as he licked his swollen lips.

'Take a seat, son.' Earl rested his shotgun with a loud thud on the wooden table, aiming the barrel at Tom.

Greg sat gingerly in his chair with his own rifle resting on the nearby freezer, pointed in the same direction.

Maddison grabbed Joe's hand and pulled him further away, making him take a seat at the distant end of the table where he leaned his rifle against his chair.

Glenda flicked on the kettle, setting out afternoon tea on the table, as a calm sense of order soon returned to the room. 'Here, dear, this'll warm you up.' She passed a steaming cup of tea to Maddison, then one for Joe.

Joe left his to cool, watching Tom at the end of the table.

'What do you want me to do?' Tom asked the room.

Joe looked to Maddison for that answer.

Fifty-six

Maddison cradled her teacup for the warmth, then peeked through the steam to Goon Two, Tom, tied to the kitchen chair at the other end of the table. He was huge, with a big bald head, a black eye and a fat top lip. 'You're going to tell us everything you know.'

'Starting with how long you've been following Maddison,' Joe demanded with bitter anger.

'The day after her uncle …' Tom hesitated.

'Was *murdered*,' finished Joe.

Glenda gasped, slapping a hand to her chest; Greg and Earl stared at Maddison in wide-eyed surprise.

Maddison plonked down her teacup and inhaled so deeply her nostrils pinched, trying to control her own hatred. 'Were you there at the train station when Eric shot my uncle in the chest?'

The realisation that she'd only been mere metres from the murderer while she was trying to save her uncle all those weeks ago, sent fresh tears to sting her eyes.

Joe slung his arm around her shoulders and gave her a gentle squeeze. She shouldn't rely on him, but couldn't help but lean into his body heat for support.

'Answer the question,' demanded Joe, his voice deep and edgy.

'I got called to pick up Eric from the car park at Croydon train station, that's all. I'd only learned about Bob's death from the papers the next day. I'm not hired for killing, see. I'm a truck driver who moonlights as a bouncer and as a driver for Eric now and again.'

'How long have you been following Maddison?'

'We were originally meant to get into Maddison's apartment to find her uncle's notes and get out. That was it, see. We were told to keep you out of it because you were the detectives' favourite barmaid.'

'My word.' Glenda raised her eyebrows as she sipped from her teacup.

'We watched your place for days, waiting to get inside. But you never left,' explained Tom. 'Until the detectives told us you were going to your uncle's funeral, so we watched you walk down the street, then we went inside.'

Maddison swallowed air at the thought they'd been following her that long. 'How did you get in?'

'Eric had the keys he'd taken from your uncle.'

'You destroyed my place!'

'I'm sorry. I tried not to break anything, but Eric went on some crazed frenzy searching the place.'

'What were you searching for?'

'Nobody could say, exactly. They said notes, a camera, and a phone. But we found nothing of Bob's, so we were told to watch Maddison, hoping she'd lead us to it.' Tom faced Maddison with sad eyes. 'The next morning, we followed you to the Flemington Racetrack. You looked so pretty.'

'Oi.' Joe snarled.

Tom dropped his head in submission. 'And that's where we lost you, see.'

'How did you know I went to Adelaide?' Maddison asked.

'Eric called that cop again. You see, Eric reckons they'd bugged your phone and heard that you were heading to Sydney. So we drove straight to the airport, where Eric spotted you boarding the plane for Adelaide. All I know is, Eric said they had someone tailing you in Adelaide until we caught the next flight out.'

'What were you planning to do to me?' It was the toughest question she'd ever asked, considering in her old world she rarely spoke out of turn. Now, here she was, interrogating a man tied to a chair. With Glenda and Greg reaching for the biscuits on the table like people eating popcorn at the movies.

Tom tried to shrug. 'Eric was trying to find you at the hotel. But when you set that fire alarm off and escaped out the back door of that hotel into the alley, we—'

'Chased me down by car.' Maddison frowned.

Joe shifted his boots under the table as if ready to attack Tom.

Glenda, Earl, and Greg sat back, raising their eyebrows at Maddison, then swivelled their heads back to Tom like spectators at the Australian Open tennis tournament.

'What happened then, dear?' Glenda asked, with Greg nodding beside her.

'Eric chased Maddison into that bikers' bar,' replied Tom. 'We had to shoot our way out, because we were getting our arses kicked by that gang. And that's when we saw you on the back of that Harley. It was a sweet ride,' said Tom with a nod. 'That bloke Match, sure could handle that thing.'

Joe scowled.

Glenda sipped on her empty cup. The china clinked, soon followed by a glug-glug from the teapot. 'Anyone else care for a refill?'

Greg and Earl pushed their empty cups forward.

Maddison took the chance to sip on hers, which was still warm. This conversation and the calmness of afternoon tea seemed so surreal, with Glenda getting a bottle of water and a straw for Tom. 'Please, do go on, dear.'

'After we'd lost you on that bloke's bike, Eric called up that copper with Match's plate details and he gave us a couple of addresses. They were all fake, see. So, the next morning, we parked out front of their clubhouse waiting for that bloke to show up.'

'Did he?' She swallowed, fearing for Mitch's safety.

Tom nodded. 'See, we reckoned that bloke must've put you on that small plane to come out here, then rode straight over to the clubhouse to confront us.'

'What did Mitch do?'

'He punched the ever-living daylights out of Eric. He flattened Eric's nose, split his lip, and gave him two black eyes, with the entire gang rushing out to back him up. We were lucky to get out of there alive.'

'How did you get out, dear?' Glenda asked with a biscuit

in hand.

'Um ...' Tom sniffed, dropping his head he muttered into his chest, 'I used the semi-automatic machine gun we kept in the boot of the car.'

Glenda gasped in horror.

'I didn't shoot anyone. Swear it. I didn't touch anyone except to drag Eric out, promising their president we'd never go back.'

'What happened next?' Glenda asked Tom, passing the plate of biscuits out to everyone.

'Well, once Eric got out of the hospital, we checked into a hotel room.'

'Did Mitch really do that much damage?' Maddison asked Tom.

'Yeah, they had to re-break and splint Eric's nose. That Match fella almost packs a punch as hard as your boyfriend here does.'

Joe's frown only deepened.

'That was a compliment there, mate. Don't mean to disrespect you none, see.'

'Sure, no disrespect. Two men coming to kill one woman in my family's home!' Joe leaned forward as if to leap across the table to strangle Tom.

'Shh ...' Maddison rubbed his large hand to calm them both down. 'Tom, how did you find out I was here?'

'That plane crash. Eric had a hunch. Hey, that was clever how your name was different. Those coppers never picked up on it in Melbourne.'

'What is your name, dear?' Glenda stared at Maddison with half-chewed biscuit in hand. Greg and Earl doing the same.

'It's Maddison,' said Joe sternly. 'Motor reg made a mistake mixing up her name order when Maddison renewed her licence. Her name is Maddison Janice Farley, not Janice Maddison Fraley.'

'Typical of motor reg to cock something up like that,' mumbled Earl matter-of-factly.

'So, you don't go by your middle name?' Greg asked.

'No, Janice is my middle name, and it's also my mother's name.' Maddison squirmed in her chair to face the seated family. 'I'm so sorry if —'

'Before anyone else jumps to any conclusions,' butted in Joe, 'Maddison has always told us the truth, but not all of it, to try and protect us from all of this.' He grabbed her hand, giving it a reassuring squeeze.

'Aren't you here for a holiday?' Greg asked.

'Maddison needed to escape from these guys, and it was purely by chance she ended up here,' replied Joe.

'What were they after?' Earl asked. 'Is it that the thing you've been writing?'

Maddison nodded, filled with a guilt-laden misery for endangering Joe's family like this. But she had to keep pushing forward, and asked Tom, 'Why am I being hunted?'

Tom shuffled in his seat. 'Um, coz they'd spotted your uncle taking photos of the boss with some people he shouldn't be seen with. See, I'd been told your uncle's got this reputation as a reporter known to ruin people's lives with the power of the pen. They weren't gonna take any chances.'

'So that's why you warned the Thurstons about the press damaging people's reputations?' Earl said to Maddison.

'Who are the Thurstons?' Tom asked.

'No one you need to worry about,' replied Joe sternly. 'You don't get to ask the questions around here.'

'Fair enough, mate. I'm cooperating, see.' Tom lowered his head. 'Ask me anything.'

'Fine. When did you realise I'd found my uncle's stuff?' Maddison asked.

'At first, we weren't sure you had anything. Those Melbourne detectives thought the same. See, it was only when you ran to Adelaide, we were sure you'd collected something from the racetrack.'

'Maddison's been here for over a week. What took you so long to show up?' Joe asked.

'We had to wait for the police reports to verify the names. Then we got told to wait for the next plane, so you didn't run again. They said you were flooded in and couldn't go anywhere. While we've been waiting, I had a holiday in Adelaide getting ready to visit Elleron Downs while Eric's been recovering from his injuries. I've always wanted to visit a cattle station. I even got new gear for this trip. See?' Tom nodded down at his new cowboy outfit.

'What happened to the real Jonathon and Christian?' Glenda asked.

'They got an all-expenses paid holiday elsewhere and were told that you'd shut down because of the plane crash and poor weather. I asked Eric the same question.'

'So, who do you work for?' Earl asked.

Tom hesitated, his Adam's apple bobbing up and down.

'Antonio Cottillard,' replied Maddison, and Tom nodded at her.

'Who?' Earl, Greg and Glenda asked Tom.

'Mr Cottillard,' replied Tom, 'builds high-rise office buildings and residential apartments around Melbourne.'

'A man who pays you to chase women around the country where that croc-bait mate of yours—' Joe rose from his chair.

'I'm sorry. I didn't know Eric was going to do that. See, all I got told was we were coming out here to search for the gear, then we'd fly back. That's it. But Eric took it personally after he got his face punched in from her biker boyfriend, see. Eric wanted his revenge on Maddison, that's Eric he's—'

'Spread out across the river system being digested by a bask of crocodiles. It's where you'll end up if you're not careful.'

'Joe, please,' said Maddison, pulling him back. 'Let Tom speak.'

Both men sat back as Glenda and Greg sipped on their tea, while Earl drummed his fingers on the shotgun handle.

'Eric told me little of his plans,' Tom said to the table, 'and you don't discuss murder with anyone. Eric only told me that we had four days to find the stuff.'

'And what about us?' Greg sat higher, putting a protective hand on his mother's shoulder.

Tom shrugged again. 'I thought his plan was that Maddison wouldn't recognise us.'

'Sounds like this Eric didn't plan too much,' said Earl.

'That's Eric, see. He'd let his temper interfere with common sense,' replied Tom candidly. 'Did Eric really get attacked by crocodiles?'

Maddison nodded.

'Where?' Greg asked.

'Dead Man's Gully,' replied Joe.

'What were you doing there?' Glenda asked with wide eyes.

A shiver squirreled along Maddison's spine as she explained. 'The termites attacked Eric, and he dove straight into the water to get away from their bites.'

'Bloody idiot,' murmured Earl. 'All of them crocs just sitting in that billabong.'

'We never did explain the dangers of the waterways to Eric, did we dear?' Glenda said to her husband.

'No, luv, we didn't.' Earl then asked Tom, 'Did your mate know anything about crocodiles?'

'Doubt it.'

'Well, that's where I found Maddison, hanging high in this tree, with half a dozen crocs surrounding its trunk, and the billabong's water the colour of blood,' said Joe sternly to Tom. 'They'd torn your mate's limbs apart and were fighting for scraps in a feeding frenzy.'

'I'm sorry you had to see that, Maddison,' said Earl. 'Wild crocodiles when they get into that feeding frenzy nothing stops them, not even gunfire. They'll attack everything that moves, and each other. It's that fight for survival, they're known for it.'

After a moment of silence, Tom asked, 'What happens now?'

They all looked at each other, unsure.

'You said four days,' replied Maddison.

Tom nodded his bald head.

'When are you expected to contact your boss?'

'When we land back in Adelaide.'

'How long have you been working for Antonio Cottillard?'

'Almost a year. I used to work at a nightclub Eric visited all the time. See, that's how we met, I saved Eric from getting his head punched in. I got the job through Eric to drive Mr Cottillard's trucks.'

'From where?' Maddison asked, slowly approaching Tom.

'From the docks to some warehouses Mr Cottillard owned.'

'What were you carrying?'

'Sea containers unloaded off the cargo ships.'

'Do you remember the names of those ships?'

'Not really. See, they came from up north and travelled down the east coast.'

'Do you remember where those warehouses are, where you delivered those containers?'

Tom gave a slow nod.

'If I were to give you a map, could you point it out?'

Tom shrugged.

'Stay there. I'll be back in a second.' She ran for the library, soon returning with the Melbourne Street directory, flicking through the pages. She slammed it down in front of Tom to point at the area of the main shipping docks. 'Where on this map are those sheds?'

'Um ...'

Glenda rummaged through the kitchen draws and pulled out a pencil. 'You can use this, dear.'

'I'll do it, Mum.' Greg took the pencil and held it out to Tom to bite down between his teeth as Joe stood protectively beside Maddison.

'There,' Tom muttered through his teeth, holding the pencil.

'That's the quarantine yards,' said Maddison. 'The legitimate side of Cottillard's business. Are there any other sheds that Mr Cottillard used?'

'A couple for special deliveries, I guess.'

'Can you show me where? Please? It'll help your situation if you cooperate.'

'I want to cooperate.' Tom gazed up at her with sad eyes. 'I swear, I was never going to hurt you or anyone here. See, I've never hit a woman. Me Nan would kill me if I did.'

'Okay, so where are these other warehouses?' Maddison tapped at the street directory.

'They were southbound.'

Maddison turned the page and waited, rubbing her fingertips together.

Tom leaned over the street directory with the pencil

poised between his teeth. 'There.' He drew an awkward circle on the street map and then dropped the pencil.

Maddison looked over his shoulder with Joe right beside her.

'We'd leave them sea containers in the middle of the night in these deserted warehouses. Someone would meet us to unclip the trailers. See, we never got out of the trucks, only stopping for a few minutes at a time. It was easy money, a thousand bucks for an hour's work.'

'How many sea containers did you deliver there?' Maddison asked.

'One. Occasionally two. Once we had five containers to deliver in broad daylight.'

'How often do you do these deliveries?'

'Depends. See, in the beginning it was once or twice a month, then he expanded, I guess.'

'To how many more?' Maddison asked Tom.

'Once a week, a couple of containers would get delivered to these warehouses, day or night. I never saw what was in them?'

'Weren't you at all curious at what was inside?'

'Nah, I guessed they were smuggling something. They weren't heavy, see, they weighed like they were empty.'

'Those containers were filled with people, Tom.' Maddison dropped heavily into a nearby chair, putting her at eye level with Tom. 'You were part of Cottillard's people-smuggling racket, where he sells those poor souls as slaves.'

'*Nooo.*' Tom's face crinkled up in horror.

'Is that true?' Earl asked with a deep frown.

'This Cottillard's making billions out of it,' butted in Joe, bitterly.

'No wonder they want you dead, Maddison,' said Greg, 'especially if this ever got out …'

'Which means everyone here is in danger. I have to leave.' Maddison stood and faced the four family members. 'I'm so sorry to have done this to all of you. I honestly didn't know what I had until after I'd arrived.'

'It's okay, dear.' Glenda came around the table to hug Maddison. 'That's what families do: we stick together. We can sort this situation out together.'

'But I can't risk any of you getting involved.' Maddison then faced Tom. 'Will your boss keep looking for me anywhere else?'

'No. They know Eric and I are out here with you.'

'Are you meant to check in with anyone?'

'No. Not until we return to Adelaide. See, we were told to not leave any phone records, nothing.'

'Good. I have a four-day window to get out of here and finish this. I won't put any more people in danger.'

'Where do you want to go?' Joe asked in a rumbling low tone.

Her heart plummeted at the thought of leaving Joe, but she had to. 'How long will it take for me to drive to Alice Springs?'

'Most of the roads are closed because of wet season flooding.'

'There has to be a way out.'

Joe took her hands and again asked, 'Where do you need to go?'

'Sydney. If I can get to Alice Springs, I'll try and hitch, or rent a car from there. I can't take any of the major airlines in case they're still watching.'

'I'll take you.'

'How?'

'By chopper,' said Joe with a glimmer in his blue eyes.

'Joe's got his pilot's licence,' said Greg with his chin up and chest out.

'You do?' Maddison arched her eyebrows at the man who was so near perfect.

'In the top shed we've got a short-range helicopter we use for the musters,' Joe explained. 'We may need to make a few fuel-stops on the way to Alice. There, I've got some mates that'll get us into Queensland where we can sneak a ride into New South Wales.' He grabbed her hand and gave it a tug. 'Come on, let's pack our gear. Dad, can you and Greg get the chopper ready?'

Maddison pulled Joe to a standstill. 'You're coming right back, aren't you? Once you've dropped me off in Alice Springs.'

'I'm not letting you out of my sight, not until we sort this whole thing out.'

'But, what about your family? And Tom?' She didn't want to put Joe at risk, he'd done too much already.

'Tom won't be a hassle, dear,' replied Glenda.

'Joe's right, Maddison. You've only got four days to get this sorted out.' Greg, raced for the door. 'I'll grab the ute, Dad, and load up the fuel.'

'I'll sort out some food for the trip, while you two get ready,' said Glenda.

'You'll want to get a wriggle on there, son,' said Earl, grabbing his wide-brimmed hat off the hook. 'I wouldn't want you flying in the dark.'

'But—' Maddison stood, unsure.

'I'd rather Joe joined you, dear. To keep you safe,' said Glenda.

'Not wrong there, luv. Joe will be a pain in the posterior worrying about Maddison all the time. He'll be no good for work distracted like that,' said Earl, stepping out the back door. 'Son, I'll see you up at the chopper. Tom, behave, or my wife will shoot you. She's a better shot than all of us combined.'

'And I'm not giving you a choice, Maddison. You don't need to do this alone, so I'm sticking with you until this is over.' Joe led her through the doorway to face the hall. 'Now, have a shower. Pack light, there's not much room. You've got ten minutes if we're going to make it to Alice before sunset.'

Maddison ran for her room to pack for Sydney, a place she was supposed to fly to in the beginning. But she hated to fly.

Fifty-seven

ALICE SPRINGS, NORTHERN TERRITORY

Slashes of a rich crimson colour stretched across an endless horizon, with shadows deepening over the red desert when Joe, with Maddison, flew the small muster helicopter into Alice Springs. With the rocky ranges in the distance, they hovered over a large junkyard full of old cars and aeroplanes. A large stretch of tarmac like a wide road, ran through the centre, its edge disappearing into the desert's dust.

Joe landed the helicopter beside a large, enclosed hangar.

'Where are we?' Maddison tried to shake the tremors out of her hands and to control her heartbeat. Even though Joe had reassured her, it had been both an inspirational and terrifying flight.

Joe had flown above winding rivers and floodplains as wide as an inland sea, as distant heavy clouds cast rainbows to curve within the sky. They'd flown over cattle and wallowing water buffaloes. Basks of crocodiles sun-baked among the incredible birdlife that filled the panoramic landscape, untouched by man. The expansive Northern Territory outback was spectacular, mesmerising Maddison to briefly forget her fear of flying.

'Welcome to Alice Springs. This is Bill and Ben's place. They're retired air force veterans.' Joe helped Maddison unclip her seatbelt.

'Is this normal to show up on someone's doorstep and park your helicopter in their yard like parking a car in a friend's driveway?'

'Kind of.' Joe chuckled, passing her the red bag. 'These guys will look after the chopper until we return.'

We? Return? 'What is this place?' It looked like a junkyard for vintage cars.

'This was an old air force base. Bill and Ben own it now. And …' He led her around the corner, opened a smaller door into the enormous hangar and pointed. 'These guys have planes.'

Maddison's jaw dropped at the assorted aeroplanes that filled the enclosed hangar. It was as if she had walked into a museum full of military aircraft.

'BILL? BEN? You around?' Joe let rip an ear-splitting whistle.

'Come in, but only if you're good looking.' An elderly male voice carried from the far side of the massive hangar.

'That's your cue, honey.' Joe gave her hand a squeeze. 'Come on, they're going to love you.' He led Maddison towards the office. 'G'day you lot.'

Elderly identical twins rose from their matching recliners to heartily shake Joe's hand with the warm welcoming of long-time friends.

'Maddison, this is Bill and that is Ben.'

'Hi.' How could Joe tell the difference? Both men had the same white hair that matched their eyebrows, and sunburnt faces. Wearing shorts, thongs, and singlets. They had wide smiles, rosy cheeks, and light blue eyes that shone brighter than Christmas tree lights. And they seemed incredibly jolly.

'Welcome, Maddison.' Bill took a bow to gently kiss the back of her hand.

Maddison giggled in surprise. 'No one's done that before.'

'It's new for me too. I've always wanted to do it, though.'

'My turn. Don't hog the limelight.' Ben jostled with Bill like boys in the schoolyard to shake Maddison's hand. 'To what do we owe the absolute pleasure of your visit, young lady?'

'We're hoping you'll fly us to Charleville,' said Joe.

'I wasn't talking to you,' said Ben, winking at Maddison. 'My dear, sweet, young lady, are you requiring transportation to Charleville?'

'Yes, please.'

'If you care to leave that troublemaker here, we'll gladly escort you.' Bill pointed to Joe.

'Oi, wait up, you two.' Joe stepped in close beside Maddison. 'I'm going with the lady, and we need a lift as soon as you can muster it.'

'I'll pay you in cash.' Maddison gripped her ruined red bag.

'And if you treat the lady right, she might even give you a tip for your troubles.'

'What sort of tip?' Bill asked, his brother Ben nodding beside him. 'Just cover our expenses and some beer money and we'll be square.'

'And a kiss on the cheek from a beautiful woman,' said Ben with his white eyebrows bobbing up and down.

'Oh, pick me.' Bill mirrored his brother's smile.

'You two, behave.' Joe protectively wrapped his arm around Maddison.

'We are,' the brothers sung in chorus.

'So, um, how soon can we leave?' After all, Maddison was on a tight deadline.

'Why don't you wait in our five-star airport lounge facilities, kept specifically for our VIP guests, while we go get ready. Feel free to use the amenities we have available.' Bill pointed to the old couch and mismatched wooden chairs spread around a square piece of carpet. Their coffee table was made from wooden crates, piled with newspapers. They even had a gramophone next to a wide-screen TV.

'Let's take the Little Ripper,' Ben said to his brother. 'She's ready to roll, and we've been looking for the perfect excuse to air out her dust.'

'Oh, good choice. The Little Ripper will be perfect for such an expedition.'

'How little a plane are we talking about?' Maddison swallowed down the fear clawing up her chest.

'You're not scared of flying, are you? You just arrived in

a helicopter,' barked out Bill.

'Maddison was in that plane crash out near home the other week,' explained Joe.

The twins cringed and faced Maddison, empathy worn in their eyes.

'We won't scare you none, Miss, and that's a promise.' Ben tenderly patted her shoulder. 'We won't be going in anything that small.'

'What are we flying in?' Maddison wiped her clammy palms down Greg's borrowed jeans.

'Our Little Ripper.' The twins pointed to a massive gunmetal grey cargo plane parked beside the hangar doors.

'Isn't she a beauty?' The brothers stared at the plane like fathers fawning over a newborn baby in the hospital. 'We could fly all the way to Singapore in the Little Ripper.'

'What about Sydney?' What about the nearest train station? *No wait, cameras.*

The twins winced, mumbling to themselves.

She looked to Joe. 'Why can't they go to Sydney?' Sydney was the last place she wanted to go, but she had no choice.

'Bill and Ben aren't allowed to enter major air space. They can only fly regionally.'

'Why?' Should she dare get into a vintage plane with these men? Did her ticket come with a parachute, or a bottle of scotch and a handful of sleeping pills? What was Joe thinking?

'Bill and Ben were part of the Royal Australian Air Force Roulettes. And, they upset the main tower at Sydney airport with their fly-bys—'

'We like to call it aeronautical acrobatics,' interjected Bill, with Ben lifting his chin in a nod.

'They scared the daylights out of the radio controllers while breaking a stack of airstrip rules.'

'You're banned from Sydney?' Maddison gawked at the twins who looked like humble grandfathers that would save puppies from pet shops.

Bill shrugged, Ben grinned, as Joe said, 'And Adelaide, Brisbane, Melbourne, and Perth.'

'We're good for Hobart and the mob in Darwin,' said Ben with Bill nodding.

'You won't do any tricks while I'm in the plane, will you?'

Fifty-eight

CHARLEVILLE, QUEENSLAND

As stars sparkled in the night sky, the humming drone of the ex-military cargo plane left Northern Territory airspace and flew into Queensland with the twins, Ben and Bill, manning the cockpit.

Inside, long bench seats ran along the plane's inner walls, where Joe stretched out with his head resting on Maddison's lap.

Gently stroking Joe's dark brown hair, Maddison asked, 'How long have you had your pilot's licence?'

'Over fifteen years. Dad has one too. Mum can fly, but she's gets too nervous to do the test.' Joe sighed. 'We used to have our own plane at the station, but we sold it with a heap of other equipment to pay the bills. We kept the helicopter purely for the musters, and with the tourists coming in and out all the time, we don't need a plane. When we're done playing tour guides, we'll get another one. We'll need it then, and Greg can get his pilot's licence.' Joe sat up, putting his arm around her slender shoulders. 'Out here, especially when the wet season floods our roads, a plane is like a car. Most stations have airstrips on them, and the smaller air charter companies are like taxis for outback communities.'

'Do you miss it? The flying?'

'Sometimes.'

'You like living on the station?'

'After seeing what the rest of the country offers, I

wouldn't want to live anywhere else. Elleron Downs is home.' He gently tucked her hair behind her ear. 'What about you? Where is home for you?'

Bill from the cockpit interrupted them. 'We're coming in to land. Please strap on your seatbelts, put your tray tables in the upright position and have all chairs facing forward.'

'And we thank you for flying with Bill and Ben's Airways,' the brothers chorused as if they were in some cheesy television commercial.

They landed softly at the small Charleville regional airport at midnight. The night air was crisp and free from humidity as Maddison climbed out of the cargo plane.

Bill and Ben slung canvas bags over their shoulders, in matching pilot's uniforms, their shiny shoes clapped along the tarmac. They left the military cargo plane in the dark and headed for the fence line where a single streetlight shone at the main gates, which led to a dark bitumen road.

'Where do we go from here?' Maddison asked Joe as they waited by the gates, without a phone signal or a car in sight. They could have been anywhere.

'We've got a car coming, milady.' Bill grinned, giving her a sweeping bow. 'We radioed a mate earlier.'

'Gawd, I hope she cleaned her car out.' Ben said to his twin.

'She'll be right, 'I'll take the shirt off me back for the lady to sit on, if need be.'

'And scare her blind with your figure.'

They paused at the sound of music.

'Sounds like Stella's coming.' Bill and Ben stared down the dark road where rock music bellowed in the distance.

A set of flickering headlights approached, belonging to an orange kombi van, spluttering and coughing, with white smoke spewing out the back. It leaned sideways as it steered around the corner with the tyres screeching and the stereo music blaring. Its horn tooted in short bursts.

'*G'day, fellas*,' yelled the driver over the music. She was wearing a straw hat in the middle of the night, madly waving at them through the driver's window.

'*Stella.*' The twins jovially waved at the woman doing circles around them in her kombi.

The vintage van screeched to a halt. Its engine putted and then sighed in relief before it chugged to a stop.

Bursting free from the front seat, her nose ring glinting in the streetlight, Stella flicked her long hair plaits over her shoulder. She hoisted up her multi-coloured, many-layered skirt and clomped over to them, showing off her leather boots and odd pair of long socks. Stella was wearing every colour of the rainbow with a warm smile and deep tan, looking like she'd time-travelled from a sixties hippy garden.

Stella launched herself with wide arms to hug both Bill and Ben, tucking one man under each arm. 'How ya doin', fellas? It's been a long time between beers, eh?'

'We can make up for it tonight,' replied Bill. 'Have you finished work?'

'Yep, all done and dusted. I've got no more buns in the oven, so it's brekkie beers for me. Who've we got 'ere, eh?'

'Joe and Maddison, this is our mate, Stella,' said Bill. 'She's the local baker.'

'Whoo-wee, well aren't you a handsome bugger.' Stella thumbed back the brim of her straw hat. 'He's a bit young for me, eh? Mind you, I heard they call them women cougars who have younger blokes.' She hooked her arm through Joe's. 'I've always wanted a toy boy.'

'What?' Joe cringed.

Maddison was unsure whether to intervene.

Then Stella, Bill and Ben collapsed into fits of laughter.

'Did ya get a load of his face?' Bill asked Ben, pointing at Joe, as happy tears fell down their rosy cheeks.

Joe stepped away from the hippy wearing a straw hat at midnight. 'What's going on?'

'It's all right, mate.' Stella playfully punched Joe on the arm. 'That pair of trouble radioed earlier and told me to stir you up a bit. I'm happily married with eight kids and four grandbabies, with more on the way.'

'Yeah, right,' murmured Joe, clinging close to the giggling Maddison. It was good to laugh again.

'Righto, you mob, your chariot awaits.' Stella heartily reefed open the kombi's side door and started shifting the junk around inside. 'Don't mind the mess, eh. I've bin cartin' the billylids and their mates' round for soccer practice. It's stinkin' cute, eh. They're only five and can't kick a bloody ball to save themselves. But we've all gotta start somewhere, right?' She stepped out of the van and faced her passengers. 'Righto, in you get, daylight's comin'.'

Stella climbed into the driver's seat and turned on the engine. Rock music exploded into the night air.

In the passenger seat Maddison playfully flicked at the sun-faded, fluffy dice that hung from the rear-view mirror.

'You've gotta put some muscle into closing that door,' shouted Stella from the driver's seat.

The side door screeched like rust on rust as Joe slammed it shut, rocking the entire van.

'Where are you mob off to then, eh?' Stella asked.

'Franklin's Transit.' Joe squeezed into the backseat, with his knees to his chest, resting his boots on a bag of soccer balls. Bill and Ben were seated in the same fashion.

'Righto, hold tight.' As the stereo blasted AC/DC, Stella gunned the engine until it backfired, it then gave an almighty roar like an ancient lawn mower. The whole van vibrated, until it jerked in a series of small kangaroo hops, as black smoke spewed out of the rear exhaust pipe, until it finally got enough momentum to roll down the deserted road.

'I've lost the switch to the volume,' shouted Stella as she steered. 'I can turn it off, but the wiring's all mucked up in the electrics. No stereo, no driving lights.'

Ten minutes later the orange kombi van screeched to a halt, forcing everyone to jerk forward in their seats.

'Righto, Franklin Transit.' Stella pointed to the brightly lit fenced yard. In the centre stood a massive shed almost as big as an aircraft hangar, with forklifts whizzing in and out of its wide doorway.

'Thank you, Stella. It was awesome to meet you.' Maddison's cheeks ached from laughter.

'Come 'ere, you look like you need one.' Stella pulled Maddison into a hug, giving hearty pats on Maddison's back as if to clear her airways. 'Good luck to you and your fella, eh.'

With a plume of smoke and an echoing backfire, the orange kombi van shuddered and shook. Its rainbow-wearing driver, and the twin silver-haired pilots, waved madly out the windows as the van lurched forward with AC/DC's *Highway to Hell* blasting from the stereo.

'What the hell was that?' Joe stood beside Maddison on the sidewalk as they both waved off the van, its tyres screeching as its body leaned dangerously sideways to take the corner. With white smoke spewing from its exhaust, it soon disappeared.

'That is the most colourful woman I've ever met.' Stella was amazing. Never in a million years would Maddison have met someone like Stella in her old world. Stella, who'd helped a friend without any ulterior motive. Just like the twins. Complete strangers who took her at face value and not for who or what she had. 'I like the twins. And Stella.'

'I didn't meet her when I worked here. She's not the type of woman you'd forget in a hurry.'

'You worked where?'

'There.' Joe pointed to the shed.

Franklin Transit was emblazoned across the large sign that hung on the front fence and on the shed 'Is it a bus station or a train station?' It was too dark to see anything else in the area.

'You're close with a train.' Joe led Maddison to the shed where a massive semi-trailer waited inside. Its bull bar was taller than Maddison, with long trailers snaking behind it longer than a city block.

'That's the biggest truck I've ever seen.'

'It's a road train.'

'Huh. And I thought your cattle truck was big, but that … Did you drive one of these?' Her neck craned up at the sheer size of the mechanical beast with shiny exhaust stacks and horns adorning its roof.

'I got paid to cruise around Australia driving one of these.'

The guy drove bikes, boats, utes, tractors, mine-sized dump trucks, road trains, and flew planes and helicopters. What couldn't he do? 'You're amazing, you know that?'

He wiped at his nose to hide his smile. 'Come on, let's find out when the next truck is leaving.'

'Will this get us to Sydney?' Not that she was excited to go there.

'Close enough. We'll find plenty of rides at the truck stops. When we hit the regional centre, we can hire a car. Are you keen to take on this next adventure?' He held his hand out to her.

She'd do anything to avoid Sydney, known to some as the Emerald City, the world she'd fled from almost a year ago. But now she had no choice. It was time for this runaway to go home.

Fifty-nine

SYDNEY, NEW SOUTH WALES

'I forgot how huge this place is. I now understand why you chose this mini and not the van.' Joe skillfully scooted their hire car through the congested harbour-city traffic. It was an enormous difference from the towering prime mover to sitting bare millimetres off the road.

'You're in my backyard now, cowboy.' Maddison gave directions, while starting to feel claustrophobic from the rows of houses, shops, traffic lights, and people swarming a capital city. It had been a long trek from Elleron Downs, and she was already missing the quiet open spaces of the outback.

'Were you born in Sydney?' Joe pulled up at another set of traffic lights. All they did was stop start, stop start.

'In Adelaide.'

'But you live in Melbourne?'

'I've been in Melbourne for about a year. My mother moved us to Sydney when I was a toddler, when she got a job with a teen magazine.'

'You never mention your father.'

'Nothing to tell. I don't know who my father is.' Inhaling deeply, she repeated a well-told tale, while staring at the grey skies that matched the towers of concrete and windows that hid the sun. 'I'm the result of a one-night stand at a university party my mother attended. His name was Tim. He was only passing through and was never seen again. On bad days my mother called him the sperm donor.'

'You're kidding?' Joe's mouth opened and closed, while hanging onto the steering wheel.

Maddison giggled at Joe's reaction. 'My mother was only eighteen when she found out she was pregnant.'

'What about the rest of your family?'

'What family? There was just my mother, and of course Uncle Bob, who was a year younger.'

'What about your grandparents?'

'I came close to meeting my grandmother once. But she denied our existence. My grandparents kicked out my mother.'

'I'm sorry.'

'Don't be.'

'What was your mother like?'

'Busy. Always busy. She was a determined woman; strength was her middle name.'

'Strong like you,' he said, patting her denim thigh.

Strength? Ha! 'I doubt that. My mother did big things with her life.' Maddison could never live up to that level of expectation. 'My mother was determined to have a better life. Dragging her newborn to university classes while working at the local rag, until she got the job in Sydney and the rest is history.' What would her mother say about Maddison's recent events?

'How did your mother die?''

'Breast cancer. Too busy to get annual check-ups. It was so severe when they discovered it, she died three months afterwards. I was sixteen.'

'I'm sorry.' Joe gave her hand a squeeze,

'Me too.' She dropped the visor to gaze into the small mirror. 'Oh, God.' She screwed up her nose. Her complexion was red and blotchy, drying out from the lack of humidity in the air. 'My mother would roll over in her grave if she saw me like this. Nancy's going to have a fit when she sees me.' She ripped off the baseball cap. Her hair was a mess, she was wearing no make-up, surviving on snatches of sleep ever since they'd flown out of Elleron Downs.

She grabbed the tied strap of her ruined red bag and dug

around for her broken hairbrush and lip gloss. It's all she had left of her toiletries, rolling around inside the bulky bag, with fewer rolls of cash and her uncle's waterproof pouch still in pristine condition.

'You look fine to me,' said Joe. 'You do.'

'Thank you.' They both hadn't stopped, except for restroom breaks, food, and coffee at various truck stops, before hustling their next truck ride. 'Is this where I say you always look ruggedly handsome? Especially with that stubble you've got happening around the chin.' Unable to resist, she tickled his prickly jawline. It was a sexy look.

Following the GPS, Joe left the city behind and turned into a suburb where leafy trees lined the street. 'Who are we going to see now?'

'Nancy McCann, who would be insulted if we don't see her first. She's my mother's best friend and my wicked godmother.'

'Known her long?'

'All my life. Nancy and my mother met at university, sharing the same internship at an Adelaide paper. Nancy came with us to Sydney and would stay in-between husbands.'

'Is your godmother a journalist too?'

'Used to be. Nancy is now an overseeing editor.' Maddison shut the visor, flopping back into her seat.

'What do you mean, between husbands?'

She shuffled in her seat to face Joe. 'Nancy's primary pastime is men. So, I'm warning you now, she is a feisty cougar, and you're about to walk into her lair.'

'Yeah, right?' Joe grinned.

'Nancy's mission in life was to marry a rich man.'

'How often did she get married?' Joe drove them past houses that got bigger and further away from the curb, where manicured lawns got longer and the fences higher.

'Five times.'

'Huh?' With straight arms holding the steering wheel, Joe gave her a fleeting side glance. 'Is she still married?'

'Divorced.' Maddison's lifestyle couldn't be any more different from Joe's. 'Now Nancy only keeps lovers. They're all younger men, she calls them her *toy boys*.'

'Are you going to protect me from this cougar? Does she have an orange kombi too? Those twins set me up with Stella.'

'It was funny.'

'So this is a joke, too.'

'Buckle up, baby, once Nancy finds out you're a real live cowboy, who rescues damsels in distress, she's gonna wanna lock you up and play till the cows come home.'

'Yeah, right? For the record, I'm a cattleman not a cowboy.'

She grinned at him, then the smile disappeared as she pointed ahead. 'There's the house. At the end of this cul-de-sac.'

'That's not a house.' Joe slowed down as they approached the black wrought-iron gates.

'Yes, it is. It's Nancy's house.' As much as she loved her godmother, she braced herself for this visit. She wasn't ready to answer the questions she'd have to face.

* * *

Joe leaned over the hire car's steering wheel to gaze up at the mansion. 'I was expecting a ground-level three-bedroom house in the 'burbs. Not a two-storey complex. Nancy obviously married her rich husband.'

Wrought-iron gates guarded manicured lawns with a sweeping driveway that led to a small water fountain. 'How do we get in?' Did this place have a butler?

'Press the buzzer on the speaker box. It's just like a front door bell.'

Joe wound down the window to press on the intercom near the gates.

'Hulloo,' crackled the female voice through the speaker.

'Theresa, it's Maddison.' Maddison leaned over Joe to wave at the camera.

'Oh, Maddy. It's you. You're home.'

'Can you let us in, please?'

'Of course, at once. I'll tell the wicked witch you're here.

You're HOME.'

There was a hum, a clank, then the gates peeled open.

No dirt crunched under the tyres as Joe entered the silky smooth driveway. Could this really be Maddison's home? 'Who's Theresa?'

'The housekeeper. Sometimes she calls herself the maid. She was my babysitter since I was four. Theresa used to live in the same apartment building as us, until her children grew up and moved out, and then she moved in here.'

'And who is the wicked witch?'

'Nancy. I guess I should warn you about that pair, too. Nancy and Theresa argue all the time.'

'So why do they—'

'Live together?'

He nodded, parking the car by the front steps that led to a huge front door.

'Theresa and Nancy have been part of each other's lives for decades. They love each other like sisters and argue like siblings.'

'How many people live here? Do you live here?'

'When my mother got sick, we all moved in together. Now it's just Nancy and Theresa. That's Theresa.' She climbed out of the car as a middle-aged woman, wearing a grey dress and flat shoes, her black hair in a tight bun, rushed down the front steps.

Theresa eagerly hugged Maddison like a mother with her child. 'Oh, my word, you look awful. Your mother would roll over in her grave if she saw you looking like this.'

'We've been on the road.' Maddison tried to straighten her hair. 'Theresa, this is Joe.'

'Hello. Are you dropping Maddison off?'

Great, they thought he was the staff!

'Um, no.' Maddison cringed, wrapping Joe's jacket tighter around herself. 'Joe will stay with me. Us.'

'Really?' Theresa stepped back, raising a manicured eyebrow, inspecting Joe from the tip of his worn boots to the top of his baseball cap.

He removed his cap, brushed fingers through his hair, and wiped his hand on his T-shirt. 'Pleased to meet you, Theresa.' Joe held out his hand.

Theresa looked at his hand and then at Joe like he was some foreign object. 'He's with you?'

Maddison wrapped her arm around Joe's. 'Yes.'

'Oh, my word.' The smile grew on Theresa's face as she clapped her hands, to then vigorously shake Joe's hand. 'How wonderful. Finally, to have Maddy home, and with a *man*. You're the first man Maddison has ever brought home. So, welcome, Joe. I'm delighted you're here.'

'Um, thanks.' *I think.*

'Mind you ...' Theresa stood back and again surveyed Joe carefully. 'You're a handsome man. Solid too.' Theresa then said to Maddison, 'You'd better watch this one around Nancy, she'll try to steal him out from under you. I hope you warned him about the witch.'

'I did, but I don't think Joe believes me. Talking about the wicked witch, where is my godmother?'

'Inside on the phone. I told her you were here, but you know how she likes to make a grand entrance. Where's your luggage? We'll get you settled inside.'

'This is it.' Maddison held up her red bag. It was wrecked.

Joe grabbed the small backpack they shared from behind the car seat. They hadn't taken much on the helicopter in their race to beat the clock.

'You're not serious?' Theresa again arched one of those plucked eyebrows.

'Nancy told me not to pack anything,' said Maddison.

'Nancy did say she was taking you shopping. Well, your wardrobe is in your room, just how you left it.' Theresa guided them through the enormous front door. 'I'll get more towels for Joe. Are you a man who eats or are you one of them models on a special vegan carb-free organic-only diet?'

'Trust me, Theresa, Joe's a real man who eats actual food. His mum's a splendid cook. She was teaching me to bake bread and knead it by hand. It's so incredibly therapeutic.'

Joe winked at Maddison. She was getting good at baking and his mum loved having Maddison hang out with her in the kitchen.

Theresa stopped in the doorway and faced Joe. 'You're not a meat-and-three-vegies fellow who eats carbs, are you?'

Joe shrugged, looking at Maddison, who nodded.

Again, Theresa clapped her hands in front of her wide smile. 'Oh, my word, I didn't think men like you existed anymore. To cook a proper meal for a man is such a change. Any preference, Joe?'

'Nah, I'm easy. I'll eat anything.' Was Theresa going to hug him?

'You're a rare find indeed.'

Joe's eyes took a moment to adjust from the outside light. The inside was huge, with marbled floors, a sweeping staircase and exotic art on the walls, reminding him of a museum. He wasn't in the country anymore. 'Don't men eat around here?'

'Not unless it's fat-free, high-protein, low-carb, organic, juiced, and God knows what with their body as their temple—except for Bob, of course.' Theresa tenderly stroked Maddison's shoulder. 'I am so sorry to hear about Bob.'

'*Oh, my darling, Sweet Cheeks,*' bellowed a female voice from the top of the staircase.

'Ah, the wicked witch arrives.' Theresa rolled her eyes as she closed the front door.

'That's Nancy,' Maddison told Joe.

Like a queen, Nancy floated down the grand marble staircase with a champagne glass in one hand and a lit cigarette in the other. She wore a flowing pant suit, her severe bob a midnight gloss, and blood-red lipstick. Her jewels were as big as the crystals in the suspended chandelier. The lady looked loaded.

'Where did *sweet cheeks* come from?' Joe whispered to Maddison.

'The cheeks of my posterior. Nancy gave it to me at birth.' Maddison rolled her eyes at him.

'Well, your butt *is* beautiful.' He chuckled at the blush brushing her fine cheekbones.

'Hi, Nancy.' Maddison hugged her godmother warmly.

'God, you look awful. Your mother would roll over in her grave to see you looking like that.' Nancy held Maddison at arm's length. 'This will not do. *Theresa.*'

'I'm standing right here, you bloody ignorant fool.'

'Oh, there you are,' said Nancy, giggling at Maddison.

'Get the team together, have them come to the house this instance. I will not have my goddaughter looking like she's crawled out of the luggage compartment of a Greyhound bus.'

'It's okay, Nancy,' said Maddison.

'No, it's not!'

'I agree,' said Theresa, by the front door. 'You could do with a pampering. You look like you've been through hell and back.'

'You've lost so much weight, darling. Those clothes are the wrong cut for you. How much cardio have you been doing?'

Would running for her life count as cardio?

Joe and Maddison glanced at each other, as if thinking the same.

'It doesn't matter, you're here now, darling, and the team will perform their usual miracles. If they ever get here.' Nancy glared at Theresa.

'Yeah, yeah, I'm calling them now. Then I'm going to find some steak and spuds for dinner and maybe even make a dessert.' Theresa's flat shoes were silent on the marble hallway that led to the many closed doors.

'That's settled …' Then Nancy's eyes landed on Joe. Head tilted, champagne glass poised in the air, her eyes slow crawled over every inch of Joe's physique, as if he were trapped under a microscope. 'Oh, my darling Sweet Cheeks, you brought me a present.' Nancy's heels click-clacked along the marble, her hips sashaying, as champagne sloshed in her glass.

Joe looked for the nearest exit.

Nancy didn't give him a chance. She lifted his hand, squeezed his bicep. 'Nice.' Ogling him off as if he was a piece of meat. 'A new toy to play with.'

Were the warnings about this woman true? He looked to Maddison for help.

'Oh, darling, you'll do wonderfully. Nice broad shoulders.' Nancy walked around Joe as if he were a centrepiece sculpture in a museum. 'Nice cheekbones. Strong, rugged features. Where did you dig this one up, Sweet Cheeks?'

'The outback. Joe's a cattleman.'

'Hmm …' Nancy's eyes flared as she poked a long red fingernail at Joe's chest. 'Solid muscle, too.'

'Um, Nancy,' said Maddison, grinning at Joe giving her a pleading look.

'Nice slim waist.' Nancy patted his stomach and raised his shirt. 'That's a full set of abs he's got there. It'd be an eight pack.' She peered over to Maddison then back at Joe as if he were a car for sale and they were checking out what was under the hood.

Joe felt like a piece of stock being judged in a cattle show prior to sale. 'Maddison?'

'Nancy, please …' Maddison stepped in closer.

'He's got a nice line from the shoulders narrowing into his hips, and a great grippable rump.' Nancy patted Joe on the backside.

'*Oi.*' Should he be flattered or run?

'You can always tell how good a lover is by their rump. It's all that thrusting and muscle control. Oh, you'll do perfectly, lover.' Nancy purred, wrapping an arm around Joe's as if he were some pet dog she'd bought from the store.

'Maddison?' Trapped in a tricky situation, Joe did not want to offend Maddison's family.

'*Nancy!*' Maddison's voice echoed in the foyer.

'What?' Nancy blinked over her champagne glass, continuing her inspection of Joe.

'This is Joe.'

Maddison reached for Joe's hand to pull him safely away from the clutches of the cougar, to then become a human shield barricading him from her godmother.

That's my girl.

Nancy looked at Maddison, unsure. 'Is there a problem?'

'Joe is with me.'

'Really?' Nancy's eyes narrowed at Maddison holding Joe's hand. 'He's *with* you?'

'Yes. Joe is staying with us. With me.'

Nancy's eyes brightened, like a globe gone full wattage, matching her pristine white teeth. 'Oh, my darling, Sweet Cheeks, you have a boyfriend.' Nancy wrapped her arms around Maddison. 'So sorry, I didn't know. I'll behave, Joe.'

'Thanks.' He sighed with relief.

'You're the first man our darling Sweet Cheeks has ever brought home.'

'Her first, huh?' He smirked as Maddison's blush got brighter, with no make-up to hide her fair complexion.

* * *

Maddison hid her face in her hands, feeling the heat radiating between her fingers.

'It's a double celebration. Come along, the bar is open.' Nancy led them into a grand sitting room where the bar stood at the far wall. 'It's so good to have Sweet Cheeks home again, and with a man!' She scooped up a bottle of champagne from the ice bucket resting on the bar and skilfully released the cork with a loud bang. 'Are you a champagne boy, Joe?' Nancy handed a fizzing glass to Maddison.

'Beer.'

'Pick your poison from the fridge behind the bar, darling.' Nancy pointed to the well-stocked fridge. 'Help yourself in this house, especially if you're staying with Sweet Cheeks.'

Maddison rolled her eyes, sipping on the cool champagne.

'Oh honey, you brought home a man.' Nancy raised her glass in the air. 'Even looking the way you do, you still brought home a man.'

'Nancy, please.' The heat rose to her ears.

Joe smirked at her from behind the bar, cracking open a bottle of beer.

It's not like she'd never brought a man here before.

Hold on?

She blinked. Then blinked again.

No way! Joe truly was the first guy she'd ever introduced to Nancy in her home.

She hadn't thought about this part of her homecoming and gulped on her champagne.

'I was getting worried you'd end up a spinster like your mother.' Nancy lit another cigarette and looked from Maddison to Joe hiding behind the bar. 'What's wrong? And don't say nothing, because something is wrong, darling. You show up nearly two weeks late, when I haven't heard boo out of you since you told me you were traipsing off to Queensland. Then I had some nosy Detective Hetter or Hatter something-or-other, from Melbourne.'

'Detective Mick Hetter?'

'Yes. You obviously know him, and by that look you're wearing you don't want to speak to him, especially when you bloody-well just show up here looking like crap with …' Nancy paused to smile at Joe, 'a *man*. I demand to know what the hell is going on.'

Maddison felt her throat squeeze as her voice creaked. 'What did you tell the detective?'

'Nothing, darling. Only that you'd schlepped off to Queensland to scuba dive the coral reef at some five-star island resort.' Nancy put her champagne glass on the bar and took a drag of her cigarette. She then blew the smoke high into the air, never taking her eyes off Maddison. 'Farkwit, my assistant, said there was nothing salvageable in your Melbourne apartment after that little break-in. Don't worry, darling, I had Farkwit put in your insurance claim.'

'Oh.' She'd forgotten about that.

'Oh? Darling is that all you have to say, oh?'

'Thank you.'

'You can thank me, darling, by telling me what the hell is going on.'

Maddison braced herself and said, 'I'm here to talk to Regus.'

'WHAT THE HELL?' Nancy's words bounced off the walls. She then scooped up her champagne glass and drank it dry.

'Who's Regus?' Joe asked Maddison from his safe space behind the bar.

'Nancy's ex-husband.'

'Which one?' Joe asked with a shrug.

'Husband number two,' replied Nancy, refilling her glass. 'Or was he number three?'

'Two,' replied Maddison.

'You should know, after all you were my flower girl in all of my weddings. You were so cute, darling. And your mother was gorgeous, as always, as my matron of honour.' Nancy waved her champagne glass at the mantel lined with assorted framed images. 'You can check out all of Sweet Cheek's photos over there, Joe. Hurry, because our ever-so-humble little Maddy gets so shy about herself, she'll hide them shortly.' She inhaled from her cigarette, then exhaled a stream of smoke towards the ceiling. 'So are you going to tell me why you're wanting to visit Regus? Or am I better off not knowing?'

'Not knowing, at this stage.' Maddison wanted to protect her godmother.

'*Fiiiine*, don't tell me then.'

'You can come with me when I talk to Regus.' Maddison could do with the moral support.

'It's a good thing I called in the team then, darling. I can't have you looking like you've rolled in from some hobo's train convention when you go to the office in the morning.'

Maddison shoved her hands into Joe's jacket that had been a comfort to her this part of the journey. 'We're on a tight deadline.' Three days to go.

'What kind of team are we talking about?' Joe asked.

'The team, darling,' replied Nancy. 'Hairstylist, beautician, manicurists, masseur, and stylists. Mmm, I'll get them to do you too, Joe.'

'Be gentle with my Joe,' said Maddison in warning.

Nancy grinned at Maddison. 'Don't worry, my darling Sweet Cheeks, *your* dear Joe is quite safe.' She leaned over the bar to give Joe another inspection. 'He is lovely. A bit rough around the edges. Nothing a bit of tweaking won't perfect.'

'I'm fine, thanks, just as is.' Joe took a swig of his beer.

'I agree.' Maddison had tried to warn him, but would this scare him off for good?

'Joe, darling, you could do with a pampering just as much our dear Sweet Cheeks needs one. I insist. I will not have you two disgrace the memory of my late best friend's legacy by walking through those halls looking like that.'

'What's wrong with how I look?' Joe frowned at Nancy. 'Besides a shave and shower.'

'No, the five o'clock shadow's a very sexy look for you. You should keep that, darling. We're just cleaning you up, that's all.' Nancy then turned to Maddison. 'Obviously, you haven't told him about the office, have you? Hmm?'

Maddison barely shook her head. 'I wouldn't go there if it wasn't important.'

'And I'll be going with her.'

Maddison smiled at Joe, a man true to his word. But was she?

'Well, my darling, Joe, you are about to walk into the snake pit and I'm only doing this for your own protection.'

'Protection from what?'

'My dear young man, you are about to walk into the house of the country's leading women's fashion magazine with Maddison Farley at your side. And my darling outback cattleman, you'd better scrub up for that.' Nancy waved her lit cigarette in the air like a magic wand. 'Because all eyes will be on you. And they are the pickiest bunch of gossiping, backstabbing, finicky fashionistas and drama queens you'll ever come across in your life. Not to mention you're going to see the king of our jungle.'

'I'm in the city, right? Do you have man-eating crocodiles shacking up with the snakes and scorpions too? Does your jungle king wear a loincloth to swing off the chandeliers?'

'I like him.' Nancy gave a tinkling laugh.

'Why do we have to go there, Maddison? We can go to his house.' Joe suggested.

'Only because that bastard lives at the office, as the obsessed workaholic he is,' barked out Nancy. Then she sighed wistfully. 'In all fairness to the man, he is the best in the business, so we shouldn't complain.'

'Who is Regus?' Joe asked Maddison.

'Haven't you been listening?' Nancy then spun around to Maddison. 'Sweet Cheeks, why haven't you told this poor man anything? Hmm?'

Maddison took a gulp from her champagne. Poor Joe.

A few hours later, Theresa led a parade of people through the main doorway to the bar. 'The team is here.' They were carrying capes, beauty cases, hair dryers, and wheeling in racks filled with clothes.

'Finally! Now that my guests have been fed and watered, we need to fix their inappropriate clothing. So, I am demanding that these two weary travellers receive some much needed magicking,' announced Nancy, the queen of this court. 'As I'm the wicked godmother, I'll be watching over you all! Now chop-chop, you have your work cut out for you.'

'Come on, Joe.' Maddison led him by the hand. 'You're going to love this.'

'Am I?'

Typical Sweet Cheeks, never telling the whole story, thought Nancy.

'My darling, Joe, just relax. They're here to pamper you, not hurt you. Now run along, get some rest, we'll talk in the morning.' Nancy waved at Joe and Maddison who were soon whisked away by the team.

Nancy lit another cigarette and sighed as Theresa approached the bar and poured herself a small glass of ouzo.

'Good to have our little Sweet Cheeks home again,' she said to Theresa.

'And with a man, too. He ate everything on his plate, no complaints, no questions. A clean plate.'

'What's happening with the wild man's wardrobe?'

'The team is sorting out clothes for Joe. The young couple had practically nothing.'

'Hmm ...' Nancy sipped on her champagne, staring at the vacant doorway where Maddison and Joe had disappeared. 'Do you think this outback Joe is with Maddy for who she is, or what she has?'

'Joe doesn't seem to know much. You should have seen his face when he walked inside.'

'Typical Maddy, never telling the complete story.' Nancy

took another sip of her champagne.

'She's just like her mother,' said Theresa.

'How do you think this blue-collar Joe's going to cope when he does find out? I hope he doesn't behave like the other men Maddison has met over the years.'

Theresa swirled the cloudy ouzo in the small glass. 'Don't ask me that. You're the one who knows what men are like. I've only been with the one man all my life. May he rest in peace.'

'Oh, puh-lease. Darling, he passed on twenty years ago. I told you, you can use any one of my toy boys anytime. I don't mind sharing.'

'No thanks, I know where they've been.' Theresa screwed up her nose. 'But our girl's home now.'

'But for how long, darling? Especially if she's here to talk to Regus, which should make for an interesting reunion.'

'Joe seems a nice man. Handsome.'

'But does he only have eyes for our Maddy? And how much does she care for Joe?' Nancy inhaled her cigarette while staring down the empty corridor, exhaling the smoke.

'You're a smart woman—

'It's about time you admitted that.'

'—who's been around the block a billion times.'

'Why, darling, I like the ride.'

Theresa rolled her eyes. 'You like meddling in people's lives, so why don't you find out how much Maddy cares for Joe? I like him.'

'You're right.'

'Which part,' mumbled Theresa over her glass.

'I'm going to have my assistant, Farkwit, prep a little surprise for that pair tomorrow.' Nancy put down her cigarette in the ashtray to scroll for the number on her phone.

'Doing what?'

'I'm going to get the best man I know, who has a gift at reading people's emotions no matter how hard they try to hide them. And he's going to tell me what he sees.'

'How?'

'Why, darling, through the lens of a camera, of course.' Nancy dialled the number, sipping on her champagne and set the wheels in motion. But a trickle of bothersome fear feathered down her spine. From the worried expression on Maddison's face, that girl was carrying a story that scared her enough to want to see the most feared man in the business.

Sixty

As the luxurious limousine sliced through the city streets of Sydney, Joe fidgeted with his tie and starchy collar. Beside him Maddison was busily staring at a tablet she shared with Nancy.

Ever since he'd arrived at the ten-bedroom, twelve-bathroom mansion with a swimming pool and private gym, he'd felt as if he'd entered some bizarre universe. A world ruled over by a five-times divorced cougar who smoked like a chimney, drank champagne like it was water, and swore worse than a truck driver.

The *team* had forced him to endure a haircut, a facial, and suit fittings from half a dozen strangers. He'd then been handfed by the housekeeper, while he was getting his callused working hands scrubbed and his nails done.

By the time they'd released him from a massage, he'd found Maddison curled up asleep on a king-sized bed where he too had crashed, exhausted from being on the road for twenty-four hours.

Only to be woken by Theresa for breakfast in bed, then sent to shower and dress in a tailored suit, tie, shoes, socks, and even the softest of jocks. They'd supplied the lot. All from some special designers.

Then he was forced to front Nancy for an inspection. This time he'd kept the cougar at arm's length while she checked him over, drinking champagne for breakfast.

But all his complaints stopped when Maddison walked down the stairs.

She'd taken his breath away. Her soft blue dress made his palm itch to follow the curves of her body. The grace of each elegant step in her heels elongated the line of her legs. Her hair, so soft and shiny, complemented the make-up that made her eyes brighten. He thirsted to draw her plump lips between his teeth before settling in for a punishing kiss, because the woman was bringing him to his knees.

But Nancy shattered his daydream, whisking them into the limousine, talking to Maddison about people he didn't know all the way to the city, where buildings got taller, traffic thickened, and the sun disappeared.

'Nancy, is this car necessary? We have a hire car,' said Maddison, as the limousine pulled up to a busy sidewalk.

'Puh-lease darling, I had that rice grain you call a car sent back. Use my car. It's in the same spot in the office basement. Keys are in my desk drawer. I never use it anymore; I prefer the limo.' Nancy leaned over and stage whispered, 'The driver has the most amazing tongue on him. When he goes down—'

'*Nancy!*' Maddison went bright red.

'I'm only fooling with you, darling. God, I only do male models that are only too eager to please me, hoping I'll promote their careers. You should try out, Joe, with your structure, I'm sure you'll find an audience to admire you.' Nancy exited the limousine.

'A try at what?' Joe followed Maddison onto the sidewalk. He craned his neck back at the black and grey high-rise full of windows. Car and taxi horns blared. Sirens echoed nearby. Exhaust fumes and cold concrete, combined with the rotten rubbish odour of a nearby trashcan, carried on the crisp breeze. A consistent stream of people in dark suits, clutching mobiles and coffee cups, flowed around them, all on an important mission at a power-walker's pace.

Again, Joe tugged at the red tie that was too tight around his neck, but his dark navy suit blended in with all the other suits surrounding him.

'Here.' Maddison undid Joe's top button and loosened his tie.

'Thank you,' Joe whispered in relief. 'I've only worn suits to weddings or funerals. It's been a while. But you look amazing.' Her delicate floral fragrance filtered through the air; it was still her scent, yet in this place, she seemed different.

'Thank you. You look amazing in that suit. Nancy chose well.' She patted his chest, and he kept her hand there.

'Besides looking incredible, are you okay?' They hadn't had five minutes alone since they'd met the godmother.

Maddison chewed her bottom lip, staring up at the building. 'I will be once we see Regus. And I'm sorry I haven't explained—'

'Come along, you two.' Nancy barged her way between the couple, wrapping her arms around theirs and escorted them through the sliding doors. 'As I was saying before, my dear Joe, if you want to make some quick money, I can get you in for a photo shoot. We're always looking for new male underwear models.'

He frowned. 'I don't think so.' He was a cattleman with a reputation to keep.

'I do hope you'll reconsider. We're always scouting for something new.' Nancy kept a tight grip on his arm, escorting them through the large foyer.

Like cattle being mustered onto trucks, a herd of people were bottlenecked at the gates by the elevators. They waved their ID cards the same way the branding tags flickered on a steer's ear. The steady stomp of assorted shoes and conversations was a constant murmur of the herd passing through electronic barriers manned by security guards standing along the fringes like ringers watching over a mob.

'Morning, Ms McCann. Welcome back, Miss Farley,' said one security guard, lifting the barrier to let them pass. While another held the doors open to a private elevator.

'Where are we?' Joe asked Maddison, finally free from Nancy's grip as they strode into the elevator.

'This is Thames Publishing House, darling.' Nancy checked her reflection in the mirrored walls of the whisper-quiet elevator as it whisked them upstairs. 'They own the entire building and everyone who's in it.'

'Is this where you send in your articles?' Joe asked Maddison.

'And they're bloody good, too,' said Nancy, commanding the centre of the lift.

'You don't say?' He was getting annoyed with Maddison

only telling him snippets of her story. Didn't she trust him?

'My darling Sweet Cheeks here has quite the talent. She's been published Australia-wide and as part of our world-wide syndication. Nearly every level inside this building runs a newspaper or magazine. There are car magazines, fishing, camping, travel, cooking, and finance. They create all sorts of magazines and papers. And this ...' Nancy inhaled deeply, pasting on a smile as the elevator doors opened. 'This is the jewel of their empire. It commands three floors, and is the highest grossing women's magazine in the country.'

'Which one?' Joe asked as Maddison dropped her head.

'Why, darling, it's *the Maddison Magazine*!'

'Maddison?' Joe followed Maddison into the foyer and reached for her hand. 'Hey, talk to me. What is this place?'

'My mother created all of this,' Maddison whispered in such a sad voice.

'Oh, my darling boy...' Nancy, again got between them, pushing them towards the reception area. 'Maddison's mother, Janice Farley, was a genius in the publishing world. Adored by all in the fashion industry, who truly mourned the woman who'd created this baby. Darling, do tell me you have heard of the magazine? Hmm?'

His damned collar was way too tight now. 'Um, yeah. I think some of our guests brought a copy out with them once.' He tried to catch Maddison's eye, but she was politely nodding at the receptionist.

Joe shoved his hand into the pockets of his suit's trousers and peered past dozens of awards to the towering golden letters splashed across the entire back wall: MADDISON.

Why hadn't she told him?

'Is Regus available?' Maddison asked Nancy, glancing over her shoulder at Joe. 'I need to speak with him.' And she needed to speak with Joe. He wasn't happy, not that she could blame him, she'd told him nothing. He'd have a hundred questions—questions she didn't want to answer.

She dropped her head in shame, avoiding eye contact with everyone in a place that suddenly seemed noisy, overcrowded, and stuffy. It wasn't just about Joe, it was also this place. She'd sworn to never walk these halls again. Yet here she was, being dragged back into a world she'd run from.

All she ever seemed to do was run away. Run from her past, her job, her apartment, and gun-wielding goons. 'I need to see Regus.' She had a promise to keep, hoping to get her life back to normal.

'Don't worry, Sweet Cheeks, you'll see that bastard soon enough. This way.' Nancy hooked her arm around Maddison, guiding them down the maze of corridors.

'Why didn't you tell me about this?' Joe asked Maddison in a low tone.

'Don't take it personally, Joe, Sweet Cheeks doesn't tell anyone. Unlike *moi*, I brag about it all the time. Few can swan around saying that their best friend created the best magazine in the country, named after their goddaughter. And I get to play the godmother to all.'

'What?' Joe raked fingers through his clipped hair in frustration.

'Nancy is the overseer to ensure they keep each issue up to my mother's high standards.'

'And it was those impeccable standards that made Janice Farley the best. God, I so miss that woman.' Nancy slowed her blistering pace to dab at her eye. 'But darling, you're here now.' She pushed through a set of double doors and into a large studio. On one side stood a clothes rack near dressing tables with lights around their mirrors. Assorted lighting was being shifted as white boards moved, creating the walls for a small stage.

Maddison stopped, recognising the scene—it was the set for a photo shoot. 'What is this, Nancy? We don't have time for a studio tour.' She turned to leave, but Nancy pulled her to a standstill.

'Sweet Cheeks, Regus will be available in an hour. So I've booked Leon to take your photos. LEON.'

Everyone in the room flinched, to stare for a fleeting second, only to then resume their blistering beehive pace.

'Do you have to holler like a hooker high on cocaine, Nancy?'

'And a good morning to you too, my darling Leon.'

Leon approached them from the shadows with cameras hanging loosely around his neck. He stroked a small grey goatee as the wrinkles deepened around his eyes to smile. 'Maddison. Oh, sweetheart, let me look at our darling little Maddy, all grown up.'

'Hi, Leon.' Maddison smiled, doing the regular round of polite air kisses to not crush the clothes and smudge the make-up. All while Joe stood sullenly on the sidelines.

'And you must be, Joe. I'm Leon, Chief Fashion Photographer for the magazine.' Leon shook Joe's hand. 'Wow, Nancy, you weren't wrong about this guy's bone structure and rugged strength.'

'Darling, I know my men. But he belongs to our darling little Maddy.'

Joe's frown was ferocious as he pulled his hand free from Leon and stepped away from the pair ogling him like a mannequin wearing a suit in a store window. 'What is going on, Maddison?'

'I'm wondering the same thing.' Maddison crossed her arms over her chest and glared at her godmother. 'Nancy, what are you doing?'

'It's for the anniversary issue,' replied Leon. 'Nancy nominated you both late last night.'

'She what?' Maddison glared at her godmother.

'Calm down, Sweet Cheeks. And don't you worry, my dear Joe, we'll be paying you for your time during the shoot?'

'To shoot what?' Joe asked.

'Cameras. Photo shoot. Magazine, darling —'

'NANCY.' Maddison's anger flared at Nancy daring to talk down to Joe like he was some country hick.

'This is for the twentieth anniversary issue.' In her Christian Louboutin heels, Nancy stepped in toe to toe with Maddison. 'You were in the magazine's first issue, darling, so we need a current photo of you for the now. It's what your mother would have wanted and what I aim to deliver. So, unless you want me to use male models parading in their underwear—'

Joe cleared his throat with a scowl that surely matched her own as she glowered at her wicked godmother.

'Well, it's obvious your dear Joe won't stand for that, so I've made room for him to be a part of it, with you.' Nancy then spun around to jab her manicured nail at Joe's chest. 'Darling, as I'd mentioned earlier, this is a way for you to make yourself a quick ten thousand dollars before we see Regus. To whom shall I make out the cheque? Hmm?'

'Ten thousand for photos?' Joe scoffed, shaking his head, stepping away from them all. 'What fantasy land is this?'

'Ten K is below average price for a special edition,' Leon replied. 'But considering you've never done it before …'

'Joe, you don't have to do anything.' Maddison stuck out her chin and faced her wicked godmother. 'I don't—'

'Don't you dare.' Nancy spun around and pointed that same nasty manicured nail at her goddaughter. 'Maddison Janice Farley, you are bloody well doing this, whether you like it or not. I was going to do this when you'd first planned to visit me a few weeks ago. So you're here now and I will NOT take no for an answer.' Nancy grabbed Maddison's hand and dragged her like a small child to the set.

Where was her backbone now?

* * *

'Bring out the models.' Nancy waved her unlit cigarette around like a maniacal orchestra conductor.

Joe frowned at the four men parading out from behind the panels wearing a variety of tight briefs. Their beefed-up bodies were slick with oil. Toned. Tanned. And barely dressed. All eagerly vying for a position to stand next to Maddison.

His Maddison.

'Listen, Joe …' Leon stood nearby, checking over his camera settings. 'You can make yourself a quick buck here. I'll make it as comfortable for you as I can. Maddison could do with the support, not that Nancy's giving her a choice, but Maddison is doing this for her mother. They're planning a special tribute to the fine woman Janice was.'

'What about those blokes? Won't they lose their pay?' Joe nodded to the male models, not keen on anyone losing out on their paycheque over him. He fully understood the burden of bills.

'Those men have volunteered to do this, with another fifty waiting to take their place.'

'Why?'

'The exposure. It's a huge coup for their careers to be seen with Maddison Farley in the anniversary edition. They'll do anything for that shot.'

Just like Maddison had told him about Nancy's toy boys.

Nancy dragged Maddison to the small stage. Her hair was glossy under the spotlights, with a hairstylist working on one side and a make-up artist fussing over Maddison's face. With Nancy barking out orders, the male models eagerly watched Maddison.

His teeth clenched, and his lips tightened at the male competition. Well out of his league.

'Come on, Joe, I'll guide you through it. It's not that hard, you'll see. After all, mate, you're just getting your photo taken.'

'Yeah, right?' It didn't feel right. He was a bloke who lived out bush. Not this. *I'm outta here.*

Joe turned for the door, when he paused to watch Maddison. Her frown flittered as she tried to settle her stance. She shared a tight smile, not her genuine smile that made her eyes shine.

He hadn't seen her real smile in a while, not since their lazy lover's afternoon at the waterfall on the station, and that felt like eons ago in a completely different world.

He'd do anything to see her smile again.

'All right …' Joe sighed heavily. 'Why not try something new?' It was just a photo. How hard could it be?

'Excellent.' Leon patted Joe on the back, nudging him towards the stage. 'Go stand next to Maddison and wait for my directions.'

Joe approached the bright lights as Leon barked out orders, sending everyone off in a flurry.

'It looks like I've been talked into this.' Joe shoved his hands deep into his trousers' pockets, in a tailored suit no less.

'Just think of the money, darling.' The whites of Nancy's eyes and teeth cast an eerie luminescent glow under the lights.

'Money's not the issue here,' Joe said to Maddison. Was that the reason she'd never mentioned any of this to him? Hell, he hated talking about money too—but this was something entirely different.

'Who do I make the cheque out to, hmm?' Nancy crowded his space. Her perfume barely disguised the cigarette odour that clung to her woollen suit.

'You don't have to do this, Joe.' Maddison's shoulders drooped as her eyes turned glassy. 'I'm so sorry for all of this. I didn't know Nancy was planning this.' She hiccupped as if to hold in her tears.

He reached for her small, icy hands to ease her pain.

'I hate doing this stuff,' she said with big sad eyes.

He crushed her into a hug, holding her to his chest. 'Hey, apparently it's for your mother, doing some commemoration to her. I'd do it for my mother if I was in your situation.'

'And we have to pay you. It's company policy, darling.' Nancy hovered over his shoulder like a groupie trying to take his autograph, with pen in hand. 'So, what name shall I write on the cheque? Hmm?'

'Elleron Downs. For the family.' He swallowed at Maddison's slight smile, which made him proud to see the hint of its return. But he wanted her full smile back. 'I taught you how to ride a quad. To fish. Shoot a gun, feed cattle, and steer a boat. I guess it's your turn to teach me something new. But I am telling no one I had a facial and a manicure.'

Her smile grew. 'Are you sure?'

'No. But I doubt I'll be able to stand around and watch four half-naked men fawn over you.' He grinned, drawing her close to his chest, where her body curved perfectly against his and he kissed her forehead gently. 'Let's hope no one I know is going to see this issue. And I'm not stripping down to my underwear, no matter how much they want to pay me.'

The laugh vibrating from her chest made him smile with her.

'Okay, let's do this.'

Sixty-one

For forty minutes, Nancy sipped her champagne and puffed on her unlit cigarette, overseeing all from the edge of the studio's shadows while Maddison and Joe were the centre of attention. Lighting was shifted. Hair and make-up checked. All with Leon obsessively snapping away.

'I need another lens change. Lower lighting,' barked out Leon. 'Okay, you two, five second break,' he said to Maddison and Joe before approaching his work table filled with camera equipment.

'Well, what do you think?' Nancy asked Leon. 'Joe didn't seem interested in the money, so that's a bonus. And the poor darling man knew nothing about this magazine. So, tell me what you saw?'

Leon removed the large lens from the camera's body. 'There's a definite chemistry between them and a powerful bond I rarely see in couples.'

'And?' Nancy tightened the grip on the stem of her champagne glass.

Leon picked up another lens and inspected the glass. 'It's good. I haven't seen Maddison smile like that, not since she was a kid. They're having a lot of fun up there.'

'I can see that.' But Nancy needed to protect her goddaughter from the losers who only lured in little Maddy for a chance to be a part of the industry. 'But does Joe only have eyes for Maddison?'

Leon clicked the camera lens into place, and grinned. 'Oh yeah, Joe's totally in love with Maddison. It's plain as day through the lens. Even with the half-dressed female models you've got parading through here to distract him, Joe never even looked at them—only Maddison.'

'Darling, do go on.'

'Joe has this easy-going mannerism that makes him likeable. He's also very wary of his surroundings. Knows he's out of his depth, yet he's still willing to try something new. Joe's definitely not the dumb cowboy you thought he might be.'

After all these years, it still amazed her how much Leon could see through the lens. 'But what about Maddison? Does she care for this guy?'

'She seems be holding back, big time. But if it's there, I'll see it.' Leon grabbed his camera. 'Clear the set. Now, you two,' he called to Maddison and Joe, who were laughing together. 'As the final shots for this session, I want you to look at each other.'

The couple grinned, goofing around like schoolchildren as Leon crouched down before them while everyone else cleared the set.

'This time I want serious faces, you two. Forget about us. I want you to imagine it's a private moment together, and I want a kiss!' Leon's camera clicked and clicked again.

Joe whispered something that made Maddison giggle.

'*I said serious here!*' Leon snapped from behind his camera.

Nancy approached the fringe of the stage's circle of light, fiddling with her necklace.

'How romantic, in front of a crowd, under the spotlight,' complained Maddison as her eyes darted around the room.

Joe wrapped his arms around Maddison, looking at her gently. 'Hey, I'll take any excuse to kiss you and I don't care where I am and who sees me. Imagine we're back on the station with no one around for miles and its only you and me.' He gently lifted her chin with his fingertips and slowly pressed his lips against hers, so softly and so tenderly.

The room fell silent.

Nancy chewed on her bottom lip with her head tilted, captivated by the couple caught up in their tender moment. It was as if they had forgotten everyone else was in the room.

Leon clicked away furiously with the camera, capturing

the tender moment.

An intern pushing a trolley burst through the doors, that banged hard against the wall, breaking the spell.

Maddison and Joe stopped kissing only to stare at each other for a mystical moment as an unspoken language passed between them. And then it was gone.

'And that's a wrap, people,' Leon proclaimed with a smile and a nod from behind the camera. 'That was great, you two. You can go now.' Dismissing the couple, he strolled past Nancy and said, 'Maddison's deep into Joe like a freefall diver swimming for that perfect pearl in the bottom of an abyss.'

'But will Maddison ever admit it?' Nancy sighed, gazing at the sweet, sensitive girl who'd always fiercely guarded herself, that got worse after her mother had died. Would Joe be the man to break through those impenetrable layers of Maddison's heart?

'Can we go see Regus now?' whined Maddison.

Oh, now what would Regus have to say about all of this? Nancy's smile widened as she opened the door to the corridor. 'This way, Sweet Cheeks. We shouldn't keep that bastard waiting.'

Sixty-two

Whisked away to the top floor, the elevator doors opened with a ding, where they were swamped with a cacophony of ringing phones, talking people, and hammering keyboards, as a fast-paced energy filled the air. And that was just in the foyer.

As Joe accompanied Maddison and Nancy further inside, the room widened to an area filled with cubicles of workers popping up their heads with phones stuck to their ears. It reminded him of long-neck turtles poking through a billabong's surface, only to quickly duck to disappear.

'Where are we going now?' Joe asked Maddison, as Nancy led them past the rows of desks filled with busy working people. How could they hear themselves think in all this racket?

'To see Regus. Look, I'm sorry I didn't warn you about any of this, the magazine, and what my mother did, and who she was.'

'Are you embarrassed by it?'

'No, I'm proud of what my mother created. It's just that people only know me here as Janice Farley's daughter and Maddison from *the Maddison magazine*. I've never been able to create a reputation for myself on my own merits. I tried. But as soon as I mention my name anywhere near people who work within this industry, they know who my mother was and the magazine.'

'I think I know what you're going through.'

'How?'

'With the station. Whenever I mention Elleron Downs, everyone knows of Dad and the Charter family name. I'm carrying a legacy my family has been running for four generations. Its why my parents encouraged me to take time away from the station, to work out who I was and to find what I wanted out of life. I got to experience it on my own, creating my reputation—not that I did a good job of it, but it's mine.' Joe pulled her to a stop to talk. 'Isn't that what you've been doing? Working as a barmaid and doing scuba diving tours in Melbourne this past year?'

'Yes. Although my gap year is almost up.'

'Gap year?' Did that mean Maddison was coming back to this place?

* * *

'Darlings, please come along.' Nancy beckoned to them. She stood beside a secretary seated behind a desk that guarded a closed door.

Maddison took a deep breath, gripping her new handbag, which held Bob's waterproof pouch, close to her chest. 'We had better get this over with.'

'Who is this Regus, anyway?' Joe asked. 'I only heard Nancy call him the king of the jungle and many other unpleasant names.'

It was time to stop keeping secrets and Joe deserved to know everything.

'Regus is Editor-in-Chief of Thames Publishing House. He's in charge of all of their magazines and newspapers.'

'Your boss?'

She nodded. 'I'm hoping Regus will know exactly what to do.'

'Do you want this story published?'

'We have to be careful with what we do next.'

'We?' He said with a spark in his blue eyes.

The word came so naturally. But she couldn't afford to think too far ahead. 'I can't let Cottillard get away with what he's done. And there's all these legal implications in all of this. Regus will know who to contact so your family doesn't get into trouble keeping that goon tied to your kitchen chair.'

'When I phoned home earlier, Greg told me they've untied Tom and have him working around the station. He can't go anywhere, and Greg's filled his head full of scary stories, telling him there are crocodiles everywhere and they're flooded in.'

'Do you trust Tom?'

'No. But I trust my parents to make the right choice.' Then he sighed heavily, glancing around the noisy office space. 'I can understand Nancy's apprehension in not visiting her ex-husband, but why are you so hesitant in seeing this guy?'

'Is it that obvious?'

'Yes. We could have seen him yesterday if he lives here, then we could have avoided that whole photo shoot.'

Joe was right.

'The last time I saw Regus we argued, and I never argued with anyone. I've always kept my mouth shut, not having the courage to speak out, or most of the time people ignore me—'

'I'd doubt that.'

'They do. Or they only sucked up to me to get to my mother.'

'What happened between you and this guy?' He threw his thumb towards the gatekeeper talking with Nancy.

'I told Regus I quit, and he called me a disappointment because I walked away.' More like ran away.

She hugged her bag tighter, staring at the closed door that led to the lion's den. 'The guy is tough. Fair, demanding, and tough, but he knows how to get the best out of people. Regus also has this uncanny ability to look objectively at a story from all angles. It's made him the best in the business. It's just …' She hesitated, licking her dry lips.

'Go on.'

'The way Regus speaks to people can be considered offensive. Politically incorrect.'

'Nancy calls him the bastard. Is he that bad?'

'Regus can be an outright cruel bastard. I said that to his face once. I'd never spoken to anyone like that before.' It's one of the reasons she'd run in shame.

But ever since her uncle's murder, her ability to speak

out had taken a leap. Shouting at the Thurstons, demanding answers from Goon One, and interrogating Goon Two while he was tied to a chair. Who was she?

'So, we're in for a warm reception then?'

'I don't know how Regus is going to react when he sees me.'

'I've got your back, baby. I'll be right here. Remember, this is for a good reason. Think of the big picture.'

She tried to find her backbone as she turned and faced the dreaded door.

Suddenly, it was ripped open.

She gasped and stepped back into Joe's chest. 'That's Regus.'

'*Kelly, tell them dickheads downstairs this is absolute tripe!*' bellowed out Regus, throwing a folder onto the secretary's desk. He rolled up his collared shirt's sleeves higher on his arms. Raking fingers through his salt and pepper hair, his scowl heightened his strong chiselled jawline, as his grey eyes hardened his distinguished features. '*In fact, tell that bunch of bent spoon-lickers, I want a full rewrite on that article or my car's headlights are gonna be brighter than their future!*' Then he saw Nancy hovering by the desk. 'What do you want? I'm not giving you any more money.'

'I'm here on a personal visit, you grouchy old bastard.'

'I'm busy, make an appointment.' Regus went to return to his office, only to stop. 'Maddy?' With hands on hips, he narrowed his eagle eyes at her.

'Hello, Regus.'

'*Where the hell have you been, young lady?* No phone call. No postcard. No story for the month. You better have a bloody good excuse—'

'*OI!*' Joe shielded Maddison behind him. 'Don't you dare talk to Maddison like that. I don't care who the hell you are.'

Regus tossed his thumb in Joe's direction. 'Who's this, Maddy? Your overpaid bodyguard dressed in Armani?'

'Darling, that is Maddison's boyfriend,' butted in Nancy, nodding at Regus.

'Her what?'

'I had Leon check him out this morning on the photo shoot. He passed.'

'True story?' Regus side-glanced Nancy, to again narrow his eyes at Maddison and Joe.

'You did what with Leon?' Maddison demanded from Nancy. 'Oh no, you didn't. Tell me it wasn't a setup?' Leon had a gift for reading people's hidden emotions from behind the lens and capturing it all on film.

Nancy smiled from behind her champagne glass. 'My darling Sweet Cheeks, it's my job to look after your welfare.'

'True story? Maddison with a boyfriend?' Regus glared at Joe with hands on his hips like an army general inspecting his troops. 'With this—'

'His name is Joe.' Maddison had expected some heat from Regus, but Joe didn't deserve this. 'You leave Joe alone!'

Regus took a step back. 'You with a boyfriend, huh?' He then grinned and his stern expression softened. 'Right. Joe, is it? I'm Regus.' He held out his hand and Joe shook it firmly, but he held Joe's hand and spoke loud and fast. 'I'll give you this lecture only once. Right here, right now. You hurt my little Maddy and I'll kick your heiny from here to kingdom come. You hear me?'

'*Regus*,' cried out Maddison in disbelief.

'Hey, if you had a boyfriend when you were a teenager—like other girls normally do—I could have done this speech years ago.' Regus then said to Joe in his hard and fast straight talk, 'I've known Maddy since she was four. She doesn't have a father, and I don't have any children. But I taught Maddy how to ride her bicycle in these halls as a kid. On the bike I gave her. And she was the flower girl at my wedding. You understand my protectiveness over the woman. Don't you?'

'Loud and clear. You just gave me the fatherly warning speech. You forgot to mention the shotgun in the cupboard.' Joe grinned.

'Huh.' Regus tilted his head, cocking an eyebrow at the lad. 'I like you.' He then nodded at Joe as if it was final. 'Come inside my office.'

The trio followed.

'So, where did you dig this one up from, Maddy?' Regus casually flung his thumb at Joe as he plonked down into the chair behind his desk, which was piled with folders and paperwork.

'Um, Joe found me.' Maddison closed the door of Regus's large office. Inhaling the familiar scent of woodsy paper and his old-school cologne, it was still full of assorted research books stacked in piles across the floor. Awards and framed photos crammed the bookcase, beside his impressive private collection of Shakespeare's works. Assorted suits and shirts hung in dry cleaner's plastic wrap on a coatrack. A leather couch stretched along the side wall, holding a pillow and a rumpled grey blanket.

'How?' Regus calmly rocked in his chair, while his eagle eyes took in the details.

Joe and Maddison sat in the guest chairs facing Regus's desk. While Nancy prowled like a caged lioness with an unlit cigarette in one hand and an empty champagne glass in the other.

'Joe pulled me out of a crocodile-infested river, from a sinking plane that got hit during a tropical lightning storm. Joe had to resuscitate me because I'd stopped breathing and nearly drowned.' She then breathed, after delivering it the way Regus liked it: hard, fast and factual.

'True story? Was that the light plane incident at that Northern Territory cattle station?' Regus remained calm and expressionless. After all, he was a newspaperman who'd heard it all before.

'Are you freaking kidding me!' Nancy stood with mouth open and arms dangling at her sides, barely keeping her grip on the unlit cigarette and champagne glass.

'I suppose I should pat you on the back there, Joe, for being a hero.' Regus gave another short nod to Joe. 'But I still had to do that warning speech, you know. I am a man true to my word. I may not have a shotgun, but I have a team of lawyers on speed dial.'

Maddison cut him off. 'That won't be necessary, Regus.'

'Just remember, if you ever want to get married, Maddy, I can give you away. I always wanted to do that. I had this wife once, she was barren. Couldn't give me no kids.' Regus slyly winked at Joe and Maddison with a glint to his eagle eyes.

'Hey, arsehole? That's because you were never home to

get me bloody pregnant.' Nancy ripped open the office door. 'I don't need this! I'll be in my office when you've finished with this bastard.' She slammed the door behind her.

'After twenty years, I still know how to push that woman's buttons to get her to leave a room.' Regus grinned. 'So, Maddy, have you finished with this whole *find yourself* drama and you're ready to come back to work?'

She took a sharp breath and blurted out the words she thought she'd never ever say. 'Regus, I need your help.'

'True story!' Regus's chair stopped rocking as he stared at Maddison for a moment. He then plucked up his phone from his paper-covered desk. 'Kelly, hold all calls. I'm not to be disturbed.' He slammed the phone back into its cradle. 'You now have my undivided attention, young lady. Because you never ask for help, so this must be bloody big.'

'Um, well …' Maddison hesitated and looked at Joe.

'Start from the beginning.' Joe gave her an encouraging nod.

'Okay.' With a heavy hand, she presented Bob's waterproof pouch. 'It all started with Uncle Bob …'

Maddison relayed the whole saga of her past three weeks to Regus, who patiently listened as she showed him the evidence Bob had gathered.

'And there you have it.' With a sigh, she collapsed back into her seat.

'Well, didn't you just dump a steaming load …' With hands behind his head, Regus rocked in his chair. 'How many days do we have left before they realise you've escaped the station?'

'Two.'

Regus sat upright in his chair. 'I've got a mate in the Federal Police, I'll call him to come and speak with you ASAP, because what you have in your possession is evidence of a crime. You might get implicated for interfering in a murder investigation, and I'll want you both covered for the legalities of this story. We'll work out a way to get the goon, held hostage at this cattle station, without getting Joe's family in trouble too.'

'Do you trust this cop?' Joe asked Regus.

'I do. He'll want to hit hard on this one, because one of

his own got murdered. But you …' Regus pointed at Maddison. 'How far do you want to run with this? It's your story.'

'It's Uncle Bob's story. You know I don't do mainstream news reports.' It was a whole different world of journalism.

'But Bob gave it to you, kid.' Regus then laced his fingers together, leaning his forearms on the desk. 'Are you going to finish it, or do you want me to handball this to someone else? Because I think, no—' Again, he stabbed at the air. 'I believe you need to take this all the way to the printers.'

'Don't you think Maddison's been through enough already?' Joe said. 'She's risked so much just to get here.'

'As if I'd put Maddy in any danger. For Shakespeare's sakes, I'm her bloody godfather.'

'*I'll finish it.*' Maddison shouted above the men arguing over her safety. 'I promised Bob I would.'

'Good,' said Regus, swinging back on his chair. 'You may be too much of an empathetic journalist for my newsroom, but that doesn't mean you have the skills and the integrity to give this story the justice it deserves.' He then flung from his chair and ripped open his office door. '*Kelly?*'

The secretary jumped to attention from behind her desk, pen and digital notebook at the ready. 'Yes, sir.'

'Call Woodcock from the AFP and get him to haul arse up here now. Tell him he's going to owe me a carton of scotch for this one.' He started to close his office door only to whip it back open. '*Kelly?*'

'Yes, sir?'

'Fetch me the bloodhounds. I want their butts up here now. *And you?*' Regus pointed to Maddison 'You go down to that office of yours, which I've kept open, and I want you to write down everything you just told me. I want your first draft on my desk before the feds get here! And don't keep it on any of the company files either. I want this one off the official company records until I say so. I'll call you when the feds get here. *Now get out of my office, I've got a business to run.*' Like a drill sergeant ordering his troops under enemy attack, he marched back to his desk 'You've got copies of all those photos and that recording, Maddison?'

Maddison nodded.

'Good. Make more. We'll give the originals to the feds to keep them happy.' He plonked down into his chair. 'Now go, because they'll keep you busy for hours when you tell them this little story of yours.'

Maddison got up from her chair, with Joe quietly following her out the door.

'And one more thing, Maddy?' called out Regus.

She faced the powerful man behind the enormous desk. 'Yes?'

He flung out of his chair and gave her a warm hug. 'Welcome back, kid, I've missed not having you around.'

'Thank you.'

'You look after her, Joe. Maddy's one in a million. *Now get out and get busy, I've got a business to run.*'

Sixty-three

'So that was Regus, eh?' Tossing his jacket over his shoulder, Joe exhaled slowly. He knew a man in charge when he met one. 'I like the man.'

Maddison arched an eyebrow at him as they passed Kelly, busy on the phone. 'Regus didn't scare you off?'

'I can see he's a busy man, and he tells it how it is at a hundred miles an hour. He obviously cares about you.' Joe slid his arm around Maddison's shoulders as they walked down the main corridor with cubicles of people busily working on either side. 'I've never had the father-to-boyfriend warning speech before. Don't think I'll want one again in a hurry, I reckon your godfather is a man who means what he says.'

'Regus is true to his word.'

'What are the bloodhounds?' Joe imagined a pair of hunting dogs.

The elevator dinged, and two geeky guys carrying laptops, sprinted up the hallway. One pushed his glasses up his nose, brushing past Maddison and Joe.

'Them.' Maddison pointed to the two geeks. 'They're the bloodhounds.'

As the two men bolted through the corridor of cubicles the room became quieter the closer they got to Regus's office.

'What do they do?' Joe asked Maddison.

'Research and background checks. If you've got a skeleton in your closet or an inch of dirt buried away, or on any public document, they'll sniff it out.' She whispered, 'they're first-class hackers.'

'Right my little bloodhounds, *close the bloody door!*' Regus's voice roared like a lion from his cave as the door slammed shut.

Joe scratched his head and looked back over the room. Maybe this really was a jungle, with Regus the lion king in his lair. Nancy the prowling cougar looking for her next male victim to play with. The female models looked like underfed giraffes, while other women dressed like colourful wild birds in a flock. Secretaries jumped to attention like a kangaroo caught under the blinding spotlights of a car. Young men sprinted like brumbies crossing a grassy flood plain. People strutted around with phones glued to their ears, talking over each other like a flock of screeching cockatoos. While more people peeked over cubicle walls like long-neck turtles coming up for air. All collectively working together like busy bush bees in a hive.

'What do think will happen next?' Joe asked as they waited for the lift.

'That depends on what the bloodhounds can find on Antonio Cottillard. They'll also look into the Federal Immigration Minister, the Police Superintendent, the detectives, and every other name I've mentioned to Regus.'

'Haven't you done that already?'

'Those guys will go much deeper. They rarely let the bloodhounds off their leash, it's impressive when they do, but it's expensive.'

'In what way?' Joe followed Maddison inside the elevator, the closing doors silencing the busy newsroom.

'The last time they hacked into a government department's database to uncover a story, it cost Regus nearly fifty thousand in legal fees and a lot of favours to save those two boys from jail.'

Joe had never realised so much went on behind the scenes for a newspaper story. 'Impressive.' So was Regus, and the lady beside him.

The doors opened to the quiet corridors of the magazine. 'Where's your office?'

'This way, the corner office.' She led him past the executive offices.

'Welcome back, Miss Farley,' said a receptionist, straightening her skirt. 'My name is Gemma and I've been assigned as your assistant.'

'Hi, Gemma.' Maddison smiled politely. 'Please call me Maddison, and this is Joe.'

Gemma opened the door to an office with a wall of windows that gave an impressive city view. Free from clutter, a large white desk dominated the spacious room, with white carpet and a matching bookcase. On one side stood a white leather couch below a framed cover of the Maddison magazine's first issue.

'As per Kelly's instructions from Mr Regus's office, you have a laptop and spare memory cards on the desk ready to go,' explained Gemma, holding the door for them. 'Is there anything I can get for you, Miss Farley?'

'Coffee please, Gemma. Joe?'

'Yes, please.' Joe stood on the edge of the white mat in his black shiny shoes. Were they going to leave marks?

'Coming right up.' Gemma closed the door.

Joe gazed at the blown-up magazine cover of a mother and child. He angled his head, recognising the eyes and smile. 'That's you and your mother.'

'That was the first cover of the Maddison magazine. It was my seventh birthday, so we had a double party celebration that day. Leon took that photo.'

'Your mother was beautiful, like you.'

'Thank you.' She wasn't happy, glancing around the room, as if it was filled with ghosts from her past.

'It must be strange coming back?'

* * *

'It's as if I never left.' Maddison stood behind the desk, slowly rolling out the white leather chair and gingerly took her seat. The only thing lying on her desk was the laptop.

It was so surreal.

It had been such a furious flurry to get here, from facing

life-and-death situations in the wilderness to exuberant luxury.

But she couldn't afford to slow down because the job wasn't over.

'I've got work to do. Is there something you want to do?'

Joe was checking out the awards and photos on the bookcase, just like she'd done at the station's library.

Poor man, thrown in the deep end. Yet still willing to hang around, practically fleeing his home to the heart of a capital city. He'd gone from wearing jeans, boots and an Akubra to a tailored suit and tie. Joe could easily pass as a high-powered executive and not a cattleman who managed a station the size of a small European state.

Then Maddison remembered Glenda's question … How would she feel about Joe if he was in her world? Would she notice him?

'I want to ring home and check on everyone,' said Joe. 'They'll want an update on what's going on.'

Maddison hadn't had time to buy another new mobile to replace the one ruined in the plane crash. Surprisingly, she'd never missed having one and Joe didn't need one living on the station, because there was no network coverage. 'Use the phone on the coffee table.'

'I won't be disturbing you?'

'No. Noise doesn't bother me when I'm writing.' She removed her coat, then raised the laptop's lid. 'I've worked in noisier places. I did this job once, tapping away on my laptop in the middle of a rock concert.' Her grin was as fleeting as the memory. 'You should go and see Nancy. I'm sure she'll give you the grand tour of the place.'

'What are you going to do?'

'I'm not going anywhere until I've finished this story.'

'In that case, I'll wait.' Joe tossed his jacket over the couch, loosened his tie more, rolled up the sleeves of his shirt and plucked a magazine off the coffee table.

'I could be hours.'

'I don't mind waiting to get a personal tour from the woman they named this magazine after. I've never read one of these women's magazines before.' He nestled back into the seat and flicked open the magazine cover.

She was tempted to lie next to him, just to slow down again. But she had a lot of work to do, her first big news story, and didn't want Regus screaming down the walls with his marching orders.

Sixty-four

As the sun set across Sydney harbour, the cityscape's lights illuminated the skyline in a twinkling display of colour as the view through the windows of Thames Publishing House.

'Right!' Regus sat at the head of the boardroom table with Maddison and Joe beside him. 'Maddison and Joe have told you their story. What are you planning to do?'

Superintendent Simon Woodcock from the Australian Federal Police stroked his tie as he sat at the opposite end, facing Regus. Officers from his unit sat on either side of him, scribbling down notes in between tapping away on their laptops. None of them wore uniforms, to keep this meeting as discreet as possible.

'When you said I was going to owe you a carton of scotch for this one, Regus, I knew it was big …' Shaking his head, Woodcock stared at the notes, photos, memory sticks and Bob's old phone. 'I wasn't expecting this.'

Regus laced his fingers together and rested his forearms on the table. 'You do understand I have a publishing business to run. I have an obligation to report this story. But before I do, I need to ensure Maddison is protected, which includes the safety of Joe and his family on that station. So, Woodcock, what are you going to do?'

Woodcock stroked his greying sideburns, still nodding to himself, as he spoke to his team. 'Set up full surveillance on Cottillard, those Victoria Police members, the Federal Minister, and the warehouses. I also want a list of movements for any ships owned by Cottillard. Get me enough evidence to raise a warrant for people smuggling and extortion.'

'What about *murder*?' Maddison gritted her teeth, trying to contain the frustration simmering to boiling point. 'Why isn't anyone rushing out the door to arrest everyone?'

'We can't arrest Cottillard yet for his part in your uncle's murder,' replied Woodcock. 'As much as I'd like to, as he's also murdered one of my own men, I want to bury him.'

'How?'

'By letting them operate as normal and hopefully we'll catch them in the act and shut his whole show down.'

'Time is short, mate.' Regus rocked in his chair, squinting with his eagle eyes. 'Allow me to crack open a box of crayons to draw you a picture here … It won't take them long to work out Maddison's gone. Once they do, this story can go two ways. They'll either get busy covering their tracks to hightail it outta the country, leaving you with dick. Or they'll declare war on my goddaughter, her boyfriend's family, and everyone they know. So how fast can you move?'

'As fast as the red tape allows us.' Woodcock then spoke to his officers. 'Get a team on a plane out to that station, undetected, to arrest that Tom. Find out everything he knows. Go through the personal effects of the guy killed by the crocodiles. Their phones, everything. Do it now.'

Two officers picked up their phones, talking among themselves as they tapped furiously away on their laptops.

'We only want our own team working on this. No outsiders. Remember, one of our own was murdered because of a tip-off from someone inside the Victoria Police. So stealth is paramount.' Woodcock then said to Maddison, 'I want you under protective custody.'

'You can't lock me up.' She wasn't the criminal.

'It's for your own protection. You'll have a police guard until this gets sorted out.'

'Why? Cottillard still thinks I'm on the station. I snuck into this city like I was an illegal immigrant—'

'Hang on, Maddy,' said Regus. 'Woodcock's right.'

'I agree,' Joe said, gently patting her arm to soothe her. 'But once you've made all of your arrests, can you guarantee Maddison's safety?'

'Good point,' said Regus, nodding at Joe. 'You know as

soon as this Cottillard gets arrested I'm releasing the full story.'

'Can't you wait?' snapped back Woodcock.

'*I am waiting,*' barked out Regus. '*The only reason I haven't gone to print is purely for Maddison's safety!*'

She blinked up at the man, who spoke hard and fast. She wanted to hug the grouch, right then and there.

'From what my little bloodhounds have dug up on that Cottillard, he is an evil little man. Selling human beings. Eluding both state and federal authorities with his operation. He's already sent two men out to kill Maddison, which he'll do again, doubling the price on her head!'

'That's why I want Maddison in police protection,' said Woodcock. 'Look, I need to build a watertight case against Cottillard, including a list of all his assets and how he got them. Everything. Which means pinning him and his crew, from the Federal Immigration Minister right down to those dirty detectives in Melbourne.' Woodcock then leaned his arms on the table, with hands open to Regus. 'Is that all you've got on this story?'

'The girl's told you all she has.'

'But I'm asking you, Regus.'

Regus kept his face expressionless. 'What do I get?'

'I promise to keep you fully in the loop with this operation.'

'All of it? None of that hush-hush company rulebook bull, either. You'll lay it all on the table and not hit that mute button and move on?'

Woodcock nodded. 'You show me, and I'll show you. Do we have a deal?'

'Deal!' Regus nodded at Woodcock. '*Kelly?*' He shouted at the closed boardroom door before he addressed Woodcock. 'I'll give you what I've got so you can slice through that bureaucratic Federal Police red tape jamming up your soup pot. My crew's legwork will give you lot a catapulting start in this race. But I want in. On everything. We can use this room and all my facilities to coordinate from here.'

'Yes, sir?' Kelly stood at the open doorway of the boardroom with pen and notebook in hand, wearing a discreet headpiece for the phone.

'Coordinate here?' said Woodcock. 'We have our own secured facilities and police systems.'

'You can access them there ...' Regus pointed to their laptops. 'This room is secure, with plenty of outside lines if you need them so we'll have full control to ensure no one leaks this out to the *wrong* people.'

'But—'

'Listen, Woodcock, how long will it take you and your boys in blue to troll through Cottillard's financials? Have you got a team of accountants and field specialists on hand? How long will it take to raise a warrant to search for the real meat and potatoes this Cottillard's got tucked away under his pillow?' Regus swung on his chair, backwards and forwards. 'Is your lot still friendly with Customs, considering your guy got murdered working with them? Do you have someone you trust enough not to blow the whistle to the harbour masters? Do you even know where to look for those crooked dicks playing pretend detectives for the Victorian Police Department?'

'We've got contacts. And we can watch the Federal politician in Canberra.'

'Oh, the Federal Minister, who runs the Immigration Department that's slower than a sleeping snail. Ever since that debacle with all those illegal immigrants escaping from those detention centres, they've done squat but point fingers at everyone else. That mob will be too busy scrambling to cover their own tracks before you put a toe in their driveway. Come on, mate, let me roll out my pizza cutter to really break the crust.'

'Fine!' Woodcock threw his hands up. 'We'll coordinate from here to begin with, depending on what you've got.'

Regus's eagle eyes glistened as the corners of his lips curled into a wry smile. '*Kelly*.'

'Yes, sir,' replied Kelly, still dutifully standing by the door.

'Fetch the bloodhound's paperwork from my desk. Make eight copies on what they've dug up.'

Kelly nodded as she scribbled.

Regus continued while staring at Woodcock. 'I want the

report from the finance team that I expected four hours ago. They've had ten hours to trawl through Cottillard's company tax returns and assets. Tell them they'd better have found something or they're all fired!'

Kelly kept scribbling, expressionless.

Regus checked his watch. 'Then check my emails. There's a report expected in ten minutes, from that bullfrog that swims in that politician's murky pond in Canberra. If it's not here in fifteen minutes, call that pompous prick up and tell him I'll crush him into a picture book that'll never get published. Once you get that report, tell him he's not to move off his lily pad until I say so.'

He rocked in his chair as Kelly took notes.

'Call Chin. Tell him to send through that stuff he had on immigration. Be sure to send him a case of cigars. Then contact Bugle, in Melbourne. Tell him I want that stuff he told me on the phone earlier in writing. Have it emailed to me in the next half hour! Call Weasel and tell him and his team of busy boy scouts to drop back, coz the feds are coming. But Weasel is *not* to stop watching that list of men, until *I say so*, no matter what the feds say.'

Woodcock frowned at Regus, who didn't stop for a breath as Kelly kept scribbling.

'Contact Fitzy from our boating magazine downstairs. He'll have the itineraries for that list of ships I gave him. Print off eight copies. Include his report from his mates in the Border Force and Port Authority. And tell my little bloodhounds ...' Regus then grinned evilly at the Federal Police Superintendent Simon Woodcock and said, 'they're off the leash.'

Kelly stopped scribbling.

Maddison gasped.

But Regus kept barking out a steady stream of instructions like a general commanding his troops. 'Tell them to go for the throat on that prick's trail. Keep them boys up in food and energy drinks. Pat them on the head occasionally and order that new IT crap I promised them as an inspirational bone to keep digging. And I want that five-star safe house fully stocked and ready for some incoming VIPs. We'll need more coffee and food in here, too. None of that greasy Chinese crap either, that last lot gave me heartburn. Got all that?'

'Yes, sir.' Kelly gave a curt nod and closed the door behind her.

'You know, Regus,' said Woodcock, loosening his tie, 'if I talked to my staff like that I'd get done for harassment.'

'You cops have gone soft. Besides, I have a reputation to keep up as the Editor-in-Chief, who's an outright cruel bastard, so I got told once.' Regus winked at Maddison.

She grimaced with a meek and mild shrug as a flood of emotions swamped her weary bones. But was it enough?

Sixty-five

Within the plush executive office of the *Maddison Magazine*, Nancy sat on the edge of her luxurious chaise lounge. Champagne glass in one hand and a smouldering cigarette in the other, she inspected the proofs from Leon's morning photo shoot. She shuffled the sheets containing thumbnail images of Maddison and Joe, peering at them through a magnifying glass.

There was a knock on the door.

'Come in.' Nancy glanced up, expecting Maddison and Joe, keen to take them to dinner.

It was eight in the evening, and they'd been with Regus, locked in that boardroom since lunchtime. She was dying to know what was going on.

Wayne, her assistant, strutted through with an ice bucket containing a bottle of champagne and a small plate. 'Here's your nightcap.' He put the ice bucket on the coffee table, then collapsed into an armchair, crossing his legs like a showgirl.

Nancy stubbed out her dead cigarette in the ashtray, then refilled her champagne glass. 'What's wrong with you now, Farkwit?'

'Wayne, remember.'

'Darling, it's a habit from the long line of assistants that swapped out their brain matter for sawdust. Be grateful for the job, and for the title as the longest Farkwit I've ever had. In a year, I may call you by name. Until then, as I told you when you first started, it's Farkwit. In this office, it's a title to be proud of. I've made you famous, like Prince and Madonna. Be grateful.' She sipped on her champagne for dramatic pause.

'Is the rant over?'

'Yes.' She smiled at Wayne, who really was the best assistant. But he also had the type of personality if she did tell him he was good, he'd get a big head and leave. And she did not want to have to train another Farkwit.

He angled his head and glanced at the images of Maddison and Joe on the coffee table. 'They're a gorgeous-looking couple.' Wayne grabbed the magnifying glass and leaned in closer to examine them. 'He's so rugged, and Maddison has always been photogenic.'

'We used little Maddy all the time as a child model over the years. Her mother would drag her out whenever we were short of money or talent,' said Nancy proudly. 'Such a shy little thing she was. Even though my goddaughter practically grew up in front of the camera, she was always trying to hide from it. Now, my darling, tell me what's happening in Regus's boardroom.'

'Well, Maddison and that tall, dark and dreamy shadow of hers that she dragged back from the wilderness, they're still with Regus.'

'Any idea who else is in there?'

'No. No one else knows what's going on up there. It's all locked down. And Kelly's being her usual tight-lipped wonder and can't or won't say when they'll finish.'

'Maddison will tell me all when it's over. I'll wait for her here. Go home, darling.'

'Will do.' Wayne flounced for the door with the empty bottle of champagne.

'Oh, and Farkwit?'

'Yes?' He stopped to catch the door jamb.

'Thank you for setting up that photo shoot for me this morning.'

He bowed. 'That's my job. But you're the one that's got to put up with the tongue-lashing from Maddison when she sees you next.' His tittering laughter followed as he pulled the door shut behind him.

'I can handle Sweet Cheeks.'

Alone in the room, she glanced over the images.

'Oh, Janice ...' Nancy whispered to the deserted room.

'How do I get your daughter Maddison to open up? I just want to see her happy.'

Her office door opened once again as she kept inspecting the photos. 'Did you forget something, Farkwit?'

'Who the hell do you think you are, lady, to call me that?' Grunted a gruff voice at the door.

Nancy spun in her seat to face the two men crowding the doorway.

One had a jagged scar along his cheekbone that blended with the acne scars around his chin.

The other man was bigger and beefier with a square jaw like a bulldog and a squashed nose.

Both wore ill-fitting, off-the-rack nylon suits that bulged in the worst places. Ugh, and their shoes were so wrong. 'Are you lost?'

'No. We're here to take you with us,' said Scarface.

'Can't, darling, I've got a better offer.' She scooped up her champagne glass and approached her desk to check her diary. Did she miss an appointment? 'I'm waiting for my goddaughter.'

'So were we.'

Nancy whirled around to face the men who lacked any form of dress sense. 'Why are you waiting for my goddaughter?'

'We're not anymore, coz there's been a change of plans.' Scarface sneered, pulling out a handgun. 'You're coming with us, lady.'

'Is that real?' She pointed at the pistol. It looked like a prop.

'Of course, it's real. Who do you think we are?'

'I have no idea. How did you get in here?'

'Listen, lady—'

'The name is Nancy, darling. Nancy McCann.'

'I. Don't. Give. A. Toss.' He snarled with his face so close she could see the pores between the acne scars and smell the mint on his breath. But his eyes were dark and cold.

What was colder was the pistol he'd jammed hard against her head, forcing her to lean at an awkward angle.

'What do you want?'

'For you to cooperate and come with us, or we'll shoot

you.'

'Shoot me? Darling, we've only just met, I couldn't have pissed you off already?'

Scarface gripped her arm.

'Ow, that hurts.'

'Look, lady, we haven't got the time, or the patience, to muck around with rich bitches like you.'

They meant business.

Nancy gulped at the fear running down her spine, fighting the sudden urge to pee.

'You can scream, but you know everyone's gone home, so we're gonna walk out nice and calm-like. Okay, lady?'

Panic took hold. Not only did she want to pee, but Nancy also desperately needed a cigarette to calm her nerves. 'I need my cigarettes and handbag.'

'Why?' The human bulldog spoke.

'Because I'm an absolute bitch without my cigarettes. Ask my five ex-husbands, they'll tell you I'm an addict. Darling, if you want me to cooperate you can't have me succumb to nicotine withdrawal and not cooperate, when I want to cooperate, and I will cooperate if you'll only let me take my cigarettes.'

'Jeezus, find her bloody smokes,' said Scarface. 'And her mobile phone too.'

The human bulldog shoved her cigarettes and mobile phone into Nancy's handbag.

'Coat too, please.' She pointed to her fur coat on the rack. 'Darling, it matches the bag.'

'Jeezus.' Scarface shook his head.

'Whatever.' The human bulldog snatched her coat off the rack. He then scooped up the cigarettes and lighter resting by the ice bucket. Taking a swig of champagne straight from the bottle, his face screwed up as if he'd swallowed glue. 'Ugh.' But his flat nose didn't move.

How did he breathe through such a flat nose?

'Why do women drink that crap?' The human bulldog dumped the bottle on top of the photo proofs.

Nancy gasped. 'You'll ruin those proofs.'

'Do we look like we give a toss, lady?' Scarface tightened his grip on Nancy's arm, cutting off the circulation.

She could feel the bruises forming.

'Come on.' He dragged her toward the door that led to the wide corridor.

'But …' How was this was happening?

'Behave,' said Scarface with the gun's cold muzzle pressed against her throat, 'and we'll give you a smoke in the car.'

'Oh, okay.' Not okay, but she had no choice.

Oh, Sweet Cheeks, what have you done?

Sixty-six

The boardroom was stuffy and crowded, its vast tabletop covered with half-empty platters of finger sandwiches and savoury pastries, in between coffee cups, paperwork, and laptops.

Kelly entered the room and nodded to Regus, who was controlling the chaos.

'Right …' Regus stood to re-roll the sleeves on his shirt with his tie hanging loose around the unbuttoned collar. 'Joe, I want you and Maddison to take my car. It's parked in the basement right next to the elevator.'

Unable to do much, Joe was glad to get out of there. He wasn't a cop or a journalist, but he was a cattleman who could drive. 'What type of car am I looking for?'

'A black BMW, I never use. It's near the lifts in the basement. There's a fuel card in the centre console, and Kelly's set you up with a mobile phone. Kelly will give you the keys and all our phone contact details.'

'Where are we going?' Joe asked Regus, a powerhouse player under pressure. He had to respect the man.

'But we're not finished.' Maddison wore a determined frown that only highlighted the dark rings under her eyes.

'You need a break, young lady,' said Regus.

'But—'

'That's not negotiable.' Regus held his hand up, silencing her. 'Go with Joe and get some rest.'

'I'm siding with Regus, let's go get some dinner,' Joe suggested.

She hugged her scary godfather, the man of the hour. 'Thank you, Regus.'

'You take care, kid, and I'll call you with regular updates.' Regus held his hand out to Joe. 'You're all right, you know that.' The two men shook hands. 'I expect you to keep an eye on Maddy for me.'

'You don't have to ask.' Joe gave a curt nod to Regus, then placed a protective palm on Maddison's lower back.

Woodcock approached them from the far end of the table. 'I've got two men assigned to watch you, Maddison. They'll be at the hotel when you arrive.'

'Any idea what's happening to protect my family?' Joe asked.

'The jet is on its way. It's scheduled to land at Elleron Downs in a few hours.'

Joe checked his watched and calculated the time difference. 'I'll call home and get them to sort out some lights for the airstrip. How many officers can I tell them to expect?'

'Six officers and a pilot.'

'Thanks.' He was damned glad to know his family weren't going to be alone out there with that Tom character for long.

'You can call them from my office, while I get my bag and laptop together.' Maddison grabbed her coat from the back of her chair.

Kelly greeted them at the door with keys and directions. The couple headed for the elevators with the sounds of Regus barking out orders in the background.

'Does Regus ever work at any other speed besides flat out?' Joe asked Maddison as they both leaned their backs against the walls of the elevator. The doors closed, and the space was blissfully silent.

'Regus lives for the job. He loves it.'

'You've got to give the guy credit; he knows his stuff. He'd make a hell of an army general the way he controls a room. I like the guy.'

'Regus likes you, and that's rare.' She raised a weary smile as the elevator doors opened to the magazine's foyer. The combined scent of summer fruits and florals greeted them as her heels click-clacked down the deserted corridors.

'This place looks different now everyone's gone.' Joe glanced at the life-sized magazine covers that lined the hallways. 'If your mother created this magazine, who owns it? Thames Publishing? Nancy? Or Regus?'

She stopped outside her open office door. 'Regus owns eighty per cent of the company's shares. The rest is public stockholders and trustees.'

'So Regus owns the Maddison Magazine then?' Why couldn't she ever give him a straight answer? What did she have to hide?

'No. My mother made a deal with Regus from the start that each year she'd get allocated shares in the magazine. When she died, she gave Nancy ten per cent and my uncle ten per cent, and the remaining forty per cent of her shares went into a trust. Uncle Bob's shares are now with the trust.'

'So this trust shares control over the magazine with Regus.'

'Nancy manages its day-to-day operations, while Regus checks every issue before it goes to print.'

'So, you haven't inherited this magazine?' Now he was getting confused. Or was she trying to avoid the question?

'Technically, no,' replied Maddison. 'I was a minor, only sixteen when my mother passed. As soon as she discovered she was sick, Regus helped my mother set up the trust to take care of my clothing and schooling expenses. They also set it up in a way that I couldn't blow it backpacking through Europe for the rest of my life. Which was a bummer, I really wanted that holiday?'

Did she say a *holiday for life*? How rich was she?

'Uncle Bob and Nancy were easy enough to convince, but Regus, he was such a ...'

'The man who's upstairs now.' Pulling everyone off their jobs and sending bloodhounds out to break laws for Maddison.

She gave a curt laugh, hugging herself as she walked to her desk and looked around the white office. 'Looking back, I owe that man a lot.'

'How many years have you been working in this office? Must have been a while because everyone in this building knows your name.'

'This was my mother's office. Not mine.' She frowned at the vacant chair behind the desk with its back to the city skyline. 'I grew up in this office, sleeping on the couch, playing in the halls of this building.'

'So you didn't work here?'

'Officially, when I was about twelve, I started working for Regus in the mailroom as a part-time job after school, while I was waiting for my mother to take us home. Home was rare, because it was normal to wake up on the couch to the sounds of my mother typing on her keyboard. Dinners would get delivered by courier for overnight stays. I'd shower in the bathroom in Nancy's office, collect breakfast from the downstairs cafeteria, on my way to meet the company driver in the basement to take me to school.'

Joe leaned his shoulder against the door frame. For the first time since they'd arrived, her protective inner walls were down, she looked so sad and vulnerable.

Maddison lifted a large award among the many on the bookcase. 'By fifteen, I'd become a trainee assistant who ran errands around the building for the secretarial pool during the school year. Then every summer holiday, while kids went on vacation, Regus got me an internship working for every other magazine and newspaper within this building except for the Maddison Magazine.' She scoffed, putting the award back on the shelf. 'I had to apply for those positions like everyone else, too.'

'No preferential treatment, huh?'

'No, Regus was harder on me than anyone else. Or so I thought.'

'Why? Considering he's your godfather.'

'Regus wanted me to gain experience from other journalists in all the other publications. I've never worked for the Maddison Magazine except to send in a few freelance articles. Regus wouldn't let me near it.'

'Why not?'

'He didn't want me to ruin it.' She laughed. 'The bastard.'

'Can he do that?'

'Yes. You see, my mother was such an extraordinary visionary, that when she found out about her cancer, she'd devised a thirty-year publishing plan.' She turned and faced the first cover of the magazine. Her hand hovered as if to stroke her mother's cheek, but she stopped only to close it into a fist, crossing her arms tightly over her chest.

And just like that her inner walls went back up.

She stood taller staring down the image of herself as a child and her voice got colder. 'Since the very first issue of the magazine, I was a sub-editor in training. Sitting beside my mother, we'd proof every edition before it went to print, ensuring it kept within that year's publishing plan. Regus and I still go over every issue—except for last month.'

From his spot in the doorway on the edge of the white carpet, he admired Maddison standing before the window that showcased the city's night skyline. It was as if she had the world beneath her feet.

It was a corporate world she looked at home in.

Nancy said the magazine was ready for Maddison to take her part anytime, and Regus had kept this office open for her, with her gap year ending.

Maddison's life belonged here in Sydney with her trust accounts, her bedroom in a mansion, limousines, and a glamourous fast-paced lifestyle.

Where was the Maddison he'd met on the station?

What was he thinking?

A woman like Maddison would get bored and eventually despise living on a hot, dusty, remote cattle station with him and his family.

Their worlds were polar opposites.

No wonder she'd never said she loved him!

Sixty-seven

'I'll call home so they can prepare for that incoming jet full of feds.' Joe reached for the phone by the couch.

'Sure. I'll go and find Nancy. She wants to take us out to dinner.'

Joe was already dialling with his back to her.

Had she done the wrong thing, over-sharing her past and telling Joe about the trust? Maddison hated talking about it; people always treated her differently when they knew.

She headed down the hallway to Nancy's office, knocking on the open door.

'Nancy, we're free to go to dinner now. Sorry, it must be quick as we're meeting ...' Maddison walked into the opulently furnished office.

'Nancy?' She knocked on Nancy's private bathroom door.

There was no reply.

On the coffee table an ice bucket stood beside the champagne bottle, the condensations water droplets trickled down its glassy sides to pool over a set of photo proofs.

'That's not like you, Nancy.' Maddison slid the bottle back into the ice bucket and grabbed a few tissues to dry off the thumbnail images.

She paused, tilting her head.

They were the images of her and Joe from earlier today.

She scowled. Sick to death of her face being used like some free prop shoved in the background. In the beginning it had been to keep costs down for the magazine to put food on the table. But it sucked.

Her hair would get pulled and teased. Her skin pores

would get clogged by caked-on make-up and her sinuses were over-sensitive from the overuse of hair spray. Her muscles would ache from pasting on a smile while standing still in awkward positions, freezing in winter showing off upcoming summer swimsuits, or sweating it out in summer wearing snowsuits!

Sure she had access to an incredible designer wardrobe, but they were just objects. Things her mother obsessed over for the magazine.

If ever she wanted her mother's attention, Maddison had to compete with all the grownups and objects of fashion.

Her mother never went to her sports games or school functions. Half the time, she never even checked on Maddison, consumed by these objects of fashion fighting for their place within a magazine.

As the days turned, the seasons shifted, current fashions were exchanged for ever-changing trends, and all those early editions of glamour disappeared. Even the woman who had started it all was gone.

The elevator dinged down the hall. Its doors swooshed open, and the familiar rumbling roll of the cleaning trolley entered the foyer. In a few moments, the vacuum cleaner started.

Maddison picked up the office phone from Nancy's desk and dialled.

'Hello?' Nancy croaked over the phone, as if dragging heavily on a cigarette.

'Nancy, it's Maddison. Where are you? Do you still want to do dinner?'

'Oh no, Maddy—'

'Nancy? Are you there?'

'Is this Maddison?' asked a gruff male voice.

'Who is this?'

'I work for Antonio Cottillard.'

Maddison gasped as if sucker-punched in the stomach. 'How did you know I was here?'

'You can thank your godmother for that.'

'How? Nancy did nothing. She knows nothing.'

'Your rock-star arrival in your godmother's limo is how. We had to look twice, what with you all decked out like some diva. We'd been told you were interstate, but the boss wanted us to keep watch, just in case. He was right.' He chuckled in an evil, gravelly tone that made the hairs on the back of her neck prickle.

'What do you want with Nancy?' Was this ever going to end? Who else was going to be in danger because of her?

'Nothing, if you give us what we want.'

'Anything. Name it.'

'Give us all the notes on Cottillard in exchange for this woman. Or we'll send pieces of her body in the mail like a jigsaw puzzle until you do.'

'Don't hurt her, please.'

'We haven't touched her. But I don't know how long our patience is gonna last. Jeezus, this lady smokes like a freaking chimney, throwing back shots of scotch and never bloody shuts up!'

'Oh.' Was Nancy being held hostage or having a party? 'Where do I meet you?' She grabbed a pen and small notepad from Nancy's desk.

'Port Botany, Hayes Dock 2. We'll make sure security doesn't bother you, it'll be shift change so they don't look too hard. Board the freighter *Zinko* to find your godmother. You have less than an hour before the boat leaves. Tell no one and come alone. Miss the boat and you can wave bye-bye to your godmother forever.'

The line went dead.

She tore off the top page with her instructions. Then rummaged through the desk drawer for the keys to the car Nancy never drove anymore.

Maddison started pacing the office floor, chewing her thumbnail to work out a plan. The original notes, Bob's phone and the pouch were all upstairs with the feds. But she'd made two copies of everything. One set of full notes and photos were with Regus, the other set were in her office with a final backup being made on her laptop beside her handbag.

With keys in her pocket, she ran on tiptoes to her closed office door.

Joe's voice was muffled inside, speaking to his family on the phone.

It took everything she had not to rush to her desk.

Joe glanced up at her, seated on the couch, cradling the phone to his ear. 'Are we going to dinner?'

'There's no rush. Take your time.' She couldn't even look at him, praying she sounded normal. She grabbed her handbag and pulled the memory stick out of the laptop. 'I'll be down the hall with Nancy.'

'Hold on a sec, Dad,' he said over the phone.

'Say hi to everyone.' Maddison tried to walk as calmly as she could, but inside she was full of jitters, ready to sprint for the corridor.

'Maddison, is everything okay?'

With her back to Joe, Maddison squeezed her eyes shut for a second, she was a terrible liar. She trembled so badly she nearly spilled out everything from her handbag. 'I'm. Fine.'

She closed the door with a resounding click that made her spine snap straight, then sprinted for the elevators, slapping at the button to summon the lift. 'Hurry up!'

Finally, the bell dinged. It was louder than a gong being thrashed in an amphitheatre as it vibrated through her bones.

'Maddison?' Joe pulled open the office door and started walking down the corridor.

Her heart rate hammered in her ears as she forced open the elevator doors to thump on the buttons.

'*Maddison!*' Joe ran for the elevator as the doors started to close. '*Maddison*, STOP.'

Hot tears blurred her vision as her throat squeezed tight. 'I'm sorry, Joe, but they've kidnapped Nancy. They're going to kill her if I don't show up. I'd never meant to involve you, your family, or anyone else in all of this. I'm so, so, sorry.'

She pressed her back to the wall as the elevator doors closed off her last image of Joe. It crushed her to see the hurt and worry in his eyes.

But she'd been nothing but a burden to Joe, to everyone, since this whole saga began. There were too many people involved. Too many were at risk, all prepared to sacrifice themselves for her. This had to end.

She scrubbed hard at the tears streaming down her face and caught her reflection in the mirrored walls of the lift. It was nothing like that wide-eyed haunted terror she'd worn when first fleeing her ransacked apartment, or the horror when she'd found out she was being followed by the gun-wielding goons.

She was now forcing herself to *not* run. She was now determined to face her fear—no matter the consequences to her own life. This had to end with her.

Sixty-eight

'NO!' Joe slammed his fists against the closed elevator doors that were whisking Maddison away.

Why didn't she wait for him to help her?

How did they kidnap Nancy?

Someone must have tipped off Cottillard. Everyone knew Maddison's name in this building, it would have been impossible to keep her visit a secret.

No wonder Maddison was sorry. It's what she'd been fearing the most, that those she cared about would be at risk because of her.

He'd seen it in her face, the fear, and the remorse, but mostly her willingness to surrender herself to the monsters to keep everyone safe. It crushed his soul.

He spotted the EXIT light above the door to the stairs. He burst through and dropped down a flight of stairs and kept on running. His lungs were short of breath, his legs burned, his heart raced, but the adrenalin coursing through his veins spurred him on.

On the ground floor, he shouldered the door open next to the elevators.

The indication panel showed Maddison's elevator was in the basement, one floor below!

Again, Joe raced down the stairs and into the basement car park.

Tyres screeched from a white Mercedes coupe coming from around the corner. The overhead lights of the car park highlighted the driver as it aimed for the exit.

'*Maddison.*' Helpless to do anything, he gripped his head

and tried to catch his breath.

Then he saw it. A black BMW.

Could it be?

Joe patted his pockets and found the keys. Juggling them for a second, he pressed the button and the BMW's lights came on as it unlocked.

In the driver's seat, he slammed the automatic luxury car into gear. With tyres squealing and smoke pouring, he tore out of the underground car park in pursuit of Maddison.

Whizzing through the light night traffic, he zigzagged, ignoring signals and signs, until he spotted her white car turning left at the traffic lights ahead.

'Where are you going, Maddison?' Joe floored the accelerator and raced after her.

But he'd lost sight of the white sports car.

'Where are you?'

He desperately peered around, almost giving up hope, when from the corner of his eye he spotted the white coupe, taking a tunnel exit.

'Dammit.' He slammed his hand on the wheel. He'd missed the turnoff, with Maddison driving out of sight.

Sixty-nine

Maddison parked the car near the docks as per the kidnapper's instructions. With her handbag secure over her shoulder, she ran down the asphalted wharves.

It was just like Melbourne airport all those weeks ago. Her skirts flicking up, her coat trailing as her heels hit the asphalt, sprinting past the stevedores, tractors and trucks towing trailers with silent cranes towering overhead, until she found dock two.

It was huge. Her neck craned up to read the name emblazoned on the ship *Zinko*, with its deck piled high with sea containers.

Maddison hurried past the crews of dockworkers manning the thick mooring lines to the loading bay and stood at the edge of the gangway. Where was Nancy?

'Oi, lady?' A stevedore in a hi-vis vest and hard hat whistled. His arm waved in the air beckoning her to come aboard.

Rubbing her cold fingertips together, a brisk autumn sea breeze brushed against her clammy skin. Unlike flying, she wasn't scared of the sea, being a scuba diver—she just didn't want to get on this boat. But she forced herself to make the first step. Then another.

Over the side, the dark sea splashed along the ship's hull. The ropes swayed, and it was as if she was standing on a skinny rope bridge between two cliff tops with the riverbed unseen hundreds of metres below. Keeping her focus dead ahead to not look down, she scampered across the wide gangway and safely onto the ship's deck flooded in lights.

'Come with me, miss.' The stevedore gave her a curt nod under his hard hat. On the starboard side they headed for the stern, passing a field of sea containers stacked like Lego bricks, creating a city-sized maze. Silent cranes stood on the foremast. Even taller was the signal mast, cluttered with assorted aerials, radar, and satellite dishes. Nearby, powerful lights above the flybridge shone like a city skyscraper.

She followed the stevedore up the stairs to the accommodation deck tucked below the wheelhouse. He pulled down a lever and swung back the heavy metal marine door, peeling it free from its waterproof seals. 'Go first right, below decks, and aim for the door at the end of the hall. You'll find the rest of your party there.'

Maddison gingerly stepped over the door's high threshold.

The marine door slammed behind her, the heavy lever locked it in place cutting her off from the outside noise. Her shallow breathing was the only sound.

She swallowed the lump in her dry throat, as she walked down the skinny corridors, passing closed cabin doors, for the metal stairs.

As she went down the stairs, she licked salt from her lips, fighting the desperate urge to run back through the marine door and into the fresh sea air to jump ship.

But she was here for Nancy.

Again, Maddison forced herself to take each step down the skinny corridor. Muffled voices and cigarette smoke greeted her, one voice she recognised. 'Nancy?' She darted into the room.

At the table sat Nancy with a lit cigarette in one hand, and a death grip around the neck of a large bottle of scotch.

'Are you okay?' She reached for her godmother's hand.

'Oh, my darling, Sweet Cheeks.' Tears glistened in Nancy's eyes, as she reached out and softly stroked Maddison's cheek. 'Aren't you a bloody idiot.'

'This must be her, eh?' The man slammed the cabin door behind Maddison.

She recognised the kidnapper's gruff tone from the phone.

Nancy pointed her cigarette at the man with acne scars

and a pistol in hand. 'Maddison, meet Scarface.' She then pointed to the door. 'The strong, silent one, blocking our way to freedom, is the human bulldog.'

'Take a seat, Maddison,' said Scarface, snatching her handbag.

Maddison dropped onto the bench seat beside her godmother, clutching Nancy's hand.

'Here, sip this. They say scotch helps prevent seasickness.' Nancy slid the bottle across the tabletop while Scarface rifled through Maddison's bag.

'A-huh.' Maddison didn't even blink, snatching up the bottle she gulped down a large mouthful. The spirit burn hit her chest and she gasped for air.

'Hits the spot, huh.' Nancy grinned, lighting another cigarette. 'Want one?'

'God, no.' Maddison shook her head. 'I haven't touched a cigarette since you made me chain smoke that packet with you when I was eleven, and you made me pay for the privilege of puking up each cigarette too.'

'What are you complaining about, darling, you never smoked again.'

'Enough of the bloody family reunion here,' barked out Scarface. 'What have you got?'

Did they know what she had, or were they like Tom who had no clue? 'A notebook, my uncle's notes.' It was her own notebook that contained copies of the photos, and her scribblings of her research, the originals were with Regus. Would they find the memory stick floating around in her bag with everything else?

Scarface emptied her bag onto the bench. 'What were you doing in that building all day?'

'I was hanging out with my godfather.' Maddison sucked at lying, but she was good at telling half-truths.

'Talking about what?'

'Um, the magazine. Catching up …' *Think!* 'He met my boyfriend and that started an argument and a load of lectures.'

'That's so true, darling. I swore Regus and your boyfriend were going to let fists swing any second.'

'How come you were alone in your office and not

upstairs with the family?' Scarface asked Nancy.

'Because Regus is nothing but a heartless bastard.'

'Regus is Nancy's ex-husband,' interjected Maddison.

Scarface nodded. 'I reckon if I was your ex, I'd keep Maddison to myself just to piss you off!'

Nancy scowled at Scarface and blew cigarette smoke straight into his face.

'Nancy, you're not helping.' Maddison then spoke to the men through tight teeth and taut face. 'You've got everything I have, as promised, we'll be leaving now.'

The two men chuckled.

'The deal was for me to give you the stuff for Nancy. You said you'd let her go.'

Scarface leaned over, narrowing his cold eyes at her. 'Plans change.'

She felt the boat sway. It was barely detectable. 'No. No. We still have time to leave.'

'You two make yourself comfortable until we're well under way.'

Nancy took another mouthful of the scotch. The human bulldog crossed beefy arms over a stocky chest with a handgun in one meaty paw, leaning his bulky frame against the one and only door out of there.

'To where?' Maddison asked Scarface as he pulled a packet of mints from his pocket.

'To Melbourne.' He popped a mint into his mouth and grinned evilly.

'But—'

'The boss wants to find out how much you know.'

'But, darling, I hate Melbourne.' Nancy raised the bottle to take another swig.

'This is not happening.' Maddison snatched the bottle from Nancy and drank. Mouthful after mouthful, she swallowed like a baby with a night-time milk bottle, hoping her nightmare would disappear.

'That'll do, young lady.' Nancy pulled the bottle away. 'You'll get drunk, start throwing up everywhere, then I'll go out in sympathy and get seasick, considering we're on a bloody boat!'

Maddison stared at her godmother with eyes wide open.

This nightmare just kept on coming, trapped on a sea voyage to Melbourne to front Antonio Cottillard himself.

There was a sharp knock on the door.

'That's our signal. Up you get, ladies.' Scarface roughly grabbed Maddison's arm, pulling her to her feet.

Maddison was too stunned to speak, staring at everything in bewildered shock.

'Where are we going?' Nancy asked, shovelling her smokes and lighter into her pocket.

'To the VIP accommodation we have for you.' Scarface waved his gun at Nancy. 'You can take the bottle and here …' He opened the cupboard. 'Here's another one to keep you warm for the journey.'

Nancy clutched the two bottles to her chest, wrapping her fur coat around them like they were babies made of gold.

Up the stairs and back on deck the blistering icy wind carried fine mists of seawater to brush against her hot cheeks. Dragged along the foredeck, Maddison glanced back to the twinkling lights of the Sydney Harbour Bridge getting smaller and smaller every passing second.

Into the shadows of the towering sea containers, they weaved through narrow corridors along the decks of the cargo ship.

'Where are you taking us now? And how long will it take us to get there?' Nancy's heels skidded on the steel deck; Maddison gripped her godmother's arm to keep them both upright.

'You should be in Melbourne in about twelve to twenty-four hours, I reckon. Or you'll get there when you get there.' Scarface stopped in front of a sun-faded blue sea container. It was exactly like the dozens that surrounded them.

The human bulldog made simple work of the large handle and pulled open the metal door to expose a gaping dark cavern.

'In you get,' ordered Scarface, waving his small handgun at the two female hostages.

'What? Darling, no. You can't expect us to go into that cave?'

Maddison gripped her godmother like a little girl all over again.

'You'll have company for the journey, they should keep the rats off you.' Scarface opened the doors wider and shone his torch inside.

'Oh dear God,' Nancy said, 'Are you seeing this, Maddy?'

Huddled inside was more than a dozen men, women, and children. They held up their dirty hands to shield them from the torchlight, shuffling as far back into the sea container as they could.

Maddison stared in horror at real live human beings, locked away in the dark like animals.

'Have a delightful trip, ladies.' Scarface shoved Maddison and Nancy inside. They stumbled, grappling with each other, as their heels slipped on the uneven shipping container floor. The door slammed shut behind them and they were plunged into a thick cloying darkness.

Seventy

Joe slowly trawled the commercial shipping piers of Botany Bay, searching for the white Mercedes. By cutting across traffic and making an illegal turn he'd managed to circle back to the tunnel. He'd followed Maddison for nearly thirty minutes, but the traffic in the tunnel meant he never quite caught up with her. But he wasn't giving up. Maddison was in trouble, last seen heading for this area.

'Where did you go, Maddison?' Various docked ships waited. Some attended by a constant stream of incoming and outgoing trucks. When a whistle blew, the dock workers started packing up.

Joe trolled through the car park as a consistent stream of stevedores drove out, until he spotted the luxury coupe on the far-right of the car park. He parked directly behind it, blocking off the white car in case Maddison ran again.

'Where are you?' Joe made his way down the docks, asking dock workers along the way. She wasn't hard to miss, a blonde woman running in heels.

They all pointed him towards dock two.

Joe jogged further down the wharf only to stop and stare at an empty dock with no ship in sight.

A couple of dockworkers stood on the edge of the wharf. Steam rose from the coffee being poured out of a thermos they shared between them.

'Excuse me, fellas, did you notice a blonde woman come through here earlier?' How far behind was he?

'Yeah, I saw her,' said one dockworker, blowing steam from his mug. 'Fancy-dressed sheila, too. I've never seen a woman run that fast in heels before. Has ya missus done a runner on ya, mate?' The men chuckled.

'Do you know where she went? Please?' Joe pleaded for information.

'She got on board that cargo ship. It was loaded with cargo containers.' He nodded with his hard hat to the dark harbour empty of freighters. 'That blonde was the last one on. They set sail as soon as soon as she boarded.'

'What was the ship called?'

'The *Zinko*. She's headed for Melbourne.'

Joe's stomach dropped as an invisible icy hand squeezed the blood from his soul. He turned and ran for the car, his mind racing even faster. Nancy and Maddison now both kidnapped, heading to Melbourne in a ship full of sea containers.

What the hell was he going to do now?

A commercial airliner flew overhead.

He was close to the airport.

But would he get a plane in time? It was nine o'clock, did he dare waste his time if he could get a seat?

Then there was the hassle of going through the airport car park to park this car, only to trudge through another car park on the other side to collect a different car, when he was already sitting in a perfectly comfortable car as it was.

What's better, sitting in the car and driving all night? Or chewing his fingernails, in between scoffing down over-priced drinks, while making a dent in the airport's floor tiles from pacing!

The car's dashboard glowed before him with the fuel gauge showing its tank was almost full.

Didn't Regus mention a fuel card?

Lifting the centre console, there it was. Along with the new mobile phone and a list of contact numbers.

'I've never chased a ship down before, but I know how to use one of these.' Setting a course on the GPS, he slammed the car into gear and raced for the nearest freeway.

Seventy-one

THE TASMAN SEA

'What do we do now?' Nancy's whine bounced off the metal walls of their stuffy prison.

'There is nothing we can do.' Maddison wrapped her coat around herself to ward off the cold as her eyes adjusted to the dim light coming through the small vents. The ship moved beneath the soles of her stilettos as the combination of stale air and body odour made her wince.

It came from the group of people huddled at the far end of the sea container.

'Let's sit.'

'Darling, I'm not sitting on a dirty floor.' Nancy swayed unsteadily in her fur coat. Jewels hung from her ears, and diamond rings garnished her manicured hands that clutched a pair of scotch bottles.

'In case you haven't realised it, we're locked in. The ship is now at sea. And we're trapped in the middle of a hundred containers. No one is going to help us. So, SIT!'

'Darling, you sounded just like your mother then.'

Should Maddison take that as a compliment?

'Help me down, these bottles are as precious as *moi*. We'll need them to survive this nightmare.'

Maddison cleared an area and they sat with their backs to the door, facing the blackness of their prison.

Nancy raised the collar of her fur coat, with the scotch

bottles tucked safely in her lap. She dug around in her pockets and lit up a cigarette. Her diamante encrusted lighter illuminated the room where people scurried to hide like rats shunning the light.

'May I?' Maddison grabbed Nancy's lighter, flicked the flint wheel to ignite the fuel, and the flame once again pitched a glow against the shadows.

The people trapped inside were of different ages and sizes, huddled together with only a few bags as their belongings and some ratty mattresses. Were they trapped? Or were they here of their own free will, chasing the promise of a better life?

'Don't smoke in here, there are children present,' Maddison said to Nancy.

'Darling, wake up and smell the nicotine. No one in this tin can is going to live long enough for my second-hand smoke to give them lung cancer and die.' Nancy inhaled so hard the room glowed an eerie orange from the smouldering cigarette.

'Stop being such a selfish sociopath.' For the first time in her life, Maddison got between Nancy and her addictions. She pinched Nancy's cigarette, butting it out, to then force the disgusting remnants through the hole in the vent.

'Hey—'

'Give me the rest of them.' Maddison held out her hand, sparking up the lighter. The people in the back hissing at her to be quiet. She was doing this for them. Or didn't they understand English? 'Nancy, I love you, but it's a disgusting habit you should have kicked a long time ago.'

'No.' Nancy hugged her cigarettes like a child.

'You will. Or I'll tip out all the scotch.'

The dancing flame of the lighter highlighted Nancy's fear.

'Please?'

'Fine. There goes our chances of sending SOS smoke signals…' Nancy dumped her cigarette packets into Maddison's hand.

'I'll give them back to you when we're in an open area.' Maddison hid the contraband in her pocket, then her godmother passed her a bottle of scotch.

Their situation was hopeless. She may as well drown her sorrows and die of alcohol poisoning to avoid what was ahead of her.

'What the hell is going on, Maddison? Why are those people cowering in here like spoiled caviar in a can?"

'Keep your voice down, I don't want to scare the children.' Maddison swallowed a mouthful of scotch, settling her back against the metal door.

'You'd better tell me what's going on, young lady, because I'm in this with you all the bloody way. They won't let me walk away free.' Nancy flung off the lid from her scotch bottle and let it roll off into the darkness. 'I want the truth and the whole truth, young lady. Not just snippets of a story either.' She took a mouthful of scotch. 'I'm waiting. Hmm?'

'Okay, okay ...' Her godmother was in this situation because of Maddison and deserved the truth and so she told her godmother everything ...

Nancy sipped on her scotch. 'So, darling, these people believe that they are being smuggled into this country as illegal immigrants, but instead they're being trafficked as slaves?'

'Yes.'

'Don't they realise this?'

Maddison shrugged.

'Where do they come from?'

'Most of them are refugees fleeing from war or persecution to seek asylum. They've come through South East Asia, into Indonesia, then into Australia by boat. The rich refugees, they catch a plane. These people are the poor ones desperate to flee from their homelands with hope for a better future.' Her research never prepared her for this, coming face to face with people she'd read about on a page, trapped in a sea-bound bunker.

'My great-grandmother fled Poland during the Holocaust.' Nancy frowned, then sighed. 'I'd forgotten what it was like to be broke and desperate.'

'I remember as a kid we were short of money and lived in the office at the magazine. And I sure as hell know what it's like to be desperate, running scared for my life.'

Maddison swigged on her scotch to dull her senses, to try and forget they were trapped inside a slow rocking tomb.

'Oh, my darling, Sweet Cheeks.' Nancy put her arm around Maddison and gave her a squeeze. 'You know, darling, it's been a long time since I sat on the ground drinking straight out of a bottle. The last time was with your mother. We'd barely scrounged enough from our coins to buy this cheap bottle of plonk.'

'I'm surprised you and my mother didn't invest in a winery.'

'We'd thought about it.' Nancy squeezed her hand. 'We just never got around to it. What with your mother busy with the magazine, and me with my many merry men.' Nancy took another sip. 'Talking about men, darling, what's happening with you and Joe?'

'Really? Do you have to ask that here? Now?' Maddison shook her head, raising the bottle to her lips.

'My darling Sweet Cheeks, the man is unreservedly, completely and totally in love with you. Even Leon picked it.'

'Let's talk about the whole photo set-up between you and Leon.'

'Oh, save the lecture, Sweet Cheeks.' Nancy waved her jewelled hand dismissively. 'I did that to ensure you weren't being toyed with.'

'I told Joe about the trust earlier.' Maddison confessed with a sigh. She missed him.

'And?'

'Joe looked at me like I was some freak. Rang his family, and that was the last time we spoke.' Except for shouting out her sorrys from the lift. A heavy wave of sadness enveloped her with its bony fingers squeezing her ribs. Would she ever see Joe again?

'That poor, darling man. You never told Joe anything about yourself, did you?'

Maddison shrugged.

'Darling, don't you think you can trust Joe?'

She gazed at their metal vault. 'Unusual circumstances threw us together. It's been pretty intense.'

'But he's still here. Give the man some credit. After all

you've been through, being chased by goons with guns, Joe has stuck by you. He's left his family and his home to help bring you here to Sydney. He's got amazing courage to shout down Regus while defending you. And no one, darling, I mean no one has the guts to do that except me. Oh, and you, that time before you ran away.' Nancy nudged Maddison. 'Why don't you want to open up to this guy? Is it because of the money?'

Maddison shrugged, picking at the edge of the bottle's label. 'Maybe because men usually became more interested in being part of the magazine.'

'Or they were gold diggers, as I'd warned you over the last couple of men you dated.'

'I give up. My mother never needed a man in her life, so why should I?' Did her mother ever feel the sting of heart ache the way Maddison felt for Joe?

'Do you want my opinion?'

'Oh please, you have the floor.' Maddison gave a drunk giggle at her clever wordplay.

'Darling, I honestly don't believe Joe is a money-sucking parasite like half of my toy boys. I tested him.'

Maddison sat up frowning. 'You didn't. How? When?'

Nancy lifted her chin, wearing a smug smile. 'Darling, you were there. Remember, photo shoot.'

'Don't remind me.' She crossed her arms in a huff, leaning back against the cold metal door.

'Darling, Joe's the first man I've ever had to convince to take a cheque. And he asked for it to be written out to his family's station.'

'Joe told us to make it out to the station before Leon took the first shot.'

'Sweet Cheeks, over the many years I have offered a cheque to people, they always thought of themselves. But Joe put his family first, which is a rare and admirable trait in our world, darling.'

'They're a tight family.' Maddison hugged her bent legs to rest her chin on her knees. She missed Glenda, with her baking sessions and her warm smile in the mornings. Greg's playful banter with her over his clothes, Earl with his dry quick quip of the day as part of his daily wisdoms. And Joe

… She missed everything about Joe.

'Hey, Nancy?'

'Hmm.'

'How come my mother never dated anyone?'

'Oh, your mother had men on the side.' Nancy grinned wryly.

'How? My mother was always working on the magazine.'

'In the beginning, Janice indulged. I guess the more popular the magazine got, the more it …'

'Consumed her.' It became her mother's most important possession. 'Don't tell me you didn't see it. You were there.' Maddison took an angry swig of scotch, relishing the heat of the burn in her chest.

'I tried to drag her out of that office, but Janice wouldn't leave.'

'Why did she end up like that?'

Nancy said nothing. Tight-lipped, as always.

'Come on, Nancy, look at where we are. No more secrets.' She frowned at herself. Is this what Joe felt like, always being kept in the dark? She covered her mouth as the burden of guilt made her stomach twist into knots. *Poor Joe.*

'You deserve to know,' said Nancy, scratching around for another cigarette. 'I'll tell you everything for a smoke.'

'Not until we get to open space.'

'But this is a conversation that demands I smoke—'

'It'll distract you. How come my mother never remarried or dated other men? She was a beautiful woman. Don't tell me work got in the way.'

'Oh, Janice and Regus shared that same trait. But back when I met your mother, we were both boy crazy.'

'What happened?'

'At university, Janice became ashamed of who she was and where she'd come from. I blame your father for that.'

'You knew my father?'

Nancy nodded. 'Tim was studying to become an aeronautical engineer when he was dating your mother.'

'It wasn't a one-night stand?'

'Darling, they loved each other.'

'Did he dump her when he found out she was pregnant

with me?'

'No. Not at all. Tim's family had discovered Janice was on a hardship scholarship. He's from old-family money and they convinced Tim to call it off, shipped him interstate, and broke your mother's heart.' Nancy sighed heavily. 'After that, your mother wouldn't let another man touch her, only to discover she was pregnant.'

'At eighteen. I know the story.'

'But you never knew that Janice was originally going to give you up for adoption.'

'Really?'

'But I saw Janice's expression change when she took one look at you. She made me snatch you back from the nurse before they took you away and she held you in her arms. You looked so innocent.' Nancy tenderly stroked the tip of Maddison's nose. 'From that moment on, Janice was going places. You could see it, and I was always going to tag along for the ride. Didn't she take us on some extraordinary adventures, from a life of squalor to the best that money could buy?' She held her bottle in the air in a salute.

'Did my father ever learn about me?'

Nancy looked at her coat, picking at some unseen lint. 'Oh, my darling Sweet Cheeks, I—'

Maddison putting her hand over her godmother's. 'Don't sweet talk your way out of this. What did my mother have to hide?'

'Don't say I didn't warn you.'

'Out with it.'

'Tim dropped out of university and disgraced his family by becoming a heroin addict. I liked to think it was because he was miserable without your mother. Sadly, he'd overdosed before your mother found him.'

'How come she never told me?'

'Janice never got over your father. It disappointed her that Tim never had the guts to stand up and fight for what he wanted. And that's why your mother worked so hard. She reinvented herself to bury her past so deep that no one would ever know where she'd come from or use it to hurt her again. Instead of addressing her past, Janice used that pain to drive herself forwards. Remember your trip to visit your grandmother?'

'Pft. The woman who refused to acknowledge my existence.' The trip to Adelaide seeing the house her mother had grown up, choked with weeds, and walls full of graffiti. 'It'd been an eye opener, visiting my mother's past. We got close then … until we came back to the office.' Maddison took an angry swig of her scotch.

'After that trip, darling, your mother returned with a plan. She renegotiated her terms with Regus and was planning to slow down once she'd achieved controlling shares of the magazine, so you two would run it together.' Nancy patted Maddison's knee. 'That's why Janice had you so involved from the beginning.'

'And we both know how that ended, with my mother being too busy with the magazine for anyone.' A magazine Maddison resented.

'That's why you weren't allowed to work for the magazine and got sent to work the crappy summer internships.'

'Pardon me?'

'When Janice discovered she was sick, your mother and Regus didn't want you to end up like them. All Janice wanted was to see you happy.' Nancy tapped on Maddison's heart.

A heart she let no one in for fear of getting hurt. Did it matter now?

'Janice honestly thought she'd be there with you, to retire at fifty and live to a hundred. But at least she was there to help you blow out the candles of your sweet sixteenth.' Nancy looked at her fingers covered in rings, stroking the fur of her coat, wriggling her designer label shoes.

Across from them, people sat in rags.

'It's amazing don't you think, darling, that when you're staring death in the face you realise all those materialistic possessions mean squat. It's the memories you make living a life that is truly too short to waste.'

Seventy-two

NEW SOUTH WALES—VICTORIA BORDER

Joe's hands tightly gripped the BMW's steering wheel, as he chased the white line down the night-time freeway. A ring blasted through the speakers as the mobile phone, resting in the console, lit up like an in-house flare.

It was the mobile phone Kelly had given him.

'Hello,' Joe spoke to the hands-free microphone, bracing himself. He'd taken a car that didn't belong to him.

'*Where the hell are you two?*' Regus's voice bellowed through the car's speakers, with other people talking in the background. 'You were meant to be tucked up in the safe house hours ago—'

'*Stop, Regus!*' And he gave it to the man hard, fast, and straight to the point just the way Regus liked it. 'They've kidnapped Nancy. Maddison went to save her. But now both women are being held hostage on a ship heading for Melbourne.'

'*How did Nancy get kidnapped? In this building? While we've had the feds here all bloody day!*' The boardroom's background noise was silenced.

'No idea. Maddison said they may have had her phones tapped and who knows how big their network is? I know they had that Melbourne detective call Nancy looking for Maddison. They could've been watching Nancy this entire time, and with us showing up this morning in the limo—'

'You would've stood out like a side of barbecued ribs at a vegan sit-down.'

'It doesn't matter how, all that matters is that they've now got Nancy and Maddison.'

'Right, I've got you on speaker with Woodcock beside me. Fill us in on everything.'

'All I know is this …' Joe explained the events calmly, but inside his heart was heavy with his guts knotted with worry.

'Joe, Woodcock here. Regus's security guy is patching us through to the building's surveillance cameras. Can you tell us where Maddison was while you were in her office talking to your folks?'

'Maddison went to see Nancy, who was supposed to be waiting to take us out for dinner.' Joe wished he'd never let Maddison out of his sight.

'What the—' Regus voice dropped a notch. 'The security tapes show you speeding through my basement.'

'I didn't want to let her out of my sight. I'm trying to help Maddison.' Joe was meant to be keeping Maddison safe but was failing miserably. 'I found Nancy's white car parked at the docks,' Joe said over the microphone, as he steered down the freeway. 'It was the wharfies who told me that Maddison was the last person seen getting onto the cargo ship. Check the security footage they have down at the docks to confirm it, because I never saw her get on. But those men told me Maddison was running full pelt to not miss that boat.'

'What is the vessel called?' Woodcock asked.

'Where the hell is it headed?' Regus demanded.

'It's called the Zinko and its heading for Melbourne with a deck full of sea containers,' said Joe.

It was as if everyone in the boardroom murmured their surprise in the background.

The first to react was Regus. 'Right, what did Maddison take with her? *And someone find me that list of ships.*'

'Maddison took her bag with her notes and the memory stick from the laptop that has copies of this whole thing.'

In the background, paper shuffled as Regus barked out orders, snapping his fingers. 'Right, we have a list of

Cottillard's boats and their shipping itinerary.'

'Is the Zinko on that list?'

'Yep. Booked to dock in Melbourne tomorrow. I bet my next lot of dividends that ship has got illegal immigrants onboard and they're taking Maddison to see this Cottillard.'

'Yeah.' Joe had already guessed that. His grip tightened on the steering wheel, worried about what that animal would do to Maddison.

'Where are you now, Joe?'

'I'm halfway to Melbourne. I'll pay you back in fuel and costs.'

'If I told you to come back, would you?'

'No. I'm not stopping. Don't ask me to turn around, Regus, because I won't!'

'I won't. I'd be doing the same as you.'

Joe could practically hear the short sharp nod of approval from Regus, the man who ruled an empire.

'Right, I've got Weasel and his eagle-eyed boy scouts in Melbourne watching the docks waiting for the Feds to show. I'll tell them you're on the way and they'll call you to rendezvous with them. My car could do with a decent run. Keep the fuel receipts for Kelly. Carry that phone with you at all times. Safe driving, Joe. I'll keep you posted.'

The silence of the car was deafening as Joe drove faster down the interstate. He tried to find some comfort that Regus and Woodcock were working out a plan to rescue those women. But how? When they were back in Sydney across state lines.

Seventy-three

MELBOURNE, VICTORIA

A loud bang came from the roof of the sea container, it was soon followed by scraping metal against metal, then they were flying on a rollercoaster ride in the dark.

Maddison gripped the metal door as the other people muffled their screams.

Then there was a hard jolt, as if dumped onto the ground.

Only then Nancy woke up. 'Ow!' She moaned, rubbing her head. 'Theresa, I need some paracetamol. And I need a new mattress, it's like a sheet of bloody metal ...' Nancy opened her eyes and peered inside their tomb.

Chains rattled, and assorted engines roared.

'*Righto, off you go,*' yelled out a male's voice outside.

The sea container shunted forward, and those trapped inside swayed with the forward momentum.

'We're on the road,' Maddison said.

'Oh crap, this nightmare is real?' Nancy groaned, sitting up she dug around in pockets. 'What's the time? And where's my cigarettes?

Maddison shrugged, pointing to the small vent. 'Daylight. I have your smokes, safe. Don't ask for them, not yet.'

'You're a hard woman .... Ugh, I need water. This'll do.' Nancy grabbed the scotch bottle she'd been cradling all night and took a mouthful, wincing at the bitter flavour. 'They could've been decent enough to get us a cabin with a toilet. How do they live in this squalor, locked in a metal box?'

'Shut up, Nancy!' Maddison scowled at her selfish godmother. 'They've been stuck in this container for who knows how long. Surviving on rationed food and water, carrying everything they own.'

'Okay, okay, Sweet Cheeks. Save the lecture. You know I'm a cranky thing in the morning. I have five ex-husbands who'll all testify to that.' Nancy brushed back her hair, wrapping her fur coat tighter around herself.

The sea container rumbled from the sound of wheels rolling on a road.

'Where are we?'

'Melbourne.'

'I hate bloody Melbourne.' Nancy thumbed over her eyebrows, dabbing at the make-up smeared around her eyes. 'Any ideas, darling, on how we're going to crank open the doors and flee from this oversized jack-in-the-box?'

'We've got no tools, no phone, nothing.'

'Well, that's obvious,' muttered Nancy.

'Right before we left Regus in the boardroom with Woodcock, they were working on a list of Cottillard's ships, trying to work out when the next shipment was to be expected.'

'Well again, that's obvious, we're the next bloody shipment.'

'I know that!'

'So why haven't all those officers hauled their butts down here to rescue us so I can have my morning cigarette.' Nancy held out her hand.

'Not a chance.' Maddison had never been so stubborn, especially against Nancy. The roles had been reversed, finally the child was playing the part of the grown up.

'You're lucky I love you.' Nancy lifted her scotch bottle to her lips. 'So what else was Regus working on? As the smartest man I know, Regus excels under pressure and would've have concocted ten different scenarios and activated three of them in ten minutes.'

'Sounds like you still admire him.'

'I never stopped loving the man. We'd still be married if he wasn't married to the job first. So, what was my ex working on?'

'Woodcock and Regus were trying to coordinate people they could trust to watch Cottillard's operations.' But no one knew they were there. No one could see there were people inside a city of containers that covered an entire ship. It was hopeless.

Did Woodcock have enough time and resources to have the police watch Cottillard's extensive operations? If so, why hadn't they done anything? And if Cottillard had been tipped off, he'd shut down and leave them all to rot—so were the police playing it safe? Or were they more worried about building a solid case against this monster, than saving two women?

'Shouldn't the feds have found the ship, at least? Darling, how could anyone miss a cargo freighter?'

'There were over a hundred sea containers on board that all looked the same. It'd be like trying to find—'

'A flawless diamond ring in a suburban supermarket's faux jewellery rack.' Nancy stroked the precious gems worn on her fingers. 'What do you suggest?'

Maddison shrugged. 'We wing it.'

'Sorry, darling, are you suggesting we flap our wings like a bunch of deranged hung-over chickens in dire need of a toothbrush and a shower?'

'All I'm saying …' Maddison took a deep breath, trying not to get upset with her godmother, who was never a morning person, not until she'd smoked a dozen cigarettes and had a glass of champagne. 'Let's be prepared for the first chance we get to run.'

'Wow, darling, doesn't that sound like a well-thought-out plan. Bravo on the effort. Hmm.'

'Hey, you don't have to be so catty about it. I'm trying, okay?' Maddison frowned at Nancy.

'Well, does anyone know we're missing?'

'Joe knows.' She gazed at her empty palms that itched to hold his large working hand, as her chest grew heavier. She missed everything about that man. Everything.

'Oh, my darling Sweet Cheeks, the more I learn about

Joe, the more I adore him. I wish you'd give him a chance and admit to yourself how much you love him. Don't be like you're your mother in leaving it too late to go get your man. Fight for it. And stop standing in the way of your own happiness. That poor darling man has gone through hell since he's met you.'

'I know.' Maddison wrapped her coat around herself, hating the cold. 'I wouldn't be surprised if Joe's had enough and gone home. I wouldn't blame him.' The further away from her, the better life would be for Joe.

'Well then, when this is all over you can haul your sweet cheeks back to wherever it is Joe lives.'

'Do you honestly believe this nightmare will end to the sounds of corked champagne and a rousing chorus of cheers? We're being sent to meet a monster.'

Nancy patted her goddaughter's hand. 'Darling, you've got some over-worked guardian angel watching over you. After all you've been through, they won't give up that easily and neither should you.'

'Yeah, right? Comforting,' mumbled Maddison.

'It's the best I can do without having had my pills, champagne, and cigarettes.' Nancy swigged on her scotch with a grimace.

'See, you can wing it if need be.' She playfully nudged her wicked godmother.

'Oh, I guess I can.' She smiled.

Outside the truck slowed down, turned, and the light from the vents dimmed. The engine echoed, as if inside a big building.

The truck stopped. Chains rattled. Metal clanked, and the container rocked.

The truck engine revved then it rumbled off into the distance, leaving them behind.

Maddison crouched down to peer through the vent. It didn't show much of anything but corrugated walls of some kind.

'Where are we?' Nancy whispered to Maddison.

'Warehouse.' Was it the same warehouse Tom pointed out on the map back at the station? She sniffed for sea air. All she could smell was the diesel fumes from the departing truck.

Men's voices approached, the large metal hinge shifted and the doors were pulled open.

With her hand shading her eyes from the light, a mixture of musky deodorant and mint carried inside on a slight sea breeze.

Sea breeze?

Maddison froze. She knew Melbourne. The road that ran past Laurie's Sports bar wasn't far from Port Melbourne's docks. She'd been up and down the Yarra River by boat, taking tourists scuba diving along the coastline of Port Phillip Bay.

She listened intently for any familiar sounds as a burst of hope ignited from her belly, spreading a tingling warmth through to her icy fingers.

'Out you get, ladies.' It was Scarface, with the human bulldog beside him. 'Hurry up, or we'll drag you out by the hair.'

'Come on, Nancy.' Maddison helped the moaning, groaning Nancy to the warehouse floor.

'My smokes please, young lady.'

As Maddison rummaged around in her pockets, the people in the back of the container gathered their belongings, speaking in an unknown language. All of them were dirty and hungry, but they wore hope in their eyes. Especially the children peering out from behind their parents.

Maddison had some idea about what happened to the adults from her uncle's photos and her research. But what happened to the children?

Two white work vans waited nearby. More men beckoned to the refugees, herding them into the waiting vehicles.

Scarface scooped up the empty scotch bottles from the container's floor. 'Jeezus. You two sheilas drank two bottles of scotch—straight. I'm impressed.' He tossed the bottles aside, where they clanged along the edge of the doorway. 'Bet you feel like crap now.'

'I've survived bigger and uglier than you.' Nancy sneered at Scarface. Her designer clothes were crumpled, her shoes scuffed, and her fur coat was covered in dirt. Make-up smeared and hair a mess, she stood with pride, putting a hand on her hip while lighting a cigarette. The wicked godmother, the socialite and queen of the hallowed halls of the magazine, looked like she'd stepped out of a nightclub after a month-long bender.

'What happens to those people?' Maddison asked Scarface.

A little girl waved at her, holding her mother's hand as they waited to climb into the waiting vans.

'Are they going to be okay?' Maddison returned the wave as awkward as her smile.

She'd tried to communicate with them during the boat trip, but none of them spoke English. But she saw how excited they were to know they were in Australia, believing they'd come to the promised land — where only hell awaited them.

The sea container emptied. Vans loaded, their doors slammed shut, and they drove out into the sunshine.

'Where do they go?' Maddison watched the van disappear around the corner, as seagulls rested on a nearby roof beneath a grey sky.

The warehouse door started to close. Did she have time to run?

She couldn't leave Nancy, who was too busy smoking, with her legs crossed as if holding her bladder. Nancy never ran anywhere — forget doing it in heels.

'Move along, ladies.' Scarface threw his thumb in the opposite direction of the vans.

'Steady on, tiger, I'm a woman with a full bladder here!'

'Jeezus.' He scrubbed at the ancient acne scars on his chin. 'Through that door there's a loo. One at a time. Age before beauty.'

'Oh darling, I've learned with age.' Nancy's voice purred with her hips sashaying as if walking along a runway during Australia's Fashion Week and not a decrepit warehouse. Nancy then slyly winked at Maddison, closing the toilet door.

Nancy was not going to flirt with these guys, was she?

'So where is this boss of yours? That sounds so gangsterish, don't you agree, darling?' Nancy asked

Maddison, as she emerged from the toilet, heading for the nearby hand basin.

Maddison dashed past her.

'What sort of manners has this businessman got, to keep us waiting?' Nancy asked.

'He won't show, not while those vans are in the vicinity,' said Maddison, now happily relieved, washing her hands. She splashed water over her face, scooping up mouthfuls. Considering the amount of scotch she'd consumed last night, she felt pretty good.

'Well, aren't you the clever little cookie?' Scarface mumbled with sarcasm. 'Let's go.'

They guided them to the far end of the warehouse and through a side door.

Maddison winced at the sunshine glistening off the water mere metres away. The strong sea breeze was invigorating as she searched for a familiar landmark while being escorted toward the waiting limousine.

The rear passenger door opened and out stepped the monster himself, Antonio Cottillard.

Maddison gasped as fear froze her veins.

Cottillard adjusted the classy coat and tie of his pinstriped suit, then removed the fat cigar wedged between his teeth.

'Who does he think he is? Al Capone?' Nancy sniggered. 'And that suit, darling, wingtips and pinstripes are only good for costume parties.'

'Nancy,' Maddison said through gritted teeth, 'you're not helping.'

Cottillard narrowed his black eyes at her, palming over his oiled black hair. 'So, this is Maddison Farley.' Cottillard was almost civil with his smile, pointing his cigar at her. 'You are one tough little lady to track down.'

'Here's their stuff.' Scarface held out their handbags.

'Burn it.' Antonio squinted at the women. 'What am I going to do with you pair?'

'We have money,' Nancy said to the man who'd made his fortune in people trafficking. 'Let us go and we'll gladly pay you and promise to tell no one of your operation.'

'Jeezus, boss, don't risk it. That overdressedchimneystack never shuts up.' Scarface glared at Nancy as the human bulldog nodded.

'Shoot them. Toss them over the side, and let the sharks deal with their bodies.' Cottillard spoke so calmly as if ordering a meal at a drive thru. Already turning his back on them, heading for the car.

'*What the hell do you do with those people?*' Maddison shouted angrily at the monster with no soul.

The human bulldog grabbed Maddison and Nancy by the arm and started dragging them to the edge of the wharf.

'I know they work in sweat shops, whorehouses, and building sites to pay off their debt to you. But what happens to the children?' Maddison was desperate to delay her destiny.

Cottillard stopped to give Maddison a sideways glance.

The human bulldog and Scarface stopped dragging them as Cottillard approached her, sharing an evil laugh mimicked by a group of seagulls. 'They get sold or put to work.'

'You arsehole.' The hatred exploded inside and she spat at him. Surprising everyone that she spat like a child, including herself.

'You bitch!' Antonio wiped at his face with his suit. 'Give me something to wipe this muck off.'

But as she kicked and lashed out in desperation, she'd somehow struggled free. She pulled at Nancy's hand. There was a huge sound of material tearing, as she took two of the longest steps in her life to freedom, aiming for the edge of the wharf.

'JUMP.' Maddison clasped Nancy's hand and leaped over the side as gunshots and shouting rang out behind them.

With gravity pushing them for over ten metres, they slammed into the icy sea water where they plummeted into the murky depths.

With their hands separating from the impact, Maddison quickly recovered. She grabbed Nancy's leg and pulled her down, dragging her to swim under the wharf.

With lungs bursting for air, the freezing water burned like icy knives jabbing at their skin as their clothes dragged them to the briny bottom. Maddison kicked harder into the shadows as Nancy struggled behind her.

Following the concrete pylons that made up the wharf structure, they breached the surface gasping for air.

Maddison covered Nancy's mouth with her hand. 'Shh,' she whispered through chattering teeth.

Nancy nodded.

Maddison led them deeper under the wharf, aiming for the dry dock in the distance.

Above them voices echoed off the water. The sounds of cars, trucks, and running boots grumbled like thunder, then a body dove off to splash into the water. Another man followed.

They were coming.

Maddison dragged Nancy, holding a finger to her blue lips as they hid behind a pylon.

A head popped out of the water, with his back to them. '*Maddison?*'

The familiar voice echoed around her. Was that Joe? Did she hear right?

'*Maddison and Nancy?*' called out the other swimmer. 'They dove down here. They can't have gone too far.'

'*Maddison, it's me, Joe. I'm here with the police.* MADDISON.'

'Joe?' Maddison peeked out from their hiding spot.

'Oh, my darling beautiful Joe.' Nancy smiled with red teary eyes and pushed Maddison on the shoulder. 'Go get your man.'

The swimmer turned around, searching the shadows with his blue eyes. It was Joe. Her Joe.

'*They're here. We found them.*' Joe signalled to the other diver.

Maddison cupped her mouth, the tears forming as Joe swam towards them.

The other swimmer shouted to the people above, '*Send down the ladder, and get some blankets ready.*'

Ropes were thrown over the side to the sounds of more people running above their heads on the wharf. Sirens wailed, and red and blue lights reflected off the water.

'Joe?' Maddison's heart burst as she swam towards him.

His arms reached around her, and she was against his

chest staring into his familiar smile, his blue eyes, and rich dark brown hair. Assorted emergency lights bounced off the water to reflect like lightning flashes. Again, the moving vehicles above them grumbled like thunder. It was just like the first time she'd seen Joe, pulling her free from the plane wreckage in crocodile infested waters, here he was again, her thunder god coming to her rescue.

'Joe, you're here.' She clung to him and never wanted let go.

'Like I was ever going to leave you behind.' He hugged her tight.

'Who's that?' Nancy pointed to the other swimmer approaching with a life jacket.

'Federal Police,' replied Joe, checking over Maddison. 'Are you two okay?'

'Yeah.' Maddison cupped his cheek, memorising the details of his blue eyes and handsome features.

'Yes, darling, we're both fine. But I'm freezing due to my coat and shirt getting ripped off my back, with my arm almost torn from my socket by Sweet Cheeks here. I'm nearly naked and I hate swimming in salt water.

'Come this way, Miss, we'll get you out,' said the police diver.

'Oh, my...' Nancy arched an eyebrow at the policeman. 'I'm with you, handsome.' Nancy glided in the water like a shark approaching her next victim.

'How did you find us?' Maddison asked Joe.

'Regus had a group of men watching.'

'Who?'

'Weasel and his eagle-eyed boy scouts. They're ex-miltary guys, who've been helping the Feds. We've been watching the boat from the second it docked. I wanted to storm it, but we didn't know which sea container you were in, but they had a plan. They had a crew following Cottillard, hoping he'd lead us to you, and this was the only container they unloaded onto a truck that drove past the quarantine yards. We knew it had to be the one,' explained Joe. 'As soon as they saw you and Nancy being dragged from the warehouse to meet Cottillard, the police moved in. But you two jumped over the side. You're quite the fighter.' He hugged her beneath the wharf as they trod water. 'That's three times I've had to do this.'

'I'm so sorry to do this to you.' Her hand cupped his cheek, as the sweep of emotions filled her. 'I love you, Joe. I love you so much.'

'Finally.' He smiled at her, resting his forehead against hers. 'I've been wondering when you were going to tell me.'

'I'm saying it now and I'll say it again. I love you.' She gripped his stubbly chin and kissed him.

'And I love you too,' he said tenderly. 'Come on, let's get out of here, this water's freezing.'

Seventy-four

Regus poured scotch into a pair of tumblers resting among the paperwork on his desk. He passed one glass with a copy of the day's newspaper to Woodcock, seated beside Maddison in the guest chairs.

'Front page news, and the biggest scoop this paper has ever had. It's sending shockwaves right across the country. Thanks for this, Woodcock.' Regus picked up the box of scotch off his desk, the bottles inside clanged as he set it down on the floor by his couch. 'Are you sure you don't want to take a couple of bottles, Maddy?'

'I've had enough scotch to last me a lifetime, thank you. Any updates on Antonio Cottillard?' Maddison asked Woodcock, who was sipping on his tumbler.

'Cottillard's locked up in his own special federal cell. We've shut down all his operations, seized his assets and frozen his bank accounts. He's awaiting trial for people smuggling, trafficking, murder, attempted murder, kidnap, and so many other charges, Cottillard and his men have no hope of seeing daylight again.'

'And those Melbourne detectives?' Maddison asked.

'We've arrested them, including that politician in Canberra, all in one big sweep. We timed it so they couldn't tip each other off.'

'Did I tell you that those beautiful bloodhounds found

Cottillard's payroll list. It had everyone, including customs officers, immigrations officers, the lot. That information was kindly donated to the feds as an anonymous tip, of course.' Regus nodded to the Superintendent sipping on his scotch.

Woodcock nodded back. 'All those names, that a concerned citizen supplied to us, are being arrested as we speak.'

'And the people Nancy and I travelled with in that sea container?' Maddison asked Woodcock. 'Please tell me those children are safe. You got to those vans, didn't you?'

'We had a team following the vans the second they left the warehouse.'

'Are they all safe now?'

'We've rescued over a hundred people,' replied Woodcock.

'No way?'

'We've raided sweatshops, construction sites, even brothels.'

'And the children?' She had to know.

'We found them all, reuniting them with their families as we speak.'

'They're safe, Maddy.' Regus tenderly patted her arm. 'And you're safe too and that's what matters to me.'

'How long will you keep running the story?' Woodcock asked Regus.

'As long as it sells papers. Right now, its headline news. But Maddison's done the best version of the entire events, set for the next issue of the Maddison Magazine. It'll be an exclusive insight into this whole sorry saga. Bob would've been proud.'

'It's the least I could do. I'd promised Uncle Bob I would.' And it was finally over. Pulled from the icy waters of Melbourne, she'd endured endless police interviews. Then, with Joe by her side, they'd flown by private jet with Nancy back to Sydney. This morning, Maddison returned to her mother's office, shut the door, lifted the lid on the laptop and started typing.

Everything went into the article, publicly thanking all of those who'd helped her along the way, dedicating it in honour of her Uncle Bob. He'd started this journey, making her swear to keep her promise, to see his story through to the very end.

But it'll be a long time before she made another promise. Even though she'd learned a lot of life lessons along the way, unearthing secrets of her past, which helped her to decide what her focus would be for her future.

She glanced at her watch as a giddy swirl of anticipation rose from her lower belly as she rose to her feet. 'If you'll excuse me, I've got a hot date.'

'That Joe is a fine fellow,' said Woodcock, also standing.

'Yeah, I don't mind the lad. He's got a strong backbone and puts his family and those he cares about first.' Regus opened his office door for her. 'Don't forget, when you two get married, I'll walk you down the aisle. I've always wanted to do that.'

'*Regus*.' The heat spread from her cheeks. 'Joe hasn't asked me to marry him.'

'It won't be long.' Regus laughed with Woodcock.

She waved at them, nodded at Kelly on the phone behind her desk, and headed for the elevators.

The lift doors opened and out strolled Joe, dressed in his own jeans and shirt, and his lived-in boots. He looked like the cattleman he was, stepping straight off the station.

No matter the clothes they'd put on the man, Joe knew who he was and wasn't changing for anyone. And why should he? He was perfect just the way he was.

Again, Glenda's question came to mind: Would Maddison still look at Joe the same in her world as she saw him on the station?

She had her answer, smiling at the man who made her heart bloom.

'Hey, am I late?' Joe asked her.

From the lady who used to always run late, she said, 'You're right on time.'

'Beautiful flower for a beautiful lady.' Joe held out a red rose and gently kissed her cheek.

'Thank you.' His romantic gesture filled her heart so much, it threatened to explode from her chest.

'Have you finished with Regus?'

'Yes. My work is done.' She smiled so wide her cheeks

ached. She was free.

'What are you going to do now?'

'Well, you've followed me all over the country and remained by my side. Even when I tried to lose you, you still tracked me down.' She slid her arms around his waist and leaned into his chest. 'So now I'm going to follow you.'

'Don't you want to stay here? Isn't this your home?'

'No. It'll always be nice to visit, but it's even better when I leave. I remembered my reasons for leaving, too.'

'Which are?'

'This isn't my future. It was my past, my childhood, and it was my mother's life. Not mine. But I have learned to accept my past, so I won't run away like some rabbit trying to escape. Not anymore. I don't want to because it helped make me the person I am today.'

'What will you do?'

She shrugged. 'I'll still oversee every issue, like I've always done. The magazine will continue to be managed by the best people in the business.' Her mother created it, and Maddison respected it. But there was more to life than having the latest in lip gloss and designer clothing.

It was the people you loved, who loved you like family, that mattered the most and it had taken the journey of a lifetime for her to realise this.

'But I'm in dire need of a holiday first. I was thinking of a remote location that's filled with an uninterrupted view of a really big sky. Somewhere in the Northern Territory outback, perhaps a family run cattle station, where we can watch the warm tropical rain fall and the grass grow. Do you have any suggestions?'

'Well ...' Joe smiled wide as he slid his arm around her shoulders and pressed the button for the elevator. 'In that case, let's go home. First, we'll have to do some shopping for Mum and Greg. I'll need your help, because I don't know how to shop, or where to go in this city.'

'I don't mind playing tour guide for the tourist. And I promise to answer all of your questions.'

'All of them?'

'Every one of them. No more secrets, I promise.'

'You already know all of mine. And I've seen how far

you go to keep a promise. So let's just promise to keep each other safe.'

'Deal.' Her smile was as wide as her full heart, as he pulled her close to press his lips against hers to kiss her as if they were the only two people in the room. And it was a kiss that tasted of a love that would last forever.

Did you like the story?

If so, your opinion matters to me!

It's true. A good reader's review is worth
a lot to this author.

So, if you enjoyed this book, please leave
a review & recommend it to your friends.

I'd appreciate it.

With much gratitude,

mel

A. ROWE

ACKNOWLEDGEMENTS

Thank you

Thank you for reading this story and to those who have helped me on this amazing journey to get here, I wish I could name you all.

Never would I have imagined that all those times I'd travelled, racing to catch a plane, train, or truck, to trek from the outback to the city that it would end up in a story. So I'd like to thank all those strangers who helped me on my many journeys of the past, present, and future adventures to come.

I'd like to thank the amazing Handbrake for not disowning me whenever I burrow down into a new story.

Thank you to the amazing Detective Sergeant Vanessa Barton for your help with the technicalities and your amazing friendship.

Thank you to my online writer friends and to the amazing editing Deb team at DNP. Thank you to Clare Burns for having a sharp eye, and to the Fabulous First Readers team for their support, I am truly blessed to have you all join me on my writing journey.

Most all, thank you to you, dear reader, I am grateful to you for taking the time to read this story. It means the world to me.

Until next time,

mel

A. ROWE

australian bestselling author

ABOUT THE AUTHOR

Australian bestselling author, Mel A ROWE, creates escapes for today's busy women to enjoy from the comfort of their home.

Delivered with a dash of drama, witty humour and quirky family units, Mel is known for reinventing romantic versions of home, taking her common characters on uncommon journeys that lead from boardrooms to billabongs as they try to find their own HAPPILY EVER AFTER.

Living in Australia's Northern Territory, Mel enjoys random outback road trips, fumbling with her camera, annoying her family with her bad singing, and making new friends in the middle of nowhere—except for water buffalos. She's been chased by a few.

Feel free to contact Mel, as her word journey continues, at

MelAROWE.com

Receive exclusive insights, and news
of upcoming releases by joining:
https://melarowe.com/newsletter/

More by Mel A ROWE

Australian Bestselling ELSIE CREEK SERIES:

The ART of DUST

DIAMOND in the DUST

CAKED in DUST

XMAS DUST

MUSTER in the DUST

ROLLED in DUST

WRITTEN in DUST

Standalone Stories:

Avoiding the Pity Party

Unplanned Party

The Football Whisperer

Winter's Walk

Run Beautiful Run

Watch for more visit: MELAROWE.COM